DARK TEMPTATION

"Go," Sloan whispered, his breath harsh and ragged, telling of the struggle being waged within him. "Tell me to release the door."

Anna closed her eyes, listening to the discordant rhythm of her heartbeat. She knew she should do precisely as he bade, but the words refused to be spoken.

"Tell me, Anna."

"I can't!" she cried out, the memory of too many long, lonely nights filling her mind.

"Then tell me what you want," Sloan commanded.

"What I want doesn't matter."

"Tell me what you want!"

What *did* she want? Anna thought. To feel? Not to feel? To remember what it was like to be desired? To experience warmth again?

"Hold me," she heard herself saying, thinking how simple the answer had been all along.

DARK JOURNEY

Sandra Canfield

BANTAM BOOKS
NEW YORK • TORONTO • LONDON • SYDNEY • AUCKLAND

DARK JOURNEY

A Bantam Book/June 1994

ISBN 0-553-56605-9

Published simultaneously in the United States and Canada

Bantam Books are published by Bantam Books, a division of Bantam Doubleday Dell Publishing Group, Inc. Its trademark, consisting of the words "Bantam Books" and the portrayal of a rooster, is Registered in U.S. Patent and Trademark Office and in other countries. Marca Registrada. Bantam Books, 1540 Broadway, New York, New York 10036.

PRINTED IN THE UNITED STATES OF AMERICA

RAD 0 9 8 7 6 5 4 3 2 1

Acknowledgments

I gratefully acknowledge the following people: John Koonce, for his pharmaceutical assistance; Dr. Nadine Keer and her pathologist friends, for their medical-forensic expertise; Dr. Christopher Rheams, who patiently answered the most simplistic of questions; Suzannah Davis, Mary Agnes Rambin, and Reverend David P. Richter, for being my guides to the Catholic Church; Janet Flicker, for being my friend and for "going to court" with me; and a huge thanks to Julie Kistler, lawyer and fellow writer, who cleaned up my leading questions and hearsay evidence. Last, but by no means least, I should like to thank two very special contributors to the book: Janice Williams, who so generously shared with me her own personal experience with diabetes; and Peggy Webb, who, one summer evening, opened up her heart and her life to me.

ONE

End of August

Anna Ramey hadn't shed a single tear over the death of her husband. She hadn't cried when she'd stood alongside his lifeless body, which had been peacefully tucked in the bed—one of many they'd never shared—in the seaside dwelling they'd rented for the summer in Cook's Bay, Maine. Neither had she cried when she'd viewed her husband laid out in the satin-lined mahogany coffin at Morganstern's Mortuary. Even so, whip-lean and black-suited Elijah Morganstern, sounding like his namesake prophet, had pressed a tissue into her hand. Mark his words, he had told his assistant, as he'd stroked his grizzled beard into a geometrically perfect triangle, it was only a matter of time until the tears fell. Expert that he was on the subject of grief, he knew, if Anna didn't, that her composure couldn't last, simply because it went against the natural order of the state of widowhood.

But her composure had lasted, through the two days of funeral preparations, through the seemingly endless mass that Father Santelices had conducted at St. Catherine's despite the fact that only a handful of mourners had shown up, and now through the equally interminable drive to the cemetery. It has lasted because Anna knew something that Elijah Morganstern didn't: crying was a luxury she couldn't afford. More to the point, it was a human activity, and being merely human was something Anna hadn't been allowed for twenty-odd years. Those around her might be made of flesh and blood, feelings and sensibilities, but life had demanded that she be structured of nothing less than steel.

Besides, she thought as the limousine windshield wipers struggled against the sudden storm, how could she cry when she was empty inside? How could she cry when she felt nothing save a cruel hollowness? Even as she posed these questions, she knew that she was lying to herself. If the summer had taught her nothing else, it had taught her that she still could feel. One part of her cherished the totally unexpected discovery, while another part wished for the comfortable, deathlike nothingness of before. It was difficult living with guilt, impossible to cozy up to shame. This last thought inspired its usual reaction. She glanced at her left hand, which now bore only the faint mark of her wedding band. She comforted herself with the knowledge that, whatever else she might be, she wasn't a hypocrite.

"Are you all right?" a quiet voice asked as the car at last turned onto the narrow gravel road of the cemetery.

Anna, her complexion pale in contrast to the simple black suit she wore, glanced up with dark blue eyes. A black hat perched atop a mass of short golden curls, many of which struggled against their confinement.

Peering through black honeycombed netting, which imprisoned Anna even as it shielded her, she studied the woman sitting across from her. For a second, she had the unnerving feeling that she was looking into the eyes of her husband, rather than those of her sister-in-law. Despite the fact that Jack had been three years older than his sister Carrie, they, with their chestnut-brown hair and gray eyes, were often thought to be twins, until disease had wasted and aged Jack far beyond his forty-six years.

"Yes," Anna said, unable to keep her gaze from wandering to the automobile's other passenger.

Anna willed her daughter to look her way, but the young woman didn't. She just stared out the rain-dappled window, the way she had since they'd crawled onto the limousine's plush seating. At the funeral Meg had chosen to sit alone, looking both younger and older than her twenty-two years. Anna wondered if Carrie sensed the dark undercurrent that had so recently sprung between a once uncommonly close mother and daughter. Did Carrie notice the way they exchanged the barest and only the most essential dialogue? Or the way Meg always found a reason to leave the room that her mother had just entered? Did Carrie think it odd that each faced her grief alone?

If Carrie felt the tension, she tactfully chose to ignore it, now as in the previous days. Instead she said, "Jack would have hated that it rained today."

Anna dragged her attention from her daughter to her sister-in-law. "I know."

Carrie smiled, temporarily forgetting that the mission they were on was a grim one. "He never could stand being shut up in the house. He always wanted to be out and doing—climbing trees, combing the beach, swimming in the bay." Carrie's smile grew. "Did I ever tell you about the time he cut a hole in the ice—it was during the coldest December ever recorded in Maine—

and we went swimming?" She didn't wait for Anna's response. "Mom almost killed us. She whipped our fannies all the way home."

Yes, Anna thought, that was the fun-loving man she'd met and married, the man who'd fathered her child, the man she'd adored heart and soul. Looking back, she was uncertain at what point the marriage had begun to go wrong. She had known about his illness from the very beginning. She just hadn't understood the implications of being married to a diabetic, a diabetic who played fast and loose with meals and medication, a diabetic who recklessly courted complications. With each failure of his body, failures that had been spawned by his own neglect, he'd added another layer to the wall he had begun building early on between them. The final straw had been three months before. The doctor's words, without a coating of sugar, came back to Anna; "How bad is it?" she asked.

"Your husband has had a stroke. He has total paralysis of the right side, his kidney function is impaired, and his speech has been affected."

"How permanent is the damage?"

"It's impossible to say. We'll stabilize him, do what we can to prevent another stroke, then start rehabilitation." Anna could tell that the doctor chose his next words carefully. "You must bear in mind that his body has been ravaged by the diabetes. You must also realize that a great deal of his recovery depends on how hard he's willing to fight."

After Jack had been stabilized, his doctor had entered him into an extensive rehabilitation program. He'd lived in a halfway house, where therapists had worked with him in an attempt to make him independent again. It didn't take long, however, for everyone to realize that Jack wasn't applying himself.

"Jack, you're not even trying," Anna had scolded him. "The therapist says that you won't do anything that she asks you to do." At this Jack Ramey had begun to scribble laboriously on the notepad he always kept at his side. "Will you please stop writing everything on that darned pad! The doctor says that you can talk. Okay, okay, I know you can't talk normally, but you're never going to talk normally again if you don't start practicing."

But her pep talk had done nothing to incite her husband to action. In fact, Jack took himself out of the program, an action everyone fought against futilely.

With each passing day he seemed to slip deeper and deeper into some dark abyss that quite frankly had frightened Anna. Furthermore, he'd become emotionally abusive in a way he'd never been before. As she had from the beginning of his poor health, she had borne the brunt of his wrath—stoically borne it. It had taken its toll, however. She'd begun to unravel at the seams. She'd begun to feel that her spirit, whatever that indefinable something was that made her "her", was being lost, drained away in ever-increasing driblets and drops.

Nearing depletion, fearing that one day she'd wake up and find that she no longer existed at all, she'd been relieved when her husband had suggested shutting up their Connecticut home and summering in the town of his youth. Anna had thought that getting away was exactly what they both needed. Perhaps the sea, symbol of continuity, could help restore her. Perhaps its magical waters could refill the emptiness that threatened to consume her. And maybe, just maybe, the memories the sea evoked, memories of a time when her husband had been happy and whole, would help Jack heal emotionally, as would being around the sister he loved.

How could she have know that life was about to play its wildest card and that, when the game was over, Jack would be dead? How was she to know that that summer, instead of being her salvation, would make her betray a vow that she held most dear? How was she to know that soon she was to become a stranger unto herself?

The limousine crunched to a stop, scattering Anna's thoughts. She glanced once more at Meg, hoping for just a measure of forgiveness, praying for even the smallest allotment of compassion. There was to be neither, however. Flinging wide open the door before the vehicle had even come to a complete halt, the young woman plunged headlong into the fast-falling August rain. Anna's heart sank.

"Meg, wait for an umbrella," her aunt called, but to no avail. Carrie glanced over at Anna. "She's upset," she said, trying to offer a viable explanation for her niece's erratic behavior.

"Yes," Anna said, not trusting herself to say more.

A huge black umbrella, wielded by Elijah Morganstern himself, ballooned into being. In the distance six virtual strangers, their heads bowed to the wind and rain, wrestled with the coffin. Anna knew that they were friends of Carrie's, fellow townsmen who'd graciously offered to act as pallbearers. One of them was Harper Fleming, a lawyer whom Carrie had been dating since her divorce. Had Harper and the other men thought it odd that Jack Ramey had no friends?

Anna stepped forward under the guidance of Elijah Morganstern, who had just whispered to the limousine driver, Arty Watteau, that now they were going to see some tears. Arty Watteau had had no idea what Elijah meant. Though it was well known in Cook's Bay that Arty, owner of the town's only limousine, was a soul so gentle that a fly need not fear for its life around him, it was also well known that Arty wasn't very bright. More to the point, his attention span was sometimes limited to that of a nanosecond. Out of the clear blue, he'd forget whom he was supposed to drive, where, and when. At those times, frightened and confused, he could always be found wandering down by the sea.

Presently Arty watched from beneath a visored cap as Anna plodded through the cemetery, her black high heels sinking into the soaked sod. She peered through the gray rain, eager for anything to take her mind off what was about to happen. Out of desperation she forced herself to observe her surroundings. Old and quaint, the small patch of land appeared to have been purloined from a nearby watchful forest, which threatened to snatch it back at the first unguarded opportunity. Wide-leafed oaks and white pines, tall firs and stately spruce, their greenery majestically blended to form a large lacy tent, encircled the cemetery.

Beneath these sentries, huddled close to the damp ground, giant ferns, with their spore-serried fronds, flourished. Moss and lichen, looking like a jeweler's proud presentation of emeralds, grew in profusion. A narrow creek, filled to overflowing with the present rains, meandered amid woods and over outcroppings of chunky rocks. Within the cemetery, grave markers stood a noble vigil, except for those few that, as though weary of their thankless job, listed at odd, irreverent angles. A squirrel, heedless of the rain, squatted before one such toppling tombstone.

Despite the umbrella, the rain drenched Anna's skirt by the time she reached the relative comfort of the green awning. She allowed herself to be shown to a chair, which may or may not have been positioned intentionally to set her apart from the others. Nevertheless, it was symbolic of how she felt now, of how she'd felt all along during the slow decay of her marriage.

Decay. It was the only physical act that her husband had left to complete in this life. At this bleak thought Anna avoided looking at the coffin with its delicately engraved border. She likewise refused to look at the gaping hole in the ground. Instead she studied the tombstone of Jack's grandparents, the newer headstone of his parents. She hadn't known the former at all and the latter only slightly. His parents had made it clear from the very beginning that their children, as seedlings of the town's founding fathers, would be laid to rest beside them. Two additional plots had been set aside for Jack's and Carrie's spouses. As it always did, the thought of being buried here, amid those she'd never known or hardly knew, next to a man who'd increasingly excluded her from his life, made her feel trapped.

The memory of the note her husband had written to her came flooding back. *i'm trapped in this body,* his unsteady hand had scrawled, slowly, painstakingly. *free me.* It had been the demons from the dark abyss talking. These black-spirited devils had frightened Anna, though in truth she'd realized later that what had frightened her most was that her husband's request hadn't frightened her enough. She should have been shocked, but she wasn't. For a heartbeat his plea had emotionally reunited them. This was the man whom she'd loved beyond all others, the man for whom she would have done anything.

"An-na, plea-zze." They had been the first words he'd attempted to speak since discovering that the stroke had affected his speech, and they had wrapped themselves around Anna's heart like a silken shackle.

Even now Anna felt her heart constrict at his entreaty. No, she didn't want to think about the pain in his eyes. She couldn't think about his pitiful plea. Instead she forced herself to listen to the ashes-to-ashes, dust-to-dust sermon that black-frocked Father Santelices was delivering. She forced herself to look at the spray of white carnations sprawled over the coffin, the mocking black hole in the ground, the motley crew of mourners. Meg once more sat beside her aunt, both displaying red-rimmed eyes. Still, Anna could not summon tears, even though she knew that they were expected of her. Occasionally she'd see someone whisper something to another. Were they talking about her? Did anyone notice that she wore no wedding ring?

As though in punishment for her lack of tears, shameful images restlessly prowled through her mind, an image of her lover's strong arms closing around her, an image of hot, eager lips devouring hers, an image of a coupling so complete that it had startled her. No, it had been the depth of her need that had startled her. In that passion-guided moment she had not cared about right or wrong, morality or immorality. She had cared only about filling the terrible emptiness that had so long dwelled within her. And he had filled her—her body, her heart, her soul. As she'd lain beneath him, the surf pounding the shore, the moon glistening in the diamond-studded sky, she'd spoken his name in breathless wonder. Then and there she'd made a vow to herself. Though the indiscretion must never be repeated, though she'd pay whatever price it exacted, she would never regret its having happened. How could she when he had made her feel alive again? Bowing her head, she prayed to be forgiven, not so much for the infidelity as for her unrepentance.

Father, forgive me, for I have sinned. . . .

"Father, we ask that You will be with those whose hearts are heavy, that You will comfort Jack Ramey's family in this special time of need. . . ."

Thunder drummed, drowning out both Anna's prayer for absolution and Father Santelices's for solace. It could not, however, drown out the hurtful memories of just how quickly Anna had begun to pay infidelity's price, a price she'd had no idea would be so costly.

"Where have you been?"

The words, more accusation than question, had been flung at Anna only minutes after she'd left her lover. Seeing her daughter had surprised Anna, since she wasn't supposed to have been home for the weekend, but rather studying for summer-school finals. Unknowingly, guiltily, Anna had run newly ringless fingers through her tangled hair, wondering as she did so if the golden curls spoke of a man's touch, wondering if there was telltale sand on her clothes.

Before Anna had been able to answer, her daughter had rushed ahead with, "You've been with *him*, haven't you?"

"Meg, listen—"

"My God, Mother, how could you?"

"Meg—"

"With Daddy lying in there?"

"Meg, will you listen to me?"

"No, I won't! I won't listen to you trying to explain why you took a lover. I won't listen to you trying to excuse yourself for acting like a bitch in heat!"

The crackling sound of Anna's palm striking her daughter's cheek had brought the confrontation to an abrupt halt. Anna had watched in stunned disbelief— had she really struck her daughter?—as tears jumped into Meg's doe-brown eyes. Disbelief had quickly turned to heartsickness when Meg, suddenly looking more like a little girl than a grown woman, had taken a step backward. Anna had taken a step forward, the instinctive act of a mother longing to comfort her wounded child. In this case a child she herself had injured.

"Meg, baby, I'm sorry."

Meg had not been interested in apologies, however. She had been interested only in fleeing her mother's presence, which she had done by racing from the room.

"Wait! We have to talk."

Meg hadn't even slowed her pace, making it necessary for Anna to catch up with her. Grabbing her daughter by the shoulder, Anna had whirled her around.

In that smug, sanctimonious way that only those who
have lived an inexperienced slice of life can display,
Meg had replied defiantly, "I have nothing to say to
you. Now or ever."

Jerking free of her mother, Meg had once more
started from the room. Suddenly putting the lie to her
own pledge, she had turned. Her eyes, cold and now dry
of tears, had found those of her mother.

"I'd rather see Daddy dead than ever have him learn
how you betrayed him."

Even had Anna known what to say, she wouldn't have
had the heart to say it. It was difficult to speak when
her heart had just been ripped from her chest and
thrown at her feet. Instead Anna had simply watched
her daughter exit the room. That night, with sleep further away than the stars, Anna had vowed to somehow
make her daughter understand. Come morning, however, Anna's goal had been altered drastically. Before
she could do anything else, she had to cope with the
death of her husband.

Thunder rolled again, and this time Father
Santelices took it as a sign to end the service. Stepping
forward, a golden cross hanging around his neck, he
spoke personally with Anna, leaving the mourners to
whisper among themselves. All of a sudden the notes of
conversation died away. In their stead an uncomfortable silence burst to life.

Anna glanced up.

A man stood at the awning's edge, just out of the
rain, but at a respectful distance from the private gathering. A waist-length vinyl poncho, lemon-yellow and
shiny with rain, fell from broad shoulders. Beneath the
slicker could be seen touches of a navy-and-gray uniform. In his hands he carried a straw cowboy hat,
which he twirled in a slow circle. Around his waist
hung a gun-heavy holster. Sheriff James Tate looked as

if he was on official business, but that he regretted having to be so.

"Mrs. Ramey," he said.

At the sight of Sheriff Tate an uneasy feeling had rumbled through Anna. At the calling of her name she stood, as though she instinctively knew that what was coming wasn't going to be pleasant.

"Harper . . . Carrie . . . Father," Sheriff Tate acknowledged as he passed among the mourners.

Harper Fleming was the only one who verbally acknowledged his greeting with a brief, "Sheriff."

When the officer of the law stood before Anna, he repeated her name. "Mrs. Ramey."

"Yes?"

"Mrs. Ramey, ma'am, I'm sorry to have to interrupt you at a time like this, but . . . well, the truth is that I needed to stop these proceedings before the body was interred. No need burying it, then turning right around and digging it up."

His statement produced gasps.

Finally Anna said, "I don't understand."

In response Sheriff Tate fumbled inside the slicker and pulled a paper from his shirt pocket.

"I have here a court order to exhume—in this case to prohibit the interment of—the body of Jack Nathaniel Ramey."

As he spoke, he passed the paper to Anna, who took it. She glanced down at it, vaguely aware that the uneasy feeling in her stomach was growing by gargantuan leaps.

Harper Fleming stepped forward and, taking from Anna what she seemed all too eager to hand to him, gave the document a lawyer's looking over. Then he pinned the sheriff with a simple question. "What's going on, Jim?"

James Tate rotated the hat a half circle, crushing the brim in the act, then said, "Well, seems that Dr. Goodman thinks that he might have acted too hastily in not performing an autopsy."

Anna's stomach knotted into squirming, snakelike coils. "I don't understand," she repeated.

"Well, now, there's nothing for you to worry about, Mrs. Ramey," the sheriff said. "Why don't you and Carrie"—he glanced over at the woman he'd gone through both grade school and high school with, cheerleader to his quarterback—"go get yourselves some rest. Then, maybe later this evening, I could come by the house and, well, maybe we could have a little talk."

On the surface his suggestion sounded unofficial. Anna, however, wasn't stupid enough to be fooled by surface appearances. And, apparently, neither was Carrie, for Anna noticed that she had latched on to Harper's arm. She also looked pale. On the other hand, Meg looked cool, collected, as though she were a participant in what was happening, yet at the same time curiously removed from it.

As for the others assembled, no one seemed to have a thing to say—until Anna made her way to the limousine. Then the rumblings began. Even before she reached the rented house, the town was already buzzing with what had happened at the cemetery. Phrases like *foul play* and *wanted for questioning* were recklessly bandied about, though in whispered tones, suggesting that one could say what one wanted to as long as one said it behind one's palm.

That evening, when Sheriff Tate arrived at the house, the reason for his visit became apparent from the beginning.

"Mrs. Ramey," he began, seated on the sofa of the living room, his hat once more in his hands, "was your husband despondent?"

Anna, who'd had several hours to agonize over the reason behind the sheriff's house call, was in no mood to drag out the interview.

"Of course my husband was despondent, Sheriff. He was a sick man. He'd been sick for a long while."

"Diabetes, right?"

"That's right, and the diabetes had been complicated recently by a stroke."

"Ken Larsen was working with him, wasn't he?"

That Sheriff Tate knew of Ken Larsen surprised Anna, though she instantly chastised herself. In a town the size of Cook's Bay, everyone knew everything—or thought he did. What did surprise her, though, was that Ken hadn't been present at the funeral, a fact she hadn't realized until now.

"Yes, he's the nurse-therapist I hired to work with Jack."

Sheriff Tate nodded. "And how was you husband's recovery going?"

"Poorly," Anna replied truthfully, because she would have bet money that the sheriff had already posed the question to Ken Larsen. Why he had wasn't quite clear to her yet. Before Sheriff Tate could say anything more, Anna said, "What's all this about? Why has Dr. Goodman decided to do an autopsy?"

James Tate ran his hand along the back of his head, buying time. Everything about his demeanor was laid-back, including the quiet voice that unexpectedly, abruptly, asked, "Mrs. Ramey, did your husband ever ask you to end his life? Did he ever ask you to help him end it?"

Anna sucked in a breath. She tried to sound properly shocked by the questions. "Of course not."

Before Anna's answer was even fully out, the sheriff stood and smiled. "Well, that's that, then," he said, adding, "Thank you for your time."

Anna rose from the chair, praying that her knees didn't buckle, praying that her behavior appeared normal. "Why in the world would you ask such a thing?"

As he walked to the front door, Sheriff Tate cocked

the hat on his head. When he turned toward her, he had a trust-me, good-ole-boy smile. "Just routine, ma'am."

But Anna grew to suspect that what was happening was not routine. In fact, it was far from it. Dr. Goodman's refusal to return her calls was not routine, nor was the fact, if rumor could be believed, that Dr. Goodman had shipped the body to Augusta for more detailed testing. The only thing that was routine was the gossip, which ran freely, rampantly.

And then it happened. Seven days after the funeral Anna was arrested. With a polite apology Sheriff Tate charged her with the murder of her husband, read her her rights, and carted her off to jail.

Anna wondered what had taken him so long.

TWO

By the following morning, a sunshiny Tuesday, the news was spreading through the quaint seacoast town like wildfire, leaving anyone who was distantly observing the phenomenon to conclude that Cook's Bay was the gossip capital of Maine, perhaps even of the nation.

At no place was the news more enthusiastically received than at Gouge's General Store. Though only in her late thirties, Inez Gouge, her dark hair pulled into a severe bun, her feet laced into sensible shoes, looked a good ten years older and acted a good twenty. She had never been married, never even had a boyfriend, unless one counted her third-grade beau, snaggle-toothed Billy Avery.

In short, Inez had no life of her own, certainly none with any excitement, and consequently, sadly, she was reduced to living the lives of others, which she did with a glee that caused the courser townsmen to refer to her as tight-assed and loose-lipped. Even the most generous-minded locals could only shake their heads over Inez's white toy poodle, who was always at her side and had huge colorful bows tied to its ears.

"Insulin overdose . . . found a note . . . never shed a tear . . ." a customer was presently telling Inez.

She caught only about every third word because she had just recalled a couple of incidents that had occurred in her store, the last one the very day of Jack Ramey's death. The incidents had involved his wife and that strange man who lived out at the lighthouse. More often than not Inez was forced to refer to people in nebulous terms because she could never remember names. That fact handicapped her as a gossip, but only made her job more challenging.

"What do you think?" the bearer of the news asked.

Inez, in reference to her recollection, replied, "I think it's very interesting."

The second the customer departed, Inez crossed the spotlessly clean hardwood floor to the counter. She pulled forth the telephone directory, thumbed through the pages, then, with a finger as lean as her mind was narrow, ran down a column. The desired number found, she picked up the telephone, dialed, and asked for Sheriff Tate. She began to fill his ear.

"You know that man living out at the lighthouse? Yes, that's the one. Well, something happened at the store that I think you ought to know about. He and that Ramey woman . . ."

When Inez had finished, with a flourish that said, *I dare you not to think that's important,* James Tate had to admit that, even considering the source, what he'd heard was well worth checking out.

At the same time that Inez was speaking with the sheriff, the gossip, which had become more swollen with each telling, continued on its appointed rounds. It made stops at the Snappy Scissors, where Doris, chattering away like a magpie, overprocessed the perm she was giving, at Carl Laraby's filling station and used-tire shop—he'd looked the word *euthanasia* up in a binder-torn dictionary, muttering afterward that it beat all he'd ever heard—and at the mortuary, where Elijah smugly insisted that everyone should have marked his word, that there was something mighty strange about a woman's not crying at her husband's funeral.

From there the news scooted on down to the wharf, to Bendy's Bait and Tackle Shop. Bendy Webber, a salty seaman whose hands were buried wrist-deep in wriggling worms, commented to a customer that he'd really liked the nice couple who'd rented the house out near the lighthouse. He remembered Jack Ramey from when he was a kid—used to fish with his own boy—and had met his wife a couple of times.

The man at the lighthouse was one of the last in town to hear. Sloan Marshall, his sweatsuit damp with perspiration, his raven-black hair tousled from the wind blowing off Penobscot Bay, was just completing his daily two-mile jog on the beach when he saw the postman. Actually, it wasn't the postman, but rather the sixteen-year-old son of the postman, who bicycled out twice a week to deliver Sloan's mail. Ever since Bobby Pellegrino had found out that Sloan had been in the service, which he'd deduced from the meager mail Sloan had received during his six-month stay in Cook's Bay, mail that had been addressed to Retired Commander Marshall, the young man had volunteered to take his dad's place.

Sloan tried to discourage Bobby's questions because, if there was one thing he didn't want to talk about, it was his military service. Talking about it always brought back painful memories he was trying hard to forget. Perhaps what Sloan resented most about Bobby, who was only waiting to turn eighteen so he could be-

come one of the Marines' few good men, was the fact
that he reminded Sloan that some things could never
be forgotten, or at best only temporarily. At a time
when Sloan had been in danger of losing his sanity, his
longtime friend Harper had saved it—but for what? So
that *she* could destroy it all over again? As life would
have it, that's how it had turned out.

"Stay away from her, man. She's a married woman."

Sloan could still hear Harper's caution ringing loud
and clear in his ears as he trudged up the stone steps
that had been carved out of the boulder as an access
from the lighthouse to the sea. With each step the
white-brick lighthouse, with its orange dome, came
more vividly into view, as did the keeper's inn. The latter was a modest four-room house, constructed of white
wood and a complementary orange roof. Its monastic
simplicity, in particular its isolation, had suited Sloan
and his somber mood.

Bobby waved and Sloan returned it, wondering what
Harper would say if he knew just how recklessly he'd
turned his back on his advice. But, then, Harper, for all
that he understood Sloan better than anyone in the
world, had no idea of the strength of his feelings for
Anna. He hadn't set out to fall in love with her. In fact,
he'd done everything he could to discourage his feelings, but the truth was that they, and Anna, had taken
over his heart without so much as a single consultation
as to what he wanted. They certainly seemed to have
no regard for what was prudent.

"Hi, Commander!" Bobby called, jumping from the
bicycle and letting it fall to the ground.

Sloan winced at Bobby's choice of greeting. "Hi,
Bobby."

The young man said what he always said: "Not much
mail."

Sloan reached for the couple of envelopes and the
obvious advertisements, steeling himself for the bar-

rage of military-related questions he knew was about to follow. Bobby Pellegrino surprised him.

"Have you heard?"

At this Sloan noticed for the first time the lights twinkling in the kid's eyes. Something had him very excited.

"Heard what?"

"About the arrest?"

"What arrest?"

Even as Sloan spoke, he could feel an unnatural stillness coming over him. It was the same abnormal calm he'd always gotten on a mission when some sixth sense told him that danger was near at hand.

"Your neighbor—Mrs. Ramey."

A fist slammed into Sloan's stomach. "What do you mean?"

"Mrs. Ramey's been arrested for killing her husband. They say it was eutha ... eutha ... euthasomething ... you know, mercy killing. They say he'd asked her to take his life, and she did." Warming to his subject, even if his facts were less than true, he added, "They dug up the body of her husband, sent it to Augusta, and guess what." It was obviously a rhetorical command because Bobby rushed ahead with, "He died of an overdose of insulin. And then there was something about a note she'd burned in the fireplace. You know, the note asking her to do him in. Miss Carrie sent Mr. Fleming over to represent her. . . ."

Sloan had heard nothing beyond the phrase *mercy killing*. A conversation he'd had with Anna that summer came racing back to haunt him.

"I believe one has the right to decide when to terminate his life. I couldn't fault someone for helping a loved one to do that. Does that shock you?"

Sloan could remember being shocked, though not by her admission. He had been shocked by his own frightening realization that, if Jack Ramey was dead, Anna would be a free woman. He had instantly loathed himself for entertaining such a base thought, but then self-loathing was something he'd learned a lot about over the past couple of years. Regrettably, he'd become something of an expert on the subject.

Bobby Pellegrino rattled on, his enthusiasm growing. Finally, as though he'd run out of steam, he said, repeating what he must surely have heard in town. "Imagine. Right here in quiet Cook's Bay."

Sloan could in fact imagine only what Anna must presently be feeling. When Bobby left, no doubt to spread more of the gruesome gospel, Sloan hightailed it for the house and, tossing the mail on the coffee table, grabbed the telephone. He dialed a number; then, as he waited for someone to answer, he picked up the phone, walked to the kitchen, and opened the refrigerator. Removing the water jug, he downed a hefty swallow. There was nothing like fear to parch a throat. But then, he was an adrenaline junkie—he'd long ago accepted that fact. Had he not been, he never would have volunteered for the harrowing missions he had eagerly taken on—and he never would have learned to endure, perhaps even enjoy, the dry throat right along with the pounding heart.

"Good afternoon. Harper Fleming's office. May I help—"

Sloan cut off the professionally pleasant voice of Marilyn Graber, Harper's secretary, paralegal, and only staff.

"I want to speak with Harper," Sloan told her.

"Who may I say is calling?"

"This is Sloan Marshall."

"Sorry, I didn't catch your voice. How are you doing?"

"Fine," Sloan answered, trying to sound civil even as his heart pounded a less-than-fine rhythm.

"Hold just a second."

"Thanks."

Sloan took another swallow of water, replaced the jug in the refrigerator, and kicked the door shut with his foot. Sand from his tennis shoes peppered the linoleum floor. He couldn't have cared less.

"Sloan?"

"Why didn't you call me?"

His friend obviously chose not to take exception to the accusatory tone. "It's been a madhouse around here. For that matter, she was only arrested late yesterday. I had to be with her during fingerprinting and booking, then I had to see to her bail."

The logic of Harper's comment took the wind out of Sloan's sails. He sighed. "Sorry."

"That's all right. I'd have called when I had time."

"Where is she now?"

"Carrie wanted her to come stay with her, but she refused. She wanted to go back to the rented house."

"I want to see her," Sloan said bluntly, even though he knew that he might well be the last person Anna wanted to see.

"No," came Harper's reply, equally blunt and in a tone that brooked no opposition.

Still, Sloan brooked it, willing to brook Anna, too, if he had to. He had to see if she was all right. "I want to see her."

"No," Harper repeated. "Listen to me, Sloan. What she's charged with is bad enough, but it's defendable. Historically, juries tend to take a sympathetic view toward a loved one helping a sick spouse end his or her suffering. Juries do not take a sympathetic view toward a third-party involvement, however innocent that involvement might be. Right off they get suspicious that the motive for murder might not have been all that altruistic."

Sloan thought of their "innocence." He hadn't intended to violate it. He hadn't intended for her to break her marriage vows. He, more than most, knew the pain involved in betraying a principle. It was not something he'd wish on his worst enemy, let alone someone he loved. He and Anna had fought the attraction until they couldn't fight it anymore. When she'd suddenly appeared on the beach that night, when she'd walked into his arms, so damned soft, so damned sweet, so damned needy, there hadn't been a force on earth strong enough to stop him from taking what she was willingly offering him.

Even now the thought of her impatient lips drove him mad, as did the thought of her hands desperately moving over his body. He'd known that Anna and her husband had ceased being lovers a long time ago, a fact corroborated the moment he'd entered her. After that he couldn't think of anything beyond her incredibly honest response. She hadn't played coy, but rather had met his every demand with one of her own. He'd never known a passion that pure, pleasure that sublime.

"Sloan?"

Sloan managed to rein in his wayward memories, but not before the pain of that night seared its way through him like a white-hot poker. He didn't want to remember her aloofness following their lovemaking. Neither did he want to recall her later telling him that it mustn't happen again. He certainly didn't want to remember the way she'd said that they must never see each other again.

"Sloan?"

He plowed his fingers through his hair. "Yeah?"

"Your relationship with her is innocent, isn't it?"

"Define *innocent*."

"Worshiping from afar." When Sloan said nothing, Harper said a slow, sizzling, "Shit!"

"It wasn't planned. It just . . . happened."

"Well, I'm sure the prosecutor, not to mention the jury, will overlook the indiscretion since it was unpremeditated," Harper said, his voice filled with sarcasm.

Beneath that sarcasm, however, Sloan heard concern, the concern of a lawyer for his client. "At least tell me that the two of you were discreet. Tell me that you didn't pull into a local motel and register under the name of Smith."

Sloan thought of the little cove midway between the lighthouse and the house Anna and her husband had rented for the summer. Isolated by a natural formation of rock and cliffs, it lay hidden from prying eyes. No, no one had seen them that night.

"We were discreet." Sloan sensed that his friend didn't sound convinced. "No one saw us. I'd stake my life on it."

Sloan could see his friend running his hand across his balding pate, down through the fringe of curly hair the color of summer wheat that skirted his head. In his mid-forties, Harper had been through many phases in his life. Throughout them all he took great pride in one fact—that he didn't give a damn what people thought about him.

"That may be precisely what you're doing, except it isn't your life you're playing with." Harper sighed heavily. "Why didn't you just go into town and get yourself laid? Hell, that waitress over at the Chat 'N' Chew would have been more than willing to oblige!"

"Because this hasn't been about getting laid, and you know it." Before Harper could reply, Sloan said, "I'm in love with her."

"You're obsessed with her," Harper said, and not for the first time.

"Isn't that what love is? An obsession? A fine madness?"

"I won't get into a philosophical discussion on the definition of love. However you define your feelings, stay away from her. If your relationship gets out, it's going to be the kiss of death for her."

Sloan echoed his friend's earlier sigh, not bothering

to hide the hurt that had his heart bleeding with grief. "There is no relationship. She's made that plain. She probably wouldn't see me even if you'd allow it. It's the penance she's determined to pay."

"Sorry, but, believe me, it's best. At least for now."

How about forever? Sloan thought, but asked, "What's she saying about this mercy-killing thing?"

"Very little. In fact, she's saying very little about anything."

Sloan knew that this was no time to mention the conversation that he and Anna had had on the subject of euthanasia. And it was certainly no time to tell him that he'd been at the Ramey house the night Anna's husband—his *lover's* husband—had died. No, Harper would shit bricks over that tidbit of news . . . and rightly so.

"Look," Harper said, "I know this is rough on you, but just lay low. And don't even as much as think about her, for fear somebody might read your mind. The two of you cannot be linked together. It'll kill her case if you are."

Later Sloan had to conclude how truly naive he'd been to believe that any word or deed could remain a secret in a town that had a thousand eyes. In less than a week, in exactly the time it took the grand jury to reconvene and issue an indictment, Sheriff Tate paid him a visit. Sloan suspected he was in trouble that Thursday afternoon when he saw the patrol car winding its way up the snow-white gravel path. He *knew* he was in trouble the second an unsmiling Sheriff Tate approached him.

"Mr. Marshall, it is my duty to inform you that the grand jury has handed down an indictment against you and Mrs. Ramey on one count of first-degree murder in the death of her husband Jack Ramey." Before Sloan could feel the earth rock beneath his feet, Sheriff Tate began to Mirandize him in a voice that sounded like a soulful Southern song.

The police station was a gray granite building, which historians proudly proclaimed as the site of the raising of a Cook's Bay militia to serve in the Great Rebellion, or the Civil War as it came to be more commonly called. As Sloan walked through the door, thankfully without the indignity of handcuffs, he thought that the place had all the charm of a dungeon. Fluorescent lights, in an attempt to alleviate the darkness, since windows were few and ill-spaced, ran along the ceiling like a serpentine maze of tunnels. They produced little more than a blinding glare that caused all inside to squint. At the same time a cool dampness seeped from the walls.

Panic flashed, reminding Sloan of the dark, damp nightmare he'd endured two years before. *Easy,* he reminded himself, *this is not Beirut. No one is going to lock you up. One phone call and you're out of here.*

As though reading Sloan's mind, the sheriff said, "You're entitled to a phone call."

At this Sheriff Tate's deputy, his only deputy, a young man in his mid-twenties whose name tag read Dicky Belinda, transferred a telephone from a nearby desk to the chest-high countertop.

In seconds Sloan had dialed Harper's office. He got an answering machine, on which he left a message. He tried not to sound desperate. Under the circumstances Sheriff Tate allowed him to make a second call. He dialed Harper's number at home, but Sloan met with a second round of bad luck and was forced to leave another message. He also forced himself to admit that he most likely was going to be locked up. At the mere thought his mouth went cotton dry.

"I'm sorry, Mr. Marshall, but I'm going to have to hold you until you can get in touch with your lawyer."

Sloan looked at the sheriff and merely nodded. He didn't think he could speak. In truth he was afraid to speak, afraid he'd disgrace himself by begging not to be locked up.

After the sheriff made certain that he understood the charges against him and his constitutional rights, Sloan was carted off to a cell. In this area of the building even less attention had been given to lighting, casting the half-dozen or so cubicles in a dreary yellow glow. Shadows crouched everywhere.

When the steel bars clanged shut behind him, Sloan's claustrophobia burst into full bloom. The stone walls crowded in around him, making him feel as though he were buried beneath them. His chest tightened, his breath grew rapid and uneven. Grabbing hold of the bars, he vowed that whatever happened, however long he was confined, he'd remain standing and not cower in the corner like some frightened animal.

He tried to think of Anna. Where was she now? Had she been brought in and re-charged? What was the official protocol under these circumstances? In the end, however, he couldn't keep his mind focused on anything other than the fear stampeding through him.

"Your government has forgotten you, Commander." The voice had spoken English, but with such a thick Lebanese accent that Sloan had had to strain to understand it. *"They have sacrificed you at the altar of their cowardice. Save yourself, Commander. Save yourself . . . save yourself . . . save—"*

Willing the voice, the past, away, Sloan did what he'd learned to do so expertly. He began to invent stories in his head. He was in Africa, climbing Mount Kilimanjaro, white-water rafting on the Zambezi River, trekking through deserts, jungles, and savanna. He had just begun to feel the sweltering heat of the sun, to see herds of wild animals grazing warily by a small lake, when he could have sworn he smelled urine and feces—his own—and only by the hardest effort did he convince himself that he was imagining the foul odors. He forced himself back to Africa.

Sloan had no idea how much time had passed when he heard the door of the cell block clank open and saw Harper appear. As his friend's footsteps beat out a curt tattoo on the concrete floor, Sloan realized that his hands had become paralyzed. He'd been clenching the bars so zealously that he no longer had any feeling in his knuckle-white fingers. He hoped to God he could pry them loose.

Harper took one look at Sloan's ashen complexion and asked the sheriff, "Is there some place other than here where we can talk?"

"Sure," Sheriff Tate said, unlocking the door.

Surprising himself, Sloan managed to release the bars and step forward.

When the sheriff caught a glimpse of Sloan's color and the perspiration glistening on his brow, he said, "Are you all right?"

"He's fine," Harper said, adding, "You wouldn't happen to have any coffee, would you?"

"At this time of day I can't guarantee that it's anything but hot and wet."

"That's good enough," Harper said.

Sloan looked up at the clock in the room they were ushered into. It was a little after seven. As close as he could figure out, he'd been in the cell for a couple of hours—a couple of lifetimes. Sloan slid into the first chair he came to, straight and uncomfortable and at the head of a table. Sloan guessed that the room, also equipped with glaring lights, was used for purposes of interrogation. At least there were no bars, and he was thankful Harper didn't rush into conversation, but allowed him time to collect himself. In fact, Harper didn't speak at all until the deputy had left a mug of questionable liquid on the table and Sloan had taken a deep swallow.

"I'm sorry. I came as soon as I got your message. I was in Bar Harbor, working on a case."

"What's happened to Anna?" Sloan asked, fitting his fingers around the mug. The warmth penetrated his rigid muscles, slowly allowing the stiffness to fade away. Even his breath was returning to normal.

"She was re-charged, but because she'd already been booked, she wasn't brought back in." Harper gave a crooked, mirthless grin. "Smaller towns often make their own judicial rules."

Sloan set the mug on the table and faced trouble as he always did—head-on. One reason that he could approach this crisis so squarely rested in the fact that he couldn't believe quite yet that it was happening. That would come later. Probably with a vengeance.

"We're standing in deep shit, aren't we?" he asked.

Harper was equally blunt. "Let me put it this way, it's deep enough that both of you could drown." Shaking his head, Harper added, "I should have seen this coming, but I didn't. I thought the worst that could happen if your relationship came to light was to complicate Anna's case, muddy her motive, give the prosecution a reason to hang her high. I never figured they'd drag you in too."

"Why did they?"

Harper looked his friend squarely in the eyes. "Because the prosecution thinks it has enough evidence, and obviously a grand jury agrees, to hang you from the same tree."

Sloan took the news without flinching. "What kind of evidence?"

"That I won't know until I've been able to take a look at their case."

First looking down at his mug, then up at Harper, Sloan said, "There's something you ought to know."

Harper gave a let's-hear look.

"I was at Anna's house the night her husband died."

Harper's look turned to one that said, "Give me some more good news."

"We'd had words. I had to talk to her."

"And did you?"

"Yeah, but not for long. She asked me to leave. She was upset."

"About what?"

"About what had happened earlier that night."

"Which was?" Before Sloan could answer, realization dawned. "Please tell me that you two didn't choose that night, of all nights, to become lovers."

"Damn it, Harper, we didn't choose it, period! It just happened!"

Harper passed a hand over his face, muttering, "Holy hell!"

"Look, nobody saw me leaving the house."

On a suddenly weary sigh Harper said, "Now isn't the time to sort all this out. Right now, in"—he checked his watch—"thirty minutes, we have to go before Judge Waynon to set bail. I'm assuming you don't want to spend the night in here."

The prospect sobered Sloan as little else could. "No, I do not."

"Then let's go," Harper said, starting for the door. "Oh, by the way, the arraignment has been set for Monday morning at nine o'clock. It appears everyone's in a real hurry to move on this."

It was only later, en route to the courthouse, that Sloan realized that his friend, his lawyer, had never once spoken of guilt or innocence.

When Sloan saw Anna sitting in the courtroom, his heart flip-flopped in his chest. He hadn't expected her to be present at the bail hearing, though in retrospect the fact that he hadn't only served to underscore his naiveté once more. Legally, he was in over his head, already beginning to drown in the shit that Harper had made it clear he was standing in. Right this moment, however, he didn't much care, as long as he could breathe his last, looking at Anna. Harper's accusation that he was obsessed with her might be right on the money. All he knew was that he'd never felt like this before. If truth be told, he didn't know whether loving this recklessly had cast him into heaven or hell.

Heaven, he thought as he observed Anna in quiet conversation with Marilyn Graber. Anna's hair, a shade more golden than the precious metal, cupped her heart-shaped face in a tangle of cheek-length curls. She in no way looked her forty-five years. Neither did she look like an adulteress. Or a murderer.

As though sensing Sloan's attention, Anna glanced up with sapphire-blue eyes. If his heart had turned over at the sight of her, it now shuddered to a momentary stop. He was immediately struck by how drawn and pale she appeared. Even so, she presented no delicacy of spirit. As always, she seemed possessed of some inner strength. As he watched, she typically balled one hand into a fist and lay it just at her breast, as though she drew her emotional energy from her own heartbeat. As always, he admired her strength even as he knew that it was something she needed to relinquish, if only temporarily. In his arms she had done just that. In his arms she had bestowed upon him the rare privilege of being strong for her.

Place and circumstance dimmed. Neither courtroom nor the charge of murder could halt his sudden descent into hell. God help him, if placed under oath, he would swear that he would do anything—anything at all—to have her in his life.

Anna lowered her eyes.

Harper nudged Sloan forward, indicating a chair on the other side of Marilyn. Sloan had just eased into it when the Honorable Howard Waynon, a giant of a man in a black robe, burst into the room and plopped down behind the bench.

"Let's proceed," he boomed without preamble.

"Your Honor, the prosecution feels that, because of the cold-hearted nature of this crime, a substantive figure of bail should be set."

Sloan glanced over at the prosecuting attorney, a tall, lean, extraordinarily handsome man. Based upon appearances alone, Sloan hazarded a guess that he owned three things: a closet full of expensive clothes, a roomful of workout equipment, and an ego too big to be comfortably housed in one human being. This last would demand that he spend every cent of what was probably a modest salary on the first two. For this man, image would mean everything.

"And what, Mr. Hennessey, would the prosecution call substantive?" the judge asked.

Without missing a beat Richard Hennessey replied, "Two million, Your Honor." As though fearing a misinterpretation, he clarified, "Per defendant."

Sloan added a fourth thing to Hennessey's possession list: balls. Exactly the size of his ego.

As though amused beyond words, Harper merely shook his head. At the same time, he curled his lips into a disbelieving smile. Slowly, he pulled to his feet.

"Your Honor, I'd like to take this opportunity to inform Mr. Hennessey that this is a courtroom, not Disney World."

"Might I take that to mean that you think the prosecution's proposal is unrealistic?"

"You might, Your Honor," Harper replied.

"Frankly, I'm inclined to agree," the judge said.

With the speed of lightning Richard Hennessey was on his feet. "Your Honor, this crime was particularly foul, particularly heinous. These two murdered—"

"Allegedly," Harper thundered.

"—an individual who was not only physically incapacitated, but also depressed. They took advantage of that depression. Surely this court cannot sanction leniency in a case of this magnitude. Surely these two cannot be allowed to commit such a crime—"

"Objection, Your Honor."

"Save your Titan's clash for the trial, gentlemen. We are here only to set bail."

Hennessey had no intention of going down without a fight. "If the court pleases, bail should be high if for no other reason than these two pose a flight risk. Neither defendant is from Cook's Bay. Mr. Marshall has been here roughly six months, while Mrs. Ramey makes her home in Connecticut. She and her husband were merely vacationing here, with no permanent ties to this community."

"To say that Anna Ramey has no ties to this community is a gross exaggeration," Harper countered. "She has family here."

"Her husband had family here."

"Your Honor, Anna Ramey is very close to her sister-in-law. Furthermore, the Ramey name has never needed defending in this community. It has always stood for integrity, from the founding fathers of Cook's Bay forward. Anna Ramey possesses no less integrity. She has no intention of fleeing prosecution. In fact, she and Mr. Marshall welcome the opportunity to clear their names."

Richard Hennessey gave a smug look that said that the state would welcome the opportunity to give them a chance to try.

"As for Sloan Marshall," Harper added, "Mr. Hennessey is right in saying that he has no ties to this community, but he has been a personal friend of mine for twenty years. I would stake my life on his integrity. Mr. Marshall has no intention of skipping out on bail."

"Next time I need a new best friend, I'll certainly

consider these two paragons of virtue . . ." Richard Hennessey began.

"Your Honor, sarcasm does not become the prosecution."

". . . but right now I'd like to set bail for two murderers."

"Alleged murderers."

"Gentlemen, you've been warned. This court is in no mood to bicker or dicker. Let's set bail . . . now."

"Two hundred thousand dollars, Your Honor," Harper offered.

"A million and a half," Hennessey countered.

"Two hundred fifty thousand."

"A million."

"Three hundred thousand."

"Five hundred thousand."

"Four hundred thousand," Judge Waynon jumped in, and with a finality that brought the proceedings to a halt. "Bail is set at four hundred thousand dollars per defendant. There will be a two percent surcharge for any bond by an underwriter."

Judge Waynon rapped the gavel, as if this legitimized what he'd just decreed. He then stood and left the bench.

Sloan had the uneasy feeling that his, and Anna's, life had just been auctioned off. He also sensed a conspiracy on the part of Harper and Marilyn to keep him and Anna apart, for the second that the judge departed, Marilyn ushered Anna out of the courtroom. No one could prevent one last exchange of glances, however. Though brief, it said a lot, and both the same thing: I'm confused, I'm scared, I'm sorry I got you into this.

The following morning, a Friday filled with the earthy smell of approaching autumn, the *Cook's Bay Chronicle* ran its largest headline to date. Not even wars, pestilence, and a storm that had almost blown Cook's Bay off the map in 1906 had merited what the printer called Second Coming type. The headline read: COUPLE ARRESTED IN HUSBAND'S DEATH. The article went on to say that what had once been thought to be a mercy killing was now being viewed as a murder for passion's sake.

Inez Gouge read the news over a steaming cup of Ovaltine. She gave a self-righteous, that's-what-I-thought smile, then announced to her beribboned poodle, "Right under the nose of her poor sick husband!" The dog made no comment.

Out on the pier Bendy Webber gave a slow sigh. He wished the police hadn't come around asking questions. That way he wouldn't have had to tell them what he'd seen the night Jack Ramey died. At the nearby filling station, a customer told Carl Laraby that he wasn't surprised, that there had always been something queer about Sloan Marshall, that it just wasn't normal for a man to isolate himself the way he had, that it made one think the man had secrets. In a room she rented above the Chat 'N' Chew, Tammie, who was waitressing her way through beauty school, felt a decided boost to her feminine ego. No wonder she hadn't been able to make it to first base with that good-looking Sloan Marshall. He'd been too busy diddling a married woman.

Across town, two attorneys scanned the morning newspaper. Harper Fleming, who'd been up half the night meeting with a bail bondsman, was in no mood to see that the case was already being tried in the press. He'd have to see what he could do about that. The prosecuting attorney, sitting in a house he hated, in a town he hated, in a state he hated, turned a deaf ear to the irritating crash of sea waves, waves he'd almost drowned in when he was a kid, just as his career was drowning now. If he played his cards right, however, this case could be his ticket out of this godforsaken place and into some prestigious New York law firm, befitting his talent and his impressively high IQ. As he sipped from his cup of coffee, he thanked God that he wasn't saddled with a moral character that prohibited cheating, because he just might have to shove a few aces up his Botany 500 sleeve.

THREE

"It's ridiculous," Carrie said that same Friday morning as she glared at the inflammatory headline of the newspaper. "That you, or you and Sloan, could have killed Jack is beyond belief. It's just ... well, it's ridiculous!"

Anna looked across the breakfast table at her sister-in-law. Scanning the sizzling print, Carrie wore an indignant expression and a tangerine-colored sweatsuit, both of which fit her to a T. With her penchant for bright and brilliant colors, bright and brilliant living, no one had ever called Carrie Ramey Douglas retiring. Neither had anyone ever accused her of lacking for an opinion, which was always formed from a tunnel point of view. In anyone less kind, this tunnel-sightedness might have been troublesome, yet in Carrie it was endearing, for it prohibited her from believing the worst about anyone or anything. Which her next comment proved in spades.

"There's a logical explanation for Jack's death. He died of natural causes, plain and simple. What else could it have been?"

Anna nodded toward the newspaper, which Carrie had culled as though it were good for nothing more than lining bird cages. "Try an overdose of insulin."

Her long chestnut-colored hair pulled back from her face with two tortoiseshell combs that always verged on falling out, Carrie shook her head in abject denial. The act caused the combs to ease just that much closer to freedom.

"There's been an error," she proclaimed with certitude. "Believe me, labs make them all the time. Dr. Goodman got a report back several months ago indicating that Maude Poole was pregnant." To underscore her point, Carrie added, "Maude Poole is seventy-five if she's a day. No, those guys in Augusta just made a mistake, and Harper will get to the bottom of it."

At the mention of Dr. Goodman, Anna recalled the weekly house calls that the aging, affable physician had made. As a child Jack had been his patient, as, indeed, had most of the residents of Cook's Bay. In fact, it had been Dr. Goodman who'd diagnosed Jack's diabetes. At a time when Jack's high-school buddies had been learning football patterns and moves to make on the cheerleaders, Jack had been learning about blood-sugar levels and how to inject himself with insulin. Dr. Goodman, who'd witnessed Jack's struggle, had apparently never forgotten. When Carrie, who'd worked as a receptionist for the doctor ever since her divorce five years before, had mentioned that Jack was spending the summer in Cook's Bay, Dr. Goodman had taken it upon himself to stop in. Anna had welcomed his friendship as much as she had his monitoring of her husband's condition.

Ever since the arrest, acting on the advice of Harper,
Carrie had taken a leave of absence from her job at Dr.
Goodman's office. This concerned Anna, for she knew
how much Carrie enjoyed her work, and how much she
thought of the man who'd become not only her em-
ployer, but also her friend.

"I'm sorry about your having to take a leave from
your job."

Carrie merely shrugged. At this the comb at one ear
fell out. Haphazardly threading it back, she said, "Actually, I'm a little miffed at Dr. Goodman. I don't know
what he could have been thinking about, ordering the
authorities in Augusta to perform an autopsy. I understand that as county coroner he has the right to ask for
one, and I suppose I understand his wanting to turn
the job over to someone else what with his being a
friend of the family, but . . ." She trailed off, then
added, "Before it's over, he'll be apologizing. Harper
will see to that."

At the mention of Harper, and of Carrie's unwaver-
ing faith in him, Anna turned her thoughts in the direction of her legal counsel. She'd never understood
what had caused the prominent lawyer to walk away
from a New York law firm so successful that its clien-
tele list read like Who's Who. He'd represented everyone from movie stars to politicians to the ordinary man
accused of extraordinary crimes. At the height of his
career, with a superlative record to his credit, he'd
cashed it all in and moved to picturesque, but hardly
big-time, Cook's Bay.

Suddenly a feeling of unreality closed around Anna,
smothering her with its dreamlike presence. Who
would have ever thought that one day she would be his
client? She and Sloan.

Sloan.

She'd tried so hard not to think about him, especially
since the bail hearing the evening before. She had

known he would have to be present, she'd even convinced herself that she could handle seeing him again, but when he'd walked into the courtroom, something inside her had burst to life, just the way she herself had come to life in his arms. The memory of their tryst on the beach, his coming to the house later that night, their heated discussion—all returned with a startling clarity. As did the thought that Jack had been only steps away, right down the hall in the first-floor master bedroom. Had he heard her slip out the back door? Had he heard her talking with her lover? Had he—

Anna jumped at the shrill sound of a whistle.

"The teakettle," Carrie explained, bounding from the chair and into the kitchen. "How about Darjeeling?"

Willing her voice to sound normal, Anna said, "Darjeeling's fine."

As though Carrie's presence had been centering her, Anna stood and walked to the window. A blood-red maple leaf, looking forsaken, drifted aimlessly past the window. Beyond, in the forest surrounding the dwelling—like a gift, the forest parted to allow a single glimpse of the sea from the house—the leaves were beginning to turn their autumnal palate of colors—yellows, golds, and oranges as burnt as sacrificial offerings. As the season progressed, nature's covenant would be completed until, finally, the trees would stand stark and bare, waiting impatiently for the first cleansing fall of snow.

Will the snow wash away my sin?

Whether it was the lack of an answer or the thought of snowdrifts or the fact that she felt alone in a way she never had before, an icy chill crept through Anna despite the warm sweatsuit she wore. She hugged her arms about her, feeling as gray as the sweatsuit's color. Gray. The color of the fog that sometimes moved in off the bay like a ghost, the color of the huge rocks that rose up like hump-backed monsters beached on their journey back to the sea, the color of oneness.

In the distance Anna could hear the sea mocking her loneliness. As the waves rushed tirelessly, timelessly ashore, crashing like thunder against the salt-encrusted boulders, spewing the foamy mist high, she could hear them whispering her name. No, it wasn't her name that the waves whispered. It was Sloan's. With each sighing of his name, the sea reminded Anna that it had not filled the empty vessel she'd become—that Sloan had.

This reminder of Sloan brought a return of a question that was never far from Anna's mind. What did Carrie think about her and Sloan being linked together? The newspaper had pulled no punches. Furthermore, Anna couldn't believe that Carrie hadn't suspected their relationship long before now. She might even feel guilty for throwing the two of them together. It had been Carrie who'd insisted, as they stumbled into the month of August, that Anna was dog-tired and needed some relief from caring for Jack at night. She'd suggested hiring Sloan, and so the two of them had tip-toed around temptation for one seemingly never-ending weekend. After Carrie had walked in on a revealing, passionate scene, Sloan had quit, with a cock-and-bull story that no one could have bought. Anna had expected her sister-in-law to say something, but she never had. Now, however, was the time to broach the subject.

"Here you go," Carrie said, carrying two cups of hot tea.

Anna returned to the table, took a seat, and plunged before her courage failed. "We have to talk."

"About what?"

"About me and Sloan."

Carrie's gaze dropped from Anna to the cup of tea, which she began to heap sugar into. "That's what makes me angriest of all," she said. "That anyone could have so misunderstood your relationship. For heaven's sake, the two of you are only friends. Excuse me, but can't a man and a woman be friends?"

Anna studied her sister-in-law, who still wasn't meeting her eyes, but rather was now busier than busy pouring cream into her tea. She honestly couldn't tell if Carrie believed what she was saying, or if she'd just chosen this way to allow her to save face.

"Look," Carrie said, finally meeting Anna's gaze, "don't worry. Harper will take care of everything."

Anna let the subject of her and Sloan drop, maybe because she wanted to believe, as illogical as it was, that Carrie didn't suspect; maybe because she wanted to believe, again perhaps illogically, that somehow Harper could take care of everything. He'd certainly done so at the bail hearing and later with the bail bondsman. In short order forty thousand, the required ten percent of set bail, had been met. Anna had come up with half of it herself, while Carrie had come up with the remainder. As collateral Anna had used the home in Connecticut and some oceanfront property that Jack and Carrie jointly owned in Cook's Bay.

"Thanks for helping out with the bail," Anna said.

"Don't be silly. We're a family." For the first time that morning Carrie's voice cracked, evincing the grief she bravely tried to hide. "Jack would want us to stick together."

Anna placed her hand atop Carrie's and gave her first smile since the hellish nightmare had begun. "Yes, he would. Of that I'm certain."

"I want the family to stick together," Harper said that afternoon.

He and Anna—Sloan had yet to arrive—sat in his law office, which was located downstairs in a monstrous two-story white clapboard house he'd bought his first week in Cook's Bay. It was the first house the realtor had shown him, and he'd fallen in love straightaway. He'd admitted later that he'd bought it not so much because of the beautiful flower gardens, the seventeenth-century white marble mantel in the room he'd made into his office, or the fact that a famous sea captain had once owned it, but rather because it was within hearing distance of the bells of St. Catherine's, a curious admission for a self-proclaimed atheist.

"In fact," Harper continued, "family solidity is crucial to your case. The jury has got to see that your family is behind you one hundred percent. I want Carrie and your daughter in that courtroom every day of the trial. To be honest, Carrie's presence is the best thing that you and Sloan have going for you. The jury has got to be moved by the fact that the sister of the man you two are accused of killing believes in your innocence."

Anna shifted in the large white leather chair. With her white slacks and white blouse, she seemed to disappear in it except for her dark blue eyes, eyes that appeared troubled by Harper's statement.

Ever attuned to signals, Harper asked, "Is there a problem?"

"No problem," Anna said, adding, "At least with Carrie. It's just that my daughter, Meg . . . she's in med school, back in Connecticut. . . . She uh, she starts a new semester soon . . . and it's . . . well, it's almost impossible to catch up if you ever fall behind."

If there had been any doubt in Anna's mind that her excuse sounded lame, that doubt vanished the instant Harper fixed her with his gaze. For a few dramatic moments he said nothing, merely stared at her with eyes that, like hers, were blue. Unlike hers, however, his were so pale that they bordered on being colorless, a fact that left one feeling that the man could see right through you. Anna suspected she'd just discovered the secret of his legal success.

"Let me get this straight," Harper said, kicking back in the plush chair that sat behind the cluttered cherrywood desk. His lazy attitude suggested that what he was about to say didn't amount to much. Anna knew better. "You're going to stand trial for murder—the murder of your husband, your daughter's father—and your daughter won't be able to attend because she might fall behind in her studies?"

Anna tilted her chin upward, at an angle that was decidedly defiant. "I don't want my daughter present."

"Why?"

Anna stood and walked to the nearest window. She knew that Harper would perceive her move as buying time, which was exactly what she was doing. She needed to decide just how much to tell this man. The vast sea of purple chrysanthemums blooming in the rock-edged flower bed offered no answer, no more than did the tree-sized hydrangea with its huge clusters of yellow-white blossoms. Neither did the bells of St. Catherine's, which hauntingly chimed the hour of four. That left Anna pretty much on her own in terms of making a decision. Having made it, she turned and met Harper's eyes squarely.

"My daughter and I aren't speaking. More accurately, my daughter isn't speaking to me."

"I see. And why is that?"

"Meg is angry."

"Why?"

To Anna's credit she didn't hesitate. "She knows about me and Sloan."

"Ah, and she's not taking it well."

Anna laughed mirthlessly. "Let me put it this way. She'd like to see me wearing a scarlet letter."

"Does your daughter's reaction surprise you?"

It was an interesting question, one Anna hadn't asked herself, possibly because she'd been too busy coping with the pain of her daughter's rejection, possibly because she just didn't want to know the answer.

Anna shrugged her shoulders, saying, "Yes and no."

"Explain that."

Could she? Could she explain in several well-chosen sentences what it had been like for her and her daughter to live with Jack?

"When illness is present in a family, it becomes a member of that family. Oftentimes the most powerful member. From the beginning Meg seemed to sense that her father was different, that we had to make concessions."

Anna paused, as though besieged with a bevy of past memories.

Brushing them aside, she continued. "She seemed to understand that sometimes the father she adored made her mother's life difficult. As she grew older, I think she increasingly felt the strain of our dysfunctional family. We never bonded against Jack, but more and more we bonded together in a sort of spiritual survival. Because we were so close, I guess I am surprised at the depth of her anger, at her total refusal to try to understand." Anna sighed. "But then maybe it's too much to expect any child, however old, however mature, to understand one parent betraying another."

"And how about you? Do you understand why you and Sloan had an affair?"

Harper had posed another question that Anna had yet to ask herself. Interestingly, it was an easy question to answer. "I understand what led to it—living with Jack wasn't easy—but that in no way excuses what I did. Whatever I did, whatever you might think of me, I do have my principles," she said with another raise of her chin, as though she defied him to deny it.

He didn't. Instead he asked, "Was your husband abusive?"

Harper slipped the question in so casually that Anna didn't think twice about answering it. "Never physically and I don't think ever intentionally. It was just that he was angry, angry at having the disease, angry with its debilitation, angry with himself for being angry. I was just the convenient object of transference."

"It sounds as if you've had therapy."

"A couple of times over the years. When things got progressively worse, we tried therapy, but it never took."

"Why?"

"Jack always dropped out after a session or two. He always claimed I was the one with the problem. Look," Anna said abruptly, "I'm not real good at talking about my marriage."

Even as she said it, she realized that, in part, she'd lied. Although it was true that she wasn't comfortable talking about her marriage with most people, she had found it amazingly easy to talk to Sloan about it. She'd told him things about her life, her marriage, that she had never shared with anyone else. Intimate things. Things that normally would have had to be dragged out of her. Oddly enough, she'd related them to Sloan without even being coaxed. The reason was probably simple. He was willing to listen to her, offering his support but never any criticism. But, then, that was what a friend was for. And he had been her friend long before he'd been her lover.

"You said that your daughter's anger both did and didn't surprise you. You've told me why it did, but not why it didn't."

"Meg adored her father, and he adored her." Anna smiled, this time genuinely. "When he was being difficult, she could always do more with him than I could. Particularly after the stroke. She was the only one who could even come close to coaxing a smile from him."

"Was he depressed?"

"He was ill. Illness generates depression."

"Then he was depressed." The question had turned into a statement that Harper waited for her to refute.

Anna didn't, but neither did she mention that her husband had asked her to help him end his life. The less said about that, the better. "Of late he was depressed."

"You said that your daughter could do more with your husband than anyone else. Was she responsible for any of his care?"

Anna was careful not to hesitate. "After the stroke we both became caregivers, along with the professional help that I hired."

"And who was responsible for giving your husband his insulin injections?"

This time Anna did balk.

Harper said bluntly, "I'm going to be asking a lot of difficult questions. It's part of my job. It's what you're hiring me to do."

Anna nodded that she understood, then said, "Before the stroke Jack administered his own injections. Following that, I was primarily responsible. When Meg was home from school—she went to summer school but came to visit every weekend or so—she often gave the shots. Of course, when the nurse we hired was on duty, he gave them."

"Just the three of you?"

"Yes."

"Never Sloan?"

"Never."

"Carrie?"

Anna shook her head vehemently. "Carrie won't stay in the same room where an injection is being given. She's one of those people who's terrified of needles."

Harper frowned, apparently surprised to learn this tidbit of knowledge about the woman he'd dated for over a year. He obviously thought it of little value, however, for he immediately glanced at some papers on his desk, changing the subject with the comment, "Your husband's time of death has been fixed at sometime between midnight and four A.M. on Saturday, the twenty-second of August. Who was present at the house during that time?"

Anna hadn't noticed the papers before and wondered just what kind of information they contained. She didn't have to wonder at the seriousness of the question. In effect he was asking who could have given her husband an overdose of insulin.

"Meg and me."

"But Carrie was present?"

"Yes, Carrie was present."

"As was Sloan," Harper added. It wasn't a question, but a declaration of the most definitive nature.

Try as hard as she could, Anna failed to keep her surprise from showing. It said clearly, concisely, "How could you have possibly known that?"

"I told him," came a soft but richly masculine voice.

Anna looked toward the doorway. When her gaze met Sloan's, she had the oddest feeling that she'd stepped back in time to their first meeting. She'd set a trap for him, there on the beach, then had waited patiently for her quarry to take the bait. What she hadn't expected was to be ensnared in her own trap—hard and fast and without the least hope of escaping. No, that day all she saw was a man who should have been a stranger but wasn't, a man tall and lean and dark-haired, a man whose eyes were hidden behind gray, mysterious-looking sunglasses. Later she would learn that he had eyes as dark as his hair, as dark as his past, eyes capable of looking at her honestly, openly, as though she was actually there. It was the same look he presently gave her.

Then and now it took her breath away.

When second bled into second, with neither Sloan nor Anna breaking eye contact, Harper said, nodding toward one of the two chairs in front of his desk, "Come on in, Sloan."

The command broke the spell that had woven itself around them. Sloan looked away first, and Anna watched as he walked across the room. As always he was dressed casually but with attention to detail. His khaki slacks bore a crisp crease, and his shirt, the same inky black color as his hair, showed a similar meticulousness. He had rolled up the sleeves of the shirt, leaving a portion of both arms bare. Beneath the black hair blanketing his arms, muscles rippled, suggesting a hidden strength. Before this summer Anna had forgotten just how sexy a healthy male body could be. It wasn't something that she would ever forget again.

Nor would she ever forget the scars disfiguring his back. Many in number and harsh in character, they had been etched into his skin with a cruel, sadistic hand. The unexpected sight of them had sickened her—not their presence, but the fact that one human being could inflict such pain on another. Without thinking of the consequences, she had traced one, then another, with fingertips guided by compassion, tenderness, a fullness in her heart on which she chose not to bestow a name. For an unsettling moment she was once more standing in the kitchen of the rented house, seeing Sloan's back, feeling the welts beneath her fingers, hearing the hissing sound that seeped from his parted lips.

Just as Carrie had interrupted the scene, so now did Harper interrupt the memory of it. Motioning Anna to the adjacent chair, he said, "There are several things I want to go over with you two today."

Anna took her seat, careful not to look in Sloan's direction. She couldn't help but notice, however, the sunglasses tucked inside his shirt pocket, sunglasses that he wore not so much for protection against the sun as to ensure his privacy, which he guarded as though it were his most valuable possession. Even now she sensed that there were things about him, his past, that she didn't know. And maybe never would.

"I want to make certain that you understand what the arraignment on Monday is about," Harper said, snagging Anna's attention. "Plus, I wanted to let you know that I entered a motion for separate trials, but the judge denied my request."

With this comment Harper did more than snag Anna's attention. The only trouble was that she didn't understand what he'd just said, a fact to which she admitted.

Harper explained. "It would be best if you and Sloan had separate trials. Even separate counsel. Of course, the state wants to try you two together, so that they can play up the conspiracy angle."

"I don't understand," Sloan said, echoing Anna's confusion. "Why would we want separate trials?"

Anna noted Harper's hesitation. Finally the lawyer said, "Separate trials would allow each of you to pursue an antagonistic defense."

"What's an antagonistic defense?" Anna asked, clearly beating Sloan to the question.

Another hesitation hovered in the air before Harper answered. "An antagonistic defense would allow each of you to point a finger at the other."

"No!" Anna and Sloan roared in unison.

"Okay, okay!" Harper said. "As your attorney I felt obligated to make the motion, but as I said, the judge denied it." Harper gave his clients a few seconds to collect their wits, then, unable to spare any further delay, said, "I want to go over what evidence the prosecution has. Keep in mind, though, that I have only the bare bones of the evidence now. I've filed discovery motions, which the prosecution will have to honor, but Hennessey will hold on to everything as long as he dares."

Separate trials and antagonistic defenses were instantly forgotten. "What kind of evidence do they have?" Sloan asked.

Harper didn't mince his words when he answered, "Substantial."

Anna, reeling from this new and present danger, felt that dreamlike world threaten to suck her into its unreal depths once more.

"The basis for the grand jury's indictment is pretty straightforward." Harper glanced down at the papers on his desk. "The male nurse, Kenneth Larsen, claims that he saw a note that Jack Ramey had written to his wife, asking her to help him take his life. He also claims that you"—here he looked up at Anna—"destroyed the note. Then there's the unalterable fact that Jack Ramey died of an insulin overdose. Add to that the scintillating rumors of an affair between the two of you, plus the fact that you"—he looked at Sloan—"were apparently seen leaving the house the night of Jack's death. Furthermore, a witness is prepared to testify that you threw something into the sea. Now I'm not certain just yet what that something was, but presumably it was the paraphernalia used to administer the lethal dosage."

The room exploded with silence. Any one of the pieces of evidence would have been damaging. As a whole, they formed an army against which one surely could not expect to do battle and win.

Hating herself for needing another's strength, Anna turned toward Sloan. He seemed as lost as she, however. Sitting quietly, he simply stared off into space. She would have sworn that his normally tanned complexion had paled, and that beads of perspiration had popped out on his brow. Even so, he was first to speak, and, admirably, with a calm voice.

"It sounds serious."

"It does provide motive, means, and opportunity, which is primarily all a grand jury is looking for. It's simply their job to say that a crime was committed and that it's possible that the defendant—in this case defendants—committed it."

"What about a trial jury?" Sloan asked. "How do you think they'll perceive the evidence?"

"Let's understand one thing right up front about a trial jury. It's the most unpredictable animal on the face of the earth. Unlike a grand jury, a trial jury has to find a defendant guilty beyond a reasonable doubt, but getting twelve separate minds to agree on what constitutes reasonable doubt becomes the problem."

Harper rose and walked to a sideboard, where he poured himself a cup of coffee. He looked toward Anna and Sloan, asking with a gesture of his hand if they, too, would like a cup. Both declined, Anna because she didn't think anything could slip beyond the silent scream that seemed lodged in her throat. God, was this really happening?

"But surely all the evidence is circumstantial," Sloan said.

"Sure it is," Harper agreed. "Anything less than an eyewitness who saw either of you, or the two of you, inject Jack Ramey with the fatal overdose is circumstantial, but . . ."

Anna was certain she wasn't going to like this *but.*

". . . the prisons are full of people who've been convicted on less."

No, she didn't like it. Not one little bit. And apparently neither did Sloan, for he uttered an explicit expletive.

"On the other hand, this is no time to panic," Harper said, obviously smelling the fear that had invaded the room like some sour perfume. He took a sip of coffee, set the cup on the desk, and pulled forward the papers he'd been reading from. Taking a pen in hand, he said, "Let's go over each point separately. By the way, Marilyn is trying to find out who this witness is who supposedly saw you leaving the house that night.

As I said, in due time we'll have access to that information. I'm just trying to get ahead of the game."

"I've already told you I was there that night," Sloan said.

"Right, but let's start at the beginning," Harper said. He had cautioned both Anna and Sloan to be circumspect regarding what they said to the police. As for Harper and his clients, they had yet to speak of the specifics of that fateful night. "The two of you had met earlier that evening on the beach."

Sloan nodded.

Harper directed his question to him. "You told me the meeting wasn't planned. Do you still stand by that?"

"Yes!" Sloan and Anna said in unison.

One quick look at Sloan, and Anna repeated, "It wasn't planned." She clung to the spontaneity of their meeting as though it were somehow a point of honor, as though it excused, at least in some small measure, what had happened that night.

"What time did the two of you meet?"

Sloan answered. "I'm guessing, but I'd say somewhere a little after eleven."

Harper looked at Anna, who indicated her confirmation.

"Okay, so the two of you met a little after eleven. Then what?" When neither Sloan nor Anna answered, Harper prompted with another question. "Did you talk?"

Anna didn't consider herself shy. Now, however, her cheeks flushed with heat. As she recalled, not much dialogue had been exchanged.

"A little," Sloan said.

"Okay," Harper said, not missing a beat, "the two of you met accidentally on the beach sometime a little after eleven, talked some, but not much, then had sexual intercourse—"

Anna must have made a sound because, suddenly, Harper halted and looked directly at her, although his comment included Sloan.

"The two of you are going to have to get used to it. Before it's over, the prosecution is going to imply much worse. Hennessey's going to do everything he can to make what happened between you sound sordid—"

"It wasn't sordid!" Sloan interjected.

"I never said it was, but it's part of the prosecution's job to make it appear that way, and make no mistake about it, he's already got enough proof of an affair to convince a grand jury that you two didn't meet to discuss the weather. Furthermore, don't underestimate Richard Hennessey. He's good."

"Great, that fact warms the cockles of my heart," Sloan said, rising, going to the sideboard, and pouring a cup of coffee.

"Forget about the affair for now," Harper said. "Let's talk about your being at the scene the night Jack Ramey died. What time were you there?"

Sloan took a long, hot swallow, as though fortifying himself. "We were on the beach for probably thirty minutes. It's less than a ten-minute walk back to the lighthouse, where I immediately took a shower. It was midnight when I walked out of the bathroom."

"You're certain of that?" Harper asked.

"Positive. I looked at the clock."

"What did you do then?"

"I paced, I tried to sleep, I paced some more. Sometime around one o'clock I headed for the house."

"What time did you arrive?"

"Between one and one-thirty, I'd guess," Sloan said, immediately making it more specific: "Probably about one-fifteen, one-twenty."

Harper turned his attention to Anna. "What happened next?"

"I saw him from my bedroom window, so I"—she

started to use the word *sneaked*, but felt that it sounded too tawdry—"I went downstairs—"

"Your bedroom is upstairs?" Harper interrupted.

"Yes. Jack had the master bedroom. It's downstairs, because of his wheelchair. Plus, this bedroom was larger than the ones upstairs. We needed the extra room to care for Jack, especially with the few pieces of exercise equipment we'd rented. Exercise equipment for his stroke rehabilitation," Anna clarified. Harper nodded that he understood. "Anyway," she continued, "I went downstairs, through the mudroom, and down the outside stairs that lead to the garage. Sloan and I talked for just a few minutes."

"Did you argue?"

"I wouldn't call it arguing. It was more a heated discussion." Anna sighed, admitting, "I was upset."

"About what?"

Anna met the question with commendable frankness. "I had just committed adultery. Furthermore, my daughter had confronted me with that fact."

Though Anna was careful not to look in Sloan's direction—he remained by the sideboard—she could feel that her last comment had startled him. She knew if she was to look up, she'd find his dark eyes, a brooding shade of brown, turned directly on her.

If Anna had avoided visual contact with Sloan, the look Harper gave his friend cut to the point. "What did you do next?"

"I returned to the lighthouse."

"But not before you threw something into the sea."

For a few silent seconds Anna could have sworn that a small war had just been launched. For those same silent seconds she had the distinct impression that Sloan was considering not answering. When he did speak, he answered only in a roundabout way.

"What I threw into the sea had nothing to do with injection paraphernalia."

His pale-blue eyes once more doing what they did best, Harper asked, "What did you throw into the sea?"

A pause. A sigh. A simple admission. "A seashell."

The sudden wrinkling of Harper's forehead expressed his surprise eloquently. "A seashell?"

"That's right. Not very lethal, is it?"

Anna had the curious feeling that now it was Sloan avoiding looking at her, though he certainly had her full visual attention, and had ever since the mention of a seashell.

"Why a seashell?" Harper asked.

There was another slight pause before Sloan, who'd obviously realized that he was going to have to explain himself, said, "Anna had been looking for a special shell all summer but hadn't been able to find one. Ironically, I'd found a shell that afternoon." He shrugged. "Maybe I was hoping she'd see it as a peace offering. Maybe I was hoping it would say what I didn't seem to have the words to say. Maybe . . . hell, I don't know what I'd hoped!"

Anna felt as if a tight fist had squeezed her heart. He'd found the kind of shell she'd searched for all summer, the kind of shell that had become far more important to her than it should have, and, typical of his caring nature, he'd brought it to her. Why, then, hadn't he given it to her?

Sloan seemed to hear the question hanging in the air. "In the midst of our argument, our discussion, I forgot the shell. Afterward I didn't think she'd want it or, for that matter, anything else I had to offer. Burial at sea seemed appropriate. For the shell and our relationship."

The fist squeezing Anna's heart doubled its effort until her breathing felt as shallow as seawater caught in an ankle-deep cove. Unknowingly, she made her own fist and laid it over her heart. She tried to drag her gaze from Sloan, but, even if her life had depended on her doing so, she could not. Sensing that her eyes were on him, Sloan, as equally compelled as she, glanced over at her. The room suddenly seemed charged with lightning, the kind that erupts out of a dove-gray sky to herald an approaching storm.

Harper obviously sensed this emotional storm, for he said, "Just a few more points, and we'll call it quits for the day."

Sloan swallowed the last of his coffee, saying in a voice filled with frustration, "Yeah, let's get it over with."

Harper obliged, turning his attention to Anna. "Did your husband write you a note asking you to help him end his life?"

"Yes."

"Did you subsequently destroy the note?"

"Yes. I burned it in the fireplace."

"Why did you destroy it?"

"Meg was coming to visit that weekend. I didn't want her finding it. I knew that it would upset her."

Harper's look said that he was perplexed. "If you destroyed the note, what opportunity did Kenneth Larsen have to find it?"

"I didn't burn it right away. When Jack proposed the idea, my first reaction was to flee. It was only after I returned to the house that I remembered the note."

"Why did you flee?" Harper asked.

"Jack's note had stunned me, even frightened me. I knew he was depressed, he'd even hinted that he'd be better off dead, but he'd never come right out with the request."

"Do you have strong views against euthanasia?"

"As a matter of fact, I have strong views pro euthanasia."

"Then why were you stunned, even frightened by your husband's request?"

"It's one thing to have abstract views, quite another to have a concrete request to act on that abstraction."

Harper's comment was to ask another question. "Where did you flee to?"

Anna glanced over at Sloan, he at her.

"The lighthouse," she said, with another defiant tilt of her chin.

"To Sloan," Harper said, saying what she had carefully avoided saying.

"Yes."

"Did you tell him about your husband's note?"

"Yes. I was upset. I needed someone to talk to."

"She didn't kill—" Sloan began, but was cut off by Harper.

"I didn't ask you that."

It struck Anna as odd that Harper wasn't asking that very thing. It seemed a pertinent question in view of the circumstances. Furthermore, why hadn't he asked if the two of them had plotted to kill her husband?

"Look, let's call it quits for today," Harper said, standing as though in dismissal. "The arraignment is Monday. Its purpose is to officially charge you with the crime and let you enter your plea. It's that simple."

Anna had stood at the same time Harper had. Again she thought it strange that Harper had assumed their innocence without asking for confirmation.

"By the way," Harper said, "I want to lay my own ground rules." He looked at Anna, his next words bringing the conversation full circle. "Rule one, your daughter *will be* in court. Rule two"—here he included Sloan—"I don't care what the two of you do with your lives following this trail, but for its duration I don't want you to see each other outside the courtroom, outside this law office. Is that clear?"

Anna looked at Sloan.

Sloan looked at Anna.

Sloan spoke. "As I told you, that doesn't pose a problem."

"Good. Oh, one other thing. When we're in the courtroom, there's to be no jump-your-bones looks. Forgive my bluntness. It's just that juries can bring back even blunter verdicts."

Anna, her cheeks stinging with embarrassment, left before Sloan. She was midway back to the house before a troubling thought occurred. Perhaps there was a simple reason why Harper hadn't asked if she, if they, were guilty. Maybe he was afraid of what he'd hear.

FOUR

Was that really necessary?" Sloan asked when Harper walked back into his office after showing Anna out.

In the interim Sloan had paced the room, had poured another cup of coffee, which he had yet to touch, and had plopped down in the chair he'd earlier occupied. He couldn't get that last image of Anna out of his mind—Anna trying to hide her embarrassment, Anna looking everywhere but into his eyes. A part of him was angry with Harper for putting her on the spot. Another part of him accepted the fact that his friend, his lawyer, was only doing his job. The angry part had posed the question, which Harper was taking his damned sweet time answering!

"You mean my telling you two not to see each other or my telling you not to look as if you're ready to jump each other?"

"Both."

Harper eased into the chair behind the desk with all the casualness of a cat curling down for a nap. His gaze, anything but casual, however, engaged Sloan's directly. From the very first time he'd met Harper, Sloan had admired his forthrightness. Harper wasn't a man to pussyfoot around anything.

"Keep a couple of things in the forefront of your mind," Harper said, not pussyfooting now any more than he ever had. "This is a closed community. Even though the Rameys have roots here, Anna is a virtual stranger, and you, my friend, are even a worse liability. You're someone who hasn't tried to fit in. Oh, not that the citizens of Cook's Bay would have allowed you anymore than cursory entrance into their small-town society, at least not without a whale of a struggle—hell, even after three years they still consider me a 'from-away'—but you haven't even tried."

Sloan knew that Harper was right. He *hadn't* tried to fit in. Polite though he'd been, he'd kept to himself. Ironically, the physical scars needed no encouragement to heal. Perversely, they seemed only too willing to do so. It was the emotional scars that had continued to fester. Like a wounded animal, he'd sensed that he'd needed isolation, which had been the single selling point of the lighthouse. When Harper had caught up with him, newly retired, he'd been traveling the country like a vagabond. With no family he'd had no clear-cut destination. Harper had offered him the lighthouse, seclusion, the opportunity to find the man he'd once been. How in the world could he have guessed six months before that Anna would so unexpectedly come into his life? How could he have guessed that only in finding her would he find himself?

". . . helps that she looks as pure as the first fall of snow."

Sloan refocused on what Harper was saying.

"Bear in mind, though, that even that first snowfall eventually turns to a messy slush. Adultery is a messy affair anywhere, but in a town as straitlaced as Cook's Bay, it alone is enough to convict you. Not that this town doesn't have its fair share of it, but you and Anna have had the poor taste to get caught at it. Furthermore, every time the story is told, her husband's halo glows brighter, while the two of you come just that much closer to sprouting horns."

Sloan had arrived at this conclusion all by himself, and though he was no lawyer, he'd already guessed at some of the attendant legal complications. "Then how are we ever going to find an impartial jury? Wouldn't it be better to request a change of venue?"

"Believe me, I've thought of that, and I might make the request yet. However . . ."

At Harper's pause Sloan asked, "However?"

"I'm not sure how much good it'll do." Before Sloan could ask the obvious, Harper explained, "This thing is spreading far beyond Cook's Bay. Three major Maine newspapers, one as far away as Augusta, carried the story today."

"Damn!"

"That isn't the worst of it. Jake Lugaric called this morning and wanted our version of the story."

Sloan immediately recognized the name as that belonging to a national newscaster, a man noted for getting the story at any cost. That he was fishing around sent a wave of panic skittering along Sloan's every nerve ending.

"What did you tell him?" Sloan asked.

"That we had no comment. That only enticed him more. My guess would be that you and Anna will make the national news tonight."

Sloan's panic flashed. To the accompaniment of a foul expletive, he jumped from the chair and began pacing the room again.

"Never underestimate the public's love of the lurid," Harper said. "Adultery is always a crowd pleaser, and so is murder, especially if it's premeditated and cold-blooded. Put them together and you've got a first-class attraction that not even Barnum and Bailey can match. And Hennessey's going to take full advantage of the press."

Sloan stopped pacing long enough to ask, "What do you mean?"

"A case like this could be the making of our hungry prosecutor," Harper explained, adding, "And he *is* hungry. Not ambitious—ambition has its bounds—but hungry. Hungry, as in a gnawing bellyache that won't go away. Hungry, as in wanting everything and not one thing less. Hungry, as in he's never going to be satisfied but doesn't have sense enough to know that yet."

Realization dawned like the sun at daybreak. "In other words, he wants everything you turned your back on."

"Exactly."

Sloan was one of the few people who knew why Harper had left New York at the height of his career. With prestigious clients aplenty, with a fashionable Fifth Avenue apartment, with a status-symbol sports car and a yacht, Harper had simply grown tired of playing games. He'd grown tired of practicing law not for the sake of practicing law, but as merely a means to other ends, namely, riches and fame. Like a pit viper, the perfect life had turned on Harper, sinking its fangs deep, injecting him with the poisonous venom of unhappiness. Suddenly he'd hated going to work each morning; suddenly he'd despised the fishbowl his life had become; suddenly he'd wanted to get back to basics, which he considered the anonymous practice of law. Regrettably, his wife had clung to the old agenda—and the fashionable Fifth Avenue apartment. She'd wanted only one change in her lifestyle: a divorce.

As Sloan studied his friend, he realized one other thing. "This case could throw you right back in the limelight, couldn't it?"

Harper shrugged and smiled. "I've been there before."

Sloan sat back down and roughly shoved his fingers through his hair. "Yeah, well, I haven't. And neither am I accustomed to being accused of murder."

An ugly slice of Sloan's past came hurtling toward him. He was growing adept at dodging unwanted memories, which a good many of his were, but this one caught him fully unaware. He laughed, though not with the ballad of humor, but rather with the song of sarcasm.

"When you think about it," Sloan said, "it's really rich. Sort of like God has a payback plan." He looked over at his friend. "If you believe in that sort of thing."

"I don't. Furthermore, I don't think this conversation is worth pursuing."

"No, no, you're wrong," the masochist in Sloan said. "If only from the point of view of irony, it's interesting. Two years ago I killed a man and, instead of being charged with murder, which morally I should have been, I was given the Congressional Medal of Honor. Don't you find that irony in the extreme? Especially since everyone is now ready to hang me for committing what's considered a similar act."

Harper ignored the question. Instead, in a weary tone suggesting that they'd had this conversation before—many times before—and that he knew there was no way for him to win Sloan over to a positive point of view, he stated, "You don't know that you killed anybody two years ago."

Sloan's reply sounded as rote as Harper's comment. "Moot point. It doesn't matter whether I killed him or not, I was—am—guilty."

"The only thing you were guilty of was being human." Harper shook his head. "No, I take that back. You weren't human. That's something you've never allowed yourself to be. What many people thought you were, I among them, was—*is*—a hero."

Sloan responded to the word as though it were the foulest thing anyone could call him. "Yeah, a goddamned hero!"

Even as he snarled the word, Sloan surprised himself. Every time he thought he was making progress, every time he thought he was further along the road to recovery, he took a step backward. But, he reminded himself, wasn't that what the military shrink had indicated would happen? In truth he'd come further than he'd thought possible, and part of the reason he'd been able to make that journey had been Anna—Anna, who'd taught him to entertain the notion of liking himself again.

"Does my past have to come out at the trial?"

"Use your head," Harper said, once more speaking forthrightly. "If this thing goes national, there's no way to stop it. Reporters are like dogs with a scent. Once one dog starts to sniff around, another joins in, then another. Before it's over, they'll have dug up every bone buried in your backyard."

"Damn!"

"Is that such a bad thing?"

Sloan's look said that Harper had to be kidding.

"Think about it. What are the mongrels going to discover?" Harper answered his own question. "That you had a distinguished military career, that you served your country with honor, that your country rewarded your valor by presenting you with the Congressional Medal of Honor. Those aren't bad things for a jury to know."

"There's more to it than that, and you know it."

"*I* know that, *you* know that, but how could anyone else? Aside from the fact that you helped liberate an

American hostage and that you yourself were captured in the process, the rest is classified. Right?"

While it was true enough that what happened next was classified, Sloan still had an uneasy feeling. He and an unsuspecting Anna were sitting on a time bomb that could go off at any minute. In a heartbeat valor could be turned into cowardice, honor could become dishonor. How could he ask a jury to understand what he himself didn't? More to the point, how could he ask Anna?

"Look," Harper said, "just go home and get some rest. And don't talk to anybody about the case."

Sloan sighed, wanting desperately for his friend to tell him that everything was going to be all right, but as gifted a lawyer as Harper was, Sloan knew that there were no sure things in the courtroom. One thing *was* for sure, though, and that was that Harper was clearly going to avoid any confrontational question concerning their guilt or innocence. Sloan decided that, at least for now, he'd let it slide too. There was something, however, that he couldn't put off.

"I, uh, I want to thank you for everything you've done."

Harper stood and circled the desk. For the first time since the arrest, Sloan looked beyond himself and to his friend. Harper seemed tired and worn, the product of too little sleep and having to defend, or prepare to defend, his best friend against charges of murder.

"I haven't done anything yet," Harper said.

"You helped me make bail."

Harper placed his hand on Sloan's shoulder and squeezed in reassurance. "That's part of my job."

At the door Sloan hesitated, then turned to meet his friend's eyes with a pair that had darkened with a fear he tried to hide but couldn't. Fear had been a constant companion, one crouched in his chest, ever since he'd been arrested and hauled off to jail. Their talk that day, indicating the seriousness of the prosecution's evidence, had done nothing to quiet that fearsome beast. In fact, with just the least provocation it would spring forward and devour him whole.

"I'm not sure that I can survive being locked up again," Sloan said.

He said nothing more, for there was really nothing more to say, a fact to which the bells of St. Catherine's chimed their testament.

"... in the small Maine community of Cook's Bay. The couple is charged with the murder of her husband, who had recently suffered a stroke. According to sources, he had asked his wife to help him end his life. Anna Ramey was arrested first for euthanasia, but evidence soon suggested to the police that something more sinister had occurred. Famed criminal lawyer Harper Fleming, who represents both Anna Ramey and Retired Commander Sloan Marshall, refused to comment on the case, except to say that he was certain his clients would be acquitted. Commander Marshall, a member of the elite Navy Seals, has a long and distinguished military career. Most recently his participation in a rescue mission earned him the Congressional Medal of Honor. Although the defense was unwilling to talk to this reporter, the prosecuting attorney ..."

Sitting before the television in the small lighthouse keeper's cottage, Sloan felt dazed. Harper had told him what to expect, and he'd thought he'd been prepared, but when he'd heard the newscaster, his hair as slick as his voice, his reputation slicker than both, say his name—Retired Commander Sloan Marshall—Sloan couldn't make himself believe that it was he to whom the newscaster referred. It had to be another Sloan Marshall, just as it had to be another Richard Hennessey now filling the television screen with his lean good looks and his limitless ambition.

". . . particularly heinous crime. Of course, the state of Maine doesn't have the death penalty, but in a case like this, one wishes that it did. I *will* make this promise to the law-abiding citizens of Maine"—here he looked as though he knew each one personally—"that I'll do my best to see that justice is done. I'll—"

Sloan snapped off the television with such force that tingles of pain shot through his hand, but he paid them no heed. Instead he listened to that hidden place inside his heart where every dark and sore memory had been categorized and filed away, never to be entirely forgotten. He heard the slamming of a door, felt himself pushed onto a cold, damp floor, saw four walls closing in on him. His pulse suddenly erratic, Sloan admitted the truth of what he'd earlier told Harper. He *didn't* know if he could survive incarceration. If he was found guilty, he would much rather just be put to a quick death, instead of dying a little every second of every day. Leave it to him, he thought on a grim note, to be arrested on a murder charge in a state that had no death penalty.

Stop it, Sloan!

But he couldn't stop the memories, now any more than he ever had. Again the fetid smell of urine and feces filled his nostrils, as did the pungent smell of fear. His heart skipped, tripped, ran a wild race.

"Your country has forgotten you, Commander. Make it easy on yourself."

But he hadn't made it easy on himself. He'd endured hanging from the ceiling by ropes tied around his wrists. During these agonizing hours, the pain would build like a slow symphony until only his pride had kept him from screaming out, had kept him from begging to be released. Finally the pain would dull as he'd slip to the edge of unconsciousness. Unmercifully, however, he never tumbled into this glorious state. And then had come the beatings, so brutal, so ruthless, that he'd thought that his captors intended to kill him. He soon learned, however, that he wasn't to be so lucky. They'd only meant to make him crave death as he'd never craved life. Tossed back into his cell after each beating, he'd crawled into the corner like some animal, where he'd proceeded to vomit up the meager contents of his stomach, much of which was laced with his own blood.

Even now, after almost a year of freedom, a vile taste lingered in his mouth. As though hoping to wash it away, Sloan walked from the living room into the kitchen, opened the refrigerator, and removed a bottle of beer. Uncapping the top, Sloan leaned his hips against the cabinet and swigged down most of the bottle's contents. The beer, malty and cool, did nothing to remove the odious taste.

Sloan tried to derail the memory he knew was coming next. *Don't think about it,* he told himself. *Play the mind games you learned to play so well. Build yourself a fantasy into which you can escape.* But even as he gave himself the order, his breath quickened. Wires. Jolts of electricity. Screams that he somehow knew were his own but that didn't resemble any human sound. Prayers for death. Please, God, let me die. Please . . . please . . . please . . .

Stop it!

Shaken, Sloan set the bottle of beer on the cabinet and walked back into the living room. He looked over at the blank television screen. He forced himself to leave yesterday's nightmare behind and to focus solely on today's. Ramming his fingers through his hair, he asked himself for the millionth time how he'd ever allowed himself to get involved with a married woman. And how he'd ever ended up being charged with murder.

Love.

Obsession.

Sloan shifted his gaze from the television to the telephone. Had Anna seen the news? Was she feeling as overwhelmed as he? Did she feel, as he, that what was happening had to be happening to someone else? As always, he had an overpowering need to protect Anna—from life, but mostly from herself because she insisted upon carrying all the world's burdens upon her shoulders.

Even as Sloan took a step toward the telephone, he could hear Harper's admonishment for him to stay away from Anna for the duration of the trial. But telephoning her wasn't the same thing as going near her, was it? Who would know if he called her?

No one.

Except him.

Except her.

Sloan picked up the phone and dialed Anna's number. He held his breath as he waited for it to start ringing. Before it did, however, he slammed down the receiver. His doing so had nothing to do with Harper's demand that he not contact Anna, but rather everything to do with Anna herself. In the past months he'd tolerated more than he'd thought any human being could. And he'd survived. Of a sorts. There was one thing, however, that he wouldn't be able to survive, that he wouldn't even come close to surviving, and that one thing would be Anna's refusal to talk to him.

Anna watched the television with what could only be called a growing sense of frightened fascination. It was the same feeling that one had while watching a coiled snake poise to strike. Fear coagulated blood and slowed response, but on a distant plane of thought one had to admire the beauty of the serpent's sinuous movements. The newscaster was good. Very good. Without implying guilt—after all, that was a matter for a jury to decide—he nonetheless had sown carefully the insidious seeds. That accounted for Anna's fear. Her fascination was due to another source altogether, however, and that source was the information she was learning about Sloan.

Though Anna knew that he wasn't comfortable doing so, Sloan had shared the fact that he was retired military. She even knew that he'd been held captive. This he'd spoken of as though it were nothing more than an inconvenience. Anna hadn't been stupid enough to buy into it. Even so, she'd realized how innocent she'd been when she'd seen the scars disfiguring his back.

". . . elite Navy Seals . . . long and distinguished military career . . . rescue mission . . . the Congressional Medal of Honor . . ."

Mesmerized, Anna listened, thinking how very little she actually knew about this man named Sloan Marshall. He must be a hero. The government didn't hand out the Congressional Medal of Honor to just anybody, did it?

Before Anna could settle on an answer, an image of Richard Hennessey filled the television screen. If Jake Lugaric had struck like a snake, the prosecuting attorney prowled with all the stealth of a sly wolf. He was setting his trap, and Anna could already feel the savage bite of teeth. What she couldn't feel was that what was happening fell under the heading of reality. Seeing her life splashed across national television in such a defamatory way left her feeling strangely detached. Surely she wasn't this Anna Ramey accused of murdering her husband. Was she?

Yes, she was, the voice of reality whispered.

Willing her panic aside, Anna closed her eyes. A picture of Meg flashed into view. Was her daughter listening to this same broadcast? At the thought of Meg, Anna wanted to rush to the telephone and call her daughter, but she knew that doing so would be futile. Hadn't she tried to reach her earlier, only to be told by her college roommate that she wasn't in? Pain knifed at Anna. She had easily enough translated the room-mate's message: Meg *was* in, but didn't want to talk to her mother.

Opening her eyes, Anna walked toward the television and turned it off. A deafening silence rained down. She felt alone. In the house. In the world. In the universe. Though the feeling wasn't new—she'd felt it often over the rocky course of her marriage—it had never been plumbed to this depth. For one crazy moment she wanted to walk—no, run—to the telephone and call Sloan. In this unreal world she'd stumbled into, his voice would serve as a beacon of sanity. Of that she was sure. Just as she was sure that she could not call him. Not after she'd so definitively shut the door to their future in his face.

Still . . .

Anna glanced over at the telephone. Fear and loneliness joined hands, sparking a recklessness deep inside her. Surprising herself, she reached for the telephone.

The shrill ring startled Sloan. In the months he'd lived at the lighthouse, the telephone had rung only a handful of times. Usually it was Harper wanting him to go for a jog, for a drink, for anything that would get him out of the house. With the newscast still playing in his head like a bad melodrama, with both Jake Lugaric and Richard Hennessey starring in the lead roles, Sloan just wanted to be left alone. Because of the telephone's insistence, however, he had little choice but to answer it.

"Hello?" When only silence greeted Sloan, he repeated in a voice just short of a growl, "Hello?"

Whoever was on the other end hung up abruptly, leaving the dial tone to buzz like an angry bee. Sloan slammed down the receiver. Terrific, he thought, now he was going to get anonymous crank calls. Heading from the living room back into the kitchen, he attempted to convince himself that he needed to put something in his stomach. He couldn't remember when he'd last eaten. To be honest, though, all he wanted was another beer.

The telephone rang again.

Sloan halted at the kitchen door, trying to decide if he was going to answer the damned thing. He decided that he wasn't. Stepping into the kitchen, he headed for the refrigerator, opened the door, and grabbed a second bottle of beer. Thinking that maybe he'd just get himself drunk as a skunk, he uncapped it. Beer foamed from the skinny neck of the bottle. Sloan wiped his hands down the legs of his jeans.

The telephone continued to ring. Sloan continued to ignore it. He took a long, deep swallow of the beer.

Suddenly Sloan put the bottle down on the counter and headed back to the living room. Maybe it was the press, and if so, he was going to give them a piece of his mind.

Snapping up the entire telephone in his large hand, Sloan disengaged the receiver and snarled, "Hello?"

Silence. Then, "I take it you saw the news."

At the sound of Harper's voice Sloan felt tense muscles begin to relax. "Yeah, I saw it."

"Hennessey looks good in those expensive suits, doesn't he?"

"Like a regular fashion plate," Sloan replied, flopping down onto the sofa and thinking that, if the over-zealous prosecutor had his way, he'd be wearing prison blues. "Isn't it bad form or something for a lawyer to be doing so much talking to the press? Isn't there such a thing as a gag order?"

"Even if the judge issues a gag order, which we might or might not get him to do, we're still going to have to contend with the press. In fact, a gag order only makes the press more determined to find someone in the know who'll break the silence." There was a pause, then, "By the way, my phone's been ringing constantly since the newscast. It appears that all the national networks want in on the action."

"I got a call myself," Sloan said.

"Who was it?"

"I don't know. They hung up." Even as he said it, it struck Sloan as odd that the press would hang up once they'd gotten through to him. "Could have been a crank call."

"You're going to get plenty of both," Harper said, cautioning again, "Don't talk to anyone."

"Don't worry."

Within the next twenty minutes Sloan's phone rang off the wall. As per Harper's warning Sloan let it ring. Finally he turned the volume to mute and went to bed, though it was not without a grudging respect for the news media. When they went after a story, they went after it tirelessly. That fact posed a threat that Sloan couldn't completely ignore, even if his skeletons were hidden in a closet marked *Classified*.

FIVE

The county courthouse looked as though it had stood for at least a couple of centuries. In fact, it was only ten years old. When the original had burned in the early 1980's, the town fathers had been distraught over the loss of one of Cook's Bay's oldest, and by far most distinctive, buildings. Consequently, with the aid of several private donations, a renowned architect from Boston was brought in. He had combined aged red brick with weather-beaten granite in a fashion just short of miraculous. For good measure he'd tossed in white marble steps that dated back to the 1800's and some Corinthian columns that predated the steps. The columns, located at the head of this impressive stairway, formed a distinguished entryway through which most court visitors traveled, remarking as they did so at the four ancient-looking turrets sitting atop the porch. As the pièce de résistance, the architect had thrown in a copper-domed cupola that glistened when the sun shone.

As Harper guided the car into the parking lot, Anna, sitting in the passenger seat, glanced at the building. She remembered the first time she'd seen it after it had been rebuilt. She had been amazed that anything could have been made to look so old so quickly. Today, however, she understood only too well. Within the span of a couple of weeks, she'd aged considerably and not very gracefully.

"You okay?"

Anna turned her attention from the building to Harper. "I'm fine."

It was a lie, of course. She wasn't fine. She hadn't been since this debacle had begun, and perhaps she never would be again. She was better than Friday night, however. Then, in a panic, she'd telephoned Sloan. No matter that she'd promised herself she wouldn't contact him, no matter that she'd made it clear to him he shouldn't contact her—she'd nonetheless been unable to stop herself. For unsteady heartbeats she'd allowed herself to be wrapped in the warmth of his voice, to let it reassure her that everything would somehow turn out all right, but then guilt, her ever-present soul mate, had forced her to hang up. She didn't deserve to be wrapped in warmth; she didn't deserve to be reassured.

"This shouldn't take long," Harper said as he pulled the car into a parking space.

The "this" he referred to was the arraignment. The night before, Harper had called and announced that he'd gotten the nine o'clock arraignment moved up an hour. With the press displaying such an avid interest, he didn't want the proceedings to take place at the appointed time. The judge, who was aware of the national publicity, had agreed. He was quoted as saying that he didn't want his courtroom turned into a sideshow.

Anna had arrived at Harper's office at seven-thirty—thirty minutes ago. She found Sloan and Harper discussing the case. It appeared that Marilyn had ferreted out the fact that it had been Bendy Webber, the man who owned the bait-and-tackle shop, who'd seen Sloan leave the house the night of Jack's death. The word at the Snappy Scissors, where Marilyn had gone at once to get the scoop, under the guise of a shampoo and set, was that Bendy had been out tending lobster traps at that ungodly hour and had seen more than he'd bargained for.

At this news Anna wondered what else Bendy Webber had seen that night. The same thing must have crossed Sloan's mind, too, for when Anna glanced his way, their gazes collided. Anna told herself to look away, but she didn't, simply because she couldn't. Sloan's dark eyes, a stunning contrast to the white turtleneck sweater he wore, wouldn't let her. At the intensity of his gaze, that of a storm at its peak, Anna felt weak, yet oddly strong. The dichotomy of feeling was not uncommon in the presence of this man.

Harper broke their silent exchange with the comment that the police were keeping close to their chests whatever it was that Sloan was supposed to have thrown into the sea. The problem was that, without the evidence, the prosecution could only surmise that it had been the paraphernalia necessary to administer the overdose. Harper considered this a definite point in their favor. The prosecution couldn't introduce into evidence what it didn't have, and without something concrete to tie Sloan and Anna to the lethal injection, the prosecution's case was weakened.

Anna allowed herself to feel a tiny ray of hope.

Before leaving for the courthouse, Harper once more went over the basics of what to expect at the arraignment proceedings. Again Anna found it strange that her lawyer spoke of entering a not-guilty plea, though to date he hadn't asked her if she'd taken her husband's life, either with or without Sloan's help. Frankly, she hoped he wouldn't ask. It would make it easier all the way around.

Following their brief discussion, Harper had transported her to the courthouse via his car, while Marilyn was assigned the task of driving Sloan. Two cars would be better at waylaying any members of the press who might manage to sneak through, Harper had pointed out, adding that it wasn't wise to let the Indians circle the entire wagon train if it could be avoided. For all that the strategy seemed logical enough, Anna couldn't help but believe that the plan was designed to keep her and Sloan apart as much as possible.

Good, she thought, though she couldn't stop her heart from turning over when she saw Marilyn's car pull into a nearby parking slot.

"Let's do it," Harper said without hesitation.

Throwing wide his door, he stepped around the car to assist Anna, all the while searching the area for the press. At the same time, Marilyn hustled Sloan forward. Wordlessly, keen eyes scouring about like that of a hawk, Harper ushered his two clients into the building through a side door, which Anna suspected had been left open expressly for them. From there they slipped into the elevator used to transport prisoners and, again silently, began the ride upward.

With their ascent Anna's heart began to pound with fear of the unknown. Even though Harper had tried to prepare them, she still had little idea what to expect. It wasn't every day that one was charged with murder. Intuitively, Anna sought out Sloan. Although gray-tinted sunglasses now shaded his eyes, Anna knew that he was watching her. Strangely, she'd suspected that he—someone—was watching her on the beach long before the two of them had ever met. Such attention from a stranger should have frightened her.

Quite the reverse had been true, however. She'd felt shielded, protected, safe as a babe swaddled in a warm blanket.

At the third floor the elevator rumbled to a stop. Pushing the pause button, an act that got both Sloan's and Anna's attention, Harper said, "Remember that this is only the beginning. We've got a while to go before we have our day in court."

During the next twenty minutes Anna watched with a growing fascination as Harper maneuvered about the courtroom. It was plain to see that he felt completely at home there. On the other hand, Richard Hennessey didn't appear as much at home as onstage, with each move seemingly choreographed for maximum effect.

Just as Harper had indicated, she and Sloan were formally charged with murder. Anna's heart jumped into her throat, where it stayed until Harper rose and entered their not-guilty pleas. His sure and steady voice boomed with such authority that it mocked the prosecution's charge. It seemed to say, "How could anyone be so prattle-headed as to think these two guilty of murder?"

After a trial date was set—two weeks from that very day—Harper again herded his clients from the courtroom and into the elevator, for a reversal of the obscure route they'd earlier taken. Far from finding the arraignment upsetting, Anna had actually found it encouraging. Wherever the road led, at least the process had begun. At least the period of inactivity was coming to a close. Harper had made it clear that the next two weeks would be chock-full of trial preparations. That was perfectly all right with her, Anna thought. Anything to keep her mind occupied, anything to keep her mind from wandering down anxiously riddled alleyways of thought.

"Everything went according to plan," Harper said to

all as the elevator moved downward. He then added, "I think we're entitled to our first sigh of relief."

As though they, too, were joining in the celebration with their own sigh, the elevator doors whooshed open. With a lighter heart Anna stepped forward, a move that delivered her right into the midst of a mob of rabid reporters. Cameras flashed, Minicams rolled, microphones pounced. One microphone, silver and black and seemingly acting on its own, jabbed Anna in the nose. She registered a sharp pain, but only vaguely. Her main concern was trying to make sense out of what was happening.

"How did you and Commander Marshall meet?"

"Is it true that you and Mr. Marshall were lovers the night your husband died?"

"Did your husband know of the affair?"

Anna heard the voices, but they sounded muted, half-toned, delivered at a somnolent speed that only distorted the words like an old record player grinding down. On one plane she thought how very normal these people looked—a blond with a radical haircut, a man with large-framed glasses, a woman who needed to lose a few pounds—while on another plane they didn't look like people at all. They looked more like a pack of yelping jackals.

"No comment," Harper said. "We have absolutely no comment. For God's sake, let us by!"

As Harper hollered this last, he stepped into the fray with his arms outstretched in a deflecting gesture. At the same time, Marilyn landed a well-aimed elbow, actually sending the blond to the floor. As she fell, she tripped over one of the wires squiggling about, pulling a Minicam down with her. Someone screamed. Another cursed. Chaos ruled, creating a momentary pathway of escape.

"Let's go!" Harper ordered.

Oddly, Anna found that her legs wouldn't obey the

command. When had they become paralyzed? And what was that running from her nose? Instinctively, she brought her hand up, swiping at the warm liquid streaming across her mouth and down her chin. When she brought her hand away, she saw that it was streaked with blood. For a reason she couldn't explain, the sight of it confused her, frightened her.

At that very moment, as though they'd sensed her confusion, her fright, a pair of arms came around her. The arms were strong, forceful, filled with purpose. In a sheltering gesture, as though she'd seen far too much in the fifteen or so seconds that had passed since the elevator had opened, a hand cupped the back of her head, partially burying her face against a chest. Anna felt the downy-softness of a sweater, the rock-hardness of the chest that lay beyond. Close to her ear she heard the steady thump-thump-thumping of a sturdy heart.

Anna had no need to wonder whose arms cradled her. She fit no arms the way she fit Sloan's, as though they had been custom-made for her, a fact she'd cruelly had to wait half of her life to discover. Just as she'd had to face the fact, hard as it was, that this chest—Sloan's chest—contained the heart that beat most like her own. In the beginning, when her marriage had been young and pregnant with lovers' promises, she had thought her and Jack's hearts had been attuned, but she'd come to realize that, rather than beating as one, they'd struck separate rhythms, at best only rhapsodizing with each other. With Sloan, though, heartbeat matched heartbeat.

"Move," Sloan commanded.

Miraculously, Anna's legs obeyed. Yes, one step, then another, followed by yet another. They walked quickly, to a pace set by Harper. Once Anna stumbled, but even as she grabbed a fistful of Sloan's sweater, he tightened his arms, drawing her to safety.

"Mrs. Ramey . . ."

"Mr. Marshall . . ."

Anna heard the voices of two persistent reporters, smelled cool air and warm sunshine as she exited the building, felt the comforting solidity of a backseat as she was pushed into a car. Without releasing his hold, Sloan slid in beside her. In seconds the engine of the car roared to life, and after a grim gnashing of the gears, the automobile lurched backward, then forward. A horn honked, warning all to get out of the way. And then the vehicle was moving—fast, fast, faster.

A fine trembling had begun in Anna, her fingers clutching Sloan's sweater fluttering with a life of their own. As always, sensing her need even before she did herself, Sloan covered her hand with his. Though her hand was by no means small, it seemed wonderfully lost in the width and breadth of his. At the same time, he angled his body, drawing her even more fully into him. Anna melted into his warmth, willing her heartbeat to settle, her breathing to steady.

"It's okay," she heard him whisper near her ear. The fact that he spoke so that only she could hear made her feel that just the two of them remained in the world.

His very voice calmed her, along with the sureness of his heartbeat. When her hand relaxed, Sloan entwined his fingers with hers. Anna knew that she ought to resist, but weeks of worry, days of being alone, hours and minutes and seconds of wondering where her life was headed—over and over, she imagined the horror of spending the rest of her life in prison—had left her only too needy. For just a few more moments she would indulge herself, knowing that her punishment lay in the act itself. Later she would remember and hate herself for this weakness.

"Is she all right?" Harper asked.

"Yeah. Just a nosebleed."

As Sloan spoke, he shifted his legs, causing his thigh to thrust against Anna's. The contact was intimate, familiar, something she'd worked hard to forget, but obviously not hard enough. Sliding his free hand into the back pocket of his slacks, Sloan pulled out a handkerchief and placed it beneath her nose. He applied pressure.

"I'm sorry about your sweater," Anna said, refering to the blood smears.

"I don't give a damn about the sweater," Sloan said, wanting to say that all he cared about was her, though he didn't because he was certain she wouldn't want to hear such an admission.

Only seconds after Harper drove the car into the double driveway of his home, Anna heard another car pull alongside. Harper threw wide his door, then opened the door to the backseat.

"Get out," he told Sloan, quietly but firmly.

Sloan didn't budge. "I'm not leaving her like this," he responded just as quietly, but just as firmly.

"Yes, you are. Now. Or you'll find yourself another lawyer."

Silence. Lawyer battling client. Friend battling friend.

It was Anna who settled the issue. Pulling from Sloan, she glanced up at him. "Do what he says."

"Listen to her," Harper said.

Second passed into second. Sloan eyed his friend, then gave Anna a lingering look before climbing out of the backseat.

"Drive her home," Harper said to Marilyn.

The older woman slid behind the wheel, started the engine, and expertly maneuvered the car from the driveway. In heartbeats she was eating up the road and leaving the house behind. Anna, holding Sloan's bloody handkerchief in her hand, didn't look back. She'd already begun to hate herself for the weakness she'd displayed.

* * *

An uneasy silence, broken only by the squeak of expensive leather and the ticking of the clock, had stolen into the room. Sloan, an empty shot glass in his hand, stood before the mantel, watching the second hand of the gold-and-glass clock irrevocably measure time. Enough of that fragile substance had elapsed, in combination with the whiskey consumed, to have placated his anger. That it had not, that the anger still burned with a far greater brilliance than the whiskey, bore testimony to the fervor of his feelings.

"You want to punch me out, don't you?" Harper asked from the chair behind his desk.

Without hesitation, still focusing on the mantel, Sloan answered, "Yes."

It was the only time during a lengthy friendship, and dozens of disagreements, that Sloan had responded thus. In fact, their friendship was the personification of opposites attracting. The only thing they'd ever agreed upon was to disagree—about politics, about religion, about any damned thing that came down the pike. Mostly they had disagreed about the military. When Sloan had burned with zeal for the Vietnam War, Harper had burned his draft card, declaring himself a conscientious objector. While Sloan had dodged bullets, Harper had emptied bedpans in a veterans' hospital. Had Harper been anyone else, Sloan might have resented his political position, but how could he resent a man who had nothing but the purest of principles and impeccable integrity?

Sloan sighed, trying to let his anger, along with the memory of a trembling Anna, slip away. Turning, he locked his gaze with his friend's and said, "What would have been the harm in our being together for just a few minutes? We would have been here in your office. For God's sake, who would have seen?"

With a calmness that provoked Sloan despite his resolve, Harper kicked back in the desk chair, saying,

"You can ask that after what just happened? With the press moving in, there are eyes everywhere. And the harm is that you're going to lose us the case before we even get to trial." Harper's calmness slipped a tad. "Believe me, that footage of you holding Anna will make the rounds faster than greased lightning."

"What was I supposed to do? Let the press devour her?"

"No, but you and Anna cannot appear to be lovers. Friends, yes. Neighbors, yes. Lovers, no."

Sloan looked at his friend as though he couldn't believe what he was hearing. "You can't be serious. Do you honestly think that there's anyone in Cook's Bay—no, no, do you honestly think there's anyone in the whole of the States who doesn't know that Anna and I were lovers? My God, every question out of those reporters' mouths had to do with the affair! They didn't even seem to care about the murder!"

"While I'll argue with the whole of the States, I will concede that there probably isn't anyone in Cook's Bay who hasn't heard that you and Anna were lovers."

Sloan looked as though this conversation was sailing well above his head. "So what's your point?"

"Let me rephrase my statement. You and Anna cannot appear to be *current* lovers."

Still, Sloan appeared lost as a goose.

"The right jury might be sympathetic to a couple who made a mistake," Harper explained. "Every person on that jury has made a mistake. We human beings, imperfect as we are, do that. But the jury wants to see that you and Anna are contrite. They want to see that you two are sorry about your mistake, just the way they've been sorry about their mistakes. They do not want to see the two of you flaunting that indiscretion. Even less do they want the slightest suggestion that you two are continuing to have an affair. One moral error is defendable, forgivable. More than that and only a jury composed of twelve active adulterers is going to acquit you."

"But we're not having an affair," Sloan said.

"It doesn't matter whether you are or not, if the jury thinks you are."

Sloan gave a look of disbelief. "The truth counts for nothing?"

"Not in a courtroom. There, there's no such thing as absolute truth. Truth is only what you can convince the jury it is."

Sloan swore.

Harper shrugged, then added, "It cuts both ways. The prosecution is going to have to convince the jury that there was an affair to begin with." Sighing, Harper said, "This Webber guy worries me. It's possible that, if he saw you leave, he also saw more."

Sloan didn't need the "more" the seaman might have seen spelled out. "Won't the prosecution have to indicate what testimony Webber will be bringing to the trial?"

"Yeah."

A sudden thought occurred to Sloan. "Meg knows."

"Ah, yes, Meg. Well, the truth is that the prosecution may have no idea that Meg knows, and even if they do suspect, they might be reluctant to call her to the stand. Loved ones notoriously make unreliable witnesses. More than one has committed perjury and, in the process, made counsel look like a fool."

"What about Carrie? Surely she has to suspect."

"Carrie is one of those rare people who sees only what she wants to see."

Sloan set the shot glass on the mantel, fingering the ship-filled bottle displayed there. He chose his words as carefully as some artist had constructed the galleon contained therein, in the end deciding for simplicity and frankness. His gaze finding Harper's, he said, "I want you to know something right up front. I won't get on the stand and say that I'm sorry about what happened between Anna and me, because I'm not."

Silence, then Harper's half laugh, a sound that said he didn't believe what he'd just heard. "Tell me something, Sloan, are you going to use this trial to punish yourself for what you think happened in Beirut?"

Sighing, Sloan plopped down in a chair in front of Harper's desk. "Stick to law. You make a lousy psychiatrist."

"It doesn't take a psychiatrist to see what you're doing."

With disquieting nonchalance laced with recklessness, Sloan said, "Maybe I'm punishing myself for what happened right here in good ole Cook's Bay. Maybe I'm punishing myself for killing Jack Ramey."

Silence returned. This time it was deep enough to drown in. The two men studied each other, gauged each other. Slowly, Harper rose from his chair, walked to the sideboard, and poured himself a drink.

"You think I'm guilty of murder, don't you?" Sloan said to his friend's back. Harper's answer was to down the drink in one swallow. "C'mon, Harper, say the word. We both know you believe I did it. Didn't you yourself tell me that I was obsessed with Anna?" He laughed sadly. "I can't even say her name without my heart skipping a beat."

Harper turned, choosing his words as cautiously as Sloan had earlier chosen his. "I don't think anything, except that you're my friend."

The answer was what Sloan had expected, and so bittersweet that it cut him to the quick. At the same time that he felt a wild exhilaration—few friendships ever soared this high—he also felt a rapid descent into depression. His friend believed him guilty of murder. At the very best, his friend was unsure of his innocence. That realization, known from the first but only now crystallized into expression, saddened him. A part of

Sloan died. But, then, the demise seemed appropriate. After all, all of this was about death—death of a marriage, death of innocence, death of a man named Jack.

Iron chains shackled his feet, forcing him into a shuffling gait. Fear, mounting with each unsteady step, caused his heart to sprint, his brow to sweat. They'd already stripped him of his shirt. He knew what that meant.

Don't think about it! They can have your body, but not your mind. Play the game. Think of the cool Colorado mountains, think of the pure fast-running river, think of the big trout waiting to be caught. Yeah, big speckled trout, cooked over a camp fire.

A door opened, a wordless shove, and he stood before The Nameless One. The three other men had names—at least Sloan thought they were names, because he heard the Lebanese words often and the men seemed to respond to them—but not the one in charge. Clearly Lebanese like the others, with a head full of thick black hair, this man stood tall, lean, vacant-eyed. There was little doubt in Sloan's mind that this individual enjoyed being the instrument of torture.

Don't think about it! Think of mountains, river, trout!

"Your country has abandoned you, Commander. I shall send you home to it, however. I have no wish to detain you. I need only a name. Give me that name and you shall go free."

"Go . . . to . . . hell," Sloan mumbled into the silence of his bedroom, thinking that, if he could only wake up, he could stop what was about to happen. But he couldn't. He never could. At least not in time to spare the nightmare's recurrence.

A length of pipe rammed into his ribs, cracking bone and tearing muscle. Over and over the pipe pounded, pummeled, pulverized.

Mountains! River! Trout! Mountains! River! Trout! Mount—

Sloan jackknifed to a sitting position. A cutting pain shuddered through his chest, making him believe that he actually had been struck, but then he realized that the pain was the result of his labored breathing. He forced himself to take several slow breaths. He wiped the perspiration from his brow. He told himself to stay calm.

As they often did, the bedroom walls started to close in on him. He'd learned not to fight the fear, but rather to give it free rein. Tonight it seemed particularly vicious, however, so he swung his feet over the side of the bed, grabbed his sweats, and wrestled them on. Grappling for socks and shoes, he slipped them on, tying the latter with quick, jerky movements that threatened to snap the laces.

He hit the front door at a run. He was only vaguely aware of dashing down the wooden steps of the cottage, of crossing the small rectangle of grass, of crunching across the gravel road. Next came the graduated stone steps that led down the rocky bank and to the beach. Though it was dark, Sloan took the steps with a confidence born of experience. He'd often negotiated these steps on murky, moonless nights. The sea-soaked sand sucked up his first footsteps, forcing him to pump his legs harder, faster. Calf muscles burned hot with the effort. By then, though, nothing mattered except the fact that he was running, that he was free—of the past, of the present, of the uncertain future.

While he'd slept, rain had moved in, expressing itself in a lightweight drizzle that moistened Sloan. Isolated patches of gray fog, like shadowy voyeurs, watched his solitary passage. On he raced, the wild sea whispering its encouragement, the light from the lighthouse flashing its coded brightness behind him. Like spent sunshine, the light grew faint, and fainter yet, until he headed into an end-of-the-world darkness. Still, Sloan didn't falter. Still, his steps were sure.

Intuitively, he was headed for Anna.

He dashed past clumps of lichen-covered rocks, bounded over and around craggy-shouldered boulders, cut through a forest that grew almost at the water's edge. Here the darkness swirled more deeply, while the sound of his steps disappeared almost entirely, swallowed whole by the lushness of leaves and needles and pungent-smelling earth. Soon he passed through the close cluster of trees, sprinting once more onto the open beach. The briny aroma of salified air, the dank fishy fragrance of sea life, hit him full in the face, along with the foolhardiness of what he was doing. Hadn't Harper told him that very day to stay away from Anna? Hadn't his lawyer made it patently clear that the success of their defense might depend on his keeping his distance?

In the end Sloan didn't know if it was Harper's warning or the stitch in his side that caused him to stop, but stop he did. Breathing harshly and quickly, he grasped at the pain shooting through his ribs and dropped to his knees. The foam-tipped sea tumbled about him, soaking him, chilling him, reminding him of the first time he'd ever seen Anna. She'd been standing ankle-deep in this very sea. It had been early summer then, a June morning plush with a pastel dawn and a spry breeze. It had been a morning that had constituted a turn in the road of his life. Ironically, he'd traveled a long way down the road before he'd discovered that he was embarked on a most perilous journey.

SIX

June

When Sloan saw the woman, he stopped dead in his tracks. He had jogged the length of this beach every morning for the past few months, and not once during that time had he come across another human being. To do so now was, quite frankly, a little disconcerting, for it shattered his carefully designed illusion that he was alone in the world. Keeping his own company, listening to his own inner counsel, had begun a healing process that was long overdue. He was feeling better about himself these days, a fact he had Harper to thank for. If his longtime friend hadn't insisted upon his joining him in Cook's Bay, he might still be roaming the country in a state of emotional chaos. Still, he was nowhere near a full recovery, and a part of him resented this woman's intrusion, this woman's invasion of *his* beach.

As he watched, the woman, standing ankle-deep in

the frothy incoming tide, kicked her feet in a kind of frisky abandon. Water splashed upon the legs of her white jeans, which had been rolled nearly to the knees. From experience Sloan knew that the water was cold this time of morning, a fact the woman verified by hugging her arms, encased in a black sweater, about her. A butter-yellow scarf had been tied around her neck, the ends of which fluttered and flapped in the biting breeze. The wind also played havoc with a headful of golden curls, which gleamed like jewels in the eager warm-rich sun.

Suddenly the woman bent, plunged her fingers into the seawater, and picked up something. She studied it, frowned—even at this distance Sloan could see the downward tilt of her lips—and gave it back to the sea. Then the woman waded ashore and, brushing the curls from her eyes, set about seriously combing the beach. In a matter of seconds she had collected several objects from the sand, each of which she tossed back, again with obvious disdain and disappointment.

She was looking for seashells, Sloan deduced, thinking that she'd really come to the wrong place for that. There were few sandy beaches in this area, and those few were serviced by a greedy sea. A limited variety of shells washed ashore—mostly crab carapace, clam, and mussel shell, an occasional big-horse mussel shell—and these usually only in fragments. Sometimes a skate egg case or a sea-urchin shell lay abandoned amid chunks of white corallike algae or a bit of deadman's-fingers sponge, but mostly the ordinary exceeded the extraordinary.

Not wanting to be found watching her, Sloan slipped behind a cluster of shiny gray rocks. They reminded him of a school of dolphins long ago beached. He'd invented a fantasy regarding them. Some merciful god, rather than let them die, had turned them into inanimate objects of beauty. Beyond this natural monument lay a cove hidden by more rocks and sheltered by a stone cliff that jutted nearly out to the sea. It was a cozy spot where Sloan often came to flee the claustrophobic confines of the lighthouse cottage.

Undeterred by the sea's scanty yield, the woman searched on, looking here and there amid the gritty sand and the knotted seaweed, occasionally wracked by strands of kelp, that formed a field of windrows. Every now and then she'd stoop to recover a shell, but after studying it she'd always fling it back. She'd then move on down the beach, repeating the pluck-and-discard process over and over. Sloan surmised that she was looking for whole shells. At one point, because the wind-tormented curls refused to stay out of her eyes, the woman removed the yellow scarf from her neck and tied it about her hair. Colorwise, it was an exact match to her hair.

Slowly, as the matin sky marbled with the colors of sunrise—pearlized pink, morning-glory blue, soft lilac, and streaks of cinnamon-brown—it dawned upon Sloan that this woman wasn't occupied in some idle, meaningless search. Instead she seemed engaged in a sacred quest, committed to a hallowed mission. Far beyond unwilling, she appeared unable to give up until she'd found a shell. Sloan couldn't help but wonder as to her motivation, even as he wondered why something—her intensity? her ritualistic devotion?—compelled him to continue his observance of her.

The woman's search continued, although she had increasingly begun to check her watch. Sloan suspected that she had to be somewhere at an appointed hour and that time was running out. Where did she have to be? And would she have to leave before finding a whole shell? This last question was answered a few minutes later. Abruptly she bent, collected something from the sand, and studied it as it lay in her open palm. Pure delight—no, a simple childlike exuberance—danced across her face. At the same time, she closed her hand, bringing it to her chest, resting it just above her heart. Had Sloan not known better, he could easily have believed that the sea had just presented her with the rarest of treasures. As strange as it was, he, too, felt the stirring of exhilaration, as though he himself had just been gifted with something. It crossed his mind that maybe his gift had been seeing this woman's delight.

What an odd thing to think.

What an unnerving thing to think.

This woman was a total stranger, someone he'd most likely never see again, which was fine by him. He was accustomed to isolation, to a self-imposed sequestration. He wanted nothing—not even the memory of a stranger's exuberance over a simple pleasure—to interfere with his solitary existence. That in mind, he headed toward the lighthouse. All the way back, however, he couldn't shake the feeling that he'd just witnessed something special.

Unaware that she hadn't been alone, Anna checked her watch. With only minutes remaining before seven o'clock, she hastily donned her tennis shoes, rolled down the legs of her jeans, then started, at a brisk walk, for the short pathway that cut through the forest and to the cottage. She'd have to hurry to get breakfast prepared on schedule. Eating meals on time was important for a diabetic—not that Jack had ever taken that kind of responsibility for his illness. Looking back, she wondered if maybe it was her fault that he hadn't. If she hadn't been so eager to assume responsibility, would he have been forced to assume responsibility himself?

Anna opened her hand and studied the shell, as though it perhaps had the answer. It didn't. The clamshell just sat mutely in her palm. White and brownish gray, with undulating swirls etched into the delicate-looking but hard husk, it was small but flawless.

Wholeness was important, fundamental. She wanted only those shells that had survived intact the trials and ruthless tribulations of the sea. She wanted only survivors.

Surviving. Regrettably, that was what life was all about. She sometimes thought how unfair it was that life wasn't about more, but there it was. She had become expert at the art of survival, especially since Jack's stroke. The last of his dignity stolen by a thief that had posed in the guise of paralysis, he had lashed out as he never had before. For the first time Anna felt herself nearing the breaking point. She had needed this getaway every bit as much as Jack. Maybe more.

Ironically, it wasn't the illness, or the complications caused by it, that had worn on her nerves. It wasn't even the venting of his frustration on her, but rather the way he had fled inside himself to a place where she wasn't welcome—something he'd done over the years, but most particularly since the stroke. His refusal to allow her to share his pain had hurt her deeply. She had taken her marriage vows seriously. Taking each other for better or for worse, in sickness and in health hadn't been sentiments she'd pledged rashly. Even though she'd felt emotionally abandoned over the years, she'd remained, and would continue to remain, by her husband's side. Duty and honor demanded no less. Moreover, try as hard as he had to kill her feelings for him, a part of her, the part where beautiful memories lived, still cared for him. Even so, on this sunny June morning, she was reluctant to return to the house. She wasn't ready to face rejection once more.

As Anna broke through the closely boughed trees, the house they'd rented came into view. Because they had arrived late the evening before, this morning had afforded her the first real look at the structure. Though simple, even rustic in design and spirit, it nonetheless had a number of sweet charms—a brick fireplace, a gambrel roof, and Doric columns supporting a small porch. When Carrie had started scouring the town for a house, she'd had three criteria to meet: it had to be fairly large, it had to have hardwood floors to accommodate a wheelchair, and it had to be near the sea—the nearer, the better. Carrie had found a house that fit the bill perfectly.

More than anything, Anna liked the location. Both forest and sea created an ambience of seclusion that she found appealing. She liked, too, what the sea salt and the sea wind had done to the house. It had worn and weathered it, causing the clapboards, an ugly brown trimmed in an uglier gray, to look as though they'd withstood the wrath of God. All in all, the house was far from a beauty, but like the shell in her hand, like Anna herself, it had survived.

Taking the steps at a clip, Anna entered the house through the back. In the mudroom she whipped the scarf from her head, allowing the crushed curls to bound to freedom, and slipped out of the gritty tennis shoes. Not even bothering with another pair of shoes, she padded on sock-clad feet through the breakfast area and into the kitchen. After placing the shell on the windowsill, she began preparing breakfast.

After a couple of false starts—it would take a while to learn where everything was located—she set the coffee to perking. Following that, and mentally thanking Carrie for so thoroughly, so thoughtfully, stocking the pantry, Anna poured two bowls of cereal, topping each with fresh bright-red strawberries. Next came two glasses of milk. She was just placing everything on a tray when she heard a sound behind her. She turned.

"How's breakfast coming?" Ken Larsen asked.

Though she'd met him only an hour ago, Anna had instantly liked the nurse-therapist Carrie had hired. He was short, probably five six, maybe five seven, with beefy arms, a broad chest, and a head full of thick, wavy brown hair. He also had a pair of laughing brown eyes and a winsome smile. More important, he seemed capable and competent. As per schedule he'd arrived promptly at six o'clock, had given Jack his insulin shot at six-thirty, and had encouraged Anna to take the early-morning walk she'd expressed an interest in. After all, she had thirty minutes to kill before breakfast would be required.

"It's almost finished," Anna replied, checking her watch once more. It was almost fifteen minutes after the hour.

"He says he's famished."

Anna knew that Ken Larsen meant that Jack had written that he was famished. She also suspected that Jack wasn't as famished as he'd proclaimed. More likely, her husband knew that she was a few minutes late. Ten to one, once she got his breakfast to him, he'd only pick at it.

"Well, I'm on my way."

"Would you like for me to carry the tray to him?"

"No, that's all right. We always eat together."

Sharing meals was one of the few rituals they continued to observe. Anna wasn't quite certain why they hung on to this one. Maybe the truth was that it was *she* who hung on to it. Perhaps she wasn't willing to give up this last vestige of a normal marriage, though even this had ceased to be normal. She tried to fill the oppressive silence with chatter, often wondering if her cheeriness sounded as false to her husband as it did to her, equally wondering why she struggled to make the effort.

Ken nodded as though he understood perfectly, adding, "I'll just take this chance to change the bed linen and to get the equipment ready for his exercise session."

Anna felt compelled to say, "He probably won't be the most cooperative patient you've ever had."

Ken smiled. "You let me worry about that."

With everything else she had on her mind, the nurse's suggestion seemed like the best deal she'd been offered in a long time.

"I thought you were hungry," Anna said ten minutes later.

Jack, slumped in a wheelchair that was wedged beneath a small table, looked up from the bowl of uneaten cereal. He gazed at his wife with steel-gray eyes that looked uncommonly clear, remarkably vibrant, despite the obvious infirmity of his body. He'd been expecting the comment. What he hadn't been expecting was for the sun to be streaming through the window, and so brilliantly that it spotlighted Anna's hair as though it had suddenly burst into a saffron flame. Dozens of curls, all ablaze with an amazing energy, bounced and bobbed about her heart-shaped face.

Before he could stop himself—he'd become adept at halting memories before they could be fully realized, especially memories of his wife—he had remembered the way her hair felt trailing through his fingers. He remembered how tenaciously those curls could cling, how soft and malleable they could be in the hands of a lover, how fresh and sunshiny warm they smelled. The memory, coming as it did from out of nowhere, from some netherworld of banished thoughts, startled him, angered him.

How had he let himself remember something so painful?

He didn't bother with an answer. That, too, might be painful. Instead he forced himself to make a mental accounting of reality. Reality was the spoon Velcroed to his right hand, the sterile-looking, definitely unromantic hospital bed he slept in, the diaper he wore should he not be able to get to the bathroom in time, the tablet and pen that had become his only form of communication. He reached for the pad with his left hand, thinking as he began to write slowly, laboriously, the way all right-handed people write with their left, that he knew Anna would prefer him to speak. He had no intention, however, of listening to his own voice. Halting and fractured, it was a stranger's voice that came out of his mouth these days.

Once finished with his brief response, he waited for Anna to turn the pad toward her and then make her own reply, which was, "I thought the strawberries were very sweet."

Jack shrugged, sending only his left shoulder upward. The stroke had paralyzed his right side, but with time partial movement had been restored. Even so, some of the simplest things—like shrugging—remained impossible.

"You have to eat, Jack," Anna said, adding, "Shall I scrape off the strawberries?"

Jack gave a quick nod. The truth was that the strawberries weren't tart, but he'd backed himself into a corner, which was where he lived most of his life—or what was passing as his life.

Anna removed the fruit from the cereal, saying as she did so, "How do you like Ken?"

Ken, who had finished making up the bed with fresh linen, had taken the dirty bedclothes to the laundry room. Jack suspected that he was giving him and Anna some time alone.

Jack bobbed another quick nod, as though to say that one nurse was very much like another.

"He came highly recommended by Dr. Goodman. Apparently, he specializes in working with stroke victims."

Victim. Jack hated the word, although he knew that none other applied as aptly. He *was* a victim, a victim of the callous roll of the die. The diabetes had come from out of nowhere, with no family history to predict it. As a teenager he'd had no idea what he'd been condemned to. In the beginning he'd pretended that his life hadn't changed, that he was the same person he'd always been, but the disease had slowly, insidiously, informed him otherwise. With each reminder he'd rebelled, even though he'd known that he was hurting no one but himself.

The truth was that he'd wanted to hurt himself—for being human, for contracting diabetes in the first place. It had been an incredibly stupid thing to do. Mostly, though, he wanted to punish himself for continuing to have dreams, wants, needs. Why hadn't those withered along with his body? Why had they remained, perversely, healthy in the face of his body's deterioration? Why had he continued to want normal things when he was incapable of achieving them? Even now he longed to make love to his wife, though to do so had been an impossibility for years. Even now he longed for her to love him, to have tender feelings for him, even though he was no longer capable of returning that love. There was no room for love when one was consumed with hate, anger, fear.

"I think the house is going to be comfortable. It's larger than I dared to hope it would be. Carrie said that it had just come on the market."

Jack let his wife talk, not even bothering with a response. None was required of him anymore. He knew that she was only trying to fill the silence. Much of the time he wondered why she bothered, except that it seemed important to her to preserve at least a semblance of normalcy.

Maybe an uglier truth, Jack thought as he struggled to bring the spoon to his mouth without spilling its contents, was that, along with hurting himself, he'd also wanted to hurt Anna. After all, she'd remained whole while he'd splintered into less and less of a human being. She'd remained vital and, more important, she'd witnessed his loss of vitality. She'd even had to care for him in proportion to that loss, an act that at best was demeaning, debasing. And through it all she'd remained lovely and desirable. Through it all she'd stood staunchly, uncomplainingly at his side.

St. Anna, patron saint of husbands who acted like sons of bitches! But, dear God, didn't she—didn't everyone—know how scared he was? Scared of another stroke, scared of being even more incapacitated. A man could be only so dependent. A man could withstand only so much humiliation.

"... the sea."

Jack glanced up.

"It's really a very pretty stretch of beach. And it's not that far away. We'll have to find a way to get you down to it."

Jack rested his right hand on the table and, reaching for the pad, he wrote in the shorthand he'd devised: *2 mch trouble*.

"No, it won't be too much trouble. Some afternoon, after the day warms up, I'll get Ken—"

Jack slammed his left hand, balled into a fist, on the table. Since the stroke the action had evolved into a way of giving a quick negative response. As always the act startled Anna. This Jack could see by the widening of her eyes, the jerk of her shoulder. He immediately regretted the harshness of his reply. Once more he wrote on the pad: *can hear sea. That's good enuf.*

Anna swallowed, sighed, said, "Whatever you say."

Jack hated the tone of her voice, a tone that had gone from animation to a lackluster dullness. Immediately he applied the hatred where it belonged—to himself. Again using the pad to communicate, he wrote: *try 2 understand. don't wnt 2 bother.*

"You're no bother, Jack," Anna said softly, stretching her hand forward in order to push some wayward strands of chestnut-colored hair from his brow.

Before she could do so, he turned his head aside. Anna's hand stopped in midair, where it remained for several seconds before she lowered it. Without another word she stood and started from the room.

Dammit! Jack thought. *Damn me!*

He pounded the table with his fist—once, twice—a clear indication that he was pleading with her to stop. Anna didn't, however. Suddenly the sound of a dish hitting the hardwood floor reverberated throughout the bedroom.

Out of nothing more than reflex, Anna turned around. Quietly, she took in the shattered bowl, the scattered cereal, the milk dripping from the table like snow-white rain. Slowly, her gaze traveled to Jack's.

He wondered if she could tell that his heart was pounding, that his palms had grown clammy, that he was sorry for hurting her—again. He wondered if she knew just how much he'd wanted her to touch him, so much that he didn't dare risk her doing so.

They were still staring at each other, two wounded creatures sizing up the other, when Ken Larsen appeared at the door.

"I heard the commotion."

With a misleading calmness Anna said, "We seem to have had an accident."

Her head held high, her chin tilted at an angle that said she was ready to receive another blow should it come, she walked from the room.

Jack watched her go, thinking that he'd drive her to sainthood yet.

Anna stood at the kitchen window. She felt nothing. It was always that way when Jack hurt her. In the beginning she felt pain, then, without its being of her own volition, she slipped deep inside herself, where feelings weren't allowed to follow. The journey, which she knew that she intuitively made out of a need to survive, invariably cost her a bit of herself, leaving her just that much more diminished. She wanted the sea to refill her, yet feared its doing so. It had been so long since she'd felt emotion. So very long.

Spying the clamshell on the windowsill, Anna picked it up and held it in her closed fist. Its sharp curves dug fiercely into her flesh, a pain she welcomed. She didn't try to explain why it was sometimes important—no, essential—to feel physically: the harsh coldness of the early-morning sea, a gentle spring rain sprinkling her upturned face, the pain of a shell held too tightly.

Opening her hand, she studied the clamshell. Though the shell was intact, though it had survived the rigors of a careless, sometimes savage sea, it nonetheless was only half of a whole. A clamshell was a bivalve, one side hinged to the other, one side a mirror image of the other. To Anna it symbolized the ultimate in survival, for few such shells could endure the constant battering of the breakers. To find such a shell had become the goal of the summer.

Interestingly, she sometimes wondered if she had some hidden agenda for wanting such a shell. Perhaps it had something to do with representing the relationship that could exist between a man and a woman. Though the symbolism could not apply to her own relationship, maybe she wanted to believe that some relationships not only could withstand adversity, but could be made stronger by it. Maybe she wanted to believe that somewhere people were engaged in the simple act of caring for one another, of feeling.

Anna replaced the shell on the windowsill. As she did so, she realized that a single drop of blood, a crimson teardrop, lay in the center of her palm. Symbol of life that it was, it should have been reassuring. She had survived her husband's indifference once more. Instead, because she couldn't cry for herself, it made her think that someone was crying for her, for all that she was sacrificing just to survive.

* * *

By the end of her first week in Maine, Anna had found nothing that even came close to resembling a bivalve. In fact, she began to realize that, as far as shells went, this expanse of beach was actually very barren. Each day she wandered a little bit farther along the sandy shoreline—was that a lighthouse in the far distance?—but her efforts were only minimally rewarded. On the second morning of her search, a windy Tuesday, she found another half of a clamshell. On Wednesday she found a small snaillike shell with delicate swirls. On Thursday, however, and again on Friday, she had absolutely no luck. Everything she found was broken and chipped. Though she knew that it was stupid, she couldn't help but feel a keen disappointment.

Checking her watch for the dozenth time that Friday morning, she gave a deep, soulful sigh. She had to get back to the house. Now. As always, a sense of oppression settled over her at the thought of returning, though she let her spirits be buoyed by the fact that her daughter would arrive later that evening. Yes, a nice weekend visit with Meg was exactly what she needed.

Sloan watched as Anna walked from the beach that Friday morning. In fact he'd watched her leave every day that week. He'd had no idea why he'd returned to the beach that Tuesday. He hadn't gone to bed Monday night with the intent to do so. He had just found himself rising at dawn and jogging back to the spot where he'd seen the blond-haired stranger, who he had concluded must be renting the nearby house. He'd tried then, and was trying now, not to consider what motivated his return. After all, she was a disruption to his isolation. After all, she had invaded his beach. If push had come to shove, however, and he'd been forced to explain his actions, he suspected his motivation had something to do with her expression of joy at finding a seashell. He had never witnessed such sublime happiness, and the fact that its source was so small a thing intrigued him. What kind of woman could find such consummate pleasure in something so incredibly simple?

On the other hand, what kind of woman could be so bereft at not finding a shell? Both the day before and today she'd found nothing, and her disappointment had been all too evident. Her frustration had loomed like a sinister cloud on a sunny day. And he had felt as disappointed as she, which he didn't understand in the least. It was as if her disappointment had become his.

Get a grip, Marshall. You don't even know this woman.

Her identity was still preying on his mind that afternoon when he visited Gouge's General Store. Every Friday he routinely bought groceries for the coming week. Since his needs were few, he saw no need traveling to one of the larger supermarkets in Camden or Rockport. Furthermore, there was a quaintness to this store that he liked—the old floor that squeaked with every footstep, the nicked counter that held the old-fashioned cash register, the white toy poodle that lay on the floor like a puddle, the aroma of roasted coffee. The only thing he didn't particularly like was the proprietress. Inez Gouge was a strange bird, who, unless he was mistaken, knew everything that took place in the town.

Setting the bread, milk, and eggs down on the counter alongside the other items he'd selected, Sloan smiled and buttered her up by saying, "That coffee smells good."

Inez Gouge, her dark hair pulled back in a bun so severe that it threatened to slant her eyes, said primly, properly, and with undeniable pride, "Freshly roasted, freshly ground."

"Then I'll just have to have a half pound," Sloan said.

Inez's look said that she wasn't in the least surprised that her customer couldn't resist purchasing some of the coffee. As she stepped toward the coffee grinder, her lace-up shoes squeaking, she said, "Plain Colombian coffee. Not that fancy doodah stuff that some try to sell as coffee. And not decaffeinated, either."

"Can't stand that fancy stuff," Sloan said.

Inez gave a snort that said she guessed not.

"Don't like decaffeinated at all."

Another snort said that Inez certainly hoped not.

In due time Inez had bagged a half pound of coffee, had plopped it down on the counter, and had begun to ring up Sloan's groceries.

"You know the house nearest the lighthouse?" Sloan asked nonchalantly.

Inez stopped. "The O'Baynon house? Or was that O'Day? Never could remember those people's name."

Sloan's heart was getting ready to take a nosedive—maybe she wasn't the gossip he'd thought she was—when she came through like a pro.

"Whichever, it's the Rameys renting it for the summer." This she said with supreme confidence as she totaled the groceries. "You know, Carrie Ramey's brother." She clucked, a sound filled with pity. "Poor man. He's had a stroke. Can't walk, can't talk. He was born here in Cook's Bay. His great-great-grandfather"—she frowned—"or would that be his great-great-great-grandfather? Whichever, his family helped to found this town. Nice family. Good Catholic people. Yes, indeed, nice family . . . poor man . . . such a brave wife."

Wife.

Sloan hadn't been surprised to hear the word. After all, most women the blond-haired woman's age were married, and even if she hadn't been, he wouldn't have been the slightest bit interested in pursuing a relationship. He was too busy fitting his own life back together to worry about fitting another person into it. Still, a vision of the stranger flitted through his mind's eye—her golden hair all atumble, her face alight with the joy of finding a shell, the shell buried in her fist and laid across her heart.

"Thirty-two dollars and twelve cents," Inez Gouge announced, bringing Sloan's musings to an abrupt end.

He reached for his wallet as she began to sack the groceries. In seconds he'd placed the money on the counter, repocketed his wallet, and picked up the two sacks.

"Thanks," he said, starting for the door.

"Why did you want to know about the Rameys?"

Sloan turned. "I, uh, I just thought I saw someone on the beach. Can't be too careful about strangers."

Inez Gouge nodded as though this made perfect sense. Then, in a voice once more filled with pity, she repeated, "Nice family . . . poor man . . . brave wife."

Pretty wife, Sloan thought, surprising himself just a bit with this admission, yet eagerly accepting the premise that a man would have to be blind not to have noticed her loveliness. Somewhere in the back of his mind, however, he made a decision not to observe her anymore. By the time he'd reached the lighthouse, that decision had traveled from the back of his mind to its fore. All in all, it was a good decision, and one he steadfastly abided by for the whole of one day.

SEVEN

The following morning, when Sloan found the small shell with its pretty iridescent lining, he told himself that he had no option. He was morally bound to see that *she* got it. He conveniently overlooked the fact that he'd sworn to have nothing more to do with the woman, the married woman, renting the house. Just as conveniently, he denied he'd jogged with his eyes downcast, searching the sand for its buried wealth.

Hastening his steps, trying to outrun the rising sun, he reached the stretch of beach where she'd appeared each morning for a week. If she held true to her schedule, she would arrive somewhere around six-thirty, hunt for shells, then make a mad dash back to the house around seven o'clock. Sloan checked his watch. It read six-fourteen. Looking about for somewhere to leave the shell, he decided to set it near a piece of driftwood, hoping that it would be found, even as he hoped it didn't look purposely arranged. He then proceeded to wait in his usual hiding place.

Six-twenty came and went. Six twenty-five followed, as did the half hour. Any minute she should arrive, Sloan thought, aware of the pleasurable sense of anticipation that had begun to build. Odd though it was, he was beginning to feel a bond with this woman. Watching her, secretly sharing her delight at finding a shell, shouldering her frustration when she didn't, had caused a kind of kinship—a friendship?—to develop. He had to keep reminding himself that they were strangers, that he didn't even know her given name, that she might well be angry to discover that he'd violated her privacy.

By twenty minutes till seven, Sloan had to entertain the possibility that she wasn't going to show up. Ten minutes later the possibility had turned into a probability. At seven o'clock, the time when she normally left the beach, probability had become reality. She wasn't coming. That plain, that simple. Sloan's pleasurable sense of anticipation turned to out-and-out disappointment, a disappointment so keen that it disturbed him. Leaving the shell behind—maybe she'd come later—he started for the lighthouse, thinking that this was for the best. He was getting too caught up in the pretty stranger's life. More to the point, she was getting too caught up in his.

Yeah, he thought, he'd let her find her own shells. She was really none of his business. This shell thing was really none of his business. Again he ignored the fact that he was playing games. He ignored the fact that, come hell or high water, he'd be there bright and early the following morning, with another shell if he could find it.

* * *

It was almost eight o'clock before Anna made her way to the beach. She'd wanted to come earlier but hadn't been able to manage it. By their very nature weekends were unpredictable. Since the nurse had Saturday and Sunday off, Jack's care on those days fell entirely to her, as did his nighttime care throughout the week. Since the stroke she couldn't remember what it was like to sleep through the night. She would get up at least three or four times to check on him, sometimes finding him awake, but more often suspecting that he was faking sleep. This weekend she had Meg to help her, which was how she'd managed a little time to herself. After breakfast Meg had insisted putting her father through his usual rehabilitative exercises. Anna had let her, simply because she knew that Jack would perform better for his daughter than he would for his wife.

This realization brought a prickling of pain, but as always, Anna went into her survival mode and the pain soon faded, allowing her to concentrate on the warmth of the sun, the sultry lure of the singing sea. She raised her face to its salty song, letting the notes wash over her, then settle deep within her. It took only minutes to realize that the ocean intended to be stingy this Saturday morning. After combing the area, which had been invaded by hungry sea gulls, she had nothing more than a handful of broken shells, all of which she returned to the sea with a frustrated sigh. She was never going to find a bivalve this way. She'd just decided to return to the house when she noted the driftwood. Maybe if the wood had washed ashore during the night, so, too, had a shell. Anna had but barely approached the water-soaked driftwood, draped with straggly strands of sable-brown kelp, when she saw the shell.

And what a sweet shell it was!

Gray, with brown and pink specks, it was small, no bigger than a quarter, and rather fragile looking, though she had only to hold it to feel its unexpected weight. Whatever animal had called this spiral-chambered shell home had not been weak. The animal's strength, combined with the flawless perfection of the shell, pleased Anna. Yes, she thought as she started toward the house, this was her favorite shell so far.

And how lucky she'd been to find it!

The following morning the sight of another shell in exactly the same spot surprised Anna, but running late as she was—it was nearing nine o'clock—she really didn't have time to do more than be grateful for whatever powers had provided, and so generously, for her. As she rushed back to the house, she thought of all that lay ahead of her. Jack had had an uncommonly restless night, necessitating that she get up even more often than usual. Finally she'd just sat up, waiting for dawn and the beginning of a new day. Even Meg had been up a time or two, but Anna had insisted that she return to bed, fearing that if she lost too much sleep, she'd doze off driving back to school. The fact that Meg was leaving that afternoon saddened her. Or was she simply sad to be left alone with Jack?

As Anna entered the house, she headed for the kitchen. There she found Meg pouring herself a mug of coffee. At the sight of her mother she reached for another mug.

"You back so soon?" the young woman asked.

"Yes," Anna said, adding, "I didn't want to be away too long from my favorite daughter."

Meg smiled, brushing back wisps of honey-blond hair that had escaped from the single lengthy braid that plunged down her back and to her hips. "I'm your only daughter, Mother."

"A mere technicality," Anna replied.

No matter how often Anna saw Meg's smile, each time she did it was like seeing it anew. She remembered with crystal clarity the first time she'd seen that smile. It had been when the nurse had placed the infant in her mother's arms. Everyone had said that a newborn baby doesn't smile, that occasionally it just appears to do so. Megan Elizabeth Ramey, though only minutes old, *had* smiled, however, and no one would ever convince Anna otherwise. And she'd been smiling ever since, a smile that never failed to brighten big button-brown eyes ... or her mother's heart.

Even Jack, a papa so proud he'd been about to pop, had agreed that their brand-new towheaded daughter had smiled. Anna remembered how he'd lovingly brushed a knuckle across the baby's small, perfect mouth and how that knuckle had gone on to caress her own cheek—a sweet I-love-you, a simple thank-you for giving birth to his child.

Anna prized these memories. They were reminiscent of a period in their marriage when she and Jack had been happy. Regrettably, that period had long since passed and would never come again. As they always did, the memories turned Anna's thoughts in the direction of her husband.

"How did the exercise session go?" As Anna asked the question, she headed for the table in the breakfast area, mug and shell in hand. Meg followed. This time she didn't smile.

"He went through the motions. That's about all."

Anna sighed. "That's what Ken Larsen says too."

"He's depressed, Mom. You're going to have to face that fact. Most stroke patients go through a period of depression."

Anna didn't point out that most stroke patients eventually overcome that depression and fight to regain their health. Instead she said, "I was hoping that coming to Maine would be more therapeutic."

"You've been here only a week. Give it time. Give Dad time."

Anna smiled, though it was a false display of optimism. "You're right, of course."

If Anna had expected her daughter to return the smile, she was sorely disappointed. Instead Meg looked deadly serious as she said, "I'm worried about you."

Anna looked incredulous. "Me?"

"You're exhausted, both physically and emotionally. You need to hire someone on the weekends and during the weeknights. Just a couple of nights a week would help. You're not getting any rest."

"I'm fine," Anna said, trying to make it sound like the truth, wishing that she didn't have contradictory circles under her eyes. When it was apparent that Meg would have said more, Anna hastened to close the subject. "Really, I'm fine."

This time Meg did smile. "It would be hard to say whether I get my stubbornness from you or Dad."

"I'd say you never stood much of a chance." Reaching for her mug, Anna added, "C'mon, drink up. I've got lunch to prepare."

Mug in midair, Meg said, "Oh, I forgot to tell you. Aunt Carrie called and said that she was bringing lunch by after mass. She said she'd be here about twelve-thirty or one o'clock."

"How nice," Anna said, relieved that at least one burden had been lifted from her tired shoulders.

She wondered, though, if Carrie's coming by was not deliberately timed. Sensitive to a fault, Carrie always seemed to know when someone needed emotional support. Anna believed that was why Carrie often chose to wear blinders. She simply needed to protect herself from other people's pain, a pain she herself felt all too sharply. Yes, she'd bet money that Carrie was coming by to be with her when Meg left for school. Even the thought of her daughter's departure made Anna's heart heavy.

"Will, uh, will you be leaving for school right after lunch?" Anna asked, trying to sound casual.

Sensing her mother's mood, Meg replied softly as she covered her mother's hand with her own, "Yes. No later than two. I've got to get back."

Fighting the loneliness she already felt, Anna replied, "I know that, sweetheart."

As though she was reluctant to do so, Meg added, "I can't come next weekend. I have this huge anatomy test the following Monday, and I need the time to study."

"I understand, Meg. You have your own life, and rightly so. Your father and I will manage fine. I have Aunt Carrie and professional help." She slipped her hand from beneath her daughter's, and, refusing to let herself do what she most wanted to—grasp her daughter's hand and hold on—she patted Meg's hand once and stood. "Let's see about folding that laundry you brought home."

Meg rose, too, picking up both her mug and the shell. "Shall I put this with your growing collection in the windowsill?"

Anna glanced down and saw the shell. Again it struck her as odd that both seashells had been in the same spot, but she simply chalked it up to coincidence.

"Please," she replied.

With Carrie's arrival a rainbow entered the house. Wearing a shocking-pink dress that should have clashed with her chestnut-colored hair but didn't, she talked her usual blue streak. The four of them ate lunch in Jack's bedroom, and for the first time that week, laughter ruled.

"Jack dared me to climb this apple tree," Carrie said, adding with a mischievous grin, "This was after he'd already tempted me to eat enough green apples to make a dozen people sick. Anyway," she said, threading back one of the combs in her hair, "up I go, and I get halfway there when he hollers out that he sees Mother coming. I knew what that meant, because she'd already told us to stay out of the tree. Well, down Jack scrambled, with me right behind him, but I lost my footing and fell to the ground."

"Were you hurt?" Meg asked, totally enchanted as she always was with stories of the past.

"Did I hurt myself?" Carrie repeated. "I landed flat on my back, knocking the breath completely out of me—I thought I was dead and prayed that I was, because if I wasn't, Mother was going to kill me. I broke my arm in not one, but three, places. Furthermore— and this is the God's truth—I sprained my ankle at the clinic while Dr. Goodman was trying to set the cast. The nurse was trying to give me a shot for pain, and I was running all over the place trying to get away from that needle."

Meg laughed. Jack smiled. Anna wondered why life couldn't always be like this.

"To make matters worse," Carrie continued, "that night I was sick as a dog from all those green apples I'd eaten. There I was—one arm in a cast and hurting like Hades, the other holding on to the toilet for dear life, and my ankle swollen to twice its normal size." Carrie looked over at Meg. "And your father didn't even have the decency to get sick from those apples, and he'd eaten far more than I had. I'm telling you, Meg, your father could always talk me into the worst kind of trouble."

Jack smiled and reached for his pad and pen. He scrawled: *I stayed with U.*

Carrie's smile softened and she reached for her brother's hand. "Yes, you stayed at my bedside all night."

The sight of Carrie's hand entwined with Jack's brought a tightness to Anna's chest. She didn't dare touch her husband with that kind of intimacy. Not without running the risk of rejection. Standing, Anna started gathering up the luncheon dishes.

"Let me help you," Carrie said.

"No, no, you sit and talk to Jack."

Anna had no sooner placed the dishes in the sink than Meg appeared.

"I, uh, I better get on the road."

Anna smiled and wiped her moist hands on a dish towel. She refused to let her daughter see how much she already missed her. Instead she said cheerfully, "You drive carefully and call me tonight, so I'll know you made it back okay."

"Yes, ma'am."

"And study hard."

"Yes, ma'am."

"And, uh, we'll see you when you can get away again."

Anna reached for her daughter just as her daughter reached for her. The hug was quick and hard. Anna wanted it that way. Otherwise she wasn't certain she'd be able to turn loose of Meg.

Motioning behind her, Meg said, "I'll just tell Dad good-bye."

Anna knew that Meg would leave after speaking with her father, that she wouldn't return for further words with her. By tacit agreement they'd settled on the ritual of one farewell. Anna suspected that Meg hated to leave as much as she hated for her to. Anna also avoided viewing her daughter's good-bye to her father, partly because she wanted to give them some privacy, partly because it hurt to see Jack display to their daughter the tenderness she so desperately needed for him to bestow on her.

A few minutes later Anna heard Carrie enter the kitchen.

"Well, Meg's off," Carrie announced.

Anna wiped a counter that was perfectly clean.

"Good. I want her back at school before nightfall."

"She looks well, even with the hectic pace of med school."

Anna smiled. "She has youth on her side."

"Yeah," Carrie said. Changing the focus of the subject, she added, "I think Jack looks good, too, don't you?"

What Anna thought was that Carrie was once more seeing the world through rose-colored glasses. Jack did not look good. He looked tired, drawn, distraught. So far the sea had failed him—them. So far it had withheld its restorative powers, although Anna hastily reminded herself that she couldn't expect too much too soon.

Obviously the question was a rhetorical one, for Carrie didn't wait for a reply. "Coming back to Maine was a good idea. And while you're here," she hastily tacked on, "you need to see about taking care of yourself. You look exhausted."

Anna glanced up from the task of loading the dishwasher. Her sister-in-law's comment surprised her. Was her fatigue so obvious that even Carrie, with her rosy view of the world, could see it?

"Of course, how could you be otherwise?" Carrie continued. "You've been by Jack's side night and day ever since the stroke."

"I'm okay," Anna said, stacking the plates in neat rows.

"You need someone to help out at night. If you could just get a good night's sleep."

"You sound like Meg."

"Then why don't you listen to us?"

"Really, I'm okay. Especially now that I have help during the day."

Anna wasn't certain why she was holding her ground so firmly. Heaven only knew that she was exhausted. It had something to do with commitment. Even though Jack seemed quite willing to turn from her, she still couldn't turn from him.

"I'm fine," Anna repeated, managing a smile that actually looked like the real thing.

"You're stubborn."

Anna's smile grew, this time sincerely. "Have you and Meg been talking?"

"No, which only proves my point." Before Anna could reply, Carrie said, "Look, I'll make you a deal. I'll get off your case if you'll meet me in town for lunch next Wednesday." At the objection she must have heard coming, she said, "Let the nurse do what you're hiring him for." There was a pause, then, "Deal?"

Anna hesitated, but only for a moment. "Deal," she said, thinking that perhaps getting out would be good for her. Besides, she had the feeling that Carrie had no intention of giving up until she got her way.

On Monday morning, when Anna found the third shell in exactly the same spot where she'd found the other two, the thought crossed her mind that someone was leaving them for her. The sight of the fourth shell on Tuesday morning left little doubt, while the discovery of the fifth on Wednesday shattered what little uncertainty remained.

But who would leave them? And why?

As Anna posed the questions, she glanced about her. She scanned the beach, as if the answers must surely be hiding somewhere nearby. Her gaze gravitated to the right, in the direction of the lighthouse. Though she couldn't see it from where she stood, she knew that it was located half a mile down the beach. She could see its beacon on clear nights, hear its horn on fog-shrouded evenings. Was someone living there? Or was it an automated lighthouse without the attendant keeper's cottage? And if it was lived in, was the person residing there responsible for leaving her the shells?

A thought crossed Anna's mind. How did whoever was leaving them know that she was collecting them unless . . . An eery feeling scampered down Anna's spine. Had someone been watching her? Had someone observed her morning ritual of searching for shells? Oh mercy, she thought, her heart sprinting, had some pervert been following her? Quickly she glanced about her again. Just as quickly, however, she realized the inanity of her fear. Whoever was leaving the shells meant her no harm. That she was absolutely certain of, though for the life of her she couldn't explain how she knew this. She didn't really *know* it as much as she *felt* it, deep in her heart, where only truth survived.

"See, I told you that you needed to get out," Carrie said over lunch later that day.

She and Anna sat at a blue-awninged table on the back veranda of The Smiling Cricket. The restaurant, crowded with noonday diners, overlooked—indeed, actually overhung—a white, lacy-looking waterfall. A stream, traipsing over tiers of jagged, irregularly spaced rocks, cascaded toward the harbor, creating in its travel the gentle gurgling sound of migrating water. Above this came the *caw-caw* of scavenging sea gulls and the honk of Canadian geese, both grown tame by their close association with people.

Anna looked up from the steaming bowl of clam chowder. She had to admit that getting out did feel wonderfully liberating. It had been hard to tell, however, how Jack had felt about her announcement that she was joining his sister for lunch. He had simply nodded and gone back to placing pegs in the holes of a square board, an exercise designed to rebuild hand coordination. Under normal circumstances, without even knowing if a defense was necessary, Anna might have tried to explain how Carrie had backed her into a corner. Anna heard herself offering no such explanation, however. After finding the shell that morning, an idea had occurred to her. Maybe Carrie would be able to give her the answer to a question that had been on her mind since that morning. Now all she had to do was find a way to ask the question without causing Carrie to counter with some of her own.

Smiling, Anna said, "You were right. I *did* need to get out."

"See, I told you," Carrie said. "And now that I have you out, I'm taking you shopping, as well."

"I thought you had to get back to work."

"Dr. Goodman takes Wednesday afternoons off, which means that I can take a long lunch break. So . . ." she added with a twinkle in her eyes, "we're going over to The Fashion Hut. They have a sale."

"I really don't need—"

"Nonsense, a woman always needs one more of something."

Anna couldn't remember the last time she'd been shopping. She certainly hadn't been since Jack's stroke. Even before that, though, they went precious few places to justify a large wardrobe. Her gray sweats had become her uniform. Her prison uniform? Maybe in a sense that's what they had become. It wasn't that, as a diabetic, her husband couldn't go out. It was just that more and more he went less and less. He always had needs that had to be met, which in the end made him appear different. Anna had guessed that he'd grown tired of being odd man out.

"By the way," Carrie added, clearly considering the subject of shopping closed, "Dr. Goodman said that he was going to stop by to see Jack. If not today, sometime soon."

"That'll be nice," Anna said. After a momentary si-

lence, her heart picking up its pace, she asked, "You
know the lighthouse out on Penobscot Point?"

"Eagle Crest?"

"I guess that's it," Anna replied, adding casually,
"Does anyone live there?"

"Yeah. As a matter of fact, a friend of Harper's. A
guy named Marshall. Sloan Marshall. He's lived there
two or three months. The lighthouse is automated, of
course, but the citizens of Cook's Bay own the keeper's
cottage, and they try to keep it rented out. You know
how property goes down when it's not lived in."

Though Carrie continued to talk, Anna found that
she was only half listening. For all intents and purposes, she heard nothing beyond the name Sloan Marshall. Was this the person leaving the shells for her?
Was this the person who must have observed her
searching for shells? Was this the person—

"Why do you ask?"

The question, though not unexpected, brought Anna's reverie to a halt. Again trying to appear noncha-
lant, she said, "No real reason. I just saw someone on
the beach, and since the nearest house is a couple of
miles away, I though maybe the lighthouse was occupied."

It was a lie and Anna knew it, but it was only a teeny,
tiny lie. Someone had been on the beach. It was just
that she hadn't seen this someone.

"Tall, dark-haired, dark-eyed?"

Anna shrugged. "Hard to tell at a distance."

"I'll bet it was Sloan. He's a real nice guy, but he
stays pretty much to himself. He's sort of a recluse."

If the man in the lighthouse stayed to himself, Anna
wondered whether she'd made an erroneous assumption. Maybe her benefactor wasn't this mysterious, reclusive Sloan Marshall after all. On the other hand, the
individual *had* kept to himself, leaving only shells as his
calling cards. For the next couple of hours, though

Anna appeared to be engaged in a variety of activities—finishing lunch, admiring the buckets of flowers blooming on the sidewalks of Cook's Bay, browsing at The Fashion Hut—the name Sloan Marshall was never far from her mind.

"Is that all you're buying?" Carrie asked, her voice filled with incredulity, her arms filled with an array of Gypsy-bright clothes.

Anna looked down at the single item in her hand. "Meg's been wanting a black belt. I thought I'd get this for her birthday next month."

"I repeat, is that all you're buying?" Before Anna could answer, Carrie asked, "Where's that blouse you liked?"

Earlier, Anna had admired a lacy, high-throated blouse that was reminiscent of the Victorian era.

"I really don't need anything." Carrie started to protest, but Anna repeated, with an authority that was hard to buck, "Truly, I don't."

After arriving back at the house, lunch and the shopping spree were soon forgotten amid the usual and persistent chores. Jack had not had the best of afternoons. Following the nurse's departure at three o'clock, Anna kept a close eye on her husband, which she continued to do after his six-thirty insulin injection, the evening meal, and on into the night. After making several trips to Jack's bedroom, somewhere around midnight she decided to try to get a little sleep.

As she pulled back the coverlet from the bed, Anna heard the rustle of paper, and glancing up, she saw the sack emblazoned with the logo of The Fashion Hut. Her outing with Carrie seemed an eon ago, as though her life were measured by a slow-ticking clock, a clock that captured time and held it prisoner. Picking up the sack, she lay it on the dresser. Oddly, her thoughts raced to the blouse she'd left behind. The truth was that she hadn't bought it because she had no one to tell her how pretty she looked in it.

Pretty.

A woman occasionally wanted to be told that she was pretty.

"You look pretty," Anna imagined Jack saying, just the way he used to a thousand years ago. *"Come here, pretty lady."*

As the sugar-sweet words danced in her head, Anna pretended that she could feel her husband's equally sweet caress—the heated brush of his lips against hers, the satiny grazing of fingertips across fevered skin, the gentle melding of one body with another. Anna closed her eyes, in remembrance of what it was like to feel pretty, in remembrance of what it was like to feel like a woman. Sadly, it was getting harder and harder to remember both.

EIGHT

Despite the fact that Anna slept little and restlessly, she nonetheless awoke early and undeniably exhilarated. She tried to ignore the excitement coursing through her, tried even harder to ignore its source, yet she failed miserably at doing both. By the time the nurse had arrived and she was ready to leave, Anna, like a mare kept waiting too long, was chewing at the bit.

Forcing a slowness to her steps, she headed for the beach, and the shell she knew would be awaiting her. But what if there was no shell this morning? What if finding the shells—five to date—in the same spot had been nothing more than an extraordinary coincidence? No, she couldn't believe that. She didn't want to believe it. Ever since she'd come to the conclusion that someone was leaving the shells for her, she'd enjoyed the warm feeling that came with that knowledge. She'd enjoyed the possibility of finding a friend.

Friend?

What a strange choice of words, Anna thought, as the footsteps she fought to curb kept quickening their pace. Try as she would, however, she couldn't think of a more appropriate word. She *did* feel some sort of bond with whomever was presenting her with the shells. Was it this reclusive Sloan Marshall who lived in the lighthouse?

Once on the beach, Anna saw that the piece of driftwood had all but disappeared. During the night the sea had reclaimed a chunk of it, leaving only a gnarled, rotted limb the pale color of ash. Anna's heart sank at the possibility that maybe the sea had stolen her shell, as well. She was suddenly quite certain that one had been left for her.

Hastening her steps, brushing the wind-teased hair from her eyes, she approached the remains of the driftwood. She saw nothing that even resembled a shell. Her heart, which had sunk earlier, now fell at her feet. Inexplicably, she felt a fierce, stabbing disappointment. As though the driftwood was to blame, she kicked it. It was then that she saw the circle drawn in the wet sand. Within the circle lay a seashell no larger than her thumbnail and as white as winter snow.

Bending, she picked up the small shell and noted its fragility and flawlessness. Carefully turning it over, she studied the interior, a delicate indentation in hues of delicate pink. As though she'd almost lost something precious, and because of that its value had doubled, Anna folded her hand about the tiny object.

Gazing in the direction of the lighthouse, she knew that there could no longer be any doubt that someone was, indeed, leaving the shells for her. Circumstance didn't have the ability to draw a circle in the sand. How did she feel about this certainty? Pleased. The bond she felt with this stranger, this unknown friend, grew stronger.

Anna couldn't pinpoint when the idea first occurred to her. Maybe it was en route back to the house, or maybe it was as she placed the shell on the windowsill. Perhaps it was as she strove to make conversation with her husband—he, too, a stranger, though she'd spent most of her adult life with him—who clearly would have preferred silence. Whatever, once the idea had occurred, Anna clung to it like a drowning woman clinging to flotsam. It would take some doing, but she was determined to set a trap for her mysterious benefactor.

Yes, she thought, it was high time they met.

The following morning Sloan awoke abruptly. As always after the nightmare, he sought to engage his mind elsewhere—on the luminous dial of the bedside clock, which indicated that it was almost the hour to get up, on the shell that he would later take to *her*, on her reaction the day before. He'd known the small shell would be difficult to find, so he'd drawn a circle around it. Had he done the right thing in doing so? Had he done the right thing by beginning the ritual of leaving the shells? Probably not, he admitted truthfully, though he just as truthfully admitted that he didn't feel a speck of remorse.

Getting out of bed, he slipped into the sweatsuit hanging from the back of a chair and laced on his jogging shoes. Walking to the kitchen, he put a pot of coffee on to perk, slid the shell into the pocket of his sweatpants, and grabbed his sunglasses. He didn't really need the sunglasses—dawn was but barely breaking across the sky—yet he always reached for them when leaving the house. They'd become a way for him to hide from others. And a way for him to hide from himself? Possibly, he thought.

The sunglasses in place, he hit the beach at his usual

relaxed jog. In less than ten minutes, with the morning sun beginning to peek above the pencil-etched horizon, Sloan arrived at the now familiar spot on the beach. The driftwood was gone entirely. Reaching inside the pocket of his sweatpants, he drew forth the shell and had just stooped to put the offering in place when he felt the presence.

Her presence.

Of that he was certain. More certain than he'd ever been of anything in the whole of his life. He felt surrounded, hemmed in, caught in a tender trap. Curiously, though, he in no way felt threatened. Instead a sense of elation, anticipation, like sparkling fireworks, exploded inside him.

Swiveling on the balls of his feet, Sloan searched for her. He scanned the beach, the rocks, the tree line. In the latter hid shapeless shadows, frightening nighttime phantoms that, by the light of day, were friendly realities. He found her standing amid the towering trees. Even as he watched, she stepped forward, substance separating itself from suggestion. She headed straight for him.

Sloan's heart began to pound.

Would she be angry at the way he'd forced himself into her life? Although from his point of view his intervention had been well intentioned and benign, it remained to be seen how she interpreted it. This consideration had no sooner taken shape than it vanished altogether, replaced by the consuming realization that he'd woefully misjudged her looks. She was not merely pretty. She was strikingly pretty, falling just short of out-and-out beautiful, with an innocent-looking face that Rubens would have painted on a cherub, a head of curly blond hair that performed playful antics in the boastful breeze, a pair of blue eyes that looked both young and old, child and woman, and something more that Sloan couldn't quite fathom.

She stopped a short distance away, her gaze meeting his fully. In response, the shell in place, Sloan pushed to his feet and waited, determined to force her into breaking the silence, wondering what those first words would be. In the end her choice surprised him.

"Why?"

Though the question had been spoken as softly as a sinner's prayer, it was nonetheless powerfully direct. Sloan liked this directness and rewarded it with the simple truth.

"Because you looked so disappointed when you didn't find a shell. No one deserves to be that disappointed if it can be helped."

If her question had surprised him, his response did no less to Anna. It had been a long while since anyone had noticed her disappointment, let alone tried to do something about it. That this man had done both moved and intrigued her. Almost as much as the toasty richness of his tan. Almost as much as the way the wind strolled through his raven-black hair. Almost as much as the way his gray-tinted sunglasses prohibited any view of his eyes. Even though she couldn't see those eyes, she felt their steadfast stare as he awaited her response.

"Disappointment is part of life," she said, again so quietly that the thieflike wind snatched away the fragile words.

The resignation in her voice saddened Sloan. Sadness? Was that what he saw buried deep in her beautiful blue eyes?

"Disappointment is part of death," he said, adding, "With every disappointment the human spirit dies just a little."

Anna cocked her head to the side, as though considering the validity of this comment. "Maybe the death of the spirit is as inevitable as the death of the body."

"No!" Sloan replied with such force that he embar-

rassed himself. He also astonished himself. He'd long
ago thought his own spirit broken, but now glimpsed a
little of his old fighting self. At least the warrior in him
appeared ready to do battle with this woman's grim enemy.

Anna smiled softly. "You're quite the impassioned
philosopher, aren't you?"

Sloan returned her smile with a crooked one of his
own. "Maybe. Maybe not."

This conversation wasn't going as Sloan had thought
their first conversation might, which was odd now that
he thought about it. Had he known from the beginning
that this confrontation had been destined? Was it secretly what he'd wanted? Was that why he'd drawn the
circle in the sand, to eliminate the possibility of any remaining coincidence? The realization that he might
have actually set himself up startled him.

Anna's voice broke through Sloan's reverie. "So,
Sloan Marshall, is it your habit to travel the world saving damsels from disappointment?"

As she spoke, she eased onto the sand. She looked as
if the beach were her home and she was entertaining a
guest that had unexpectedly dropped by. At her silent
invitation Sloan joined her. Though her conversation
was warm and friendly, he couldn't help but take note
of her body language. With her legs bent at the knees,
and her arms banded about her legs, she had placed a
barrier between her and him. But, then, wouldn't a psy-
chologist tell him the same thing about his sunglasses?

Rather than concentrate on this last, he focused on
the fact that she'd managed to surprise him once more.
"You know my name."

"I asked Carrie. After I'd concluded that it must be
you leaving the shells."

"And what did Carrie tell you about me?"

"That your name is Sloan Marshall, that you're a
friend of the man she's dating, that you have dark hair

and dark eyes, and that you're a recluse. Are you?" she asked, threading her gently tangled hair back from her eyes. "A recluse, I mean?"

Sloan wondered where her yellow scarf was. He understood now why she wore it. Otherwise, the wind whipped her hair into a frenzy. A delightful frenzy, but a frenzy nonetheless.

"You didn't wear your scarf," Sloan said, indicating to her that he knew her routine, and well.

Anna drew a hand to her neck. In the face of the scarf's absence, in the face of Sloan's knowledge of this detail of her life, she felt bare, vulnerable. She wasn't sure she liked the feeling.

"I dressed in a hurry," she said.

"It was important to catch me in the act, huh?"

"You didn't answer my question," Anna said. "Actually, you haven't answered my last two. I'm beginning to suspect you're deliberately avoiding them."

"I don't even remember them," Sloan said, lying through his teeth. He wasn't comfortable with personal queries.

"Are you a recluse?"

As Anna repeated the question, she wondered why she was being so persistent. She decided that reclusiveness suggested a drama that was irresistible. She had never met a bona fide recluse before. Even as this thought crossed her mind, she acknowledged it as the falsehood it was. In her own way she, too, was a recluse. Oh, maybe not a physical recluse, but an emotional one. Life had forced her to hide out. Was Sloan Marshall hiding out, too? Suddenly Anna had the strongest urge to yank away the concealing sunglasses, to peer into his eyes, to probe their depths.

"Am I a recluse?" Sloan repeated, stalling as long as he could before answering. "I guess I must be if Carrie says I am."

"Why?"

Sloan grinned, though his heart turned over once. This wasn't a subject he wanted to go into. Now. Ever. "It's a prerequisite for being an impassioned philosopher."

Anna smiled knowingly. "I think you're avoiding an answer, but never mind, we'll go back to the original question. Is it your habit to travel the world saving damsels from disappointment?"

"Actually, you're the first damsel I've ever tried to save from disappointment."

"Why me?"

Sloan stared at her through the silver-tinted shades that secluded him from the world. The words he was about to speak were the truest he'd ever spoken and, because of that, the most disturbing. "I honestly don't know."

"But you have been watching me?" she asked, silently adding, *through those very glasses?*

"Yes. Does that upset you?"

"Should it?"

"Does it?"

"No," she replied, wondering if perhaps she shouldn't be upset by the very fact that she wasn't.

"Look, just so we know where we stand, I know you're a married woman. I mean, I'm not coming on to you."

"I didn't think you were," she returned hastily, not wanting him to think that was what she'd thought. It truly hadn't been, which probably spoke volumes about how she saw herself. Maybe she'd concluded that her husband's inattention had something to do with her undesirability? It was more question than answer and one she didn't want to pursue.

Sloan was just as eager for a disavowal. "Well, I'm not," he said. "Boy Scout's honor."

There was something so youthful in his manner, so

boyish, that Anna couldn't help asking teasingly, "Were you a Boy Scout?"

Sloan grinned back. "As a matter of fact, I was." Suddenly his grin disappeared, lost in the need to reaffirm his position, to define their relationship.

"Look," he said, "I know this sounds crazy. I, uh, I can't explain it even to myself, but I feel like we've become friends. I've watched you, I've brought you shells, I've seen your excitement, I've . . ." He groaned. "Am I making a fool of myself?"

Anna had been touched to discover that he'd felt the same as she had. "No, you're not making a fool of yourself. Actually, I feel very much the same."

Sloan both felt and looked relieved. "The truth is, I guess I could use a friend right now."

Though the remark was cryptic, though she wanted to pursue it, Anna didn't. Instead she replied, "The truth is that I guess I could too."

Sloan thought her reply interesting, but he didn't ask her to expound on it. "It's agreed, then, that we'll be friends?"

Suddenly reality struck. Things were moving fast. Maybe too fast. After all, she really didn't know this man. "Let's agree to think about it."

He'd spooked her, and if he was truthful, he might be a little spooked himself. "Fair enough," he said, giving her, and himself, the room they needed.

"So," Sloan said finally, breaking the nervous silence that had descended, "you're Carrie's sister-in-law."

"Yes."

"You're married to her brother."

At the mention of her marriage, Anna's heart skipped a beat. This was one subject she didn't want to discuss. It was altogether too painful, and so, as she always did when pain closed in, she disappeared inside herself, using up a little more of herself in the process of getting to this safe place.

"Yes," she answered. Simple. Blunt. Encouraging nothing else.

"How long have you been married?"

Pause, hesitation, then, "Twenty-four years."

"Do you have children?"

"A daughter. Meg."

"Pretty name," Sloan said. And as though it were information that should be stated and gotten out of the way, he tacked on, "I'm divorced. No children."

"I'm sorry."

"Don't be. The divorce was a long time ago."

"I meant about your not having any children."

Sloan shrugged. "I guess it was fate." Silence, another awkwardness. "Someone said that your husband had a stroke."

"Yes," Anna said. Standing, dusting her pants, she stated flatly, "I've got to go."

Confused, Sloan stood as well, wondering what had brought the conversation to such an abrupt halt. The comment about her husband having had a stroke? Whatever, he'd done more than spook her this time. He'd chased her off. Completely.

Sloan did not wonder about the look in her eyes, however. As he'd suspected earlier, it *was* one of sadness. If he had found it difficult to witness her disappointment, he found her sadness impossible to bear.

"I'm sorry. I said something I shouldn't have."

"No," Anna said, lowering her eyes before he read more than she cared for him to. She took several steps backward. "I've just got to go. I have to cook breakfast." Those several steps became several more, all executed with a growing haste.

"Hey, wait!" Sloan said, indicating the shell sunning in the sand. "Don't forget your shell. It's not the best of the lot, but it *is* whole."

Anna retraced her steps, picked up the shell, and

studied it. She then looked up at Sloan. "Thank you. For all the shells."

"Why do they have to be whole?"

Again it wasn't something Anna wanted to go into, and so she hid just that much further inside herself.

"I really have to go," she repeated, starting from the beach as resolutely as she'd earlier crossed it.

"Are you going to be here in the morning?" Sloan called after her.

"I don't know," she tossed over her shoulder without looking back.

"I'll be disappointed if you're not!" he shouted.

Again Anna didn't look back. She just kept walking toward the throat of the path that would take her to the house, to her husband, to her stale marriage. "Disappointment is part of life."

"Hey!"

This time the tone of Sloan's voice, commanding, demanding, stopped her cold. She turned.

"You settle for too little," he said.

"You ask for too much," she countered.

They stared at each other.

Sloan stood in exactly the same spot, his hands in his pants pockets, the wind tousling his black hair, the gray shades of his glasses glistening in the blossoming sun. He looked more enigmatic than ever. Abruptly, from out of nowhere, a question formed in Anna's mind, in Anna's heart. It was a simple question, but one that seemed of prime importance. In fact, she couldn't remember another question that had ever seemed this important.

"Do you really have dark eyes beneath those sunglasses?"

A mild panic fluttered through Sloan. She was asking him to remove the glasses, but for a reason he didn't understand, he couldn't. Was he afraid that she'd see too much, wonder too much, ask too many questions? Whatever, he hid behind a grin.

"Yeah," he answered. "I'll show you tomorrow."

Anna couldn't help but smile at his obvious ploy. She chose to say nothing, however, but rather started once more for the house. No sooner had she then she heard his cry.

"Hey!"

Anna once more pivoted toward him.

"Do you have a given name?"

A grin still played at her lips, while a feeling that could only be called recklessness—Lord, when was the last time she'd felt reckless!—roamed her heart.

"Yes," she answered. "I'll tell you tomorrow."

With that Anna left. Sloan watched her, thinking that both of them had made a commitment, even as both had held on tightly to their privacy.

Later that afternoon Dr. Goodman arrived unexpectedly. He had been in the neighborhood, he announced, which was difficult to believe since the rented house was virtually isolated. Jack was glad to see him, as was Anna. Though she'd met the good doctor only a handful of times over the years, she'd always liked him. Kind-hearted and gentle-handed, he epitomized the small-town physician, although his appearance suggested more that of an absent-minded professor. His hair always needed a little more combing, his clothes a little more matching, his life a little more organizing. His demeanor was misleading, however, for he was bright, an excellent doctor, and the lead cellist in the Cook's Bay Symphony.

When Anna showed Dr. Goodman to Jack's bedroom, Ken discreetly took a break; Anna then departed for the kitchen to make coffee for their guest. When she returned to the bedroom, she served coffee, then started to leave.

"Join us," Dr. Goodman said.

The doctor's request startled Anna, and in her astonishment she glanced toward her husband, who sat in the wheelchair, which once more was wedged beneath the small table. She worried that her action might be interpreted as seeking permission, and yet that was precisely what she was doing. With Jack's mercurial temperament, she always walked on eggshells trying to please him. With his normally functioning left hand, he indicated for her to take a chair near him. Whether his gesture was sincere or not, Anna couldn't have said, but she did as bade.

"How's that daughter of yours?" Dr. Goodman asked. If he'd noticed the silent exchange between husband and wife, there was no evidence of it.

As always, because of the distortion of his voice, Jack let Anna take the lead. She smiled, genuinely. "Meg's doing great. Working hard in school."

Adding a dash of cream to his coffee, Dr. Goodman replied, "Well, I'm afraid she's going to work a lot harder before they make her a doctor. Does she have any idea what branch of medicine she wants to specialize in?"

"I think she's leaning toward internal medicine," Anna said, tactfully not mentioning that she personally thought her daughter's decision had something to do with her beloved father's illness.

"Good choice," the doctor replied, turning his attention to Jack. "So, tell me, how do you feel you're doing after the stroke?"

Anna knew that the question had been carefully calculated to draw Jack into the conversation—whether he wished to be drawn in or not. It crossed her mind to wonder, too, if the doctor's insistence on her staying might not have been as meticulously orchestrated. Did he want to observe them together, to determine how the stroke was affecting the family unit? If so, would he see the strain, the disharmony that dwelled just below the surface?

The direct question obviously took Jack by surprise. Furthermore, it demanded a personal reply. Slowly, Jack set down his cup, one specifically designed so that the disabled might avoid spills. Anna knew how he loathed the cup, but it did allow him a degree of independence. Reaching for his pad and pen, Jack began to scribble a response. After several seconds Jack angled the pad so Dr. Goodman could read the note.

"Well, now, Jack, recovery following a stroke is often slow. You can't let that discourage you. I've seen Ken work miracles, so give him a chance, give him a little time."

Time.

Anna took a step back into that finite, yet insubstantial thing called time. Though only hours before, the incident on the beach, the meeting with Sloan Marshall, seemed to belong to a world of a thousand yesterdays. In fact, she couldn't swear that it had happened at all. On the other hand, the incident seemed to defy time, to have occurred within its own temporal framework, to be possessed of a reality so substantial that it couldn't be denied.

Had she really committed herself to meeting him there on the beach the following morning? The question was really a moot one, for no sooner had she arrived back at the house, than she'd realized that the following morning was a Saturday. With Ken off, Jack's care rested in her hands, which meant that she couldn't leave him alone.

Certainly not to meet a man!

"You shouldn't be relying on that pad and pen . . . need to exercise your vocal cords . . . strengthen your speech . . ."

Anna caught odds and ends of the continuing conversation, but deliberately turned loose of them in favor of the mental dialogue running through her head.

"The truth is, I guess I could use a friend right now."

And that was the whole crux of the matter, wasn't it? Anna thought. Could a man and a woman be just friends? Oh, she knew what Carrie would say, that the question was positively archaic. Enlightened times allowed men and women to be friends. Then what was the problem? The problem was that she wasn't an enlightened woman. When you'd been married to the same man for twenty-four years without so much as another man flirting with you—okay, so Jack's boss had come on to her a time or two—it seemed strange to have any other man enter your life in any capacity. More than strange, it seemed unseemly, inappropriate.

Which was the really crazy thing about Sloan Marshall's suggestion that they be friends. She'd bet every dime in her bank account that he'd meant nothing unseemly and inappropriate by it. A woman could sense the intentions of a man on the prowl, and Sloan Marshall was not such a man. She'd sensed nothing but sincerity. The man had asked her to be his friend, and God only knew she needed one.

So what was the problem?

"Anna?"

So why these second thoughts about meeting a man whom she'd begun to think of as a friend long before she'd met him?

The thudding of Jack's fist on the table scattered Anna's thoughts. When she glanced up, Dr. Goodman was standing and Jack was staring at her. Immediately she came to her feet, offering no apology for her obvious inattention.

"Take care," Dr. Goodman said, giving Jack a pat on the shoulder. "And give yourself time to recover, okay?"

Jack gave a nod.

"Thanks for stopping by," Anna told Dr. Goodman when she'd shown him to the front door.

"My pleasure," he said, similarly patting Anna on the shoulder. "If you need me, call me."

"I will."

Dr. Goodman was halfway out the door when he turned. "You know, you could take a little better care of yourself."

Anna gave a sheepish grin. "Do I look that bad? You're the third person in a week who's told me that."

"You look tired. Get some rest."

The words rang in Anna's ears long after the good doctor had departed. They were sound enough, but totally impractical. Even if she'd tried to get some rest, it would have been an impossibility—what with Jack soiling the bed and the linen having to be changed and washed, what with Ken leaving at three o'clock and Jack withdrawing into himself, meaning simply that he was embarrassed about soiling the bed.

When the telephone rang at six-thirty, Anna reached a weary hand to silence it. "Hello?"

"Have you put on dinner?" Carrie asked.

"Yes. Pot roast."

"Darn. I was hoping to catch you before you did."

"Sorry."

"Is there enough for three?"

"Sure, but I thought you had a date with Harper."

"*Did* have a date. He has a client he's got to go bail out of jail."

"Come on over, then," Anna said, brightening at the prospect. She told herself that she could use the company, a buffer between her and her husband. And maybe Carrie's presence would give a boost to Jack's mood.

"Look, how about me staying the night? I could give you a little relief."

Anna tucked the phone between her ear and shoulder as she began to scrape a carrot. "Have you been talking to Dr. Goodman?"

"I don't need to talk to him to know you're wasted." Carrie pulled out her own carrot and dangled it. "Just think. Eight full hours of uninterrupted sleep."

It was more than Anna could resist. "Dinner will be ready at seven."

Later Anna wondered if it was really a good night's sleep she'd found irresistible, or the fact that maybe she'd have a chance to go to the beach come morning—to get out of the house, to find a shell . . . to see Sloan Marshall.

NINE

From the moment that Anna saw Sloan on the beach, she thought how foolish her second thoughts had been. Their friendship needed no justification. Uncomplicated and pure, it simply *was*—like air and water and flaming fire. Even so, like all budding relationships, it would have to be constructed one cautious step at a time. And it would have to be built in secret, for although Anna knew of its innocence, she wasn't naive enough to believe that all would share her opinion. Particularly not in a small, idle town like Cook's Bay.

When Sloan saw Anna approaching, he threw his hand up in a wave, which she returned. He then went back to casting crumbs of bread before a horde of ravenous sea gulls. He was still wearing the tinted sunglasses despite the fact that curtains of clouds continued to gather in the sky. It had rained during the night, hard, fast, furious, and to the accompaniment of an angry wind that had churned the ocean like a cooking cauldron. When the wind had finally departed, it had left behind a wide, wild range of debris—a huge pile of driftwood, a piece of lumber from a nearby pier, shells galore, snakelike kelp, and chunks of coral. The threat of rain remained, cloaked in the cool folds of an embittered breeze, a tangy tartness that stung the air and swarmed above the tired, worn sea.

Sloan had been afraid that the bad weather might keep Anna from the beach. Anna had feared the same, just as she'd feared that Carrie would ask why she wanted to go out when rain seemed imminent. Carrie hadn't asked, however. She'd simply, practically, told her to take a raincoat with her.

Transferring the garment from one arm to another, Anna, as though she'd known this man forever, called out, "Hi!"

"Hi!" Sloan called back with the same familiarity.

Anna stopped where she was, not wanting to scatter the gulls snapping up the bits of bread that Sloan tossed their way. A feathery sea of gray and white rose and fell, wavelike, about him. Slowly, like a master wading among his worshipful flock, Sloan broke from them and started toward Anna, causing a number of the skittish fowl to take flight abruptly.

Anna smiled. "Who are your friends?"

Sloan smiled back. "There were only two when I started feeding them. Before I knew it, their friends and relatives had shown up. Big time."

"Maybe there are a few carrier pigeons among them."

Sloan's smile widened. "Maybe. The message *did* get carried pretty fast."

He stopped in front of her, thinking myriad things at once—that he'd been worried that she wouldn't show up even if the weather permitted, that there still appeared to be a hint of sadness in her eyes, that her hair, which spilled about her in a silken disarray, looked far more golden than he'd remembered. As this last thought skipped through his mind, she untied the yellow scarf from her neck and, battling the brassy breeze, drew it over her hair, knotting the ends beneath her chin. The confinement of the sassy curls, while undeniably necessary, nonetheless seemed a shame.

At the same time, a bevy of stray thoughts wandered through Anna's mind. Sloan seemed taller than she'd remembered, while his smile seemed broader and friendlier, and his shoulders wider. It also seemed to her that his sunglasses were darker, a shade of gray as impenetrable as . . . As what? Secrets? Did this man have a secret? But, then, didn't everyone?

"I, uh, I didn't know if you'd come," he said.

"I didn't for sure, either," she answered truthfully, thinking of the hours she'd spent weighing the issue.

"Why did you?"

"Because I'd like to be your friend," Anna said, smiling as she added, "I've never been friends with a man before."

Sloan shrugged, saying, "I've never been friends with a woman before, but my guess is that a friend's a friend."

"I suspect you're right," Anna said, feeling the need to change the subject to one less serious. "It looks as if it's going to rain again."

"Yeah," Sloan agreed, relieved that Anna wanted his friendship as much as he wanted hers. And that was all he wanted from her. He'd questioned his heart thoroughly about this and was satisfied with the answer he'd found.

By this time one of the more brazen gulls had followed Sloan, begging with its shrill cry for another handout. Ivory with a pewter-gray breast, the plump bird halted and cocked its head in consideration of the two human beings. Its black, beady eye seemed to say that one couldn't be too cautious.

"Here," Sloan said, passing the plastic bag of bread bits to Anna, "see if you can get him to come to you."

As he spoke, Sloan slowly squatted, one jean-covered knee digging into the impressionable sand. Anna eased beside him, one of her jean-clad knees taking a position near his. Both felt a rush of cool moistness.

"Come on, boy," Sloan coaxed as Anna held out a handful of bread.

"Come on," she tempted in a soft, singsong whisper that Sloan was certain the bird couldn't resist. What, or who, could turn its back on such sweetness?

The sea gull, however, looked thoroughly skeptical.

"I've seen this bird on the beach before," Sloan said quietly. "Down by the lighthouse."

"How can you tell?"

"Look at its leg. It's scarred."

Anna lowered her gaze to the animal. Sure enough, just above the point where a webbed foot flared out, a callused scar knotted the skin.

"It probably got caught in a fisherman's line," Sloan explained.

"Ah, poor thing," Anna cooed.

"Scars don't hurt," Sloan said.

Something in the matter-of-fact way Sloan made the pronouncement caused Anna to glance up at him. At the same time, the wary bird fluttered its wings, as though having decided not to take a chance with these two strangers.

"Easy, easy," Sloan crooned in a molasses-thick voice that Anna thought could have easily persuaded the devil toward acts of charity. It certainly caused Sloan's comment about scars to flee entirely.

"C'mon, boy," she repeated, edging forward, proffering her bread-ladened palm.

The motion, though slow and steady, scared the bird, and with a squawk of protest it sailed into the air.

"Darn!" Anna said.

"Don't worry. It'll be back. If not tomorrow, then the next day. It takes a while to build a relationship."

Anna's gaze once more found Sloan. Though he wasn't looking at her, she was certain that his words had been intended to apply to more than building a relationship with a wild creature. The words had been intended for their relationship, which was every bit as fragile, as friable, as theirs with the bird. Maybe even more so.

After the gull's departure Anna threw the rest of the bread to the remaining birds. Sloan produced a raincoat of his own, a navy-blue garment that had been thrown over a pile of rocks. Spreading out the raincoat, he sat down on it. Anna followed suit, once more pulling her knees upward and banding her arms about them. Just as one could see the beach from the house from only one spot, there was also one spot on the beach where one could see the house. Not wanting to see or be seen, Anna had been pleased with Sloan's choice. Had it been deliberate? Had he, too, realized that it was best for their friendship to remain unknown?

Neither Sloan nor Anna spoke as they watched the birds gobble up the food—but, then, the silence didn't seem to need filling. Anna couldn't help but compare it to the silence she and her husband shared. She always felt the need to saturate it with sentences, to pack it full of words, however mundane, however inane. As though the sea, as well, saw no need to interrupt the quietness, the waves whispered ashore, folding gently over themselves in a kind of hushed, reverent rapture. In the distance, though, thunder rumbled, a disgruntled reminder that the rain would soon be returning. Overhead, clouds trembled.

"Are you going to tell me your name?"

Sloan asked the question as he and Anna watched some small birds, newly arrived on the scene, scavenge among a heap of driftwood. Their long pointed beaks picked and probed into the wet sand.

"Uh-uh," Anna said, adding, without even looking in his direction, "Not until you take off those sunglasses."

Anna could feel the slow smile crawling across Sloan's lips. She could also feel her heartbeat quicken just the tiniest bit, the way heartbeats often did in the throes of game playing. And they were playing a game, a harmless game of wait-and-tell, wait-and-show. Curiously, each discovered that he, she, wasn't eager for the game to end too quickly, and so Anna postponed it with a question.

"What goodies are the birds searching for?"

Without missing a beat Sloan said, "Buried treasure."

It clearly wasn't the answer Anna had expected. She glanced over at Sloan, who glanced over at her.

"There are those who would tell you sand fleas," Sloan said, "but the truth is that it's buried treasure. To be more precise, jewels—diamonds, emeralds, rubies as red as blood, sapphires as blue as the deepest sea."

Anna looked more than a little incredulous. She also looked more than a little intrigued.

Sloan nodded in the direction of the driftwood. "Surely you can see that's a nineteenth-century schooner washed ashore in last night's storm. It was wrecked a hundred years ago and washes ashore with every storm." As though to prove his point—that the driftwood was, indeed, a schooner—he indicated, quite specifically, with his hand. "Fore. Aft. And of course, although it's hard to tell, my guess is that it was a three-masted vessel."

Totally mesmerized, Anna asked, "Is that large for a schooner?"

"Yeah, although this ship was special for reasons other than size."

"What reasons?"

"Well, for one thing, it was brand new. As a matter of fact, this was its first voyage, and it was state-of-the-art. Very elegantly appointed too. Lots of gold, plush satins and silks in the stateroom, china and silver in the dining room."

"I had no idea schooners were so luxurious."

"Not all of them, but as I said, this was a special ship. It had been built for a very specific purpose."

Sloan noted that Anna had turned loose of her knees, had lowered them, and now actually sat facing him. This realization warmed his heart. At the same time, he knew he wasn't being fair. He was still hiding behind his glasses.

"What purpose?" Anna asked, so caught up in the story that she only marginally heard the warning roll of thunder. Overhead, the clouds began to thicken, to darken.

"The man who commissioned the ship to be built, an ex–sea captain, lived right here in Cook's Bay. Two years before, he'd traveled to England and had met this lady with whom he'd fallen instantly in love. Now, the only problem was that she was a great deal younger than he and very beautiful, and he thought that he had absolutely nothing to offer her. He didn't know that she'd fallen in love with him, too, because of his gentle, caring ways."

When Sloan paused, Anna said, "Go on."

"Well, he came home to Cook's Bay, heartbroken because he thought he'd never see her again, and thinking that was best for her. She, on the other hand, waited for him to write, and when he never did, she wrote him."

"How brazen for a hundred years ago," Anna said, sucked into the story as though it were quicksand.

"You bet your navigational compass it was."

Anna grinned, thinking that she'd probably done more grinning in the past couple of days than she had in a long while. It felt good.

Sloan had noted that, as his story had progressed, the sadness he'd seen in her eyes had begun to diminish. In fact, at present her eyes sparkled very much like the sapphires he'd spoken of. That was reason enough to continue with the story.

"They corresponded for a while, and finally our sea captain asked her to be his wife. Now, he honestly thought that his proposal would so shock her that it would drive her away, but to his utter surprise, she accepted."

Anna's grin grew. "Of course."

"He commissioned this schooner to be built just to go fetch his bride. They did a lot of fetching in those days."

"Oh, yes, lots."

"Once it was finished, he sent for her. As a wedding present he also sent a chestful of jewels that he'd collected from all over the world."

"What was the name of the ship?"

Sloan paused just long enough to make Anna realize that he was inventing this story as he went. She'd thought at first that he'd merely been repeating a local legend, but, then, in retrospect, how likely was that? He was a stranger to this area. Suddenly her interest was piqued, not only by the extemporaneous story, but also by the man telling it.

"The *Mary Jane*," he said, adding, "There was a beautifully carved figurehead of her on the bow." He sighed. "An exquisite work of art done by a master sculptor."

The story begged to be completed, even though Anna knew the ending would be a tragic one. To underscore this, thunder pealed and lightning streaked. As though in anticipation, the sea shuddered.

"The ship sank, didn't it?" Anna asked.

"On the way back, not more than ten miles off this very shore. An unexpected storm came up. Not a single person on board survived."

"And our sea captain?"

"He went mad. Lived for another ten or twelve years, but never spoke another word, except once a year. On the anniversary of the wreck he'd call out her name, as though to tell her that he hadn't forgotten her. When he died, according to his wishes, he was cremated and his ashes were scattered on this very stretch of sea. Now, I know what you're thinking," he said. "That this is a sad story."

"But it isn't?" Anna asked, curiously, desperately wanting it not to be.

"Not in the least. Many say, and I believe it, that once a month, at the full of the moon, the beautiful figurehead rises from the sea, takes human form, and walks this very beach in search of the man she loved. If you listen carefully, you can hear her call his name. Just once. Just the way he'd called hers for all those years."

"And does she find him?"

Sloan grinned. "You bet your navigational compass she does."

Anna didn't return his grin. She'd been too moved by the story, too moved by Sloan's sensitivity. What an interesting man this stranger from the lighthouse was!

"For one night, every month, they become lovers," Sloan said, adding, "Then, hand in hand, they walk back into the sea." He paused. "End of story."

Sloan wasn't certain what he'd expected Anna's reaction to be, but he hadn't expected her simply to stare at him. The stare was unnervingly prolonged, but the intensity of it was what unstrung him the most. She looked very much as though she were seeing right through him, which her next question proved.

"You made that up, didn't you? Right this minute."

Yeah, Sloan thought, she had the ability to see more than he wanted seen. He was vaguely aware that it had begun to rain, giant, plump drops that struck him like bullets fired from a gun. He stood, instinctively wanting to flee the rain, instinctively needing to flee her question.

"It's no big deal," he said flatly.

"Yes, it is." Anna came to her feet as well, because Sloan had, and because she, too, had become aware of the rain, which was growing harder by the second. Thunder growled, no longer in the distance but directly overhead. "Not only are you an impassioned philosopher, you're an extraordinary storyteller, a poet of the soul."

"Look, it's no big deal," Sloan repeated. "I've had lots of experience."

What an odd thing to say, Anna thought, *unless* . . . "Are you a writer?"

"Not hardly. Just a survivor."

The comment was obscure, leaving Anna more fascinated than ever; but if it was clear that she might have asked more, it was equally clear that Sloan had no intention of supplying any more answers. He seemed to regret what he'd already said.

Snatching up both raincoats, he said, "C'mon. You don't need to be out in this weather."

Thunder clapped and lightning forked, a white-hot streak that emblazoned the black sky. A gust of wind, chilly despite the fact that it was the middle of June, tore from out of nowhere, partially ripping the scarf from Anna's head. A half-dozen or so honey-colored curls sprang free and were immediately soaked in the deluge that had begun to pour from the hostile heavens.

"Hurry!" Sloan shouted, throwing a raincoat about Anna's shoulders. Anna huddled beneath it, even as the birds fled in search of shelter. "Go on! Get out of this!"

As Sloan spoke, he threw the other raincoat about himself but then hesitated, as though delaying his departure until he saw Anna safely on her way.

She needed no further encouragement and started off in the direction of the pathway. After taking only a few steps, however, she turned and called out, "Hey!"

Even above the storm Sloan heard Anna. He, too, had taken only a few steps, but in the direction of the lighthouse. He pivoted toward her. Through the sheet of gauzy rain, their gazes met.

"My name is Anna!" she hollered, not fully understanding why it was important that he not leave before possessing that knowledge, but knowing that it was.

Anna.

Like a warm fire the name wrapped itself around Sloan. Yes, he thought, her name would be Anna—a simple name, a name to match golden curls, blue eyes, and a purely featured face. Her sharing her name had been sweet—incredibly sweet—but, ironically, her doing so created a storm within him every bit as great as the storm raging around him. He knew what was expected of him in return—removal of the sunglasses—yet he felt vulnerable, scared. By telling her the story, he'd already told her more about himself and his past than he'd intended. Suddenly the walls of his life started closing in on him like the walls of his tiny prison. All he wanted was to get out. Now.

"Please understand," he wanted to plead, but instead he shouted as he waved good-bye, "See you tomorrow, Anna."

Anna waved and began to run homeward. Though disappointed, she wasn't surprised that Sloan hadn't removed his sunglasses. She'd suspected all along that he was hiding behind them. What other conclusion could

she draw when he wore them with such consistent in-
appropriateness?

But what was he hiding from?

What had he meant about being a survivor?

And why did she consider it crucial to have these answers?

"I've been worried sick about you!" Carrie cried as
she threw wide the door of the mudroom. "And so has
Jack!"

Drenched to the skin and chilled to the bone, Anna
raced up the steps, flying past her sister-in-law and into
the house. The warm house. The dry house.

"Where in the world have you been?"

Out of breath, Anna gasped, "On . . . the beach."

"I know you've been on the beach, but why in heav-
en's name didn't you come back sooner? Before the
storm broke?"

"Got caught," Anna said, telling herself that she
wasn't really lying.

"You better get out of that raincoat. It's soaked." Before Anna could reply, Carrie reached for the garment,
saying, "Now aren't you glad I made you carry it?"

In the process of stripping the coat from Anna's
shoulders, one of the combs in Carrie's hair tumbled to
the floor. It landed near the puddle already forming
from the rainwater dripping off Anna's shoes. Anna
bent to retrieve the comb.

Eye to eye with the hem of the raincoat, Anna realized that it should have been gray but was, instead,
navy-blue. Her heart turned over. Slowly, she came to
her feet, while her gaze rushed to Carrie's face. Carrie's expression said that she hadn't yet noticed that
her sister-in-law had left with one raincoat and had returned with another.

"Here, let me have that," Anna said, passing the

comb to Carrie and taking—she forced herself not to snatch it!—the raincoat.

"That's all right. I can—"

Anna interrupted with, "There's no point in your getting wet too."

Carrie was left with only the comb in her hand, which she threaded back through her hair. Anna immediately tossed the raincoat into the nearby washing machine and closed the lid.

"Don't you want to hang that?" Carrie asked.

"I'll let it dry a little first," Anna said, stooping to untie her wet tennis shoes and peal away the soaked socks. "Right now I'm going to take a quick shower, change clothes, and cook breakfast."

"I've already cooked breakfast," Carrie said.

Carrie's comment caused Anna to check her watch, which read seven-forty. Stunned, she said, "Oh, Carrie, I'm so sorry. Time just got away from me."

"That's all right. I was glad to help."

For the remainder of the day, Anna had little time to consider what had happened on the beach. Carrie left at midmorning, again relegating Jack's care solely to her. Carrie had been right about Jack's having been worried when she was out in the storm, a fact that touched Anna, perhaps in greater proportion than it should have. It was the first time in a long while that he had shown any real concern for her. He always seemed too wrapped up in himself.

By the time evening arrived, Anna was, as usual, exhausted; so was Jack. His rehabilitative exercises, combined with the extra strength it required to perform the most mundane actions, always left him tired, and often cranky. The continuation of the storm did nothing to brighten spirits. With the dreary rain ceaselessly pounding the windowpanes, depression sat heavily upon two chests.

At six-thirty Anna administered Jack's insulin; then

at seven o'clock they ate dinner. Once more Anna found herself talking about anything and everything. Why did the silence shared with her husband seem so awkward, when that shared with Sloan had seemed so natural? A little after eight-thirty Jack scribbled on his pad that he was ready for bed.

"That sounds like a good idea," Anna said.

Within the next thirty minutes they performed the nightly ritual. She helped Jack to the bathroom, then into the bed. Both activities were taxing, leaving Anna's arms aching and Jack's brow peppered in perspiration. She pulled the cover up over him, checked to see that there was water in his bedside pitcher, and placed the bell he used to summon her within easy reach. Next, she lowered the light, and after wishing him a good night, she started from the room.

She was halfway to the door when the bell tinkled. Turning, she saw her husband reach for his notepad and begin to write. She crossed back to his side, patiently waiting for him to finish. When he had, he angled the pad toward her. It read: *stay with me.*

Uncertain that her eyes hadn't deceived her, Anna turned up the light and reread the message. Forced to conclude that she hadn't misinterpreted the words recorded there, she glanced up at her husband. He was looking at her. Wrestling with the pad, he penned another note: *bad day. hate rain.*

A warm feeling flashed in Anna's chest. She smiled. "It has been pretty miserable, hasn't it?"

In response Jack wrote: *stay 4 while.*

She dimmed the light once more and retucked Jack beneath the cover. Then she drew a chair forward and, curling her feet up under her, settled into the cozy softness. The room grew quiet except for the rain pattering against the roof and the windows. Anna thought that it sounded like a stranger knock-knock-knocking.

The stranger in the lighthouse.

The stranger in the bed beside her.

The warm feeling that had burst to life at Jack's request for her to stay cooled at the realization that she still could not touch him, or ask him to touch her. No, he would reject both loving gestures.

Anna thought back to that morning on the beach—to Sloan's story, to his comment about being a survivor, which was one thing they had in common, to his refusal to remove his sunglasses. What did all of it mean? She was still trying to find answers when sleep pulled her into its slumberous embrace.

Anna awoke with a crick in her neck and a right foot that felt as though it had been shot full of novocaine. Noticing that Jack was still asleep, Anna pushed from the chair and hobbled to the kitchen. It was still raining, not the hard rain of yesterday and last night, but a lazy, slow-dancing drizzle. Even had she been able to leave Jack, which she hadn't, the weather didn't permit a trek to the beach. She wondered what Sloan would do today.

Had he realized that they'd mistakenly exchanged raincoats? The thought brought an image of the coat still crumpled in the washing machine. She'd meant to hang it up after Carrie had left but had simply forgotten amid all the chores she'd had. She hurried to the mudroom, opened the washing machine, and pulled out the garment. Though no longer wet, it contained a hundred and one wrinkles. Shaking it out, she pulled a hanger from the rack and fitted the shoulders of the coat around it. It was as she did so that she saw the tag inside.

It read, and most interestingly so: Commander Sloan W. Marshall, United States Navy.

TEN

The scarred sea gull returned on Monday. Swooping out of the sky, it landed a short, though wary, distance from where Sloan and Anna were combing the beach for shells.

"There's your friend," Sloan said quietly.

"Where's the bread?"

Sloan nodded toward the raincoats that lay discarded on the sand, each waiting to be claimed by its rightful owner. "In the pocket. Actually, I brought potato chips instead of bread."

Anna glanced up, meeting her reflection in the silver lenses of his sunglasses. She was certain now, beyond a shadow of a doubt, that his wearing the glasses meant something. She was equally certain that, in due time, she'd find out what that something was.

"You're going to give him potato chips?"

"What's wrong with potato chips? Hey, remember that this guy is used to worms."

"Worms at least sound nutritional. Potato chips are junk food."

"Take 'em or leave 'em," Sloan replied.

Their conversation had consisted of nothing more than featherweight banter ever since they'd met that morning. Sloan told himself that his good mood had to do with the storm's passage. Anna told herself that her good mood was simply the result of getting out of the house. Each suspected that the real reason for their cheerfulness had to do with again being in each other's company.

Anna sighed, as though resigning herself to the inevitable. "Hand me the chips."

For the next few minutes she tried to entice the bird to eat out of her hand, but he would have no part of such incautiousness. Failing that, she attempted to lure him to her feet, but again the bird obviously considered that too close for comfort. At last a disappointed Anna tossed the chips a safe distance away. The bird, who limped slightly from its old injury, gulped down the food.

"You'll win him over," Sloan said, adding, "Hunger eventually leads to recklessness."

Anna looked up, her gaze once more colliding with impenetrable silver. She wanted to see this man's eyes. She surmised that that due time she'd been waiting for was now.

"Tell me something," she said. "Are you from another plant?" At Sloan's startled look she continued, "Yes, that's it, isn't it? You're an alien. With eyes totally unlike ours. That's why you can't, won't, take off the glasses."

Sloan grinned, though his heart quickened. He didn't want to take off the glasses, yet oddly, he did.

"You've discovered my secret," he said. "Actually, I'm from a planet in another galaxy."

"Let me guess," she rushed on. "Everyone on this planet has eyes that are red, feral, slanted, and glow in the dark."

Sloan gave a you've-found-me-out look. He also fought at another grin. "Darn, can't keep anything from you, can I? Bet you didn't know, though, that my eyes can burn human flesh and melt human bones."

"No!" Anna exclaimed, as though totally stunned.

Sloan fought a smile. "Yep."

"I'd be in danger if you took off the glasses?"

"Probably."

"I'll chance it. Take them off."

The thud of a heartbeat, the silence of a pause, the tremor of something akin to fear—all the heart-loud sounds of a dare. Should he? Would he? He answered the question by abruptly stripping the glasses from his eyes.

Anna had certainly seen her share of brown eyes, but never a brown so vivid and bold. The color reminded her of a moonless midnight. He'd been right about one thing: she suspected that they could burn flesh and melt bones. At least feminine flesh and bones.

She saw, too, what could only be called pain. It was smothered, but far from extinguished. She realized that she'd been in far greater danger than she'd thought, simply because his pain spoke so elementally to her heart.

Ignoring the questions she'd have liked to ask, she said instead, "That wasn't so difficult, was it?"

Sloan started to answer cavalierly, but decided not to insult his new and tender friendship with Anna. Consequently, he responded with a simple, honest "No," hoping that she would ask for nothing more.

She didn't, for one simple reason. If she asked questions, so, too, might Sloan. Like the sea gull, both were careful, not quite ready yet to commit.

Anna smiled. "Does this mean that you're human after all?"

Sloan relaxed when he realized that Anna wasn't going to pursue the subject, although her question troubled him. He could hear Harper's charge that his problem was his inability to face his humanness. He guessed Harper was right when he heard himself answer Anna.

"Being human is intolerable." Sloan immediately tried to lessen the severity of his remark. Smiling, he added, "On the planet I come from."

Anna didn't return his smile. "It's often not even allowed here on earth."

Neither had much to say after that.

Tuesday morning, another fair day in a fair month, the sea gull was waiting for Sloan and Anna. At their approach the bird cocked its head and gave a screech that sounded like a chastisement for their tardiness. Although it once more refused to eat from Anna's hand, it did reward her by feasting on the cookies crumbled at her feet.

"Cookies?" Anna had asked, trying to look stern despite the smile lurking about her mouth.

"Take 'em or leave 'em," Sloan had replied, a twinkle of laughter in his brown eyes, eyes Anna had been delighted to see had been freed from their prison.

The sea gull had taken them quickly, ravenously, then had flown off in the direction of a bank of billowy white clouds cruising in a clear sky.

"What are you making?" Anna asked when Sloan dropped to his knees and began scooping up sand.

"A castle, but it's not just any old castle," Sloan said, working the sand quickly.

Anna grinned. "Somehow I just knew it wasn't."

"Well, it isn't. This is a very special castle over-looking the Loire River in France. A beautiful princess by the name of Fiona lives there. She has everything that any princess could possibly want, yet her heart is heavy and as cold as the winter snows blanketing the castle grounds, for her prince is missing and thought to be dead."

Anna listened, once more fascinated by Sloan's story-telling skills. Again she wondered what he'd meant about having had experience creating such fantasies, and about his being a survivor.

"You amaze me, Commander Marshall."

Sloan halted when he realized what she'd called him.

Anna wasn't certain how she would have described the look that spread across Sloan's face. Surprise? Dis-comfort? She knew without doubt that she'd been wise to pick her moment in broaching this subject.

"How did you know?" He tried to make the query sound as if her knowing didn't matter in the least, but Anna knew better.

"The label in your raincoat."

Sloan nodded, as if to say that he should have known.

"How long have you been in the navy?"

In one quick swipe of his hand Sloan razed the castle he'd been building so meticulously. Anna wasn't even certain that he knew what he'd done.

"Actually, I'm not in the navy," he said, no longer meeting her gaze. "I was, but I'm retired now." Abrupt-ly Sloan pulled to his feet, saying, "I should let you get back."

Feeling that she'd been summarily dismissed, Anna rose as well. "I'm sorry. I didn't mean to upset you."

"You didn't," he said, though Anna knew that she had, simply because he avoided looking at her, simply because, for a reason she didn't understand, he'd pulled within himself. More important, he'd pulled away from her.

* * *

It was obvious Wednesday morning that the sea gull wanted to take the nuts from Anna's hand but couldn't quite garner the courage to do so. She wondered if that symbolically represented her relationship with Sloan. When Sloan had met her that morning, sans sunglasses—she wouldn't have been surprised to find him once more wearing them—he'd posed, or rather reposed, a question that had left her feeling as cornered as he must have felt the day before.

"Why only whole shells?"

The cuffs of their jeans rolled to midcalves, they had waded out into the sea in search of another shell to add to Anna's growing collection. Anna glanced up at Sloan. She had avoided answering this question once before but decided to respond truthfully this time.

"I respect survival."

Sloan knew that her remark was telling. What was she struggling to survive? And could she possibly know as much about the topic as he?

"Surviving is important," he said. "But not at just any cost." He wondered what she'd think about him if she knew the price he'd paid to survive, then answered his own question. She'd probably think what he thought about himself—that he was a coward.

In answer to his comment she said, "Maybe you're right. I used to think that surviving was all that mattered. Just getting through the day, getting through the night, getting through . . ." She started to say "getting through the heartache," but instead repeated, "Just getting through."

Another telling comment, Sloan thought. "But now you don't?"

She shrugged. "I don't know. Sometimes the price just seems too high."

Anna thought of the feel-nothing world she fled to when hurt, and of how the trip took its toll, leaving her less and less whole with each voyage. She thought, too, of how, condemned to that world, she longed to feel. All of this made her think of the bivalve shell she was searching for.

"I'm looking for this shell," she heard herself saying.

At the end of her comments about what this shell represented to her—survival, the endurance of relationships, maybe even feelings themselves—Sloan asked a simple question. "What is it you want to feel, Anna?"

Her answer was equally simple. "Anything."

"Hi!" Anna said, rushing onto the beach on Friday morning.

She stopped short at the sight of the sea gull. The bird hadn't come the day before but now sat waiting for her.

Sloan smiled, for no other reason than that Anna was smiling. God, her smile made him feel good! After her baffling remarks about wanting to feel anything, then her refusal to say more, he longed to know that she felt as good in his company as he felt in hers.

"I told you he'd be back, and I just have a feeling that today's the day. Frankly, I don't think he'll be able to resist this treat."

Anna slipped slowly to Sloan's side and sat down beside him. The bird stood only inches away. That it hadn't flown at Anna's approach was encouraging.

"Do I dare ask what you've brought?"

"Gumdrops."

Anna looked up at Sloan. "You've got to be kidding."

Passing her a bag of candy, Sloan said smugly, "Take 'em or leave 'em."

Opening the bag, she scooped out a handful of soft morsels and held them out. "C'mon, boy," she whispered. "I know this is a little unorthodox, but this idiot beside me says you're going to love gumdrops."

Sloan chuckled softly. The bird took a step toward Anna and the treat she offered.

"C'mon," Anna repeated.

The bird took another tentative step, then another. It looked at the bits of candy, looked at Anna, looked once more at the candy. Suddenly, as though having made up its mind, it waddled right up to her hand and began to eat from it.

Sloan had never seen anything as magical as the smile that broke across Anna's face. It could have lighted the darkest of nights. He could have easily believed that he had survived the last two years only to witness this sweetest of all phenomena, and, whether she recognized it or not, she *was* feeling something.

"I told you he was a candy-holic," Sloan said quietly.

Anna glanced up at Sloan. The smile at his lips, the warmth in his eyes, touched her. It was the look that one friend gave another when sharing a special moment. Yes, she thought, though only a week had passed, this man had become her friend. Her very best friend.

"Yes, you told me," she returned.

Her voice was soft and gentle and washed over Sloan like molten honey. Yes, this woman, whom he barely knew, had become his friend. His very best friend.

Soon enough the sea gull departed, seeming to wave a fond farewell with the beating of its wings. Anna watched the small beast sail high and free and wished that its soaring spirit might be hers.

"Will you tell me about your marriage someday?" Sloan asked, intuitively knowing that this subject lay at the heart of her struggle to survive, her need to feel.

"Yes," she answered without hesitation, as she continued to stare out to sea. "Will you tell me about your military service someday?" Like him, she too knew the source of his pain.

"Yes," he answered, watching the same horizon as she.

Each knew the other would keep those vows, simply because friends didn't break promises.

Anna didn't go to the beach at all on Saturday. Meg came home unexpectedly—to Anna's delight—and even though Anna searched for a few minutes when she might slip seaward, the opportunity never presented itself. Sunday morning, likewise, proved as impossible. Sunday afternoon was another matter, however. Out of the clear blue, Father Santelices stopped by to see Jack.

Tall, handsome, and rakish in appearance Father Santelices, who was in his late thirties, looked more like a good-for-nothing ski bum than a priest. In truth the Catholic Church didn't have a shepherd who was more devoted to the care of his flock. At least that's what Anna had heard about the soft-spoken, gentle man whom she showed to Jack's bedroom.

In a strange way she thought his unorthodox appearance fitting, for Jack himself was far from the quintessential Catholic sheep. On the one hand, he thumbed his nose at the Church—he hadn't been inside of one since the christening of his daughter—while on the other hand, the basic Catholic tenets were so ingrained in him that they might as well have been locked within his DNA.

While Father Santelices and Jack visited, she made a mad dash to the beach. She knew that it would be the greatest of coincidences if Sloan was there, and, indeed, he wasn't, although he had left a message for her. Printed in the sand, far enough up on the beach that the tides wouldn't destroy it, was a single word: *Hi!* With a smile at her lips, Anna wrote *ditto!* beside Sloan's message, then sat down to enjoy the sea. She willed her mind to be blank, just to absorb the sight and sound of frolicking waves. Instead Sloan's question played through her mind.

"Will you tell me about your marriage someday?"

Anna sighed. What would she tell Sloan? How could she explain feelings so mixed that even she couldn't decipher them? In the end she told them with far more ease than she ever thought possible.

"I'm sorry I'm late," Anna said that following Monday morning as, gasping, she plopped down beside Sloan.

She had run all the way from the house, afraid that Sloan wouldn't wait for her, afraid that she'd find another message written in the sand. In her haste she'd thrown on her old gray sweatsuit and had merely made a pretense of passing a brush through her hair. Her scarf forgotten, the breeze greeted her by tossing the golden curls end over playful end.

"I was beginning to think you weren't coming," Sloan said, feeling a tremendous sense of relief that she had. It had seemed like forever since Friday, and he couldn't shake the notion that maybe his question had driven her away. But here she was, her hair attractively atumble, her clothes delightfully scrambled into, her soft voice becomingly battered by her effort to regain her breath.

Swiping corkscrew curls from her eyes, she said, "Carrie came by unexpectedly. She brought Jack some homemade soup. His favorite—chicken noodle."

Anna realized that, though only in a marginal way, she was talking about her marriage. She'd even called Jack by name, which she hadn't done before in Sloan's presence.

Sloan seized upon the name. Even more important, he seized upon the fact that she'd divulged this information without being asked.

"It sounds like Jack and Carrie are close," Sloan commented, trying to keep the subject alive without making it appear obvious.

"Very close," Anna said, her breathing beginning to return to normal, "but, then, Carrie never does anything by half measure, relationships included."

"Does that mean the two of you are close too?"

Anna didn't even have to consider the question. "Yes. She's far more than my sister-in-law. She's my friend. Actually, I guess she's more than that." At Sloan's silent encouragement Anna explained. "If I could be like anyone, I'd choose to be like Carrie."

"Why?"

"She's so . . . so . . . I don't know. No, I do know. She's so free-spirited. She's unimpressed with life's rules. She's quite able and willing to make her own."

"That suggests that you feel you don't."

Anna laughed. "Are you kidding? I'm the consummate rule player. I've played by the rules—I've never been sure whose rules, but I've played by somebody's rules—of being a good wife. I've played by the same somebody's rules of being a good mother." Anna sighed. "Actually, I think I've been a good mother." No sooner was the statement out than she amended it. "No, I'm *certain* I've been a good mother."

The implication was clear, although the subject was as treacherous as quicksand. "But you're not certain that you've been a good wife?"

"No, I'm not certain. I've tried to be, but trying doesn't make it so, does it?"

"No, it doesn't," Sloan said, thinking that he'd tried to be a good soldier.

For quiet moments they stared at each other; then, as though she'd be unable to stop herself from saying more if she continued to look into his eyes, she turned her gaze away and toward the sea. Waves tumbled about, tripping one over the other before rushing ashore. The waves slowed, however, coming inland as though suddenly hesitant to reveal themselves. The way she was hesitant to offer more?

"Living with someone who has a chronic, debilitating illness isn't easy," Anna said.

Sloan knew this admission had cost Anna. "I'm sure it isn't."

Sloan's caringly delivered words mingled with the sea's murmur. Again Anna didn't trust herself to look at Sloan.

"Don't misunderstand me. Jack's done the best he could. It's just that he's not an overly patient man." She shrugged. "But, then, maybe I'm not an overly patient woman."

"You strike me as being the most patient person I've ever met."

At this Anna did glance over at Sloan. Her gaze merged with his—blue with brown, honesty with honesty.

"Make no mistake, Sloan. I'm not a saint."

"Neither am I."

This time Sloan was first to look away. A silence swelled between him and Anna.

"You don't have to tell me anything you're not comfortable with," Sloan said as the silence wore on.

"I know."

Another silence followed. A flock of sea gulls flew overhead. Both Sloan and Anna wondered if their feathery friend was among them. And crazily, the bird reminded Anna of an incident she hadn't recalled in years.

"The Green Parrot," she said softly, as though she had to sneak upon the memories to capture them.

Sloan looked toward her, but said nothing. He noted that she again sat with her knees drawn up and her arms draped about them. Instead of shutting him out, however, he sensed that this was more a holding of herself together.

"Jack and I had been married for only a few months." She looked over at Sloan. "He'd had diabetes since he was in high school, so I knew that he had the disease when I married him."

"How did you meet him?"

"In college. He was studying to be a geologist, and I was studying to be a teacher."

"A teacher?"

Anna smiled. "An elementary-school teacher. I loved kids, wanted to have a houseful of them." The smile faded. "I never got to be a teacher. Neither did I get the houseful of kids."

"Why?"

"I married before I graduated, and though I intended to finish school, the money was tight in the beginning, and then Meg came along and, well, one thing led to another. I just never went back to school."

Sloan knew that she had slickly avoided an explanation for why she'd failed to have a houseful of children. He didn't push.

"Anyway," she continued, "we met and married, and I thought that Jack handled the diabetes pretty well. Looking back, I had clues to the contrary but wasn't smart enough to decipher them."

"What do you mean?"

"Diabetics must live by a strict code. They must avoid certain foods. They must eat at certain intervals. They must keep a watch on their blood sugar. They must keep an eye out for complications. The list goes on and on and on."

"What kind of complications?"

"More than you want to hear about."

Sloan knew of one very basic complication of diabetes and wondered if that had been the reason Anna had had to give up her dream of having children.

"It took living with Jack on a daily basis to discover how he was abusing himself. In fact, he was doing more than that. He was daring the disease."

"Why?"

"Who knows? Out of anger, to punish himself, to prove he was normal when he knew he wasn't." She shrugged, repeating, "Who knows?"

"So what about this Green Parrot?"

Memories as chill as a frosty morning rushed at Anna. "As I said, diabetics have to live by a strict code. They have to eat at a given time. On this particular night Jack's boss had taken us out to dinner at a fancy restaurant called the Green Parrot. The reservation was for six-thirty, which meant that we'd probably be eating by seven o'clock, which would have been fine . . . if that's how everything had turned out."

"But it didn't."

Anna sighed. "Not hardly. Once we got there, we found out that his boss had forgotten to make a reservation, and because it was a Saturday night and the restaurant was popular, we didn't even get seated until almost eight-thirty."

"And?" Sloan pursued when she paused.

"Jack had taken the insulin about six-thirty, so here was this hormone running around in his body, waiting and wanting to do its job, but with no food to do it on." Anna sighed. "I sat there worried half out of my mind at what I knew was going to happen. Sure enough, Jack began to shake, though he covered it well. His thinking began to slow down—not the confusion that comes with too much sugar, but a dullness of the mind. Here again, though, he covered it well. His boss didn't seem to notice. He just went on talking like everything was perfectly all right."

Even after all these years Sloan could hear the panic in Anna's voice. It took little imagination to draw a mental picture of a young woman, a young bride, frightened for her husband.

"What happened?"

Anna looked over at Sloan. "I believe the saying is 'Everything went to hell in a handbasket.' Actually, it didn't get that far, but it was well on its way. I knew Jack was in trouble. It was only a matter of time until he became nauseous and began to perspire. At that point he could have fainted."

Sloan could feel Anna's growing restlessness. She had stepped back in time.

"The sad thing was that it was all so unnecessary," she went on. "All Jack had to do was call the waiter over, tell him what was happening, and ask that something be brought to him—orange juice, bread, candy, anything at that point. But, no, he was willing—no, preferred—growing ill, perhaps even fainting, rather than appear different in front of his boss, who knew that he had diabetes, anyway."

It struck Sloan as odd that Anna's voice had not risen, even though the incident had clearly frustrated her then and now. Had she denied herself anger along with all other emotions?

"So what did you do?"

"I sat there as long as I could. Finally I excused myself on the pretense of going to the ladies' room. I headed in that direction, but I veered off and went into the kitchen instead." Anna smiled. "Restaurants do not like customers coming into the kitchen. Anyway, to make a long story short, I cornered the waiter, told him what was happening, and pleaded for him to bring some bread to the table. But not to say anything when he did."

"And did he?"

"Oh, yes. If there's one thing restaurants like less than customers in the kitchen, it's customers fainting in the dining area."

Sloan had to grin, which made Anna join in.

"And so everything ended all right?"

Anna's smile disappeared. "Not really. When the waiter brought the bread, Jack looked over at me. He knew what I'd done, and I honestly thought for a moment that, out of defiance, he wasn't going to eat. But he did. I guess he needed the food more than he needed to be defiant. Shortly afterward we ordered, dinner came, and the evening ended, surprisingly with our companion never knowing what had gone on."

"Why do I think there's more to this story?"

"When we got home that night, he jumped all over me—verbally. He told me that I was never to do that again, that the disease was his responsibility. Not mine."

"At the risk of playing devil's advocate, he was right."

"Of course he was. The only problem was that he refused to accept responsibility, which meant that I had to accept it for him or sit idly by and watch him pay the consequences for his irresponsibility. In retrospect I should have let him sink or swim on his own, but he was my husband, I loved him, and he was soon to become the father of my child. I didn't want anything to happen to him."

I loved him. The words, tumbling about in Sloan's head and heart, were eloquent in their simplicity. Anna Ramey was a woman who'd love long and hard and deep. She was a woman who'd do what she had to do to protect those she loved—even if it was from themselves, which her next words proved.

Smiling, she said, "I got smart real fast. I never again got caught."

Sloan smiled. "Good for you." A few seconds passed before he added, "But even with your clandestine help, complications arose."

"They were inevitable."

"And then came the stroke."

"Yes, and that was the straw that broke the camel's back."

"Your camel or his camel?" Sloan asked perceptively.

Anna pondered, then replied, "Maybe both our camels. Don't misunderstand me. I love my husband. I'm devoted to my marriage, but ..." She glanced back toward the sea.

"But what?"

"I could have lived with the disease, I could have lived with the complications, I could have lived with the stroke, but"—her voice cracked—"I can't live with being shut out of his life."

When she turned toward him, Sloan fully expected to see tears in her eyes, but they were dry. As dry as brittle dreams blowing in a reckless wind.

ELEVEN

"Damn!" Sloan said on Tuesday morning.

It was obvious that Anna wasn't going to show up, and he knew precisely why. Accepting the fact with what dignity he could muster, he wrote a greeting in the sand and, placing a shell nearby, headed back for the lighthouse. Sloan went to bed disappointed and wondering if he'd ever see Anna again. It was, therefore, with great relief that he saw her, the yellow scarf fluttering at her neck, waiting for him Wednesday morning.

"Hi," he said, sitting down beside her. "I missed you yesterday."

"Jack slept poorly Monday night." Hesitation, pause, then a burst of honesty. "But I probably wouldn't have come anyway."

"I know," Sloan said, being just as direct.

Anna glanced over at him. Was it possible that he *did* know? Did he understand that she felt as though she had betrayed Jack? More than that, did he understand that she was worried that somehow she'd made herself appear small and selfish in Sloan's eyes?

"You know?" she asked.

"Yep," he responded. "But I know how to remedy how you're feeling."

"You do?" she asked, starting to smile simply because of Sloan's whimsical approach to something that could have been a difficult topic.

"I do. It's very obvious that the emotional scales have become unbalanced. You've shared something very personal, very painful, with me, and I have yet to share the same with you. In short, you're naked and I'm fully dressed. Metaphorically speaking, of course," he hastened to add.

Anna's grin grew. "Of course."

"What I need to do here is tell you something personal and painful. So what do you want to know?" He knew what she wanted to know; it was the same something he didn't want her to know. Or maybe he did. He wasn't sure anymore.

Anna knew something, too—that Sloan wasn't near as casual as he sounded. Cutting right to the chase, she said, "Tell me why you hide behind sunglasses. Tell me about your military career."

Sloan nodded, cleared his throat, and replied, his gaze conveniently avoiding hers, "There's really not that much to tell."

"Tell me what there is. And look at me when you tell me."

Sloan forced his gaze to hers. "I served in the navy for almost twenty-five years, and about a year ago I retired."

"Why?"

Sloan swallowed. "I didn't feel that I had anything

more to give to the Navy. I, uh, I'd gone through a traumatic episode and needed to put my life back together."

"What kind of traumatic episode?"

Sloan sighed, ran his hand along the back of his neck, and faced the inevitable. "I was commandeered for a special mission, along with several other men. We were sent to free an American held hostage in Beirut, which we did. Unfortunately, I ended up being captured. They held me a while, then let me go."

Two things crossed Anna's mind. One, this must be what he'd survived. Two, his matter-of-fact tone was inappropriate to the gravity of the admission.

"You were sent to liberate a hostage but were captured in the process?"

"Yeah," he replied, in a manner that said, "Now wasn't that silly of me?"

Anna had seen movies and clips on television about people being taken hostage, and remembering them now sent a shiver scurrying along her spine. She gave a disbelieving shake of her head.

"And you think that was no big deal?" she asked.

"Hey, people have been held prisoner ever since there've been opposing sides."

"Did they . . ." She knew the word *torture* was appropriate—the word that was often used to describe what happened to hostages—but she just couldn't say it. Even so, horrible images flashed in her mind. "Did they hurt you?"

Sloan had been asked a lot of things in his life, but no question had ever sailed so swiftly and so surely into his heart. It had everything to do with the possessive way she'd asked the question, the way she was pleading for him to answer in the negative, as though it really made a difference to her if he was in pain. He didn't want to lie, yet the truth was far too harsh for her.

He smiled, hoping the smile appeared genuine.

"You've been watching too many movies." He then added, "They kept me in a small room, bound some of the time, without any sunlight. That was the extent of it." *Lie, lie, lie!* he thought, and while he was at it, he'd give her another. "That's why I hide behind sunglasses. I'm just not as comfortable with the sunlight as I used to be."

Yeah, that sounded believable. She'd never guess that he hid behind them in the hopes that no one would see the craven coward he was, that no one would witness his shame.

Anna wanted desperately to believe that he was telling the truth, but something in the way he averted his eyes left her with the feeling that he wasn't telling her everything.

"Are you telling me everything?"

Sloan's gaze once more meshed with hers. "Yes," he said, knowing that the coward had become a full-fledged liar, simply because he had to safeguard this woman's good opinion of him. Abruptly Sloan grinned, saying, "So are we both naked now? Metaphorically speaking, of course."

Anna still had the nagging feeling that he was withholding something, though the grin on his face seemed so sincere that she concluded she must be mistaken. "Yes," she said, smiling. "Metaphorically speaking."

"Good," Sloan said, rising and starting off down the beach. "C'mon, I want to show you something." Sensing her objection, he turned and, while continuing to walk backward, said, "It's not far. You've got time."

When Anna stood, she was once more looking at his back. She ran to catch up with him. Falling into step beside him, she asked, "Where are we going?"

"You'll see," was all Sloan would say.

The cove was small and sheltered, like a little world unto itself. Large rocks formed one side, salty-looking cliffs the back, while a dense hunter-green forest, one tree seemingly trying to out-tower the others, made up the third side. At sea a rash of bobbing buoys, in a rainbow of colors, marked lobster traps. Once Anna stepped inside the cove, a silence, a serenity, enveloped her.

"How beautiful," she whispered, as though she'd walked inside a church. She had the feeling that all things worldly had been denied admittance here. Only those things righteous, only those things pure and wholesome, were allowed. Even the wind had ceased to blow, as though nature, feeling it too reckless, had checked it at the entrance.

"Yeah," Sloan whispered back in a tone filled with reverence. "Isn't it gorgeous? Sometimes, especially at night when I can't sleep, I just come here and sit."

Anna wondered if his inability to sleep had anything to do with the past, his captivity.

"Come here, let me show you something."

Anna followed Sloan to a small pool, isolated in a basin formed by a cluster of rocks and left behind when the tide swept back out to sea. The bottom of the pool was encrusted with pink algae and lumpy green sponge. Sea anemones clutched at the sides and under overhanging rocks, shielded from waves and sun. Barnacles fished for their daily food. Both Sloan and Anna were content to watch the small miracle of life in the silence they had grown so comfortable with.

Finally, after checking her watch, Anna announced with obvious regret, "I've got to go."

They started back, once more to the mute tune of silence, as though leaving this haven was an occasion for sadness.

At the entrance of the cove, Anna turned, smiled, and said, "Thanks for showing me this."

"You're welcome. Will I see you tomorrow?"

"Yes," she answered, then added, "I've got to go."

" 'Bye," he said as they stepped out onto the open beach. .

The wind, as though lying in wait, rushed at Anna, tumbling her hair, whipping the scarf around her neck. She brought it upward in an attempt to tie it about her head. The wind had other ideas, however. It snatched the silken scarf from Anna's hands and, billowing it like a runaway butterfly, carried it out to sea.

"My scarf!" she shouted.

Sloan dashed from behind her and raced out into the incoming tide. He lunged for the scarf just as it disappeared beneath the frothy wave. Anna was certain that it was gone for good when Sloan, a big smile at his lips, held his hand heavenward.

"Got it!" he called, wading back to shore.

Anna's lips burst into a big smile as well, though she couldn't honestly say whether it was because of the recovery of the scarf or simply in reaction to Sloan's smile. He seemed so inordinately pleased with himself.

"Got it!" he repeated when he stood before her.

Anna thought that he looked more like a little boy than a fully grown man, a little boy bearing his gift.

"What a soggy mess!" Anna cried.

"Is it ruined?" Sloan asked, squeezing the water from the sheer fabric.

Anna barely heard the question. She was too busy seeing Sloan's fist. His large, wet fist. Why had she never noticed before just how large his hands were? She watched as his large, wet hand moved toward her upturned palm. In seconds the sodden scarf lay in her hand. It wasn't the scarf that registered with Anna, however. It was the stroking of Sloan's fingers, slight, but oh so real, as he grazed the side of her hand. Or maybe it wasn't the side of her hand. Maybe he'd touched her wrist. Maybe even the back of her hand. Or her palm? She couldn't tell, because all of a sudden her entire hand tingled.

She glanced upward, wondering if he, too, was feeling what she was. She thought he was, for an odd look had slipped into his eyes. But then, he had reason to look at her oddly. He'd asked her a question, and she'd made no attempt to answer it. Now, what exactly was that question? Something about the scarf, wasn't it? Yes, the scarf.

"No," she said, "it isn't ruined."

"Good," he replied in a voice that, had Anna not been so distracted, she would have noticed sounded far huskier than usual.

"I've, uh, I've got to get back," she said, motioning vaguely behind her.

"Yeah," Sloan said. "You, uh, you ought to get back."

Another good-bye from each of them, and Anna trekked across the sandy beach toward the house. Sloan watched her go. What in hell had just happened? One moment he was fishing her scarf out of the sea, the next he felt as if a bolt of lightning had streaked out of a perfectly clear sky and struck his hand with a simmering softness. He had barely touched her, and yet a fiery sweetness had consumed him.

His reaction was baffling.

And it concerned him. He and Anna were friends. Moreover, she was a married woman committed to the vows she'd taken. He of all people understood the consequences of breaking a vow, of betraying a principle. He'd never let Anna do that. Which, of course, she wouldn't, didn't even want to, which made this whole line of thought foolish beyond words.

By the time Sloan had reached the lighthouse, he'd convinced himself that all was well, that his reaction had been perfectly normal. It had been a long time since he'd been with a woman, a long time since he'd experienced a woman's softness. Furthermore, he might have a lot of shortcomings, he might be a coward and a liar, but he was not the kind of man to covet another man's wife.

* * *

Her reaction was perfectly understandable in light of
what she'd been feeling these past weeks, Anna concluded as she prepared breakfast. For whatever reason,
she had been preoccupied with touching, any contact
that would verify companionship and caring, any caress, however small, that would prove that she was still
alive, still a woman. How many times had she lamented
that Jack could not, would not, give her what she
needed?

Yes, it all made perfect sense.

That accepted, she went about her normal routine.
Breakfast transpired as usual. Afterward she couldn't
find enough to do. She washed a load of clothes, dried
them; then, while they were as warm as the beach
memories she was avoiding, she folded them. She
rinsed the yellow scarf and ironed it. Following that,
she wrote Meg a letter. As she was doing that, it
dawned on her that she wasn't writing at all. She was
just staring at her hand—the hand Sloan had touched.
As though by magic she felt his fingers, silky with the
salty moisture of the sea, skim across her skin. Warm.
His touch had made her feel warm and alive and—

Anna reined in her thoughts. She wrote a closure to
the letter, slipped it into an envelope, then hastily addressed it and, even more hastily, looked for something
else to occupy her time. She was aware of an uncomfortable urgency building within her. Once more she threw
herself into activity, this time the preparation of lunch.
She served it at noon with a generous portion of prattle.
The effort grew tiring, though. At the same time, the
sense of urgency took on painful proportions.

In midsentence she stopped talking. If Jack noticed,
he said nothing He merely continued to eat, slowly,
painstakingly. Anna, too, ate—not that she tasted a
bite of anything, though she did hear inordinately loud

sounds. The clatter of silverware. The clink of ice cubes. The spiraling crescendo of that urgent feeling.

Anna's eyes dropped to her husband's left hand. It rested on the table, quite near her own left hand, fingertips almost, but not quite, touching fingertips. One gold wedding band called to the other.

Do it, her wedding ring whispered. *You have the right. After all, this man is your husband.*

If her life had depended on it, Anna couldn't have stopped herself from doing what she did next. In fact, it didn't even seem as if she was the perpetrator of the act. Some stranger, too long denied her needs, perhaps hoping to rout the warm memories of Sloan's touch, reached for the nearby hand. Everything happened in the span of seconds—heartbeats, really. Anna felt her husband's hand, remembered how gently it had once moved over her body, how tenderly it had held their daughter. She felt the hard gold band of his wedding ring. She felt—not saw, for she was afraid to make eye contact—her husband's surprise. And then she felt his hand pulling from hers—slowly but resolutely. Anna's gaze rushed to Jack's.

"Don't!" she pleaded in a rough, raw voice she didn't even recognize as her own.

The look in Jack's eyes was equally unfamiliar. It seemed so distant, so detached. This detachment frightened Anna and made her plead all the harder.

"Please, Jack, I need you!"

For a fleeting moment she thought she saw a crack form in the wall standing between them. She thought he was going to reach for her hand, but when it moved, it was not toward her, but toward the pad and pen that had become his constant companions. Anna's heart grew heavy. It grew heavier yet when she read his note.

wasting your time 2 need me.

Anna's blue eyes darkened with an emotion that she

could only call anger. Who was this stranger who'd moved into the body of her once-loving husband?

"What do you mean I'm wasting my time?"

Another pause to write. As she waited, Anna's heart began to throb. With anger, with dread of what the stranger would write next.

i don't exist anymore—emotionally or spiritually.

"That's absurd, Jack. Of course you exist."

Another pause. An increased throbbing of Anna's heart.

no & it would B better if I didn't exist physically.

Anna read the message, then reread it to make certain that she hadn't misunderstood. Surely, he didn't mean . . . Suddenly her heartbeat thundered in her ears. Suddenly her anger exploded. She ripped the sheet of paper from the pad and balled it into a wad. At the same time her gaze hurried to his.

"I won't listen to this nonsense," she said.

The very quietness of her delivery made her statement all the stronger, as did the fact that she rose from her chair with an innate dignity. Slowly, she crossed the room, walked out of it without once looking back, and without a word to the nurse, whom she passed in the hallway, moved toward the back of the house.

Only when she heard the door slam did she realize that she was negotiating the back steps. She felt the warmth of the noonday sun, smelled the freshness of a summer day, saw the house fading into the distance. At first her pace was slow, but then it grew faster and faster until her feet flew across the familiar ground, through the woods, to the pathway that led to the sea. Her breath came heavy, heavier—a wild beast that chased her onward. She had no idea where she was headed. She knew only that she was fleeing the stranger who had once been her husband.

* * *

Jack listened to the silence. It swelled like an unorchestrated symphony, sending shrill, empty notes to blare inside his tender soul. Within his chest, his heart raced to its own dark music.

Father, I have sinned.

How have you sinned, my son?

I have hurt my wife.

Jack folded his left hand into a fist, an angry fist. How could he so callously hurt Anna? And yet, wasn't it more cruel to lead her on? He could never again be husband to her wife, a fact the touch of her hand harshly reminded him of. It didn't matter that he wanted to be. It mattered only that he couldn't be. She needed to be free. He needed to be free.

It would be better if I didn't exist physically.

Jack's heart picked up its tempo. The thought of death frightened him even as it brought him peace. He was so tired of fighting, of struggling, of traveling a road that seemed to be going nowhere. No, of late he was certain where his journey was taking him—to an eternal destination. What would Father Santelices have said if he'd known what Jack was contemplating? Would he have spoken of the endless damnation of Jack's soul? Of a sin so unpardonable that even God could not forgive it?

Jack sighed, wishing that Anna was there to take his hand, knowing that, if she were, he would once more shun her touch.

Father, I have sinned.

How have you sinned, my son?

I have become a stranger to myself.

Sloan had no idea what force compelled him, a restlessness he could neither define nor ignore, yet the second he saw Anna, he knew that it had been meant for him to return to the beach. Something was wrong. He could tell this merely by her appearance. She sat with her knees drawn upward, her arms clasped about her legs. Ironically, the position had bowed her back, making her look incredibly vulnerable. As did the fact that she sat totally, unnervingly motionless as she stared out at the sea. If she saw his approach, she acknowledged it, him, in no way. Even when he eased down beside her, assuming a pose identical to hers, she spoke not a single word. She just continued to stare straight ahead.

Finally, softly, Sloan asked, "What's wrong?"

Never glancing his way, Anna answered, "Nothing."

Sloan let her response stand for two heartbeats. "Friends don't lie to each other." He conveniently overlooked the fact that he'd lied to her about his captivity.

"There's noth—"

"Don't, Anna."

Anna angled her head in Sloan's direction. Though she tried, she couldn't hide the fact that something was troubling her. Worse, that spark of life had died in her blue eyes, her lovely blue eyes. Without even knowing what had happened, Sloan knew that Jack Ramey was to blame for that death. It did not make him feel charitable toward the man.

"You don't have to tell me what's wrong," Sloan said. "But don't lie to me."

Her usual numbness, both comforting and scary, had replaced Anna's anger, and now she felt nothing. Absolutely nothing. Not even when she'd seen Sloan walking toward her, not even when he'd sat down beside her, not even now as she stared into his caring eyes. She looked away, wondering how much, if anything she wanted to tell this man.

She thought back to the way Sloan's fingers had brushed her hand earlier that day, knowing that incident had fathered what had transpired between her and Jack. Just as what had—or rather what hadn't—happened between her and Jack over the past years had made her overly sensitive to Sloan's touch.

"Jack and I haven't been lovers for years," Anna said, unable to believe she was being so frank. She'd never made this admission to anyone before. She blamed the numbness, which in part was culpable, but she also knew that the man sitting beside her had a way of making her want to share her thoughts and feelings.

Her statement in no way surprised Sloan. He'd suspected Jack's impotence was the reason there had been no houseful of children. He further suspected that the topic of discussion had something to do with what was troubling Anna, but he let her find her own way of telling him that.

"As time went on, I adjusted to that fact," Anna said finally. She thought of her lonely bed and of more lonely nights than she could count, and added, "One adjusts to what one has to."

Again Sloan said nothing, though he could painfully imagine the price she'd paid.

"I learned to live with celibacy," Anna said. "What I couldn't learn to live with was . . ."

Her voice faltered. The numbness that had claimed her partially receded, allowing a glimpse of her earlier anger to return.

Sloan saw the flash of anger. She was feeling, which was far healthier than not feeling, but again she was paying a dear price.

"What couldn't you live with, Anna?"

The query came so softly, so sweetly, that Anna had no choice but to respond. But, then, it would have taken little persuasion, for she wanted—no, needed!—to tell this man just how much she was hurting.

"All I wanted was an occasional touch, a hug, someone to hold my hand, some contact!" She had willed her voice to sound normal, but the anger had a will of its own. On some level she acknowledged that the anger felt good. "He won't touch me, and he won't let me touch him!"

Though a part of Sloan wanted to deck Jack Ramey for his insensitivity, another part of him understood. How could a man remember what it was like to make love to this woman, then touch her knowing that the touch must be limited because of his incapability?

"I reached for his hand, and he pulled it away." Anna's voice thickened. "Even when I begged him, he wouldn't let me touch him."

Sloan heard the hurt, the desolation of spirit, that lay behind her anger. No matter the circumstances, he couldn't imagine any man not responding to this woman's need. He couldn't imagine any man having the option. He himself had spent the better part of the morning trying to forget the gentle touch of her hand, and here she was pleading with her husband for what he—Sloan—would die to give her.

A part of Anna wanted to show Sloan the note crumpled in her pants pocket, but another part couldn't bring herself to do it. She couldn't believe that Jack was serious about wishing for death. He was depressed. Nothing more.

"What can I do to ease your pain?" Sloan asked, again so softly that his voice, like a log-fed fire, warmed Anna.

Take my hand. The words whispered in Anna's head, in her heart. They seemed as natural as the currents, the tides, of the ocean, yet they shouldn't have.

Let me take your hand, Sloan thought, admitting that maybe his pain would be eased by that act. For pain was exactly what he felt at being near her and not being able to touch her. Dear God, when had touching her become so important? Ever since that morning's silken memories, came the reply.

What would he do if I took his hand?

What would she do if I took her hand?

The questions didn't wait for answers. As though each had no say in the matter, as though it had been ordained from the start, Sloan reached for Anna's hand even as she reached for his.

A hundred recognitions scrambled through two minds: warmth, Anna's softness, Sloan's strength, the smallness of Anna's hand, the largeness of Sloan's, the way Anna's fingers entwined with his as though clinging to him for dear life, the way Sloan's fingers tightened about hers as though he'd fight to the death to defend her.

What would it feel like to thread his fingers through her golden hair?

What would it feel like to palm his stubble-shaded cheek?

What would it feel like to trace the delicate curve of her neck?

What would it feel like to graze his lips with her fingertips?

Innocently, guiltily, Sloan's gaze met Anna's. They stared—at each other, at the truth boldly staring back at them.

With her wedding band glinting an ugly accusation, Anna slowly pulled her hand from Sloan's. She said nothing, though her fractured breath spoke volumes.

Sloan's breath was no steadier when he said, "I swear I never meant for this to happen."

Anna stood, Sloan stood, the world spun wildly. Anna took a step backward as though by doing so she could outdistance what she was feeling.

Sloan saw flight in her eyes. "Anna, wait. Let's talk."

But Anna didn't. She took another step, then another, and then, after one last look in Sloan's eyes, she turned and raced from the beach.

"Anna, please . . . Anna . . . *Ann-nna!*"

TWELVE

September

"Anna . . ."

Sometimes, even though months had passed, Anna thought she could hear Sloan calling her name. Always she remembered his anguish, a jagged, serrated sound that tore at her heart.

"Anna . . ."

She wanted to turn back that day on the beach, but she'd been afraid. Not of Sloan, but of herself. If she'd turned back, she would have seen herself for what she'd become: a woman who had begun to feel something for a man other than her husband. In the end she'd had to confront that woman, anyway.

"Anna!"

Anna jerked her head up, startled to find herself sitting in a chair in Harper's office, and even more startled to find him staring at her with a look that indicated he'd just said something to her and expected a reply. Sloan, who stood at the window overlooking the garden, had turned, obviously curious as to why she hadn't answered. Their gazes met, and in that brief moment Anna suspected that Sloan knew all too well her mind had wandered into the past. Did he know, though, that her hand, which she'd unthinkingly brought to her heart, tingled as if he'd just touched it?

"Are you all right?" Harper asked, drawing Anna's attention.

He sat behind his massive desk, which smelled of lemony polish and scarlet roses. Anna imagined that the latter had come from Carrie's garden, the last brave blossoms of a blighted summer.

"Yes," she said into Harper's questioning eyes as she lowered her hand to her lap.

Satisfied with her response, Harper began to leaf through sheaves of paper, his attitude one of total commitment to the upcoming trial.

"What we need to go over today," he began, "is what you can expect from the prosecution's case. As you both know, the prosecution is obligated to submit its list of witnesses and the sum and substance of its case against you."

Sloan stepped from the window and toward the vacant chair located adjacent to Anna's. On one plane she considered Harper's remarks; on another she noted that Sloan was wearing the white sweater he'd worn exactly a week before, at the arraignment hearing. The splatter of her blood was gone.

Harper passed a sheet of paper to both Sloan and Anna, saying, "The list of prospective witnesses is about what I expected, give or take a witness or two."

Anna read hastily through the list, her gaze shuddering to a stop at one of the names.

"They're calling Meg as a witness?"

"Easy, Anna," Harper said. "Let's take this one step at a time. Okay?" At Anna's silence, which was more a result of shock than acquiescence to her lawyer's plea, he proceeded. "Let me begin by summing up the prosecution's case, which, pulling no punches, is as follows: The prosecution will contend that, perhaps inspired by Jack Ramey's request to help him end his life, the two of you so plotted. Not as the mercy killing you might like your actions to suggest, but as cold-blooded, premeditated murder. Now, if the prosecution is feeling charitable, it might also contend that the two of you, in some convoluted pattern of thinking, actually believed that you were being merciful. After all, you were doing what Jack Ramey himself desired, and he probably cared little for your motivation or for the fact that the two of you benefited from the deed. Wouldn't you two lovers have reasoned—and perhaps with some logic, the prosecution might suggest—that ending Jack Ramey's life would be best for everyone involved?"

"His death would be best for everyone."

"My God, Sloan, what are you suggesting?"

"Nothing. God, nothing! I'm just saying that we're caught up in the bitterest of ironies."

Anna could still hear the stunning words ringing in her ears, in her conscience. What had shocked her most about Sloan's comment was that it had mirrored her own thoughts. God forgive her, she had thought the same thing! A quick, furtive look in Sloan's direction told her that he, too, remembered the conversation, a conversation that had taken place the very night Jack had died.

Harper shuffled some papers, then spoke again, drawing both Anna and Sloan back to the present. "The prosecution will also introduce evidence that the two of you believed that your time was running out."

"What does that mean?" Sloan asked.

"Inez Gouge is prepared to testify that she overheard the two of you talking—that you told Anna about a job you'd applied for and were subsequently offered, and that the job would necessitate your leaving. That you wanted Anna to go with you."

"Damn!" Sloan said.

"Does that mean the conversation did take place?" Harper asked.

"Yes," Sloan admitted. "All except the part about Anna going with me. There was never any mention of that."

Harper made a note before moving on with a question that took Anna by complete surprise. "Tell me about the large needle and syringe that Carrie borrowed from Dr. Goodman."

Anna looked incredulous. "The one we used to inject fruit with liqueur?"

"That's the one. Carrie's told me about it, but I want to hear it from you."

"It was for the Fourth of July party Carrie gave." Harper nodded, indicating that so far her testimony was matching Carrie's. "She'd read in some fancy cuisine magazine about injecting fruit with liqueur, so she borrowed a big needle and syringe from work."

"How did it get to your house?"

"As I mentioned before, Carrie hates needles, so she brought everything to me—the watermelon, the cantaloupe, the honeydew melon, and the needle and syringe—to do the injecting. She forgot the needle and syringe when she left, so I just put them in the back of the silverware drawer. We both kept forgetting them when she came to visit."

"What does this have to do with anything?" Sloan asked.

"The prosecution is going to assert that this needle and syringe were used to administer the fatal overdose of insulin."

"That's absurd!" Anna said.

"But it *was* in the house?" Harper asked.

"Yes, it was in the house," Anna replied.

"Who knew it was there? Other than you and Carrie?"

"I don't know," Anna replied.

"Meg?" Harper prompted.

Anna shrugged. "I don't know."

"Jack?"

Again Anna shrugged. "I don't know."

"Did your husband ever go into the kitchen?"

"Yes," Anna said. "Sometimes Ken would wheel him in just for a change of routine. Jack's days could be long and boring." She didn't mention that hers often fell into the same category.

"Then he possibly knew of the needle and syringe?"

"Possibly," Anna said.

Harper looked over at Sloan. "Did you know they were there?"

"Yes." There was a pause during which the two men looked at each other. Then Sloan added, almost challengingly, "I had occasion to go into the kitchen when I worked there that one weekend. It was impossible not to see the needle and syringe when the silverware drawer was open."

"So, actually, anyone who opened that drawer probably saw the needle and syringe?" Harper asked.

"I don't see how anyone could have missed them." Sloan said.

"Well, one thing's for certain. Ken Larsen saw them and is prepared to say that they disappeared shortly after Jack's death."

"I haven't any idea what happened to them," Anna said. "With all the chaos that needle and syringe were the very last things on my mind."

"Just as I suspected, the police can't prove what happened to them, either," Harper said. "Right now, however, that's the least of our worries."

The comment ensnared Anna's and Sloan's complete attention.

Harper pulled no punches. "There's bad news and there's bad news. Which do you want first?"

Sloan laughed sarcastically. "Why don't you give us the bad news?"

Again Harper went straight to the heart of the matter, even as his gaze went straight to Sloan. "Not only will Bendy Webber testify to seeing you at the scene of the crime, and to witnessing your throwing something into the sea, but he will also testify to seeing the two of you on the beach earlier that evening. In short, he saw the two of you kissing, saw the two of you disappear into the cove. Though he didn't actually see the two of you have intercourse, the prosecution will use his testimony to place the nooses around your necks. Afterward, Inez Gouge will tighten the nooses by testifying to conversations she heard in the store. Meg will be used to kick the blocks out from under you."

Anna turned a ghostly shade of white. Her stomach rolled over, creating an empty, nauseous feeling. She honestly thought she was going to lose what little lunch she'd managed to eat.

"Meg's going to testify against me, us?" she asked, the tone of her voice begging Harper to tell her that she'd misunderstood what he'd said.

"I'm sorry, Anna," Harper said. "I was hoping that the prosecution wouldn't call your daughter, but I suspect that Hennessey went on a fishing expedition, hoping that Meg did suspect something, and that she would admit to it."

"Have you spoken with Meg?" Anna asked, thinking how paradoxical it was that Harper might have spoken with her daughter when the same daughter hadn't returned a single one of her innumerable phone calls.

"No, but I've seen her statement, in which she mentioned the fight you two had that night. If it's any consolation, she's listed as a hostile witness. She isn't testifying of her own volition."

Obviously, it wasn't much consolation, for Anna's color, what little had remained, drained away entirely. And the nausea grew. Placing her hand over her stomach, swallowing, Anna prayed she wasn't about to disgrace herself.

"Get her some water," Sloan said.

Harper immediately rose and walked to the door of the adjacent room. "Marilyn, bring us a glass of water, will you?"

When the secretary entered the room less than a minute later, she apprised the situation and walked toward Anna. She handed her the glass, which Anna took. The glass was cool, and that, in and of itself, was reviving.

"Take a sip," Sloan said softly, so softly that his voice wove itself into Anna's agitated being, calming her, soothing her, making her want to tumble into his arms. She glanced up at him with eyes that asked why, after all that had happened, couldn't she be immune to him. "Go on. Take a sip."

Anna brought the glass to her lips and drank. She took a deep breath before saying, "I'm fine." She smiled faintly at the three people hovering like mother hens. "Really, I am."

After Marilyn exited the room, silence lingered.

"You want to call it quits for the day?" Harper asked Anna.

She shook her head. "No, I do not. Let's go ahead." As though to prove her point, she asked, "What about Carrie? She's listed as a prospective witness."

"Her testimony's going to concern the needle and syringe—establishing the fact that it was available as a murder weapon. Look, I know that Meg's testifying is a blow, but we'll get through it. And as for the rest of the witness list, well, let's don't get excited about it. Some of the people on the list may never testify. A lawyer tries to cover every base by including the name of anyone he might want to call to the stand, however improbable that witness's testimony might be. Then, too, some of the names might be nothing more than shills."

"What does that mean?" Sloan asked.

"Sometimes a lawyer will list the names of witnesses whom he doesn't intend to call. Just to throw opposing counsel off the track."

This prompted Sloan to ask, hopefully, "What about Nichols? Do you think he's a shill?"

Anna had seen the name on the list but had no idea who the individual was, except that the title in front of his name suggested that he had something to do with the military. That was interesting, since Sloan, even though he'd shared part of his past with her, nonetheless had been suspiciously evasive.

"If Hennessey doesn't call him, I will." At Sloan's obvious objection Harper said, "Hennessey's going to use him to establish that you were a lean, mean fighting machine, programmed to kill, but he'll also have to concede that you were awarded the Medal of Honor. That can only help the case." Harper paused, then added, "Remember that Nichols can testify to only so much."

Anna thought the last remark an odd one—but, then, maybe it was only her imagination. Heaven knew that she wasn't thinking too clearly these days, certainly not at the moment.

"Can the two of you stand the other piece of bad news?" Harper gave no time for a response, as though the quicker the news was announced, the less painful it would be. "Jake Lugaric might be coming down to cover the trial."

A fog-thick silence settled over them as the news sank in.

"*The* Jake Lugaric?" Sloan asked.

"From Channel Thirteen?" Anna asked.

"*The* Jake Lugaric from Channel Thirteen," Harper

answered. "The only real-life, truly authenticated vampire. The man who sucks people dry of juicy stories. The man who knows whose palm to grease to get what he wants."

Sloan swore. "I don't believe it."

"The good news—"

"Good news?" Sloan parrotted. "You mean there is some?"

"The good news," Harper repeated, "is that I've talked to the judge about issuing a gag order, and he's agreed to it."

"Which means exactly what?" Anna asked.

"That no one involved in the case can talk to the press. If they do, they can be held in contempt of court." Harper grinned. "That's good for us, bad for Lugaric." The grin faded, as though Harper had just remembered more. "By the way, there will be no change of venue. Both Judge Waynon and I agree that it would serve no purpose. Like it or not, people have heard about the case. If they hadn't, Lugaric wouldn't be gracing us with his bloodthirsty presence."

Harper then went on to discuss a couple of other minor trial points, but Anna found that her concentration was shot. Furthermore, her hands had begun to tremble, forcing her to set down the glass. What she wouldn't give to feel warm and safe again, but the truth was that she deserved to feel neither.

Sensing Sloan's eyes on her, she looked toward him and was struck all over again by the majesty of the simple color brown. It was as rich as the raw earth, as elemental as his raw sexuality. She knew that she should deny that sexuality, but she could have more easily denied her next breath.

We're in this together, his eyes said.

Anna glanced away, thinking once more that she didn't deserve the solace he was offering.

"We'll need to meet another time or two before

Monday," Harper said, unaware that he'd lost his audience, "but for the most part we're set. I want you to look and act innocent. I want the jury to see that you're upset by this horrendous accusation that's been leveled against you." Harper paused. "Is there anything either of you wants to say, to ask?"

Clearly puzzled by Harper's dismissal, Sloan asked, "When are we going over our testimony?"

Harper's hesitation seemed unusually long. "I, uh, I'm not certain that either of you testifying would be a good idea."

Sloan looked as though he couldn't possibly have heard what he had. "We're not going to testify in our own behalf?" Before Harper could respond, he said, "A defendant always testifies in his own defense."

"That's not true," Harper said.

"Okay, so a few don't make it to the stand because they'd hurt their cases. . . ." Sloan paused. "Is that what you think? That Anna and I would make bad witnesses?"

"No, of course not."

"What, then?"

"It's not necessary that you take the stand."

"I'm no lawyer," Sloan said, "but even I know that when a defendant doesn't testify, it looks fishy to the jury."

"The jury will be instructed not to interpret such an omission as guilt."

"Well, you can tell them all you want to, but we both know you're running a red flag up the pole."

"Look," Harper said, "Hennessey's going to play hard and fast, particularly about the affair."

"That's my point," Sloan insisted. "That jury is going to hear how immoral and unprincipled we are. As you said yourself, it's Hennessey's job to make the affair look cheap and tawdry. It wasn't, and I want the jury to know it."

"And are you going to keep your cool when he starts asking you all those intimate questions? Like how long had you wanted to take the wife of another man as your lover? Like how did she feel in your arms when you finally did? Like how did you feel knowing that she was never going to be yours as long as her husband was alive?"

With each question Sloan squirmed just a little more. Finally he shouted, "Yes, I'll keep my cool!"

"Like you are now?"

Sloan made no reply for several moments, then said simply, quietly, "I want to testify."

Anna could feel the fevered current sparking between the two men, the two friends. The air sizzled with it. In the next room Anna heard the ringing of the telephone. Neither man appeared to notice, a fact confirmed when Harper seemed surprised at a knock on the door. Marilyn cracked the door open and stuck her head in.

"Can you talk to Sheriff Tate about another case? He says it's important."

"Yeah," Harper said, looking over at Sloan as if to say, *Use the time to settle down.*

When Harper took the call, Sloan rose and walked to the window. Ramming his hands in his pants pockets, he stared out at the yellow yarrow blooming like patches of untamed sunshine. He felt Anna's approach, and the frustration inside him began to abate. She was like that. She could calm him, soothe him, heal him of pains he'd thought unhealable. On the other hand, she could stir his blood, his emotions, hotter than they'd ever been stirred. Because of this he forced himself to keep staring straight ahead.

"He doesn't want us on the stand because he thinks we're guilty," Anna said matter-of-factly.

Sloan had hoped to spare Anna this concern; but,

then, what had been the realistic chances of her not guessing the same thing he had?

"Maybe," Sloan said, softening the blow as much as he could, aware that she wasn't looking in his direction any more than he was looking in hers.

She made a sound that was half sigh, half laugh. "How can we hope to convince a jury when we can't even convince our lawyer?"

"It's his job to convince the jury, and he's a damned good lawyer."

"Maybe he's right. Maybe we shouldn't take the stand." She hesitated before saying, "I really don't want to testify."

"You don't have to, but I want to." Pause, then, "I'm sorry about Meg."

Again Anna's response was matter-of-fact, so matter-of-fact that it sent chills down Sloan's spine. "Meg is my punishment."

Unable to stop himself, he looked over at her. He saw only her profile, shrouded in a multitude of curls. She wore an unadorned black skirt and blouse. Her attitude, her appearance, made her look both severe and serene. The severity was right on the money. He'd never met anyone so harsh on herself. The serenity, however, was really nothing more than a lie. Not an intentional one, but a lie nonetheless. It masked the fact that she refused to let herself feel.

"What happened to the woman who wanted to feel?"

Anna turned her head until her eyes met Sloan's. Smiling faintly, she said, "She got what she wanted . . . and it hurt."

"And so she's hiding away again?"

"She has to survive."

"No!" Sloan said forcefully, plaintively. "Don't lose that woman I made love to one night, the woman who made love to me."

Anna shut her eyes, and Sloan could feel the memories

washing over her in the same way they washed over him—a sweet tide of remembrance. He could also see her hands trembling. They'd been trembling the first time he'd kissed her. They'd been trembling the night he'd made love to her.

"Tell me you don't regret that night," Sloan said, his tone begging, pleading—trembling.

Anna opened her eyes, blue eyes, honest eyes. She could no more have lied to him than she could have grown wings and flown. "How can I regret the only time in my life that I've ever been really alive?"

In that moment Sloan accepted one fact as truth. They could bury him in a thousand prisons, they could hang him from the highest tree, they could burn him in the hottest of hells—nothing mattered except the fact that Anna didn't regret that night.

THIRTEEN

July

Cook's Bay loved to celebrate the Fourth of July. That Saturday morning, bands marched through the middle of town trumpeting songs that stirred patriotic hearts and set spirited feet to tapping. By noon the bay had filled with yachts flying their colors high and free and blaring their horns in festive discourse. That evening, in a tradition as old as the town, guests partaking of a picnic milled about the lawn of the old Ramey home, an imposing white two-story structure with red shutters and a brighter red door. All across the front of the house, crimson geraniums bloomed madly, while to one side a rose garden flourished, a garden in which nothing but red roses grew. Because of the home's location, on a ridge overlooking the sound, it afforded an impressive view of the grand fireworks display that would take place at nine o'clock that night.

"Having fun?" Carrie asked, her bubbly voice making it obvious that she was.

For the occasion Carrie wore white pants and a T-shirt that electrically blinked with red and blue stars. A similar pair of red stars, these relying on Carrie's perpetual motion for glint and glimmer, dangled from her ears. In startling contrast Anna wore a simple white blouse, black slacks, and a watch that seemed to be ticking off time with an unnatural slowness. The hour hand appeared unwilling to move beyond eight o'clock.

"Yes," Anna replied in answer to her sister-in-law's question.

It was a lie, but there was no need spoiling Carrie's merry mood. The truth was that Anna might have actually enjoyed getting out of the house had it been under other circumstances, and had she felt that Jack was enjoying himself. But he wasn't. He was miserable. Even Meg, home for the holiday and her birthday, had commented as much. Ever since his oblique reference to death, the subject had hung between him and Anna like unfinished business. Anna knew that her daughter would have been worried if she'd known about the note, but Anna had destroyed it.

Just as her relationship with Sloan had been destroyed. She had not been back to the beach, had not seen Sloan, but neither had she, to her shame, been able to forget the feel of his hand entwined with hers.

"Jack's having a great time, isn't he?" Carrie asked. "I knew it would be good for him to get out."

As she spoke, the two women looked over at Jack, sitting in his wheelchair, a blanket draped about his legs despite the summer warmth. Anna said nothing in regard to Carrie's comment, though it never ceased to amaze her how her sister-in-law could avoid seeing the obvious. Or avoid admitting the obvious, for she had betrayed herself by suggesting that Jack needed something to bring him out of the doldrums.

"Everyone is asking me what I did to the fruit," Carrie whispered conspiratorially, then grinned wickedly. "Of course, I'm not telling a soul. Let them die of curiosity. Oh, excuse me," Carrie said. "I see the mayor's wife, and if I don't greet her personally, they'll crucify me at the Snappy Scissors." With this Carrie, winking like a neon sign, sped off in the direction of a woman who was bony thin, but tall and regal looking.

Anna sighed, not so much out of boredom as from plain, ordinary fatigue. Between Jack's nocturnal demands and her own restlessness, she was sleeping poorly. Why hadn't she realized that her friendship with Sloan was turning into something more? Unlike Carrie, she did not delude herself into thinking that it had not. But when, at what moment, at what sigh, at what heartbeat, had laughter and conversation become less important than something as simple as touch?

Anna lay the question aside, knowing that she hadn't a clue to the answer. Instead she looked about her, concentrating on the overflow of guests. She saw the prim, matronly woman who ran the general store. Next to her was the tall mortician, who was discreetly trying to shake a beribboned poodle from his leg. Anna turned her head in search of other diversion. Wasn't that Harper Fleming? Yes, it was, and he was talking to a man who had his back to her. Slowly, as though on cue, the man turned. Despite the fact that the sun was sinking, he wore sunglasses.

Anna's first reaction was to believe that she had somehow, like a gifted magician, conjured up Sloan from her subconscious. Her second reaction was that there was no way she could invoke an image that real, any more than she could control the sudden rapid beating of her heart. She turned away quickly, knowing she didn't want to turn away at all. Certain that Sloan hadn't observed her, Anna stepped back toward the safety of her husband and daughter. How could she avoid running into Sloan? Fortunately, Meg supplied her with an answer.

"I don't think Daddy's going to make it to those fireworks. He's looking pretty tired."

Although Carrie would have a fit if they didn't stay, Anna was more than willing to risk her sister-in-law's disappointment.

"You want to go now?" Anna asked, seizing this avenue of escape. Looking around, trying not to sound too eager, she added, "Meg, why don't you go tell your aunt we're leaving?"

Jack made a guttural sound that could be interpreted as a negative. Her heart jumping in her chest, she felt hound-to-hare panic. They had to leave. They simply had to. She couldn't face seeing Sloan again, not after what had happened when they'd last been together.

"Carrie won't mind," Anna said, gripping the handles of the wheelchair. Under other circumstances the image of her turning the chair so quickly that it wheelied on its side might have been comical. Now it didn't even come close to amusement.

Jack halted her with a grunt, then scrawled on a pad: *a little longer.*

The hare increasingly smelled the scent of danger, compelling Anna to give it one more try. "Jack, Carrie really won't mind."

"I won't mind what?"

Anna whirled, eager to do battle with Carrie, to explain Jack's fatigue and his need to leave, which was really *her* need, but no one had to know that she was fleeing the dark-haired man standing so calmly, so handsomely, across the way. Anna had just opened her mouth to speak when her gaze collided with that of the man, the dark-haired man, standing so calmly, so handsomely, not across the way, but beside Carrie. Not one word found its way past the lips of the hare. In fact, the hare seemed totally incapable of anything beyond drinking in the sight of the hound.

Meg, eyeing first her mother, then the object of her mother's rapt attention, finally said, "Daddy's tired."

"Oh, no, you don't, Jack Ramey," his sister said. "You can't leave before the fireworks. This'll be the first time you've seen them since we were kids. Don't you remember what fun they are?"

At the stricken look on Carrie's face, Anna knew that her cause was lost. She was caught in a velvet trap. Unknowingly, her hand went to her hair, her fingers trying to bring some order to the militant curls in a way that onlookers might have translated as primping.

"Besides," Anna heard Carrie say, "I've brought someone I want you two to meet. This is your neighbor, Sloan Marshall. He lives down in the old lighthouse." Turning to Sloan, Carrie added, "Sloan, this is my sister-in-law—"

"Anna and I have met," Sloan interrupted, his voice quiet and even, his gaze, no longer hidden behind sunglasses, steady and sure.

Anna wished fervently that he still wore the sunglasses. His night-dark eyes were both penetrating and sensitive—an emotionally lethal combination. Slowly, it dawned on her that everyone was waiting for her response, her explanation to Sloan's unexpected comment.

"On the beach," Anna said hastily, hoping that she didn't sound like a complete idiot.

"I jog on the beach every morning," Sloan explained. "I run into Anna every now and then."

"Yes," Anna said. "Every now and then."

Carrie frowned. "You asked me about him once, didn't you? About the guy who jogged on the beach?"

"Yes, I did," Anna said, but not wanting to dwell on

that, she hurried ahead with introductions. "This is my husband, Jack. Jack, Sloan Marshall."

With a naturalness that Anna envied, Sloan smiled and nodded in Jack's direction. "Nice to meet you."

Jack nodded back.

"And this is my daughter, Meg."

Sloan's smile widened. "Hi."

"Hi," Meg replied, but only, Anna noted, after the slightest of hesitations.

"Just look at all of you," Carrie said chidingly. "Not a one of you has anything to eat or drink."

"We ate earlier," Anna said simply, knowing that Jack would hate her mentioning that his health required it.

As always, when reality intruded, Carrie seemed surprised. "Oh, yeah, right. Well, you've got to try the fruit punch. It's wonderful." Looking over at Sloan, Carrie said, "I've got sodas, wine, coffee—"

"Fruit punch is fine," Sloan said.

"Fruit punch," Anna echoed when Carrie looked her way.

"C'mon, Meg," Carrie said, "help me."

As Meg fell into step beside her aunt, she glanced back at the three adults left behind. Again Anna noted her daughter's behavior. Meg, however, didn't seem to be the only one watching her. Anna could have sworn that so was Jack. At this Anna concluded that her guilt had taken control. Neither Meg nor Jack had any reason to suspect that she and Sloan were anything more than what they'd admitted to being. Nonetheless, she felt the need to fill the growing silence, and fill it she did with an inanity extraordinaire.

"It's a lovely evening for a party, isn't it?"

As the evening wore on, Sloan was certain of a number of things: that Anna was far lovelier than the evening, that no hour had ever passed more slowly, or awkwardly, and that, as much as it pained him to admit it, he both liked and understood Jack Ramey.

As regarded Anna's loveliness, she had no idea how pretty she was. Dressed simply and wearing little makeup—only a hint of lipstick was his guess—she, quite frankly, took his breath away, especially the idle and sexy way she raked her fingers through the curled confusion of her hair. Had he not known better, he would have sworn that she was inviting him to do the same. Of course she wasn't, and that fact defined their relationship. She wasn't free to invite him to take any personal liberties, because she was a married woman. God, how he'd worried about what had happened at the beach! God, how he wanted to talk to her, to apologize!

When he realized there wasn't going to be a chance to talk to her, and that his presence was making her uncomfortable, Sloan had tried to break away, but every time he did, someone stopped him—Carrie, Harper, even Jack. Minutes away from the onset of the fireworks, Carrie had decided that Jack's chair needed moving to a site that would afford him a better view. Totally oblivious to her brother's plea that he be allowed to remain where he was, Carrie had insisted that Harper and Sloan pick up the chair and set it on the brick pathway. No one had any choice but to do Carrie's bidding, and so Sloan and Harper had done so with as little fuss as possible.

The incident had left Sloan with an intimate understanding of Jack Ramey. It had also fostered a grudging respect. Aside from the initial objection, Jack, an obviously proud man who'd just been humiliated, had said nothing. He'd simply pulled quietly into himself, not being rude, but not being overly friendly, either. Sloan could see himself in Jack's place, coping with embarrassment, contending with a disease that set him apart, comparing himself to every able-bodied man he met. Yes, he could understand Jack Ramey, just as he could understand the emotional coldness that Anna had had to live with. If the coldness in some small way excused his allowing his friendship with her to develop into more, his understanding of Jack's plight negated the excuse . . . and made him feel like the sorriest of heels in the bargain.

At exactly nine o'clock the first starburst of fireworks flowered in the night sky. At the spangled eruption of red, the guests, seemingly in tandem, murmured an *ohh*. That was followed by a loud *ahh* at the showering of blue lights. Thereon the guests in tandem sounded like an unconducted choir, and over and over people pointed upward as though witnessing visions never seen before. Carrie, who stood behind Jack's chair, acted more child than adult and, at each blinding flash of light, squealed with a consummate delight that Harper, Meg, and even Jack found contagious.

Sloan and Anna stood slightly, but not conspicuously, apart from the others. That fact led Sloan to initiate their first private conversation that night.

"Anna?"

She glanced over at him—all dark hair, dark eyes, dark angles in the secret shadows of eventide. Even his voice was dark, with the same urgency Anna had heard on the beach. The only difference was he now spoke her name quietly.

He, too, looked over at her. His eyes mirrored the urgency of his voice. "Are you all right?"

"Yes," she answered. "Are you?"

Sloan shrugged, at the same time executing a small, forced smile. "Guess it depends on your definition of *all right*."

Anna looked away, the beauty of his smile, however forced, creating a painful longing in her heart. "Yes, I guess it does."

Sloan knew this meant that Anna wasn't faring any better than he was. The misery-loves-company side of him wallowed in this fact, while his nobler side hated the thought of her being in pain, especially pain he'd caused.

"Look," he whispered. "I've given what happened a lot of thought"—hell, it was all he'd thought of—"and I want you to know that it wasn't your fault. It was mine. I let things get out of hand. I should have seen where this was leading."

A huge *boom-boom* cannoned, brightening the sky with light as yellow as the daytime sun. Anna didn't notice. She saw only Sloan. She should have known that he'd try to take the blame.

"I want one thing understood," she said, her words spilling over Sloan like molten gold. "What happened was not any more your fault than mine. I, too, let things get out of hand. I, too, should have seen where this was leading."

Sloan appreciated the fact that Anna wasn't denying that their relationship had changed. But, then, Anna wasn't one to run from the truth.

"Anna . . ."

Her gaze, summer warm, melted into Sloan's, making him uncomfortably aware that he was a man, that she was a woman—a married woman. He glanced away, though it didn't lessen his need to tell her what was in his heart.

"When I first met you," he said, "I told you that I wanted to be your friend. I meant that. I swear I did."

"I know."

But Sloan needed to make certain that she understood. "If I had known how this was going to turn out, I would never have left that first shell."

"I know."

"I would never have approached you."

"I believe I approached you," Anna corrected.

"You know what I mean."

"Yes, I do."

"I just wanted to be your friend," he repeated, hesitating. When he continued, his voice had grown husky. "I can no longer be just your friend."

Suddenly she, too, had to make him understand her position. "Surely you know that there can be nothing more between us. Jack and I have our problems, but we're married. I took vows—"

"I'd never ask you to break them!" Sloan interrupted, speaking more loudly than he'd intended.

Harper glanced back toward them, silencing them both, causing two hearts to race with the fear of discovery.

Finally, during another loud round of cheers, Anna braved one more remark. "We can't see each other again."

Overhead, a cluster of crystal-colored lights exploded in a dazzling display, then drizzled down like diamonds raining to earth. Both Sloan and Anna, their faces upturned, stood silhouetted against this bright finale. It heralded the end of the Fourth of July festivities . . . and the end of a relationship that had never really had a chance to begin.

"All right!" Meg proclaimed the next afternoon. As she spoke, she plucked a thin black belt from rustling wrapping paper and encircled her waist with it. "And it goes great with the black jeans Aunt Carrie gave me."

"Does it fit?" her mother asked.

"Yeah," Meg said. "How did you know it was what I wanted?"

Anna smiled. "I'm not totally obtuse. The dozenth time you mentioned needing a black belt, I got the message."

Meg, her hair flowing about her shoulders like sunshine about the day, tried to smother a smile but didn't succeed. "I mentioned it only four or five times."

"However many, I got the message."

"What about the jeans?" Carrie asked. "Do you think they'll fit?"

Meg picked up the jeans and checked the tag in the back. "They should fit fine. They're my size."

"They better," Carrie said, looking refreshed despite her late evening. "They were on sale."

"Thanks, you guys," Meg said, hugging her aunt and her mother. She then turned to her father, hunched in his wheelchair, and planted a kiss on his cheek. "And thank you, too, Daddy."

In contrast to his sister, Jack looked exhausted, although Anna and Meg had taken him home right after the fireworks and put him straight to bed. As usual, he'd slept poorly. Which meant that Anna had slept poorly, too, though, in all honesty, much of her restlessness had come from seeing Sloan again. Knowing she was wading into treacherous waters, she forced Sloan from her mind and watched as Jack smiled and scribbled on his pad: *happy 22nd birthday*.

Meg hugged her father, this time tightly, and in return Jack slid his left arm around his daughter. Anna was reminded of the special bond that existed between this father and this daughter. Noting that he clung with a fierceness that she hadn't known he was capable of, she wondered if maybe he, too, was starved for human contact. Why, then, wouldn't he let her near? Why was it that only another man would?

"C'mon," Anna said, perhaps a bit too brightly, "let's cut this birthday cake."

"Yeah," Carrie said, pushing the coconut cake toward her niece. "Eager little hands were baking this at five this morning."

Taking the knife her mother handed her, Meg asked, "You were up at five this morning, Aunt Carrie?"

"I didn't say my hands were doing the baking. Eager little hands over at Millie's Bakery were."

Everyone smiled.

"I want a huge piece of Millie's cake," Meg said.

"Of course you do, darling," Carrie said. "We all do."

In short order three pieces of cake graced three plates. At Jack's rapping of his knuckles on the table, the women looked up. Jack nodded toward the cake.

"You know you shouldn't have sweets," Anna said.

In response her husband nodded once more toward the cake.

"Jack, please—"

This time Jack struck the table, one sharp rap in defiance of Anna, in defiance of his disease. A pregnant silence stretched out, seemingly into infinity. All the while Jack's will battled with Anna's.

"Couldn't he have one piece?" Carrie asked, her gray eyes wide, her voice uncertain.

"No." The response came quickly, unequivocally, from Meg. "He can have two bites and no more."

The silence grew. Suddenly Jack grinned and scrawled: *yes, dr.*

The tension of the moment was broken—but, then, so was Anna. She ate her cake in near silence, contributing only what she had to to the conversation. As soon as she could do so politely, she slipped from the bedroom and into the kitchen. Sweet solitude enveloped her, sterling silence surrounded her. She stared at the windowsill filled with shells. Instead of fleeing into her emotionless world of survival at Jack's treatment of her, she was actually feeling anger for the second time, and it felt good. Darned good! Before she could stop herself, she longed to share the news with Sloan.

"Mom?"

Anna whirled, looking as guilty as though she'd been caught with her hand in the cookie jar.

"Are you all right?" Meg asked.

"I'm fine," Anna said, turning back around. She picked up a dishrag and began wiping a perfectly spotless counter.

"Two bites of cake won't hurt him."

"That's not the point, is it? He shouldn't have sweets, and he knows it."

Pause. Then, "Mom, I know things are a little rough right now, but give him time. Okay?"

Sighing, Anna stopped cleaning the counter. Her gaze met Meg's. A part of Anna wanted to say that she was out of patience, that she didn't have any more time to spare—didn't anyone see that she was slowly disintegrating, disappearing into thin air?—but another part of her, the mother part, responded to her daughter's plea.

Anna smiled. "Everything's going to be all right."

Meg smiled, too, but Anna thought the smile less than hearty. That, combined with the uncharacteristic way Meg averted her gaze, alerted Anna that something was coming. In this case forewarned was not forearmed.

"Who's this Sloan Marshall guy?" Meg asked, stepping to the refrigerator and extracting a quart of milk.

The question struck Anna like an open palm to her face. She'd convinced herself that her paranoia had been responsible for her idea that Meg suspected something. Now she didn't know what to believe.

"What do you mean?" Anna asked.

Still, Meg didn't glance her mother's way as she began to pour, oh so casually, a glass of milk. When she spoke, though, her question had gone from being indifferently asked to being bluntly posed. "Who's Sloan Marshall?"

Anna willed her voice to sound relaxed and her hands not to reattack the counter. "Exactly who your aunt said. He's the man who lives in the lighthouse."

"How do you know him?"

"Just as I said last night, I've seen him jogging on the beach."

"How many times?"

To Anna's credit she managed a genuine-enough laugh. "I don't know. I didn't keep count." Pause. "Why? Is it important?"

"I don't guess so. It's just that you seemed to know each other."

"We've spoken. Several times. He's friendly. I've been friendly back." Again Anna hesitated, this time steeling herself to ask one more question. "Why are you asking about Sloan Marshall?"

Meg finally looked her mother fully in the eyes. If there was anything other than the familiar in her daughter's, Anna didn't see it. Then, dropping the subject as quickly as she'd raised it, Meg said, "No reason."

Anna should have breathed a sigh of relief, but she didn't. Long after Meg had left for the drive back to Connecticut, Anna remained unsettled by her daughter's query, and by the subtle insinuation in her voice. What did Meg know? Or think she knew? Anna told herself that it didn't matter, because she wouldn't be seeing Sloan again. That thought consoled her. It also saddened her, no matter how much she tried to pretend it didn't.

The following week was a nightmare. On the eve of Meg's birthday Jack took a turn for the worse, although Anna didn't realize it until the next day. Ordinarily an early riser, Jack was drowsy when Anna tried to awaken him, a fact she mentioned to Ken when he arrived. By noon Jack had been consumed by a thirst that no amount of water could satisfy. On the other hand, he'd completely lost his appetite. At three o'clock, the hour that the nurse usually left, Anna asked Ken to remain on duty, which he did. By three-thirty Jack's breathing had become heavy, his pulse rapid. An ambulance was called.

What Anna remembered most about waiting for the

arrival of the ambulance was the consummate fear in Jack's eyes. Normally proud, normally defiant, he looked like an animal caught in the headlights of an oncoming car. Would the vehicle strike him dead? Would it swerve at the last lifesaving second? Or, and Anna knew that this was what Jack feared most, would he slip into a coma, that sinister place where one was neither alive nor dead?

"It's going to be all right, Jack," she whispered, holding his hand tightly, letting him hold hers.

But as she sat in the waiting room of the small hospital, she knew that she had lied to Jack. Maybe things would be all right this time, but what about the next? Or the next? He was on a collision course, a fact she'd denied until now, a fact he'd already accepted. That acceptance, the realization that the end—or worse, a living death—might be near was what had frightened him.

She had been as frightened as he—her heart drumming, her throat dry, her heart making desperate deals with God. She was as trapped as Jack. They both lived in a world from which there was no escape, a world neither had chosen, a world neither deserved. With each progression of the disease, the boundaries of that world grew more narrow, more confining, until, like exhausted mice ensnared in a go-nowhere maze, they ceased even to try, content only to sit and be consumed by their plight, their fright.

Ultimately, a kidney infection was blamed for the acidosis episode. Jack spent a couple of days in the hospital before being sent home with an adjusted, and higher, dose of insulin. Anna breathed more easily. In another couple of days she realized that her doing so had been premature. As was often the case for diabetics, the infection proved difficult. Only one thing proved more so, and that was Jack himself. A man who'd shunned attention in the past, he now demanded

it. He wanted his blood sugar monitored far more than
was necessary. He panicked at the slightest symptom,
certain that he was having another acidosis attack or a
hypoglycemic attack. When he developed a headache,
he was certain that a stroke was soon to follow.

Anna knew that he was scared. She tried to take this
into consideration but found it harder and harder to do
as his abuse grew. If his health was taking a roller-
coaster ride, so were his emotions. His reasoning had
grown cloudy and illogical. He needed her, then resented her for responding to his need. He wanted her
near, yet didn't want her to see him weak, vulnerable,
human. His depression mushroomed.

And so, with the passage of each day, Anna grew
more weary. On Friday afternoon of what was possibly
the worst week of her life, she announced to Ken that
she was going into town to get a few things at the general store. It was either get out of the house or go cer-
tifiably crazy.

The creaking of the old wooden floor, polished with a
glossy patina reminiscent of aged brass, soothed Anna's
frayed nerves, although to be honest, the hissing of a
hundred hellfires, as long as she was hearing them outside the house, might have proved as comforting. Only
the *yip-yip-yip*ping of a white poodle, wearing the most
garish rhinestone-studded collar, violated the serenity.

"Here, boy," Anna heard the store's owner call.

The dog hesitated, then trotted off toward its owner.
Inez Gouge had nodded politely, primly, to Anna as
she'd entered the store. To Anna's surprise she'd inquired about Jack's health, although she didn't remember his name. Apparently news of Jack's stay in the
hospital had made the rounds of the town. Inez seemed
genuinely concerned, which Anna thanked her for.

The dog had started barking just as she came to the
aisle containing cosmetics. Though few in number and

basic in purpose, the products spilled mockingly before Anna. These days she was lucky to get a slow bath instead of a fast shower, and lipstick was all the makeup she could manage. But, then, as she'd already admitted, she had no man to look pretty for.

Anna smiled sadly as she reached for a plastic-encased tube of mascara. When was the last time she'd worn mascara? She honestly couldn't remember, any more than she could remember the last time Jack had told her she was pretty.

Did Sloan think she was pretty?

Anna had no idea where the question came from and was so appalled that she quickly replaced the mascara on the rack as though it were the guilty culprit, as though it had spawned the wayward thought. When she first heard the softly spoken, "Hi," she wondered if it was just another manifestation of her renegade imagination.

She prayed it was.

She prayed it wasn't.

When she turned, she prayed for forgiveness, for she realized that, throughout the past difficult week, even though her sick husband had been at the fore of her mind, the man standing behind her had been at its back.

FOURTEEN

"Hi." Anna meant her response to be a greeting. Instead it sounded like an endearment.

"I thought that was you," Sloan said, knowing darned well that it was Anna. He saw her in his mind's eye every waking moment and dreamed of her every night, or more precisely, when he could sleep for thinking of her. In short, the week had been a nightmare.

Anna speared her fingers through her hair, and Sloan experienced a jab of jealousy. He would have liked nothing better than to be the one threading his fingers through her frothy golden locks.

"I, uh, I came after some groceries," Anna said, recognizing the idiocy of her comment even as she made it.

"Yeah, me too. I always stop in for a few things on Friday." Sloan grinned. "You know, laying in bachelor provisions for the coming week, things like beer and pretzels, beer and peanuts, and beer and beer."

Anna smiled, wondering how a man with such a devastating grin had managed to cling to a bachelor status. "Sounds nutritious. Especially the beer."

Grins faded as each faced a moral dilemma. Anna asked herself if it was better for her to admit that she found a man other than her husband attractive or to lie to herself and pretend she wasn't attracted?

Sloan wondered if a man was less culpable if he admitted desiring another man's wife. How low had a man sunk when he lied to his best friend? When Harper had asked after Carrie's party just how well he knew Anna, Sloan had implied not well. Harper had said nothing more, but Sloan had felt uneasy. Just the way he felt uneasy now. He knew that Inez Gouge had eyes in the back of her head. Even as he thought this, he felt a pair of staring eyes. Glancing toward the end of the aisle, he saw the dog peering around the corner.

Turning back to Anna, he said, "It's just the dog."

Strangely, the remark lent an illicitness to the conversation, as though each clearly understood that they must be careful. That in mind, Sloan chose his next words with deliberation.

"I understand your husband's been ill again." At Anna's look of surprise he added, "Carrie told Harper. Harper mentioned it in passing."

"Yes," Anna said. "Jack came down with a kidney infection."

"How's he doing?"

"Not well."

"I'm sorry to hear that," Sloan responded. A pause. A heartbeat. Then, "How are *you* doing?"

Anna wanted to tell him that she wasn't doing well, either, that she felt trapped and afraid and lonelier than she could ever remember feeling. She wanted to tell him that she felt herself slipping into the shadows of life, the substance of her being growing faint, color-less, ephemeral. She wanted to tell him these things, but she'd been programmed to say another.

"I'm fine."

"You don't look it," Sloan said bluntly. "You look exhausted."

In any other woman he would have thought that she stood nose to nose with a breakdown, but women like Anna didn't break. They just bent and bent and bent again, until the winds of adversity sailed smoothly over their arched shoulders. Furthermore, people even stopped noticing that they were bent.

Anna surprised herself by smiling. "That kind of flattery could go straight to a woman's head."

Even though she smiled, Sloan sensed that his statement had upset Anna. He wished that he hadn't been so frank.

"I never meant to imply that you weren't pretty, only that you look tired."

Several things crossed Anna's mind at the same time: that Sloan looked tired, too, as though he wasn't sleeping well; that the little dog was back; that maybe she was just fishing for a compliment. Her response proved the latter.

"Am I?" she asked. "Pretty?" She had cast her line deep into turbulent waters.

Her question floored Sloan, not so much that she had asked it, but rather that she'd needed to ask it. But she had—desperately. He could see that desperation in the depths of her beautiful blue eyes.

Before he could answer, she turned her head away, saying, "I'm sorry. That was a stupid question."

Her profile, except for the tip of a finely pointed chin, lay hidden in a flock of silken curls. Sloan wanted, more than he'd ever wanted anything in his life, to slip a crooked finger under that chin and return her gaze to his. He didn't, because the action would have been inappropriate in a public place. No, that wasn't the reason at all. The truth was that if he touched her, he feared that his whole being would go up in white-hot flames.

"Anna, look at me."

Sloan's voice washed over Anna, warming the coolness of her embarrassment. Still, though, she could not look at him. Why had she asked such a patently ridiculous question? It was all that mascara's fault!

"Anna ... please."

It was the word *please* that she couldn't resist. Slowly, with a seeming loss of will, she angled her head until her gaze locked with Sloan's. She saw his eyes darken. She saw his Adam's apple bob down and up as he swallowed. She heard him whisper, "You're incredibly pretty."

She would have liked for his response to mean nothing to her, but it did. In fact, it meant too much. It was the first time in a long while that she'd felt pretty. It felt good, but it was the wrong man making her feel that way. She looked away once more.

"I've missed you," Sloan said in a thick, ragged voice. He hated himself for saying it, for putting Anna on the spot, but the words, entrapped in his heart, would not be denied. They were the reckless harvest of too many restless nights.

"Don't," Anna said, looking about guiltily. "Not here."

Not here. Not now. Not ever. Because I don't belong to you!

She hadn't spoken these words, but Sloan heard them as clearly as if she had. They cut. Deeply. Painfully. Soberingly. Sloan cleared his throat, then said, "I've applied for a job, and if it comes through, I'll be leaving Cook's Bay."

It took a moment for his statement to sink in. When it did, a dark feeling, one that emptied her stomach, her soul, tore through Anna.

"Where?" she heard herself asking, trying to sound matter-of-fact, as though his announcement in no way involved her.

"The North Sea."

"The North Sea?" Her voice rose; her heartbeat quickened. The North Sea? Without a map she didn't know precisely where that was, but she *did* know that it was on the other side of the world.

"Yeah," Sloan said, hoping to come across just as matter-of-factly. "The job would entail underwater diving for an oil company."

"Diving?"

"A skill I learned in the navy." Before Anna could say more, Sloan added, "I've known about the job's availability for a while, and, uh, well, I called about it this week." *After I thought I'd go crazy thinking about you.* "They said they'd let me know."

"When?"

"Could be days. Could be longer. Depending on the drilling date."

Tell me not to go! Sloan pleaded, knowing that he had no right to wish this. Absolutely none.

Don't go! Anna wanted to cry, but she had no right to do so. Absolutely none.

Instead Sloan said, "It's better if I go."

"Yes, it is," Anna replied.

And so they stood looking at each other, knowing that they'd spoken the truth, knowing that the truth hurt.

Suddenly the dog barked. Anna and Sloan jumped as if they'd been shot. Sloan whirled around; Anna looked toward the end of the aisle. They expected to see the dog. They did not expect to see Inez Gouge holding the dog and scrutinizing them with an intensity that made the canine's interest look mild. How long had she been standing there? What had she overheard? And did the two of them look as guilty as they felt?

Sloan turned back to Anna and said in a voice that carried, "Please give your husband my regards." The very calmness of his tone suggested that there was no need to assume that Inez Gouge had heard anything.

"I'll do that," Anna said.

"Good to see you again."

"You too."

With that Sloan walked away, leaving Anna with a pounding heart, with a heavy heart. There was the distinct possibility that she'd never see him again. She told herself that she hoped she didn't. Maybe because of that, as she plucked items from the shelves, she watched him out of the corner of her eye, as though trying to store away final memories of him.

All he bought was a six-pack of beer, which he paid for as he talked to Inez Gouge with a normalcy that Anna envied. He then walked from the store, and perhaps from her life, without even once looking back.

Anna waited for her survival numbness to settle in, a numbness she would have welcomed, but it never came. Instead she was left with a raw hurt, making her wonder if she really wanted to feel after all. And what was the source of her hurt? Sloan's leaving or her staying? He had just walked out of the door, headed toward the rest of his life, while she was stalled, trapped, in a world whose tomorrow would be exactly like today.

A cold panic seized Anna. She tried not to blame Jack for condemning her to this prison, yet there was no one else that she could blame. And there was so little satisfaction in accusing something as uncaring as fate.

"Will this be all?" Inez Gouge asked in a normal, unaccusatory voice.

Anna's gaze swept across the items she'd automatically spread out on the counter. Some she didn't even remember placing in the shopping basket. She didn't

remember much of anything except Sloan telling her
that he was leaving.

*"I've applied for a job ... I'll be leaving Cook's Bay ...
North Sea ... North Sea ... North ..."*

"Mrs. Ramey?"

"Am I? Pretty?"

"You're incredibly pretty."

"Mrs. Ramey?"

Anna glanced up.

"Will this be all?" Inez Gouge repeated.

"Yes," Anna said, but no sooner had the word left her
lips than she countermanded it. "No!" she said.
"There's one more thing."

Slowly, resolutely, Anna walked from the counter,
down the third aisle. Without hesitation she pulled an
item from a rack and returned to the front of the store.
She placed the item on the counter.

"Add this, please," Anna said.

If Inez Gouge thought the eleventh-hour purchase of
mascara peculiar, her expression in no way reflected it.
Instead she punched the cost of the cosmetic into the
cash register and totaled the amount of the purchase.

Had her life depended upon it, Anna couldn't have
explained why she'd purchased the mascara. She'd
known only that she hadn't had a choice. Something as
basic as breathing, as fundamental as a heartbeat, had
compelled her.

If the week before had been hell, the one that followed was doubly so. While Jack's physical health appeared marginally better, his emotional health dipped
to the lowest it had ever been. He ranged from being
belligerent to being nearly catatonic. For hours on end
he would lie facing the open window, from which the
sound of the sea drifted in. This song, of surf and sea
gulls and ultimate simplicity, seemed the only thing ca-

pable of bringing Jack any peace. As for Anna, there was no peace at all.

Restless and worn, she roamed the house like a prisoner. When she could withstand the confinement no longer, she'd slip off to the beach, hoping against hope that Sloan would be there, hoping against hope that he wouldn't. He never was. Had his job offer already come through? Was he getting ready to leave Cook's Bay? Had he already left? When the questions became more than she could bear, Anna would turn her attention to hunting for shells. Though she collected a couple more whole shells, it became consummately clear that there were no bivalves to be found, which didn't surprise her. Bivalves didn't survive any more than relationships— not the one with her husband, not the one with the man other than her husband.

"Have you heard about your neighbor?" Carrie asked on Wednesday.

She had stopped by after work to check on Jack. Indeed, everyone seemed to have stopped by that day. Both Dr. Goodman and Father Santelices had called on Jack, which Anna had appreciated, although Dr. Goodman had left her a little concerned. A sore had developed on Jack's leg, which might prove problematic for the future. Anna's heart had turned over at the mere thought of complications that might result in amputation. With Jack's vanity, he would never be able to tolerate that. Just as she now feared that she wouldn't be able to tolerate what her sister-in-law was possibly about to tell her—namely, that Sloan was no longer in Cook's Bay.

"Heard what?" Anna asked, willing herself to sound only mildly interested, even though the coffee she was pouring missed the mug and splashed onto the counter.

"He's leaving Cook's Bay. He's accepted a job somewhere. I can't remember where. At some oil company, though."

At the realization that he hadn't left yet, Anna breathed more easily. "I know Harper will miss him," she said.

"Yeah, he will."

"When is he leaving?" As she asked the question, again with what she hoped was indifference, she mopped up the mess she'd made on the counter, then handed a mug to Carrie.

"Apparently not for a week or so. The oil company called yesterday saying that he was hired, but that the drilling schedule had been delayed."

Anna felt greatly relieved, though she had no idea why. His leaving was inevitable, and as such, it would be better if it happened sooner rather than later. Furthermore, she had no intention of seeing him again. Still, knowing that he was at the lighthouse brought her a measure of comfort.

That evening, as Anna and Jack dined, she tried to put thoughts of Sloan from her mind. She always tried to put thoughts of Sloan from her mind while around her husband. To do otherwise constituted a betrayal. As always, Jack was quiet. Atypically, so was Anna. She simply had run out of small talk. Even so, she felt compelled to make a comment at one point.

"If you'd like something else, I could check the refrigerator for leftovers."

Jack shook his head.

"Would you like for me to cut the chicken up into smaller pieces?"

The question angered Jack, though for the life of her Anna couldn't understand why. She—someone—had been cutting his meat ever since the stroke. What was the big deal about cutting it into smaller pieces? If she didn't understand the reason behind his anger, she understood all too clearly the sharp shake of his head. It was an emphatic no. She said no more.

As the silent meal progressed, Anna discovered that

she was no more hungry than her husband. She picked and probed and remembered an article she'd once read about caged animals refusing to eat. She thought of her prison, her cage, made all the more confining by the absence of bars. Once more panic gripped her. Ironically, she thought of the unopened tube of mascara on the dressing table in her bedroom. She still didn't fully understand why she'd bought it, although she thought it had something to do with this trapped feeling she'd had ever since Jack's health had worsened. Somehow it represented a key to her prison. Unlike Sloan, she had nowhere to run except back to the past, a past in which it had mattered that she was pretty, a past in which she had felt whole and, more important, like a woman.

The rude clanking of silverware brought Anna back to the present. She glanced up to discover that Jack, clearly embarrassed, clearly irate, had dropped his knife after attempting to cut his meat. Anna made no move to collect the utensil from the floor. As unobtrusively as possible, she simply passed hers to him. He grasped it with a vengeance and began to hack at the pieces of chicken breast. As Anna feared, the plate, which had slid closer and closer to the edge of the table with each stab of the knife, eventually tumbled off. It hit the floor with a deafening crash, exploding like buckshot.

Though her heart hammered, Anna calmly stood and walked around the table. She avoided looking at her husband as she stooped to clean up the debris. A deep guttural snarl broke the silence. She looked up. Jack, his face red with rage, shook his head so vehemently that she feared it would fly off his shoulders.

"It has to be cleaned up," Anna said.

The snarl grew.

"Jack, please be reasonable."

He reached for his pad and pen and began to write—

hard and fast and almost illegibly. Nonetheless, when the pad was turned toward her, Anna read: *leave it alone. leave me alone.*

The words had been calculated to hurt. And they did, with all the force of a hand slapping her face. Anna stood slowly, regally, with the knowledge that something had just snapped within her. But even as she turned and walked from the room, the hurt, the pain, slipped behind the curtain of nothingness. She climbed the stairs to her bedroom feeling deathly numb.

The numbness increased until it began to frighten Anna. Never before had it lasted this long. Never before had it been this paralytic. She felt as if her movements had been reduced to slow motion. Worse, that the movements didn't belong to her, but rather to someone else who stood nearby watching. And she was cold. Coffin cold. At nine o'clock, almost two hours after the incident, Anna slipped down the stairs, only to discover that Jack had somehow crawled back into bed by his own power. Had he managed to go to the bathroom? Was he asleep? Or was he merely pretending to be? Anna surprised herself by not caring whether he was or wasn't. Neither did she care that the broken plate and food still lay scattered on the floor.

Dear heaven, she was cold. And numb.

Mounting the stairs, she stripped her clothes and, turning the water as hot as she could stand it, stepped into the shower. Almost instantly the bathroom filled with steam so thick that Anna could hardly breathe. But she didn't care. She was getting warm. Hanging her head like a rag doll, she pivoted slowly, letting the water spray her neck, her back, her hips. She was aware of the needles of water prickling her skin, yet, again as though she were anesthetized, she registered only pressure, not mild pain.

Why couldn't she feel?

Maybe it was only with her husband that she didn't feel. Enough emotion assailed her in Sloan's presence.

Shutting off the shower, she stepped from it, ran a towel through her wet hair, and draped herself with another as she walked into the bedroom. Immediately the image in the dresser mirror caught her eye. Easing onto the stool, she studied the woman captured in the silvery portrait. She must still exist, by very dint of the fact that she cast a reflection, but just as the reflection was trapped within the mirror, so, too, was she trapped.

"I've applied for a job . . . in the North Sea."

"Have you heard about your neighbor? He's leaving Cook's Bay."

Leaving . . . going away . . . free as a bird . . . but she was trapped, trapped, trapped . . .

Anna reached for the mascara. Methodically, she tore away the plastic wrap. Slowly, she twisted the cap. Purposefully, she removed the wand and began to sweep the thick chocolate-brown color onto her eyelashes. Within minutes a lushness framed her eyes. As though the mascara contained magic properties, as though she could now see more clearly, Anna took an inventory of her features. Damp corkscrew curls, the color of butter, clung to her head, while her eyes, though disclosing her fatigue, still shone with a feminine mistiness. Touching a cheekbone with her fingertips, Anna concluded that time had treated her face kindly. Yes, she thought, she was still pretty.

"Hey, babe, you look pretty," came Jack's voice from the past.

Immediately she heard another voice, her own. *"Am I? Pretty?"*

On the heels of this came Sloan's slow, sexy reply. *"You're incredibly pretty."*

Warmth flushed through Anna. Even though she knew it was inappropriate, she welcomed it. Feeling anything was better than feeling nothing. Besides, it had been a very long while since she'd felt anything sexual. Any desire she might have had had been buried deep beneath the sobering fact that her husband could not satisfy it. And so she had banished desire, exiled any feelings of sexuality.

Or had she merely pretended to?

In answer to the question, images bombarded her—images of warm kisses and hot hands, images of sighs, moans, moments of supreme bliss. With a gentle tug the towel fell from Anna's breasts. The mirror showed them to be full and firm. At the brush of her fingertips, a pinkish-brown nipple pouted, and her breath caught. Yes, she'd only pretended to bury her desire. It was still there, ready to burst to life at the right man's touch. She closed her eyes, imagining that man's caress. She didn't even begin to pretend that man was her husband.

The images shamed her.

The images pleasured her.

The images made her feel.

Shaken, longing for something she could never have, Anna stood, donned her gown, and crawled into bed. Sleep eluded her, though, adding to her restlessness, her fatigue. Throughout the fitful night one question kept plaguing her: at what point, thought, or deed, did a woman became an adulteress?

It was odd, Sloan thought, as he lay in bed staring into the dark night, that at one time coming to Cook's Bay had saved his sanity. That same sanity was now threatened if he didn't leave this quiet seacoast town. Even Harper had sensed the change in him, the escalating impatience.

"Why are you in such a hurry to leave?" his friend had asked earlier that day.

"I'm not in a hurry," Sloan had answered, then

added, "Yeah, maybe I am. Don't you think it's about time that I get on with my life?"

"What I think is that your sudden need to depart has something to do with Anna Ramey."

Sloan had halted his pacing of the lighthouse cottage—pacing was what he did best these days. His friend's comment had startled him, though it shouldn't have. Harper had never been a fool. Neither was he noted for mincing words.

"Damn, Sloan, she's a married woman!"

Sloan had plowed his fingers through his hair. "Don't you think I know that? Why do you think I want to get the hell out of Dodge?" Sloan had sighed, saying, "Look, nothing's happened between us. I swear it."

Unless one counted X-rated fantasies, Sloan could have added, but hadn't. Neither had he mentioned the countless cold showers he'd taken.

"Stay away from her," Harper had said.

"Yeah," Sloan had replied, meaning it heart and soul.

But it didn't keep him from wanting her, Sloan thought as the long night wore on. It didn't keep him from wondering what her kiss would be like. Tentative? Certain? Sinfully sweet? Nor did it keep him from wondering what kind of lover she'd be. More than anything, he wondered if she wondered what kind of lover he'd be.

He had pushed her too far this time, Jack thought as he lay wide awake. He'd known it the moment he'd seen the stricken look on her face.

Yes, the sea seemed to murmur. *You were unfair, even unkind.*

Yes, he knew that too. What he didn't know was why he'd done it. It was just that he was so tired, so very tired, of the daily struggle.

And so very tired of being afraid? the sea suggested.

Yes, that too. He wanted to be brave, but bravery wore all too thin when called upon for too long.

I understand, the sea said. *And you mustn't blame yourself.*

Come morning he would apologize, Jack thought. He would tell Anna how very sorry he was.

The sea made no comment. Looking back, Jack thought the silence telling.

Anna dreaded going into Jack's bedroom, and yet she knew she must. She had left the broken plate, the scattered food, for Ken to clean up. She'd simply told him that there had been an accident, offering nothing more as to why she hadn't dealt with it herself. Neither did she explain why, for the first time, she hadn't joined her husband for breakfast. It was now midmorning, and she couldn't avoid the confrontation any longer. Besides, with the nurse in the laundry room washing last night's soiled bed linen, it seemed the appropriate time for her and Jack to spend a few minutes alone.

When she stepped into the bedroom, Jack indicated that he'd already written her a note. Anna was surprised. Wordlessly, making momentary eye contact, she walked to where he sat, his shoulders stooped, as though he'd visibly aged overnight. In contrast, there seemed a youthful eagerness about him. He already had the tablet slanted toward her.

i'm sorry, it read.

Anna wasn't certain that her eyes hadn't deceived her, so she reread the note. Before she could finish with it this second time, Jack was writing an additional message.

forgive me.

Anna glanced up at her husband. His gray eyes pleaded with her. This man, watching her with such expectancy, was the kind, gentle, loving man she'd married. This was the man she'd wanted back in her life for so long, the man she'd prayed would return to her.

What she hadn't anticipated was her reaction to seeing him again. In a blinding flash of clarity, she realized that she no longer loved her husband. Somewhere along the way, during the dark of some lonely night, at the dawn of some heartbreaking new day, she'd fallen out of love. No, she hadn't fallen out of love, she'd been driven out of it. The wall that Jack had built around himself had finally grown so steep that she had stopped trying to scale it. She felt relieved—he could no longer hurt her—but mostly she felt a profound sadness.

Something in her demeanor, perhaps her prolonged lack of a response, perhaps the way she simply stared at him, must have alerted Jack that all was not going as he'd hoped. The expectant light in his eyes dimmed, then died. Anna thought she saw a sadness that matched her own. She saw something more, as well—a resignation, a look that said he wasn't surprised.

Adjusting the notepad, smiling ruefully, he wrote: *2 little, 2 late.*

"Jack—"

He stopped her with a shake of his head, this time a gentle shake. It was far more powerful, far more compelling than the sharp, angry shakes she'd seen so often following the stroke. As though collecting his thoughts, he just sat. Anna had opened her mouth to speak when Jack once more began to pen a note.

When finished, it read: *divorce me.*

Anna studied the words. They were simple, yet complex; forthright, yet shrouded in vagaries, for even though the law could break the ties that bound man to woman, husband to wife, there was no way that the emotional ties could ever be severed. Not completely. Not satisfactorily. Not in a way that the heart couldn't remember. While it was true that she no longer loved him, it was equally true that she still cared for him. This was the man she'd shared several good years with, the father of her child. Ironically, perhaps more now than ever before, Anna felt an intense loyalty to him.

"No, Jack," she said, "I won't divorce you."

why?

Anna smiled. "Because you're my husband. Because we married for life—for the good times and the bad. We married until death do us part."

Slowly, laboriously, he wrote: *help me take my life.*

He'd hinted at this very subject before, and now he stated it boldly. Anna discovered that there was a big difference between hinting and stating boldly.

"Jack, don't do this," she pleaded.

He ignored her. *simple. insulin overdose. no one would question.*

So macabre was his request, and his composure, that even though her heart was pounding, confirming her shock, her fear, Anna seemed incapable of registering the true significance of what he was asking. A part of her said that this conversation was happening; another part of her said that it wasn't.

Jack sensed that he was losing her. *i'm trapped in this body. free me.*

Anna had had enough. It was time to flee, to run, to escape. She was halfway to the door when she heard Jack speak.

"An-na. Plea-zze."

She turned, simply because she had no choice. His voice sounded small, fractured, the words slurred and overpronounced. Even so, there was an eloquence, a dignity, about them, which made them sail swiftly, surely into her heart. But all too quickly the moral magnitude of this plea returned to her, and the only thing she could think of was escape.

FIFTEEN

When Sloan heard the knock on the cottage door, he cursed. The absolute last thing he wanted was company. He'd worked hard on this bad mood, and he didn't want anyone messing around with it. And so he yanked open the front door, resolved to get rid of the caller with a few well-chosen words. He was not prepared for what he found gracing his doorstep.

His lips moved as though to call her name, but in the end Sloan uttered not so much as a single syllable. He merely stared at the breathless woman. He guessed that she'd run the entire distance from her house to his. Even had she not been panting, the moist tendrils of hair plastered to a damp forehead would have suggested haste. As would have the patch of sweat spotting the front of her gray sweatshirt.

"I need . . . a friend," Anna gasped.

Sloan remembered telling her not too long ago that they could no longer be just friends, but at this moment, starved for the sight of her, knowing that something was wrong, he'd have been any damned thing she wanted him to be.

Wordlessly, he pushed open the creaky screen door.

Wordlessly, she edged past him.

Though her mind was muddled, Anna noted a dissimilar number of things all at once: the cottage was sparse, stern even, in appearance; she was out of breath—God, was she out of breath!; she was also cold—how could she be cold when she felt flushed, when warm beads of sweat ran between her breasts?; and last, but by no means least, she knew that she shouldn't be here, but she didn't care. She had to be with Sloan.

Anna's gaze connected with his, and she offered the only explanation she could for standing in the middle of his living room. "I had nowhere else to go."

In truth she had slipped into automatic pilot, unaware of where she was headed until the lighthouse, and the keeper's dwelling, had come into view. Once she'd known her destination, her pace had quickened.

Her coming to him, for whatever reason, pleased Sloan, and he didn't care one hoot in hell that it shouldn't have. He'd had all he could take of denial.

Nodding toward the sofa, sensing that she was about to drop from exhaustion, he said, "Sit down."

Anna did, feeling her legs shaking from overexertion. Her hands trembled, too, from a surfeit of emotion. She watched as Sloan walked from the room, and didn't even have the energy to question where he was going. Instead she lay her head on the back of the sofa and closed her eyes. She was still in that position when she heard Sloan speak.

"Here."

Though she could have remained forever lost in the

satin folds of his voice, Anna forced her eyes open. He stood before her, tall, lean, magnificently muscular in a pair of faded jeans and a worn T-shirt. Though it was already midmorning, his rumpled hair had seen no comb, his stubble-shadowed face, no razor. Her guess was that he'd recently crawled from bed. Had she burned in hell from the questioning, she, nonetheless, wondered what kind of lover he'd be.

Sitting up, she reached for the glass of water.

Sloan noted that her hand trembled as she drew the glass to her lips, lips that wore not a trace of lipstick, lips that he'd sell his soul to taste. Her breathing had slowed, however, until her chest rose and fell with a more normal rhythm. Beneath her sweatshirt he saw the outline of her full breasts. He didn't even try to censure the thought that came next. He wanted to touch her breasts. He wanted to touch all of her, just as he wanted her to touch all of him. He wanted them to be lovers.

He stepped a safer distance away.

"What's wrong?" he asked.

Anna took another swallow of water, set the glass on the coffee table, and said casually, "Jack asked me to help him end his life."

Sloan blinked, paused for several moments, then said in disbelief, "What?"

Calmly, too calmly, Anna pushed moist strands of hair from her forehead and said, "My husband asked me to kill him."

Sloan said nothing as he allowed her statement to sink in. When it did, he replied, "Jesus Christ! You can't be serious."

"Oh, but I am," Anna said. "Dead serious." When she realized her apt choice of words, she gave a short laugh. "Pardon my pun."

Sloan made no response. His legs now every bit as unstable as Anna's, he eased into a nearby chair. For what seemed an eternity, neither he nor Anna spoke. Finally his gaze pinned her. "What did you say?"

She shook her head. "I honestly don't remember. I was so stunned, so shocked. He had hinted at it once before. Something about everyone, including himself, being better off if he was dead, but this time he came right out with it." She sighed unevenly, a clear indication that emotions rippled beneath the surface of her deceptive calmness. "He meant it. He wasn't just being dramatic."

"Jesus Christ!" Sloan repeated, this time in a solemn whisper.

Another silence descended. Into this one slithered a base thought that Sloan immediately loathed himself for. If Jack Ramey was dead, Anna would be free. And if Anna was free . . . Sloan couldn't even allow this thought to reach a conclusion. How could he entertain such a sick notion?

Anna's thoughts ran along similar lines. *I'm trapped in this body. Free me.* At some point during the long, exhausting run to the lighthouse, Anna had realized that in freeing Jack she'd likewise be freeing herself—from an ongoing nightmare, from a loveless marriage. My God, how could she even think such a terrible thing!

Restless, Anna stood and walked to the nearest window. It was a perfect summer morning, a wonderful time to be alive, a strange time to be discussing death. With clear, bright sunshine streaming in—truth could not hide in the sunshine—there was one other thing she must admit. To herself. To Sloan.

"What frightened me most about his request was that it didn't frighten me enough."

Anna had realized this as she'd raced toward the lighthouse. She'd realized one other thing, as well. Though Jack's request had stunned her, she'd curiously felt closer to him than she had for a long while. He'd turned to her in his hour of need, placing his faith in her. Just the way he had during the loving years of their marriage. For one moment she'd turned cold with fear as she'd considered just how far she might be willing to go to honor the love they'd once known.

"What do you mean?"

Anna turned toward Sloan, the toasty warmth of the sun hugging her shoulders. Even so, she continued to feel cold, continued to feel as though a frigidness had invaded her being, had permeated every cell. Could this man make the cold disappear? Could this man warm her? And why couldn't she leave these questions as untouched as she herself must remain? She forced her mind back to Sloan's query.

"When I was ten years old, my dog was hit by a car." Anna could tell that Sloan didn't quite understand how this answered his question, but that he was prepared to wait her out. "She was a beautiful blond-and-black collie. I had named her Ribbons because she was so soft. Anyway, she dug her way out of the backyard. She was bad about that. One afternoon she got out and was struck by a passing car. To this day I remember the horrible thud and the pitiful little moans she made as she lay there in the street."

Anna seemed lost in a maze of painful memories. As stupid as it was, Sloan wanted to rush to her and comfort her for something that had occurred more than thirty years before. He couldn't stand the thought of her ever having been, ever being, in pain.

Finally Anna stepped from the past and continued. "The vet told us that it would be best to put her to sleep, that she was fatally injured, that it was only a matter of time until she died, anyway."

"And so you did?"

"Yes." Anna sighed fretfully as other disturbing memories closed in. "That same year my grandmother died of cancer. Toward the end she was in a great deal of pain. I remember how she'd just lay in the hospital

bed and moan, those same pitiful little sounds that
Ribbons had made. With the naiveté of a ten-year-old,
I asked Mother when we were going to put Granny to
sleep. She, of course, explained to me that you couldn't
put people to sleep. Only animals. To the child I was,
that made no sense. It defied all logic. And I'm not
sure the adult I became understands it, either."

"A lot of people agree with you."

This appeared to be all the encouragement that
Anna needed. "I believe one has the right to decide
when to terminate his or her life. I couldn't fault someone for helping a loved one to do that. If life has ceased
to have quality, meaning, perhaps it's even our moral
duty to help those we love meet death mercifully."
Anna hesitated, realizing the magnitude of what she
was saying. "Does that shock you?"

Sloan thought of the unbearable suffering he'd been
through when held prisoner. How many times had he
prayed that someone, anyone, would kill him? How
many times had he wanted to kill himself if he'd but
had the means? And after his release, when he'd had to
face his cowardly actions, there had been a time or two
when he'd seriously considered ending his emotional
torture.

"No," he said, "You haven't shocked me. Sometimes
death can be a friend."

Anna was so caught up in her own crisis, she didn't
hear the personal note in Sloan's reply. "I'm not saying
I'd be a party to a mercy killing—I'm not certain I'd
have the courage—but I couldn't fault anyone for taking his or her own life or for helping a loved one do so.
If one is ill and isn't going to get better . . ." She trailed
off.

Sloan thought that of all the people he knew, Anna
was most likely to have the courage. She was strong.
Circumstances had forced her to be. She also felt
deeply. Only someone who did could muster the kind of

moral conviction needed to commit such a controversial act. Again he found this line of thinking troubling, and so he picked up the trail she had abandoned.

"And your husband isn't going to get better?"

Anna didn't even have to ponder the question. "Only qualitatively. He might get better, but he'll never be well. In the end the diabetes will kill him. Tomorrow. Next month. Next year. In five years." She shrugged. "It's anyone's guess."

Anna thought back to Dr. Goodman's visit the day before. The usually optimistic physician had seemed, for the first time, guarded and cautious, almost as though he was making certain that she understood the seriousness of her husband's condition.

"The kidney infection isn't getting any better," she said. "Plus, there's a place on Jack's leg that Dr. Goodman's worried about. And, of course, Jack has ceased even the pretense of trying to recuperate from the stroke." Anna smiled sadly. "Not that he ever gave it much of a try. He was tired of the struggle even before the stroke, which I guess is the crux of the issue. One has the right to decide for oneself when the struggle should end, when—" Suddenly she stopped. Running her fingers through her hair, she said, "My God, I can't believe I'm standing here discussing this so calmly, so rationally."

The crack in her voice, the tremble in her hands, told Sloan that she was far from calm. In fact, she had been badly shaken. And he wanted to pull her into his arms and comfort her, protect her. He wanted to make love to her until all the ugliness in the world, all the ugliness in their lives, disappeared. The admission should have been a carnal one, but Sloan realized that it didn't *feel* carnal. Maybe because making love to her seemed natural—just the way everything that had happened between them had seemed, from the beginning, natural, normal, destined.

Anna apparently read his thoughts, for she said, "I want more than anything for you just to hold me, but I can't ask you to. It would be unfair to Jack. Unfair to you. Unfair to me."

Her honesty stunned Sloan.

"The really ironic thing is," she continued, needing to share one more thing with Sloan, "I realized this morning that I don't love him." She repeated the words, as though trying them on for size. "I don't love my husband. And maybe I haven't for a while. I guess I've just been in the habit of thinking I did."

This admission walloped the breath from Sloan.

"What do you mean?"

"Just that." Anna sighed. "Last night he was so emotionally abusive." She went on to tell Sloan about the incident at dinner. "This morning, when he apologized, I saw a glimpse of the man I used to love. Regrettably, it no longer mattered. I no longer loved him. The truth is that he hurt me so often that I stopped feeling anything when I was with him. It was a way to survive the pain."

She laughed, and Sloan could have sworn that the uneven notes bordered on hysteria. Little by little the strain she'd been under, capped by the events of the morning, had taken their toll. The fact that she was usually in control only served to make the contrast so stark, so disquieting.

"Funny," she said, her eyes too bright, "I feel only when I'm with you, things I shouldn't feel at all . . . because I'm married. I no longer love Jack, but I'm committed to him. He's the father of my child, the man I vowed to love and honor and obey . . . but I don't love him. I don't feel with him. . . . I feel only with you."

Sloan realized that she'd begun to ramble, a kind of disjointed discourse. Her trembling had increased, a fact she herself was obviously aware of, because she suddenly, tightly, hugged her arms about her.

"Don't," Sloan begged hoarsely as he came to his feet. He had no idea whether he was pleading with her not to ramble, not to fall apart, or not to say what she was saying. Maybe he was pleading with her not to make him feel more helpless than he could ever remember feeling. God, he wanted to take her in his arms!

"I thought I wanted to feel, but I don't."

"Anna, please . . ."

"I thought feeling anything would be better than feeling nothing."

". . . don't do this . . ."

"Why did you do that, Sloan? Why did you make me feel?"

". . . to you . . ."

"Why, Sloan?"

". . . to me."

"Why! she cried. "Why did you do it?"

Her chest heaved, her eyes, tearless as usual, shone with accusation and with pain. More pain than Sloan could bear. He took a step toward her, then stopped himself. If he touched her, he'd be lost. There'd be no turning back. He wanted to tell her to leave, that her presence overwhelmed his senses, played havoc with his control, but he said nothing, because he didn't have the moral strength to do otherwise.

Anna saw Sloan's tentative step; she saw the pain in his eyes. She knew what her presence was costing him. It was costing her the same thing, but she couldn't make herself leave. But, then, neither could she continue to confront the hurt she saw in his eyes. She turned away and back toward the window, pleading with the sun to warm her, if only for a minute. She felt cold, so cold, and the trembling now seemed to be coming from deep inside her.

Leave, Anna told herself, *before you beg him to hold you.*

Leave, Sloan pleaded, *before I take you in my arms.*

Now, while you can.
Now, while I'll let you.
Go! Anna ordered.
Go! Sloan commanded.

Silently, without looking back, Anna walked toward the door. She grasped the doorknob and tried to turn it. It wasn't an easy task with her shaking. She tried again. This time she twisted frantically—she had to leave while she could!—and was rewarded by the handle giving way. She pulled. The door opened—a half inch, an inch, an inch and a half.

From out of nowhere a hand appeared and closed the door.

With a detached objectivity Anna studied the hand. It was large, masculine looking, with long, lean fingers. Just above the knuckle of each finger grew a tuft of coal-black hair. Hair similarly sprinkled the back of the hand, which tapered to a wrist both slender and strong in appearance. From there the black hair raced wildly, sexily, up a muscularly corded arm.

Though he wasn't touching her, Anna sensed Sloan's presence behind her—a daring intimidation, a sweet temptation. *Trapped.* There was that word again, the one she'd used so often of late to describe herself; yet this time she didn't detest the word. In fact, right this second she loved the word above all others. This time she was gloriously trapped . . . between Sloan and the door—imprisoned not by contact, but by the need for it. She wanted to feel his body against hers, more dearly than she wanted another breath.

"Go," Sloan whispered, his breath harsh and ragged, telling of the struggle being waged within him.

"I can't," she said softly, unevenly. "You're holding the door."

"Tell me to release it." Sloan's voice had grown dark, demanding, demon riddled.

Anna closed her eyes, listening to the discordant

rhythm of her heart. It seemed to fill her head with deafening thunder. She should do precisely as he'd bade her, but the words refused to be spoken.

"Tell me, Anna," Sloan begged, desperate for her to exert the control he'd lost. "Dammit, tell me!"

"I can't!" she cried, the memory of too many long, lonely nights crowding her heart.

Anna heard Sloan's rough intake of air, even as she felt his other hand splay against the door, penning her.

"Then tell me what you want," Sloan commanded.

"What I want doesn't matter."

"Tell me what you want."

"Sloan . . ."

"Tell me what you want!"

What *did* she want? Anna thought. To feel? Not to feel? To remember what is was like to be wanted, desired? To feel warm again?

"Hold me," she heard herself saying, thinking how simple the answer had been all along.

Even if he'd had the will to continue fighting against his own need, Sloan didn't have the strength to ignore hers. And so, willingly defeated, he gave in to the inevitable. His hands fell away from the door frame, hovering only momentarily before settling on her upper arms. His touch was hesitant, light—that of a butterfly landing on a delicate flower. Gently, he turned her around, their gazes meeting briefly but boldly. Then he pulled her into his arms.

The act was so incredibly natural that Anna wondered why she'd fought it. Surely there could be nothing wrong with enjoying the fortresslike strength of Sloan's wide chest. Surely she couldn't be faulted for cozying her cheek against his massive shoulder, or for banding her arms about him and hanging on with all her might. Even as she rested against him, she could feel her cold body, like a thief, stealing his warmth.

It felt so right to hold her that Sloan thought he'd

fought, in vain, against something that hadn't even needed fighting against. And he realized that now that he'd touched her, he was lost. Now that he'd touched her, he had to go on touching her for a little while longer. He excused his reasoning by reminding himself that she was still trembling, a fine shivering, as though she'd been lost in the middle of a winter storm. Maybe he was trembling too. He couldn't be sure.

He was certain, though, that his face was buried in her hair and that he smelled the clean fragrance of shampoo, which he found supremely intoxicating. Just the way he found the swell of her breasts sexy, along with the tiny sigh she made as she settled against him.

"Anna," he whispered, simply because it seemed important, vital, to say her name.

She felt his breath, her name, on her hair. Her name had never sounded so sweet, so filled with life. Her own life had been so barren for so long that she instinctively turned her face toward his.

He, too, acted instinctively, doing what he'd wanted to do so often. He threaded his fingers through her silken hair, drawing the playful curls back from her face. When her forehead came into view, he planted a small kiss there. He hadn't intended to do so, but it had seemed like the right thing.

Anna moaned, liking the feel of his hot breath on her skin. In fact, she liked it so much that she felt compelled to say, "Don't make me feel. I don't want to. I mustn't."

"No," he whispered, "I won't make you feel."

Sloan wondered if Anna heard the contradiction in her words. In the past she hadn't wanted to feel, because it hurt. Now she thought she mustn't. Even so, as she spoke of not feeling, she nuzzled Sloan's nose with her own. Nature kicked in, and he nuzzled hers. He realized that their lips were close. So close that their breaths were mingling. So close that temptation was banging on the door of their consciences.

"Don't," she whispered.

"No," he whispered back.

Though she'd willed herself to feel nothing, she sensed her vulnerability. And why was she moving her head just that little bit to cause his lips to hover above hers?

"No," she whispered, as his heated breath washed over her, "we can't. *I* can't."

Even as she spoke, she felt a sense of expectancy, an anticipation, and her heart thrummed loudly, painfully as she waited for the kiss that she'd known all along was coming, simply because it must, simply because neither one of them could stop it.

"No," he repeated, but he knew he was lying. He was going to kiss her—no matter what she said, no matter what he said.

His lips closed over hers, softly, tenderly, as though he'd kissed her a hundred times before. Anna didn't play coy. She kissed him back, and she felt. All kinds of things. Simple things, like astonishment. How could she have forgotten so completely the beauty of something as natural as a kiss? And yet, part of her had not forgotten, for feelings of pleasure traveled seemingly well-worn pathways, making her feel giddy, making her heart race, making her blood hum a heated song. Amid the astonishment, amid the pleasure, she nonetheless felt a little frightened.

"No," she said when his mouth eased from hers, "I don't want to feel."

"Yes, you do," Sloan responded, angling her chin upward so he could deliver tiny kisses all along the length of her neck. Her skin tasted slightly salty.

She moaned again. "No."

"Yes," he countered, dropping a kiss at the hollow of her throat as she arched her head backward.

"No," she repeated, but she was aware of seeking out his lips even as she spoke.

She lowered her head.

He raised his.

When she again felt his warm breath beating against her lips, she whispered one more feeble protest, "No!"

Sloan's lips claimed hers with the purest of affirmations, and the world exploded. This kiss was nothing like the first. It had neither gentleness nor simplicity. This kiss was rough and raw, the product of too much denial, too much need. Desire ruled, and Anna opened her mouth to Sloan at the slightest hint of pressure. When his tongue slipped inside, mating with hers, sweetly, silkily, she heard one word screaming in her head, her heart.

Yes!

Yes, to all the times she'd wanted to defy the denial she'd forced upon herself. Yes, to all the lonely nights she'd lain awake wanting what she couldn't admit to wanting. Yes, to Sloan's kiss. And yes, to the wonderfully complex feelings roaming through her. Her head spun, her heart palpitated, her blood boiled. She felt hot and cold, light and heavy, full and empty. She felt like a woman. She felt *human*. And, dear God, it wasn't a bad thing to feel!

Sloan loved the way her response was so honest, so open. She wanted him as a lover, and she wasn't playing games to the contrary, a fact that fueled his own desire. When her knees threatened to buckle, he backed her against the door, gently urging the proof of his own need against her.

Anna had forgotten what an aroused male felt like. She had forgotten how truly awing, how beautiful, a man's body was. She had likewise forgotten how heady it was to be the inspiration of such masculine power. Making love with this man would be so right. In fact, nothing in the whole of her life would ever be this right. Suddenly that made it seem wrong. It would be easier than anything she'd ever done, to become this man's lover. But that would be a betrayal not only of Jack, but also of herself. How could she live with doing either?

Dragging her mouth from Sloan's, Anna said, "I can't." Her eyes, dark with passion, pleaded for understanding, pleaded with him to know that she wanted to, but she couldn't.

They stared at each other, both breathing hard and fast, two pairs of lips wet and warm from the other's kisses. Slowly, Sloan released her and stepped away. He turned his back to Anna. She could see his shoulders heaving with the effort to regain control of his emotions, of his body.

"Sloan, I—"

Without looking in her direction he held up his hand, indicating for her to give him a little time. In the silence that fell between them, Anna heard the ticking of a clock, the clanging of a distant buoy.

"I'm sorry," she said.

Sloan pivoted toward her, and she could see the passion still clouding his eyes. Taking a deep breath, he said thickly, "I want you to understand something. I want you, in every way that a man can want a woman. I want you more than I've ever wanted anything or anybody."

"I want you too," Anna replied. "But this is wrong. What's happening between us is wrong."

"No," Sloan said, crossing back to her. "What's happening between us isn't wrong. Only the timing is wrong."

With a tenderness that melted Anna's heart, Sloan drew the crooked knuckles of his hand across her cheek. She couldn't help leaning into his caress.

"You belong to me," he said. "You've belonged to me from the first time I saw you on the beach. I didn't know it then, but I do now. I don't care if you have a husband. It wouldn't matter if you had a hundred. You belong to *me!*"

Sloan spoke with such a fierce possessiveness that it startled him. He could never remember feeling this passionately about another human being. Perhaps about anything. How had this woman so bewitched him? How had she managed to make him care so much? So much that he wouldn't let anybody hurt her. And that anybody included himself.

"Ah, Anna," he said, "I'd give anything to be an uncaring son of a bitch. I'd give anything to be able to live with saying or doing whatever it would take to make you my lover, but I can't do that. In the end you'd hate yourself, and me." He laughed. "We defy our own code of ethics at our own peril."

Anna didn't hear the harshness of Sloan's laugh, or the fact that he'd shared more of his past than he'd intended. She heard only his next words.

"Don't come back, Anna," he said, his voice eerily stripped of all emotion, although his body throbbed. "If you do, I can't promise that I won't be a son of a bitch. In fact, though I'll hate myself for it, I'm pretty sure I'll do anything I can to make you my lover."

And so, Sloan sent Anna home, to a husband she didn't love, a man she was shackled to because of vows that had been pledged . . . till death did them part.

Anna returned home more shaken than she'd left. As she entered the house, fearing that her thoughts might be transparent, she tried to erase from her mind the events of the last hour. Even so, she felt different, and worried that she looked it. Could a woman hide the fact that she'd just been kissed by a man other than her husband? Could she hide the fact that she'd wanted to make love to this man, or that her body still hadn't cooled from that heated need?

Knowing that she must find a way to go on with her life she forced herself to check on Jack. She expected to find him halfheartedly going through the motions of exercising. He wasn't. Instead he merely sat in the wheelchair, staring out the window toward the sea, although there wasn't a view of the ocean from that location. The nurse was arranging the covers on the bed.

"Finished with the exercises so soon?" Anna asked, striving for a normalcy she didn't feel.

Ken turned, hesitated, said, "We, uh, we decided not to do them today."

Surprised, Anna glanced over at Jack. He ignored her, making her suspect that what Ken had really meant was that Jack had refused to do the exercises.

"I suppose it won't hurt to miss a day," she said.

Still, Jack acknowledged her presence in no way, which Anna realized might be for the best. She, too, would ignore him—kindly, benignly. In particular she would ignore the grim request he'd made of her. There was no other way to handle it. Now if only she could ignore Sloan's telling her that she belonged to him, the feel of his lips sweetly claiming hers, his body making it all too evident that he desired her as she desired him.

"Oh, your daughter called," Ken said.

The mention of Meg was like ice-cold water being thrown at her. It also put the last hour into a whole new perspective. Meg must never—never!—find out what had transpired at the lighthouse.

"I told her that I thought you were down on the beach. She said to tell you that she'd be home for the weekend." At Anna's look of surprise he said, "Something about a couple of her classes having been canceled."

"That's great she's coming home," Anna said, meaning it, yet regretting, too, that she wouldn't have the time alone. Maybe she was afraid her daughter would take one look at her and start asking questions that she didn't want to answer. Meg had already proved herself too inquisitive where Sloan was concerned.

"You ready for that coffee?" Ken asked, addressing Jack. Jack said nothing, merely sitting passively as Ken took hold of the handles of the chair. "We're going to have coffee in the breakfast room," Ken said to Anna. "A little change of scenery might be nice."

Again Anna suspected that Ken's remark had fallen short of his meaning. Ten to one he meant that his patient was depressed and he hoped a change in surroundings would help perk him up.

"That's a good idea," Anna replied.

As the chair was wheeled past her, Anna wondered if Jack would make eye contact with her. He didn't. In seconds she heard them in the kitchen, with Ken delivering a one-sided conversation about the weather. Anna suspected that, even if Jack had taken pad and pen with him, the nurse would still be talking to himself. At the thought of the pad Anna glanced around and saw it lying on the small table. She stepped forward, picked up the writing tablet, and read: *don't want to*. That was followed by two more entries, obvious responses to Ken's queries about why Jack didn't want to exercise: *tired* and *don't feel well*.

Sighing, Anna dropped the notepad back onto the table. As she did so, a thought occurred to her, leaving a frown on her brows. She picked up the pad again and flipped back a page or two. At the sight of the messages Jack had written earlier, messages that could easily be interpreted as a plea for her to help him end his life, Anna's heart skipped a beat. What if Ken had seen them? Immediately came the answer that he hadn't. How could he? Jack kept the pad with him, and he'd already covered that page with another.

Even as Anna began to relax, another unsettling thought came to her. What if Meg was to see it? The answer was obvious. Meg mustn't. Discovering the depths of her father's depression would do nothing but upset her. Hadn't she herself been upset to learn the somber turn of Jack's thoughts? No, Meg had quite enough on her mind dealing with her father's illness and medical school. Anna ripped the page from the pad, folded it in quarters, and stuffed it inside the pocket of her pants. She'd decide later what to do with it.

Later came after Ken had left for the day. Before going he'd mentioned to Anna that Jack's depression seemed to be getting out of hand, that perhaps he needed professional help to deal with it. For a moment Anna wondered if he'd seen the note, after all, but concluded that she was just being paranoid again. Jack's recent behavior, particularly his refusal to do his exercises, was sufficient indication that his depression had gone beyond the norm for a person recovering from a stroke. Anna had agreed that calling in a mental-health expert was a good idea. Right now, though, she needed to get rid of the note.

Her plan formulated, she walked to the living room and pulled back the screen of the fireplace. Burning the note would perhaps burn Jack's plea from her mind. Placing the folded paper inside the fireplace, she struck a match. Eager flames lapped at the fragile sheaf. As quickly as the fire burst to life, it began to die, to fade into nothing more than a heap of gray ash.

Anna willed herself to think of nothing, not of pleas or pledges or passionate kisses. It just seemed better that way.

SIXTEEN

September

Anna thought that the courtroom looked and sounded like a three-ring circus. In the first ring performed the newly selected jury, which the court had taken two hard days and nights, and both side's every peremptory challenge, to seat. The net result, nine men and three women, had pleased Harper, who had stated right up front that they wanted as few women on the jury as possible. Women, he insisted, were less likely to be forgiving of infidelity. So far the jury's performance had consisted of being sworn in. Following that, court had recessed for fifteen minutes and the jury had filed from their sequestered box; Anna watched them, torn between thinking that they looked like ordinary people, and knowing that they weren't. The fact that they controlled her and Sloan's future made them quite extraordinary.

Restless, Anna glanced toward the second ring of the

circus. It consisted of the gallery, which contained the usual interested spectators, plus the press. Of this latter, which seemed to be a species unto itself—Homo gawkus—there was a God's lavish. In fact, so many reporters had shown up that the judge, fearing that the entire courtroom would be reporters and nothing else, had restricted the press to the first five rows on the prosecution's side. This had delighted Hennessey, since it meant having his audience nearby, but it had displeased the reporters, who were virtually held captive. If they got up, they risked losing their seats. All except Jake Lugaric, who appeared and disappeared very much like the vampire Harper had accused him of being. His place was always held by a black-haired woman with a complexion paler than a corpse, a sight that further enhanced his ghoulish mystique.

Anna watched as Jake Lugaric reentered the room, with a dramatic flair that suggested he practiced entering rooms. Dark-haired, dark-eyed, and dressed in a rumpled tweed sports coat, he passed among the spectators, handing out sparkling smiles and an occasional autograph. He created as much news as he reported, and accordingly, word floated around town that he'd arrived at the courthouse only at noon, leaving the impression that he couldn't waste his valuable time on jury selection, only on the trial proper.

"I see that Dracula has returned from the crypt," Harper said.

The comment forced Anna's attention to what she considered the third ring of the circus, the area occupied by the prosecution and the defense. Richard Hennessey and his assistant, an incipient little man who gave the impression of never having been excited in the whole of his small life, had their heads bent together, while Harper and Sloan had opted for a little exercise, which had meant a walk to the water cooler and back.

"I wonder how he knew the jury was nearing selection," Sloan said.

"Yeah, I wonder," Harper said. "Maybe the cadaver who holds his seat." Then, in a quick change of subjects, Harper said, "Look, I know we've gone over this before, but let's hit it one more time. Remember that the gag order prevents saying anything to the press, plus no outbursts, no matter who says what. On the other hand, it's perfectly all right to show that you're concerned. As I've said before, the jury wants to see that you're human."

Anna didn't know how to tell Harper that she couldn't show what she wasn't feeling, and these days she wasn't feeling much. She just felt dazed, as though she moved about in a cloud, which was all right with her. She'd tried feeling, she'd tried being human, and had discovered that both were a whole lot less than they were cracked up to be. However, when the jury took their seats, when the judge bustled in, when the bailiff proclaimed that court was in session, fear gnawed at Anna's composure.

Sensing this, Sloan whispered, "It's going to be all right. I swear."

Anna knew that the promise was as valuable as fool's gold, yet Sloan's having made it consoled her anyway.

"Is the prosecution ready?" boomed Judge Waynon, a big, beefy man.

"We are," Richard Hennessey replied.

"Is the defense ready?"

"Ready," Harper responded.

"The prosecution may then make its opening statement." Richard Hennessey was half out of his chair when Judge Waynon leaned forward in his, piercing the crowd of onlookers with a pair of heated green eyes. "Before we begin, however"—Richard Hennessey eased back in his chair—"I want to make one thing perfectly clear to this courtroom. This court will not tolerate any disruption in these proceedings. Not for even so much as a New York minute. Any, *all*"—this word thundered throughout the room—"violators will be removed."

The silver-haired bailiff tapped, as though for emphasis, the gun that hung low over his too-snug brown uniform.

When Howard Waynon had given the crowd time to absorb his warning, he announced, "Let's begin, Mr. Hennessey."

Richard Hennessey, every blond hair in place, his navy suit impeccably pressed, needed no further prompting. As quick as a flash he sprang to his feet, adjusting first one cuff, then the other, of his stiffly starched pure linen shirt. He approached the jury box and stood exactly midway of it, one manicured hand on the railing. He looked as though he were about to have a confidential chat with his very best friends.

"Ladies and gentlemen of the jury, it is fact that on the night of August twenty-second Jack Ramey met his death in the form of an overdose of insulin."

The word *death* bounded about the cavernous room like a ricocheting bullet, striking the walls papered in mint-green and mauve, the pews worn shiny with occupancy, the dark-wooded judge's bench, where the word *justice* had been carved so carefully. Justice. Anna wondered if justice would be served by the end of the trial. And exactly what was justice in this case?

"It is also fact," Hennessey continued, "that there were three people in the house that night with Jack Ramey—his sister, his daughter, his wife. While all three unquestionably had the means and opportunity to administer that lethal overdose—the insulin used to achieve death was kept right there in the house—only one of the three had motive."

Anna heard the words, even felt their chill, but on some elemental plane could not accept the fact that they were being said of her. The words, the implication, were simply too harsh.

"I will present witnesses who will testify to the unhappiness of the Ramey marriage, to the fact that Jack Ramey, depressed and ill, begged is wife to help him end his life, to the fact that she burned that note so as not to incriminate herself"—a perfectly planned pause followed—"and her lover."

This word produced the hoped-for results—shock on the jurors' faces, rumblings of disgust from the audience.

"Yes, ladies and gentlemen of the jury, her own daughter will testify to Anna Ramey's shameless infidelity, while another eyewitness will place her lover"—here Hennessey looked over at Sloan—"at the scene of the crime that night."

Anna heard the restless whispers, the rap of the judge's gavel, but mostly she heard Richard Hennessey's spellbinding voice. He was good. Really good. With the kind of sincere delivery that had her half believing that he regretted what he was having to say. Of course, the other half of her knew that the delivery was calculated to stir up everyone's righteous indignation. Yes, Richard Hennessey was good, and that fact frightened her, but she'd burn in Hades before she let him see her fear.

"There were others present the night Jack Ramey died, but no one benefited from Jack Ramey's death except the two people you see seated at the defense table. And these two had everything to gain—her freedom, their future."

Richard Hennessey said something more about the jury's not confusing the murder with a mercy killing; then he charged that Anna and Sloan must not be allowed to escape their deserved punishment. Anna watched as Richard Hennessey, as satisfied as a man after good sex, took his seat.

A silence followed, a silence that challenged the defense attorney to be as good, as convincing. For several drawn-out moments Harper made no move, although the eyes of the entire court were trained on him.

Finally the judge asked, "Mr. Fleming, does the defense wish to make an opening statement?"

Anna felt the brush of Harper's chair as it was slowly pushed from the table. With the same unhurriedness the lawyer rose.

"Yes, Your Honor, the defense does."

"Please do so, then."

One hand in his pants pocket, the jacket of his steel-gray suit unbuttoned, Harper approached the jury with an obviously troubled look. Even after he stood before them, he seemed to be searching for words. Finally, as though he knew that he was taking up the court's time, he spoke.

"Well," he said in a deep sigh, "that was a fine opening statement. No, no," he amended, "it was more than fine. It was moving, stirring. I'll tell you the truth, I myself was about ready to stitch a scarlet *A* on Anna Ramey's chest."

This produced titters of laughter among members of the jury and the audience. Richard Hennessey, however, didn't crack a smile.

"And I'll confess one other thing to you. My first inclination was to petition this court to simply dispense with these proceedings, to take these two murderers, these two adulterers"—here Harper waved his hand in the direction of his clients—"lock them in the deepest cell of the dankest prison, and throw away the key." Pause. "That was my first inclination."

Harper paced alongside the jury box, making that august body wait for what he had to say next. When he at last stopped, he looked one juror squarely in the eyes and said, "My second inclination was to junk the first, to realize that I'd been taken in by a smooth con artist. Fortunately—for you, for me, for my clients—our judicial system demands more than the prosecutor standing before you with his moving, stirring allegations. He has to prove, beyond a reasonable doubt, that my clients are guilty of what he alleges they are. In short, ladies and gentlemen of the jury, he has to convince you"—he pointed to several individual jurors—"that Anna Ramey and Sloan Marshall are murderers. And he can't do that, because they're not."

This produced hushed talk in a room that had grown silent. Judge Waynon tapped the gavel. The talk died away. Anna waited with the same expectancy as everyone else in the room to hear Harper's next comment.

"Without Mr. Hennessey's moving, stirring rhetoric," Harper continued, "I'm going to tell you what the facts of this case are. I'm also going to tell you what my clients are guilty of, and, yes, they *are* guilty of something. Fact number one," Harper said, holding up his index finger, "Jack Ramey did die of an insulin overdose, but we don't know who administered that fatal overdose. Fact two"—a second finger joined the first—"Jack Ramey did ask his wife, via note, to help him end his suffering, and Anna Ramey did destroy that note. Fact number three," Harper continued, adding a third finger, "Anna Ramey and Sloan Marshall were lovers."

The announcement came so unexpectedly that for a breath-held moment it appeared that no one could believe what he'd just heard. Suddenly talk erupted, and Judge Waynon pounded his gavel. Richard Hennessey looked as though he would have liked to object to the admission. How dare the defense admit so glibly to something that he was going to take great pleasure in forcing them to own up to?

Harper's affirmation of her affair with Sloan took Anna as much by surprise as it did everyone else. She sucked in a sharp lungful of air, feeling that Harper had somehow betrayed her. Oh, she knew that the affair would come out, but she hadn't anticipated Harper confirming it during the first few minutes of the trial. She sensed that Sloan was equally surprised.

Even so, he whispered, "Take it easy."

She felt dozens of pairs of eyes burning her with their curiosity, their condemnation. Her inclination was to hang her head, but she wouldn't. In fact, she forced herself to tilt her chin higher.

"The truth of the matter is," Harper continued, as though he was unaware of the commotion he'd caused, "that Sloan Marshall and Anna Ramey were lovers on one occasion, and that occasion, ironically, occurred the night Jack Ramey died."

A round of murmurs washed across the spectators.

Another tap of the gavel, this time with a warning from the judge. "Mr. Fleming will be allowed to conclude, or I'll clear this courtroom."

The murmurs ebbed away.

"I would remind you, though," Harper said, again as though there had been no interruption, "that you have not been impaneled to decide the guilt or innocence of my clients regarding infidelity. You shall be concerned only with whether they committed murder. And herein, ladies and gentlemen of the jury, lies the flaw in Mr. Hennessey's opening speech. He's asking you to conclude that having an affair necessarily leads to committing murder. Ladies, gentlemen, we all know that can't be true. If everyone having an affair went on to commit murder, our graveyards and prisons would be bursting at the seams."

A smattering of laughter broke out. The prosecutor didn't join in.

And neither did Harper, for when he spoke again, he went directly to the heart of his defense. "No, Anna Ramey and Sloan Marshall did not commit murder that fateful night. They were not the ones to benefit most from Jack Ramey's death. All I ask of you is that you keep an open mind, and an open heart, and I'll give you a viable alternative—that's called *reasonable doubt*—for what happened that night."

With that Harper recrossed the room and took his seat. He left everyone, jury, gallery, and clients alike, wondering just what that viable alternative might be. Anna knew that he'd purposefully left everyone hanging. Shrewd. Hennessey might be good, but Harper was shrewd. Seasoned. And supremely convincing. This last was particularly impressive, Anna thought, when one considered that Harper had managed to plant seeds of doubt concerning her and Sloan's guilt even though Harper himself was uncertain of their innocence.

Below his breath, where only Anna and Sloan could hear, Harper said, "I had to steal his thunder."

Anna knew that it was an explanation for having admitted to the affair. It made sense, but still it stung.

"Call your first witness, Mr. Hennessey," Judge Waynon ordered.

Once more with eagerness Richard Hennessey complied. "The prosecution calls Kenneth Larsen."

It took a few seconds for Kenneth Larsen to make his way from the holding room and be sworn in. He then stated his name and occupation. Anna had never seen him wearing a suit, and he looked like a stranger, a fact underscored by his refusal to glance in Anna's direction.

Hennessey strutted forward, as though he now recognized Harper to be a worthy opponent and relished the idea of doing battle with him. "Mr. Larsen, would you begin by telling this court how you came to know the Ramey family."

"I was hired to take care of Jack Ramey."

"In what capacity?"

"I was hired to be his nurse and his therapist."

"What were your qualifications for those positions?"

"As I said, I'm an R.N.—a Registered Nurse. I'm also

an accredited physical therapist, specializing in stroke rehabilitation."

"How did this latter relate to Jack Ramey?"

"Mr. Ramey was a longstanding diabetic and he'd suffered a stroke, which is not an unusual complication of diabetes."

Hennessey had continued to step forward until he now stood to the right of the witness, careful not to obstruct the jury's view. "What kind of recovery was Jack Ramey making?"

"Poor."

Hennessey affected surprise. "Oh? Had the stroke been that severe?"

"Though partially paralyzed, though he probably never would have recovered one hundred percent, he could have improved. I've had patients who've had similarly disabling strokes and, recoverywise, have fared much better."

"To what do you attribute his lack of improvement?"

"Disinterest. From the beginning he only went through the motions. The last month or so of his life he refused to do even that."

"In your opinion, why was that?"

"He was depressed."

Harper rose. "Objection, Your Honor. With all due respect to Mr. Larsen, I've heard nothing among his credentials that would qualify him in the area of mental health."

Hennessey looked as though he'd just been waiting, wanting, the objection. "The prosecution would contend that, while Mr. Larsen isn't professionally qualified to treat depression, he has nonetheless been trained to recognize it."

"Objection overruled."

Smugly, Hennessey turned his attention back to the witness. "So your medical opinion is that Jack Ramey was depressed?"

"That's correct, and at first it didn't overly concern me. Recovering stroke patients are often depressed."

"Was there a point at which it began to concern you?"

"Yes, it began to concern me on the sixteenth of July."

Again Hennessey feigned surprise, as though this announcement were news to him. "Please tell this court what happened on July sixteen to cause you to be concerned."

Ken Larsen told of arriving at his usual time to discover the bedroom floor strewn with broken porcelain and food, of how Anna Ramey had not had breakfast with her husband that morning, which was not her custom, of how she'd visited him later, then left the house, seemingly upset, of how he himself had found, accidentally, the note that he believed sent Anna Ramey fleeing from the house.

"Note?" Richard Hennessey inquired, as though the witness hadn't been coached up one side and down the other.

"The stroke had affected Jack Ramey's speech, and although he could talk—in fact, he should have been rebuilding his verbal skills—he refused to. Instead he communicated with a pad and pen."

"I see. Tell us about the note you found."

"This was the first time that Jack Ramey had refused to do his exercises. In fact, he adamantly refused. I didn't push him, because it was clear that he was upset. I just wheeled him to the window the way he asked me to. He could hear the ocean from there, and he just sat listening to it. At least I guessed that was what he was doing."

"Objection, Your Honor. What Mr. Larsen guesses is of no concern to us."

"Sustained. Please move ahead to the note, Mr. Larsen."

"The pad that Jack Ramey wrote on had been left on the edge of a small table. As I passed by, I knocked it off. I picked it up and began to straighten the pages." Feeling the need to clarify, he added, "It was a small legal pad, where one page folds over the other. Anyway, when I was turning the pages, one caught my eye."

"What did it say?"

"Something about freeing him, that he was trapped in his body. Then there was the word *easy*, followed by *insulin overdose*, then something about no questions being asked." In regard to the latter, he said, "I assumed he meant that no one would question his death because he was ill."

"Objection, Your Honor. Assumptions fall into the same category as guesses."

"Sustained."

Hennessey appeared unperturbed. "How did you, as a reasoning human being, interpret the note?"

"As a plea for his wife to end his life."

Harper stood. "Your Honor"—Hennessey started to interrupt, but Harper cut him off—"the defense stipulates that the note was, indeed, a request from Jack Ramey to his wife to help him end his life. The defense also concedes that Anna Ramey burned that note in the fireplace later that day. Perhaps, with these facts entered into the record, we can move on?"

"Yes, perhaps we can," Judge Waynon agreed.

Hennessey had wanted to milk the note for all it was worth and wasn't thrilled with having to move on, but he did, salvaging what he could.

"Did Jack Ramey ever mention the note to you?"

"No. He never even knew that I saw it."

"Did anyone else mention the note?"

"I waited for Mrs. Ramey to tell me about it, but she never did. When I left that afternoon, I suggested that her husband might need professional health care to deal with his depression."

"What, if anything, was her response?"

"She agreed that he needed professional help."

"What happened then?"

"To my knowledge she never called in any professional help."

All along the way Harper had made several whispered comments to Marilyn Graber, who sat directly behind him. He'd also made notes to himself. At this last question and answer, he scribbled a question to Anna: *Why didn't you call in professional help?* Anna took the pen and wrote: *His physical health worsened.* Harper nodded his head.

"Mr. Larsen, what medical equipment did you routinely use in connection with Jack Ramey's illness?"

"The usual disposable needles and syringes. It was my responsibility to keep the supply stocked."

"Did you ever notice any other needles and syringes in the Ramey home?"

"I did. I saw a large syringe, fitted with a large needle, in the silverware drawer in the kitchen of the Ramey home."

"Tell us when you saw it there."

"On several occasions."

"When was the last time you saw it?"

"The day before Jack Ramey died."

"And were that syringe and needle there the morning after Jack Ramey's death?"

"No, they were not."

"What medicines, if any, did you use in the treatment of Jack Ramey?"

"Primarily insulin. Two kinds were always kept on hand—regular insulin and Novolin."

"When was the last time you saw the bottle of regular insulin?"

"On the day Jack Ramey died."

"You're certain there was a bottle of regular insulin in the house on that day?"

"Positive."

"One other question. Did you have occasion to notice the atmosphere in the house?"

"Atmosphere?"

"As regarded the relationship between Anna and Jack Ramey."

Again Harper objected. "Your Honor, now the prosecution would have us believe that Mr. Larsen is a marital expert."

"After having been part of the household for almost three months, he must assuredly have formed an opinion."

"My point precisely. All he can give the court is his opinion." Suddenly Harper had a change of mind. "On second thought, Your Honor, the defense will withdraw its objection."

Though he'd gotten what he'd wanted, Hennessey now looked skeptical, as though he wasn't quite certain he wanted Ken Larsen's opinion, if Harper was going to let him have it without a fight.

"Proceed, Mr. Hennessey," the judge urged.

Richard Hennessey turned his attention back to his witness. "How would you characterize their relationship?"

Without hesitation Ken Larsen answered, "Strained."

"Thank you, Mr. Larsen. The prosecution has no further questions of this witness."

With that Hennessey briskly crossed the floor and took his seat. He leaned over and said something to his assistant. The prosecutor was all sharp features and crisp movement, while Harper, who rose slowly from his chair, gave the impression of casualness, of a man who had time and wouldn't be rushed. He walked toward Ken Larsen as though greeting a visitor in his home. He smiled.

"Mr. Larsen, I have only a few questions. Am I correct in assuming that during your medical career you've nursed a significant number of patients?"

"Yes, of course."

"And of that significant number a—" Harper paused. "Let's use the word *significant* again. A significant number were stroke victims, as was Jack Ramey?"

"Yes."

"You've had occasion, then, to observe the family unit more than once in the throes of a health crisis?"

"Yes."

"Had you never, before observing Anna and Jack Ramey, witnessed any strain in a marital relationship because of health problems? Was their situation unique?"

"Yes. I mean, no, it wasn't unique."

"The truth is, is it not, Mr. Larsen, that illness creates strain within a family? Any kind of illness. Certainly something as chronic as diabetes, as traumatic as a stroke."

"Yes, that's true."

"In your opinion, was Anna Ramey a good wife?"

The question came so smoothly, so naturally, that it took Richard Hennessey a second to realize that it had been asked. When he did, he jumped to his feet. "Objection. Calls for a conclusion."

Harper dragged his hand across his balding pate. "Your Honor, I'm not certain that I understand Mr. Hennessey's objection. This witness's conclusions, opinions, were quite acceptable to the prosecution only minutes ago. What's happened to discredit them?"

"Objection overruled," Judge Waynon said.

Harper turned back to the witness. "Was Anna Ramey, in your opinion, a good wife? For example, did she share in her husband's care?"

"Yes."

"Did she visit with him?"

"Yes."

"Did she take her meals with him?"

"Yes."

"Did she encourage him?"

"Yes."

"Did she act caringly, lovingly toward him?"

"Yes."

"I repeat: in your opinion, was she a good wife?"

"Yes, in my opinion she was a good wife."

"Isn't it true that she was such a good wife that she herself was physically and emotionally exhausted from the trauma of caring for her husband? Isn't it true that her daughter, her sister-in-law, Dr. Goodman, even you yourself, were concerned about her?"

"Yes, that's true."

In an apparent change of subject Harper asked, "You said earlier that when you saw the note Jack Ramey had written asking his wife to help him end his struggle, you were concerned. Am I remembering correctly?"

"Yes, I said that, and yes, I was."

"Do you think it possible that Anna Ramey might have been concerned too? You did say, I believe, that she left the house upset."

"Yes, I saw her leave—I was in the laundry room and she sailed right past me—and I'd say she was upset."

Harper frowned. "Huh. That would be an odd reaction for a woman just waiting for the opportunity to do her husband in."

"Objection! This court isn't interested in Mr. Fleming's musings."

"Of course it's not, Your Honor, and I withdraw my"—he paused—"musing."

"Mr. Fleming's comment shall be stricken from the record," Judge Waynon said. "Proceed."

"Thank you, Your Honor." Harper turned back to the witness on the stand. "Mr. Larsen, are you a parent?"

Ken Larsen's face brightened. "Yes. I have a four-year-old son."

"Your Honor," Hennessey said, "this witness's private life has no bearing on this case."

"I would ask for a little leeway here, Your Honor," Harper said.

"Granted."

"Thank you." Harper stepped closer to the witness stand. "Mr. Larsen, as a parent, do you ever protect your son from harm?" At the blank look on Ken Larsen's face, Harper added, "For example, do you keep him from running into traffic? Do you keep poisons out of his reach?"

"Of course."

"Then you do everything you can to see that your child isn't hurt, both physically and emotionally?"

"Yes, that's the role of a parent."

"Ah," Harper said, and the single exclamation indicated that he was well pleased with the witness's response. "And you'll stop protecting him when your son reaches what age?"

"I'm not sure I understand."

"When your son reaches what age will you consider your parental obligation over in terms of protecting him?"

"I'm not sure that a parent ever relinquishes that obligation."

"Is it even remotely possible that, when Anna Ramey destroyed her husband's note—the same note that had upset you and Mrs. Ramey herself—she was merely protecting her child? The way any caring parent would? Knowing that her daughter was coming home that weekend, knowing that the note, if seen, would surely upset her, too, might she not have tried to spare her?"

Ken Larsen looked as though this thought had never crossed his mind. Finally he conceded, "I suppose it is possible."

"Now, Mr. Larsen, you seem to attach a great deal of importance to the fact that Anna Ramey didn't call in professional help for her depressed husband. If you were so worried, why didn't you go over her head and talk to Dr. Goodman? You were, after all, the health professional on the scene."

"I thought about it—"

"But never did it," Harper said, taking a calculated risk.

"No, but only because his physical health deteriorated. He spent some time in the hospital, and even when he came home, he was on shaky ground."

"You felt at that time that his physical health took precedence over his emotional health?"

With visible relief Ken Larsen answered, "Exactly."

"Isn't it possible that Anna Ramey felt the same?"

Again, as though this idea were a novel one, the nurse concluded, "Perhaps."

"Let me ask you a question or two about this mysterious syringe and needle that were kept in the silverware drawer." Harper frowned again. "You know, I'm a little confused about something. Jack Ramey died on a Friday night, and you showed up on a Saturday morning, but you didn't normally work on Saturdays, did you?"

"No, I didn't. Dr. Goodman called to tell me of Jack's death. I went by the house to pay my condolences."

Harper nodded. "Of course. I should have realized." No sooner had he said this, however, than a frown once more crinkled his forehead. "But I still don't see how you came to know of the syringe's disappearance. With the court's permission, I'm going to refer to this as a syringe, although we know there was a needle attached to it."

"The record will so note," the judge said.

"The family was having coffee," Ken Larsen explained. "They asked me to join them, and because I knew my way around the house, I got my own. I needed a spoon to stir the cream in my coffee, and when I opened the silverware drawer, I noticed that the syringe was gone."

"In the midst of all this emotional chaos, you noticed that a syringe was missing?"

There was a hesitation, followed by, "Well, actually, I realized it later."

Harper didn't try to hide his surprise. "Later?"

"Your Honor," Richard Hennessey said, "does it matter when Mr. Larsen realized the syringe was missing?"

"Two people are on trial for murder," Harper said. "I'd say that entitles the jury to every fact they can get."

"Agreed. Proceed, Mr. Fleming."

"When did you realize the syringe was missing?" Again Ken Larsen hesitated, casting a furtive glance in the prosecutor's direction. "Let me see if I can jog your memory. Isn't it true that you remembered that the syringe was missing only when the prosecutor specifically asked you about it?"

"It was missing," Ken Larsen said.

"Isn't it true that it was only after Jack Ramey's death had been ruled a murder, only after you'd had time to recall the note, only after the prosecutor had asked you about the syringe, that you conveniently remembered—"

"It was missing."

"—that it was missing?"

"It *was* missing!"

"Your Honor," Richard Hennessey cried, "Mr. Fleming is badgering the witness."

Before the judge could rule, Harper asked, "You're one hundred percent certain?"

"Your Honor!"

"Mr. Fleming," the judge cautioned.

"Yes!" Ken Larsen said, defiantly.

"And can you tell this court with the same one hundred percent certainty what happened to it? Can you tell this court who removed it from that drawer?"

"Your Honor!"

"Mr. Fleming!"

"No!"

"No further questions." Harper was halfway back to his seat when he turned. "Sorry, Your Honor, I do have one last question." Ken Larsen was already standing, as though he couldn't wait to get off the witness stand. "Is it possible that Jack Ramey knew of the syringe's presence in the house?"

"Yes, I suppose it's possible."

"Could he have removed it from the drawer?"

"I don't see how. He was partially paralyzed. He couldn't navigate the wheelchair on his own."

"Not at all, or for any great distance?"

"He could move it a little bit, but—"

"Then he could navigate it?"

"Barely."

"Is that a yes, Mr. Larsen?"

"Yes," the nurse admitted, grudgingly.

"Did you ever push him into the kitchen?"

"Yes, but—"

"Are you one hundred percent certain that Jake Ramey didn't remove that syringe from the silverware drawer?"

Ken Larsen had just been hoisted by his own petard. He'd already admitted that he couldn't testify with one hundred percent accuracy who had removed the syringe from the drawer. If so, he certainly couldn't testify to who hadn't.

"No," Ken Larsen said.

"Thank you, Mr. Larsen. No further questions, Your Honor."

"Mr. Hennessey? Redirect?"

"Just one question, Your Honor," Richard Hennessey said, jumping to his feet. "Mr. Larsen, given Jack

Ramey's disability, given the fact that he had difficulty maneuvering his wheelchair, would you be surprised to learn he had removed the syringe?"

"Yes."

Harper let it stand, simply because the gallery was abuzz with the idea he'd newly planted—that Jack Ramey might have killed himself.

"Because we're approaching the dinner hour," Judge Waynon said, "I'm going to recess this court but reconvene it at seven o'clock. I think it in everyone's best interest if this trial is concluded as soon as possible. Does either the prosecution or the defense object with continuing into the evening?"

Hennessey stood and with his usual enthusiasm said, "No, Your Honor."

Harper stood too. "No objection, Your Honor."

"This court is then recessed until seven o'clock."

"All rise," the bailiff ordered, and those in the courtroom came to their feet just in time to see Judge Waynon, his black robe flapping about him, vacate the bench and disappear through a door.

A hundred voices rose at once, each seemingly in a different key. It sounded like a chorus gone wild. The members of the press rushed out as though the courthouse had suddenly caught on fire—all the reporters except Jake Lugaric.

"The son of a bitch," Harper rumbled.

"Want to try another exit?" Marilyn asked.

"No, we're not going to give him the satisfaction," Harper said.

"I'd love to deck him," Sloan said.

"Don't even think it," Harper ordered. "The press would have a field day with your violent nature." Harper gave a devilish grin. "On the other hand, I could knock him into the middle of next week and get by with it."

"What if I deck him?" Anna said, feeling exhilaration at the upbeat ending to the nurse's testimony.

Harper laughed. Sloan smiled. Anna felt warmed by Sloan's hand, situated at the small of her back. Strong and solid, it whispered that he was there. She had no right to enjoy his nearness and couldn't grow accustomed to it, but nonetheless, for the time being, she reveled in it.

"How do you think the trial went today?" Jake Lugaric asked, meeting the group midway of the aisle. The cadaver held a microphone forward. "You think you can make this suicide thing stick?"

"No comment," Harper said, trying to hustle the defendants past him.

Anna was aware of Sloan slinging an arm possessively about her waist. She also made the idle observation that, up close, Jake Lugaric wasn't nearly as attractive as he was at a distance. Though his smile was nice enough, his face bore evidence of pockmarks. His clothes, though of good quality, looked as though he'd slept in them. And his hair, obviously greased to glisten, simply looked as if it needed a good shampooing.

"How do you think the jury is going to take to an open admission of infidelity?" he asked, now being forced to walk backward as the foursome barreled down upon him. The cadaver followed.

"No comment," Harper repeated, pushing forward. "Just let us by."

Throwing both hands into the air and backing away, Lugaric said, "Yeah, yeah, no problem."

The foursome passed by, headed for the nearby door.

Lugaric called after them. "Surely you don't expect the jury to believe that you two screwed only once."

The arm at Anna's waist tightened. Harper's voice said, "Keep walking. He's only trying to antagonize you."

"He's doing a hell of a good job," Sloan snarled.

"Hey, Commander . . ."

The group had almost reached the door.

". . . what really happened in Beirut?"

Sloan whirled to face a cool, challenging, confrontational Jake Lugaric. Sloan's complexion paled, as if the reporter had just drained him of every drop of blood. In its place came fear, a dark, chilling fear that lingered like a menacing fragrance.

SEVENTEEN

Lugaric's only fishing around," Harper said.

The drive from the courthouse to Harper's office had been a quiet one, except for a few exchanges concerning the trial. Harper again had explained why he'd admitted to the infidelity, while Marilyn had expressed her opinion that the trial had opened well and in their favor. Harper, however, had cautioned against any premature celebration. Throughout the limited conversation, Anna, who'd sat in the backseat with Marilyn, had said nothing, and Sloan had sensed she knew that he and Harper were only waiting for an opportunity to be alone. The second that the two women disappeared into the kitchen to prepare sandwiches, Sloan and Harper huddled together.

"He must know something, or thinks he does, or he wouldn't be fishing around." Sloan, whose heart had yet to settle down, was still shaken from the reporter's earlier question.

"Hey, Commander, what really happened in Beirut?"

When Sloan realized that Harper hadn't contradicted his comment, he asked, "You think he knows something, too, don't you?"

Harper shook his head. "I do not. If Lugaric knew something, it would already be news." Shucking his suit coat and tossing it over the back of the chair, Harper said, "Look at it logically. Lugaric is a man whose talent is ferreting out the garbage in people's lives. He can probably smell it a mile away. Even if there's nothing to smell, he's suspicious and is going to give anything and everything a sniff. He probably came up against those classified documents and is doing nothing more than sniffing around. He probably only wanted to see what your reaction would be."

Feeling that he was suddenly choking, Sloan gave a harsh laugh as he loosened the knot of his black-and-red tie and unfastened the top button of his shirt. "Well, I certainly gave him every reason to suspect that there was something to smell." Then, in his own defense, he said, "He took me by surprise."

"Your reaction wasn't out of line. The part of your past that's public record justifies a strong reaction. My God," Harper said, his voice rising to the occasion, "what man wants to be reminded of being held hostage and tortured?"

"Keep your voice down!" Sloan whispered.

Harper looked incredulous. "Don't tell me Anna doesn't know about your past."

"She knows I was held hostage, she knows I was tortured." A bittersweet memory assailed Sloan, a memory of Anna's fingertips tracing the scars on his back. He turned loose of the thought while he still could. "Look, she doesn't know anything more, and I don't want her to."

"And what do you think she'd do if she did?"

"I don't want to find out."

For a full minute neither man spoke. Finally Harper did. "This is all moot. The documents are classified."

"You said yourself that Lugaric was good at knowing which palm to cross."

"Okay, although I don't think it's that easy to access government documents, I'll concede that anything's possible, but what's the worst that could happen?" Harper answered for Sloan. "It'll make the news, which none of the jury can listen to. There's no way that this kind of testimony can be introduced into the record. It'll have to come from a military source—Nichols—for any of it to have validity, and Nichols can't testify to anything that's classified. So what in hell's the harm if your past does come out?"

Sloan's voice was rough and scratchy as he repeated what he'd said earlier. "I don't want Anna to know."

Harper hiked his hands to his hips in total disbelief. "Do all roads always travel back to Anna?"

Sloan said nothing. In the end it was perhaps the most eloquent of answers.

Richard Hennessey was pissed. To add insult to injury, the son of a bitch was late, according to the prosecutor's imitation Rolex watch. Sighing, he thrummed his fingers against the steering wheel of his red second-hand Porsche, which was parked on one of Cook's Bay's many back roads. The flanking forest cushioned all sound, creating a suffocating silence that Richard Hennessey hated. Once he got to New York, he was going to get an exclusive apartment on a busy downtown street, where he could throw wide the windows and listen to the hustle and bustle of life.

The Ramey murder trial was his ticket to that life but only if he won a conviction. The direct examination of Kenneth Larsen hadn't gone quite as he'd planned, but, then again, it hadn't been a disaster. Hennessey snorted. He was glad as hell that he wasn't in a position to have to convince a jury that Jack Ramey had taken his own life. No, he didn't care how good Fleming was; he wasn't going to make that dog hunt. The truth was that Anna Ramey and her lover were guilty as hell, and even if they weren't, they'd never be able to prove their innocence. Either way he was going to ride their coattails to New York, to freedom, to something better than this goddamned dead town. And the first thing he was going to do was buy himself a brand-spanking-new sports car and a real Rolex.

Checking his watch, which said that he was due back in court in exactly thirty-three minutes, Hennessey said, "Shit! Where is he?"

In answer to his question he heard the whine of an engine and saw a rented car pull into view. It contained a man and a woman—a very pale woman. Jesus, wonder if he was fucking her! Before the car had come to a complete stop, Hennessey threw wide his door. The man got out of his car, while the woman remained inside.

As the man strolled forward, Hennessey realized that he'd never really liked him. They'd gone to the same college and had been fraternity brothers, but they'd barely known each other. Hennessey had thought the guy far too arrogant, far too egotistical. Still, the guy had one quality that he admired: like himself, he was an opportunist.

"What in hell do you mean calling my office?" Hennessey demanded.

"Evening to you, too, Mr. Prosecutor," Jake Lugaric said, totally unruffled by Hennessey's rebuke.

"I thought we agreed not to contact each other."

"Yeah, well, we did," Lugaric said, leaning back against the Porsche, as though sensing that the act would annoy Hennessey. "But that was before I came across something I thought you might be interested in, and if you don't mind my saying so, you might want to show a little gratitude. Considering the fact that the prosecution's not exactly off and running."

Hennessey's face reddened as though he'd been slapped. "What do you mean by that?"

Lugaric shrugged. "Nothing, except Fleming managed to defuse the infidelity issue and plant the seed that Jack Ramey did himself in."

Hennessey's blush deepened. "The trial's only begun. And the infidelity issue is still very much alive. A jury finds defendants guilty for all kinds of reasons, most of which they aren't aware of themselves. All I need is a jury who wants to punish them for having a good time while the husband suffered. And as for the suicide seed being planted, trust me when I say it's never going to sprout." He paused, then added, "And will you get the hell off my car?"

Lugaric pushed from the gleaming vehicle. "My mistake. I pegged you as the kind of guy who liked to keep an ace in the hole. Just in case you needed it." He gave a wave and started back toward the rented car. "Catch you later, counselor."

Lugaric was halfway to his destination before Hennessey's curiosity got the better of him. "What have you got?"

"Nothing you need," Lugaric called back without even turning around.

"What in hell have you got?"

Lugaric halted as he was getting inside the car. He eyed the impeccably dressed prosecutor, then retraced his steps. He told him what he had.

"You've got nothing," Hennessey said.

"Not that I can prove yet, but believe me, I've got a nose for news. Something happened in Beirut, and for a minute today Marshall was scared as shit that I knew what it was. It has something to do with these classi-fied documents I keep bumping into. Trust me on this."

"You can't get inside classified documents, so how are you going to prove anything?"

"Everything can be gotten into." Lugaric looked at Hennessey meaningfully. "If there's enough money."

Hennessey looked aghast. "You can't seriously be suggesting that *I* provide you with the money. I could be suspended—hell, even disbarred!—for that kind of improper conduct."

Lugaric laughed, showing an even row of pearly whites. "Hennessey, you're a hoot! You contact me about making this trial into a media event—'Whatever you have to do,' I believe you said—and now you're worried about improper conduct."

"I'm washing your back, you're washing mine. Expo-sure is as good for you as it is for me."

"Like I said, Hennessey, you're a hoot." Lugaric started back toward the car. "Think about it."

"I haven't seen anything to be impressed with so far," Hennessey called after him.

Lugaric turned. "Nothing newsworthy has happened yet. But it will. And I have a real talent for being on hand when it does."

Hennessey watched him go, thinking again that he really didn't like this arrogant son of a bitch. But, then, he liked dreary Cook's Bay even less.

"Tell this court how you came to suspect foul play in the death of Jack Ramey."

Court had resumed at seven-o-five when the prosecu-tor, with profuse apologies for being late, had charged into the courtroom. He had immediately called Sheriff Tate to the stand. The officer of the law, sworn and seated, his straw hat in his lap, had laboriously an-swered questions about his job and his investigation. Finally they'd come to the crux of the matter.

"Well, to tell you the truth, I didn't suspect foul play in the beginning."

Sloan thought that the response was less than Hennessey had wanted, though the prosecutor did an admirable job of covering up his annoyance. Sloan also thought that Sheriff Tate, though he must surely have testified innumerable times before, was not comfortable doing so.

"And why is that, Sheriff?"

"Well, you know, the man was ill. At least that was the rumor going around town. He'd even been hospitalized a time or two over at the Good Shepherd. I had no reason to suspect that his death wasn't the result of his illness."

"At what point did your opinion change? When did you suspect foul play?"

"Well, it wasn't exactly one given moment, but a building up of facts. You know, several things piled on top of each other."

Again Sloan could tell that Hennessey's patience was wearing thin. In fact, the man had seemed edgy since entering the courtroom. Plus, though he'd been immaculately groomed before, he now looked a little disheveled. His tie was askew, his cuffs uneven, and the new-penny shine of his tasseled loafers had been dulled by what looked like a white powdery dust.

"Tell us about the first thing that led you to suspect foul play," Hennessey insisted.

"Well, Kenny Larsen came to me and told me about the note that Jack Ramey had written to his wife and how he thought she'd burned it, because the note was missing and there was a little heap of ashes in the fireplace."

"That was when you got the court order to halt interment and, in conjunction with Dr. Goodman's wishes, sent the body to Augusta?"

"That's right. I had no choice, but I don't mind telling you, I thought it was a waste of time. You could have knocked me over with a feather when the report came back."

Hennessey ignored his witness's voluntary speculation. "And then you arrested Anna Ramey?"

"Yes."

"When did you suspect that Sloan Marshall was involved?"

"Well, I heard a rumor about a possible affair, and then, when I questioned Bendy Webber, he told me about seeing Sloan Marshall leave the house the night Jack Ramey died and about his throwing something into the sea. Plus, Dr. Goodman remembered that Carrie had borrowed a big syringe from him and hadn't returned it. In fact, she'd told him that she'd left it at the Ramey house and couldn't remember to get it. Then, when I asked Kenny about the syringe, he remembered it was gone the day after Jack Ramey died. Then there was the missing bottle of insulin. Well, as you see, everything just added up."

"Objection," Harper said. "Sheriff Tate is implying that everything added up to murder, when in fact it added up only to a grand-jury indictment."

"Objection sustained," Judge Waynon decreed. "The jury will in no way consider Sheriff Tate's response as affirmation of guilt. It is the purpose of this trial to determine guilt or innocence."

Hennessey proceeded. "Sheriff, you mentioned that a bottle of insulin was missing."

"Yes, one was."

"Mr. Larsen testified that two types of insulin were used to treat Mr. Ramey—regular insulin and a type of insulin called Novolin. Do you know which bottle was missing?"

"The regular insulin."

"Sheriff, according to your investigation, what has been established as the time of Jack Ramey's death?"

"Between midnight and four A.M."

"Who was the last person to see him alive?"

"Carrie Douglas, his sister. She saw and spoke to him right at midnight. Anna Ramey found the body about six o'clock and called Dr. Goodman, who was on the scene about six-thirty."

"Did anyone report seeing Jack Ramey during those intervening hours?"

"No one."

Sloan sensed movement at his side and glanced over at Anna. She had removed her hands from the table and placed them in her lap. She didn't look his way.

"Did Mrs. Ramey tell you that she didn't check on her husband?"

"When questioned as to her movements that night, she said she didn't check on her husband."

"Thank you, Sheriff," Richard Hennessey said. "I have no further questions."

As Harper rose and began to approach Sheriff Tate, the officer began to knead his hat. Harper smiled.

"I have just a few questions, Sheriff."

Sheriff Tate looked relieved.

"How did you first hear the rumor concerning the affair?"

The sheriff hesitated, then said, "Inez Gouge. She called and told me what she'd seen and heard in her store."

Harper nodded, as though not in the least surprised. "And when did you discover that the bottle of regular insulin was missing?"

"When I arrested Anna Ramey."

"You looked around without a search warrant?"

"I asked her if I could look around, and she gave her permission. That's a perfectly legal search."

"You're absolutely right, Sheriff, it is. But didn't it strike you as odd that a woman guilty of murder so readily allowed you to search the premises? As the murderer, she would have known what you'd just learned from the Augusta investigation, that is, that Jack Ramey had died from an overdose of regular insulin. Surely she suspected what you were searching for."

"People do strange things."

Harper pursed his lips as though in deep thought. "Don't you think it goes beyond strange that a woman would use a specific kind of insulin to kill her husband, a kind of insulin of which there was only one bottle in the house, and not bother to replace that bottle? Wouldn't she at least try to hide what she'd done? Remember that her husband had died in the early morning hours of the twenty-second of August, and you didn't arrest her until the thirty-first. She'd had ten days to cover her tracks." Before the sheriff could answer, Harper added, "Wouldn't you say that her behavior indicated that she had no idea that you'd find that bottle of insulin missing?"

"Objection. Mr. Fleming is demanding a purely speculative response. Sheriff Tate can't possibly know what was going through Anna Ramey's head."

"Sustained."

"Sheriff, will you tell this court why the syringe and empty bottle of insulin haven't been introduced as evidence?"

Sheriff Tate had the grace to look flustered. "We don't have them."

"The truth is that you don't know what happened to them, do you?"

"No. We assume that Mr. Marshall threw them into the sea."

"Your Honor, please instruct this witness that this court is interested only in facts, not assumptions."

"The witness is so instructed."

"Now, according to your investigation," Harper continued, "how many people were in the Ramey house on the night Jack Ramey died?"

"Four people—Jack Ramey, Anna Ramey, their daughter Meg, and Mr. Ramey's sister."

"One last question. You said that when the report came back, you were surprised to learn that Jack Ramey had died of an overdose. I believe your exact words were, 'You could have knocked me over with a feather.' Why were you so surprised?"

"Anna Ramey didn't strike me as a murderer."

Richard Hennessey bounded to his feet. "Objection. Calls for a conclusion as to what does and does not constitute a murderer."

"Question withdrawn," Harper said, adding as he headed back to his chair, "I have no further questions of this witness."

"Redirect, Mr. Hennessey?"

"No, Your Honor."

"The witness may step down," Judge Waynon said. "Call your next witness, Mr. Hennessey."

"The prosecution calls Dr. Philip Goodman."

During the time it took for the bailiff to produce the physician, Sloan glanced over at Anna. Dressed in a navy suit, she looked tired, drawn, and pounds thinner than the first time he'd seen her. After the way she'd picked at her food at dinner, he couldn't understand why she wasn't skin and bones. Nor could he understand why she hadn't mentioned the incident with Jake Lugaric. Surely she'd wondered about it. Or maybe Harper was right, after all. Maybe Anna, maybe Jake Lugaric, had simply assumed that he'd reacted to being held hostage. The thought was reassuring, and so Sloan allowed himself to believe it.

Sloan's attention shifted back to the witness stand as Dr. Goodman was sworn in and took his seat.

"Dr. Goodman," Richard Hennessey began, "other than as a practicing physician, do you serve Cook's Bay in any other medical capacity?"

"Yes, I'm the coroner."

"As such, did you perform an autopsy on Jack Ramey?"

"No. Autopsies are not routine. They're performed only under a number of conditions, one of which is the suspicion of foul play."

"And you didn't suspect foul play was involved in the death of Jack Ramey?"

"No. Jack Ramey had a history of health problems, problems that had been particularly unstable of late."

"So you did what with the body?"

"From the condition of the body—temperature, lividity, and rigor mortis—I merely estimated the time of death, which I set between midnight and four A.M., then sent the body on over to the funeral home."

"How did you find out that Jack Ramey had died?"

"His wife called me. About six o'clock."

"And you were at the Ramey home when?"

"By six-thirty. At the latest."

"And what was Mrs. Ramey's condition?" At Dr. Goodman's frown the prosecutor added, "How would you describe her behavior?"

"I, uh, I guess she was pretty normal. You know, in control. Doing what had to be done."

"Was she crying?"

"No."

"Did you have occasion to witness her sister-in-law, Carrie, and her daughter, Meg?"

"Yes."

"And what, if anything, did you see?"

"They were crying. Not hysterically, but crying."

"I see," Richard Hennessey said. "So here was a woman whose husband had just died, and she wasn't shedding a tear?"

Harper pulled to his feet. "Your Honor, this whole line of questioning is bordering on the absurd. What has Anna Ramey not crying got to do with anything?"

"It goes toward showing state of mind. It acts as a barometer of her feelings."

"Your Honor, I'll parade a hundred psychiatrists through this courtroom to testify that grieving people do not always cry."

"Does the prosecution want such a parade of experts?" the judge asked.

"No," Hennessey conceded, then hastily added, "But Dr. Goodman's testimony is valid since he was first on the scene. He reported simply what he saw. I'm not asking for an interpretation of it."

Judge Waynon sighed. "I'm inclined to allow the testimony to stand—the prosecutor does have a right to question Dr. Goodman concerning what he witnessed that morning—but I'll allow the testimony on the understanding, Mr. Hennessey, that you move on. Enough is enough."

Hennessey looked pleased as punch. "Yes, Your Honor." Turning his attention back to the doctor, he asked, "When did you first suspect foul play?"

The doctor scratched his chin, hemming and hawing as he did so. "I guess the truth is that I didn't suspect anything even when Sheriff Tate came to me with information about the suicide note. I mean I couldn't ignore it, but I didn't want to jump to such serious conclusions."

"Of course not. What did you do then?"

"I recommend that the body be sent up to Augusta."

"Why didn't you perform the autopsy?"

"Frankly, I didn't want to get involved. I knew the family and felt that I should step aside. Plus, I knew that the experts in Augusta had the skills and tools at their disposal to do a thorough job."

"And when the forensic report came back, what did you conclude?"

"I had to accept the fact that Jack Ramey had died

of an overdose and that, possibly, Anna Ramey was involved."

"What else did you conclude?"

"Kenny, Jim, and I—"

"The nurse and Sheriff Tate?"

"Yes. We got to talking about how the fatal dose could have been administered, and I said that a big syringe would be the thing, and then I remembered that Carrie—Carrie Douglas—had borrowed one from me."

"Had she returned it?"

"No. She said that she left it at the Ramey house."

When Harper didn't object on the grounds of hearsay, Hennessey announced, "No further questions of this witness."

Harper rose and stepped forward. "I'm going to keep it simple, Doctor, though"—here Harper turned his attention to the judge—"we would reserve the right to recall this witness during our case in chief."

"So reserved," Judge Waynon said. He turned to Dr. Goodman. "You will remain on call until you testify in the case for the defense or until the defense has rested."

"Yes, Your Honor," Dr. Goodman replied.

Harper moved to stand right beside Dr. Goodman and smiled. "It would be my guess, sir, that you've practiced medicine a while."

The good doctor beamed. "Closing in on forty years."

Harper shook his head in disbelief. "Forty years? Imagine that. I guess during that time you've seen just about everything—suffering, tragedy, the highs and lows of the human spirit, and probably a few miracles thrown in."

"Your Honor," Hennessey said, "while the state is duly impressed with the scope of what Dr. Goodman has seen over the years of his practice, I hardly see its relevance to this case."

"Show relevance, Mr. Fleming, or drop the subject."

"Yes, sir," Harper responded. Addressing the doctor, he said, "Has it been your experience that illness is as traumatic on a family as it is on the patient?"

"Without question."

"Some families cope better than others?"

"Certainly."

"In your opinion, how did Anna Ramey cope?"

"Objection," Hennessey threw in. "Speculative. Calls for a conclusion."

"I'd say that after forty years of practicing medicine and observing human nature, Dr. Goodman has earned the right to present an opinion as to how Anna Ramey coped. If nothing else, how she coped in comparison to other families the doctor has witnessed. I would remind the court that Kenneth Larsen was allowed to testify in this area. I can't believe that Dr. Goodman, with more years of experience, has less credibility."

"Overruled. Proceed."

Harper repeated the question. "How did Anna Ramey cope?"

"Bear in mind that I hadn't observed her over the years, but, from what I saw following her and Jack's return to Cook's Bay after his stroke, I'd say she was coping well. As well as could be expected under such difficult circumstances."

"Would you say that Anna Ramey was a woman in control of her emotions? Let me rephrase the question. Did you ever see Anna Ramey break down and cry?"

"No."

"Is she the first widow you ever saw not cry?"

"Oh, no. Shock is a great emotional insulator."

Harper frowned, as though a thought had just occurred to him. "Wouldn't you find that kind of behavior—I mean not crying—odd coming from a woman who'd just killed her husband?"

"Objection. Calls for . . ."

"Wouldn't you think she'd be crying her eyes out?"

". . . a conclusion of the witness."

"Just to show everyone how much she was grieving?"

"Objection!"

"Question withdrawn," Harper said, though of course it was obvious, particularly to the prosecutor, that his opponent's point had been made. And well.

"Only a couple more questions, Doctor," Harper said. "How sick was Jack Ramey?"

"He was very ill."

"I know what I'm about to ask is a difficult question, simply because you took an oath to honor life above death: but did Jack Ramey have a lot to live for?"

"Objection! Speculative."

"Let me rephrase the question. In your best medical judgment, what was Jack Ramey's prognosis?"

"It's difficult to say with complete certainty."

"The court understands that, Doctor, but surely you can give us a reasonable, educated prognosis, one based on similar cases."

The doctor sighed, then repeated what he'd said only seconds before. "He was very ill. The diabetes had taken an ugly turn. We'd adjusted the insulin dosage, but still the disease remained erratic. Of particular concern to me was a kidney infection that refused to respond to treatment. Bear in mind that he had already suffered kidney damage from the stroke. He was possibly headed for renal failure, which would have meant sustaining his life by dialysis. He also had an ulcer on his leg that was resisting treatment. The ulcer had appeared in July and continued to worsen, probably because he spent so much of August confined to bed. The ulcer might have meant amputation of the leg at some point. It's not uncommon for a diabetic to lose a lower limb."

"Did Jack Ramey know how ill he was?"

"Definitely. It is my belief that he was afraid."

"That he'd die?"

"That he wouldn't. That his health would keep deteriorating, and that his life would become less and less viable. He seemed particularly obsessed with the possibility of another stroke, which might leave him even more incapacitated than he already was."

"When you heard about the suicide note, were you surprised?"

"No, not really."

"One last question. Can you tell the good people of this jury that Jack Ramey did not end his own life?"

The doctor paused, giving the question his fullest consideration. Finally he said, "I can say, unequivocally, that I would be surprised to discover that he had."

Voices clamored through the courtroom, followed by the pounding of a gavel. The voices dropped but didn't die, provoking the judge to reissue his warning.

"I'm prepared to clear this courtroom."

The voices fell away, leaving an unsettled hush, into which Harper asked, "Can you, Dr. Goodman, say with complete certitude, with one hundred percent absoluteness, that Jack Ramey didn't commit suicide?" Pause. "Yes or no."

"No, but—"

"Yes or no."

"No."

"No further questions.

"Redirect, Mr. Hennessey?"

Hennessey answered the judge by jumping to his feet and asking, "Why would you be surprised to discover that Jack Ramey had committed suicide?"

"I'm not sure that he was physically capable of it. After all, he was partially paralyzed, and injecting the vein in his arm, which in the opinion of the Augusta pathologist is how the overdose was administered, would be tricky at best. Plus," the doctor said, as though the thought had just crossed his mind, "even if he'd managed to inject himself, wouldn't the equipment—the syringe, the bottle of insulin, maybe even a tourniquet—have been found with him?"

Hennessey looked over at Harper and asked smugly, "Yes, wouldn't it?"

The courtroom held its breath for Harper to make some kind of rebuttal, but when it became obvious that he wasn't going to, the judge asked, "Mr. Fleming, anything more of this witness?"

Looking pleased, and not at all disturbed by Dr. Goodman's comment, Harper replied, "No, Your Honor."

Hennessey appeared a little surprised. As did the judge. As did Sloan, who glanced over at Harper in expectation.

Harper whispered, "Trust me."

"Call your next witness, then, Mr. Hennessey," Judge Waynon demanded.

A sense of restlessness roamed through the courtroom—people shuffled on the benches—creating the impression that everyone thought that Dr. Goodman would be the last witness for the evening. The clock on the wall, and rear ends weary of sitting, proclaimed that it had been a long day. Even Sloan, who'd watched as purple skies had given way to black, had been surprised at the continuation and concerned about Anna, who looked increasingly tired, although she'd uttered no complaint by either word or deed.

"The state calls Dr. Samuel Buseick."

Dr. Buseick, the forensic pathologist from Augusta, had a full head of brown hair, a trim mustache, and wire-framed glasses. The latter, coupled with a scholarly air, suggested that he'd spent a lot of his life in books. When he began to recite his curriculum vitae, it became clear that he had, indeed, pored over many a volume.

Midway through his narration Harper interrupted. "Your Honor, the defense recognizes that Dr. Buseick is an expert in the field of forensic pathology."

Judge Waynon, who shifted in his chair—was he tired, too? Sloan wondered—said, "Let the record so state the defense's recognition."

"Dr. Buseick," Hennessey began, "you were in charge of the autopsy of Jack Ramey?"

"I was."

"In a nutshell, Doctor, what did you conclude?"

"That Jack Ramey died of an overdose of insulin. I would guess somewhere between fifty and a hundred units."

"You sound positive about the overdose."

"I am positive."

"How can you be so certain?"

"There are sophisticated tests for such a determination."

"Would you explain to this court what those sophisticated tests are?"

"Certainly. They primarily have to do with the analysis of body fluids to determine both the glucose level and the insulin level. For example, in the case of glucose we can study the fluid from the eyeball. In an insulin overdose the glucose level of such ocular fluids is extremely low. On the other hand, other body fluids will reveal abnormally high levels of insulin."

"And you can still make these determinations on a body almost a week after death?"

The doctor smiled faintly. "It's a greater challenge, but it can be done. It *was* done in the case of Jack Ramey."

"From a forensic point of view, how do you think the lethal dose of insulin was administered?"

"Jack Ramey received fifty to a hundred units of regular insulin—"

"This regular insulin has been mentioned before," Hennessey interrupted. "Exactly what do you mean by regular insulin?"

"Many diabetics take two types of insulin—fast acting and intermediate acting. Regular insulin, given subcutaneously—"

"Forgive my interruption again, but what do you mean by subcutaneously?"

"Introduced beneath the skin. Diabetics usually inject themselves in the thighs, buttocks, abdomen."

Hennessey nodded his understanding. "Please go on."

"As I was saying, regular insulin, given subcutaneously, begins to take effect within fifteen to twenty minutes, while intermediate-acting insulin will take an hour or two. At one time both of these had to be taken separately, but today the two can be found in one solution, which, according to medical records, Jack Ramey was on. He took a type of insulin known as Novolin seventy-thirty." Anticipating the need to supply further information, Dr. Buseick added, "Seventy percent NPH Human Insulin Isophane Suspension and thirty percent Regular Human Insulin Injection."

"But he didn't die from an overdose of this Novolin seventy-thirty?"

"No. He died from a massive overdose of regular insulin, which I believe was injected directly into a vein. In this case I suspect it was injected into the vein of the subject's right arm. I found what might have been evidence of a bruise beyond the norm."

"You say 'beyond the norm.' What does that mean?"

"Diabetics often display bruising, especially when the disease is long-standing and acute. Plus, he'd ben hospitalized. His hospital records indicated that he'd had several intravenous injections."

"Back to this regular insulin. Why would Jack Ramey have owned a bottle of it if he normally took this Novolin seventy-thirty?"

"Most unstable diabetics keep fast-acting insulin on hand. In case of an emergency."

"Why do you think that the dosage was administered via vein rather than subcutaneously?"

"A dose that high injected directly into the vein would cause death more quickly than a subcutaneous injection."

"How quickly?"

"It depends on a number of things. For example, the body weight of the individual. It wouldn't take everyone the same length of time to expire. Just how recently one had eaten would be another important factor." Showing himself to be a seasoned trial witness, the doctor said, "I would think in Jack Ramey's case, considering his body weight, considering the time of his last meal, it would have taken only minutes."

"We've heard a great deal at this trial about a large syringe. Why wouldn't a syringe and needle ordinarily used to administer the normal dosages of insulin be just as good? Why go to the trouble of using a larger one?"

"A smaller syringe wouldn't hold fifty to a hundred units, thereby making multiple injections necessary."

"Can you think of any reason, other than to cause death, that fifty to one hundred units of insulin would be injected into a vein?"

"No. Even to counteract a traumatic episode, one wouldn't use a dosage anywhere near that high."

"No further questions."

As Hennessey resumed his seat, Harper rose. He didn't step forward as he normally did, but rather remained at the defense table.

"Can your sophisticated technology, technology that clearly indicated that Jack Ramey died of an insulin overdose, tell this court who injected that fatal dose?"

"No, of course not."

Positioning himself behind Anna, Harper placed his hands on her shoulders. "Can your sophisticated technology indicate that Anna Ramey did?"

"No."

Moving to stand behind Sloan, he repeated, "What about Sloan Marshall? Or Anna Ramey and Sloan Marshall together?" Here Harper put a hand on both clients' shoulders.

"No."

"Objection. The witness has answered the question. Three times now."

"What about Jack Ramey himself?" Harper continued before giving the judge time to rule. "Can your sophisticated technology eliminate him entirely?"

"No."

"Mr. Fleming, if you don't mind, I'd like the opportunity to rule on Mr. Hennessey's objection."

"Sorry, Your Honor."

The judge gave a yeah-sure-you-are look, then proclaimed, "Sustained. Move ahead."

"One last question," Harper said. "If a man was paralyzed on his right side, which arm would he inject, if wishing to give himself an overdose?"

"If he had use of only his left hand, one would expect the injection to be administered into his right arm."

"And did you not testify that you suspected that Jack Ramey died of an overdose injected into his right arm?"

"I did."

"No further questions."

"Redirect, Mr. Hennessey?"

"Do you have any forensic evidence, however small, to suggest that Jack Ramey injected himself?"

"No. As I said before, such a determination is beyond my forensic capabilities."

"No further questions, Your Honor."

And so, Judge Waynon dismissed the witness and recessed court until nine o'clock the following morning. Everyone in the courtroom gave a sigh of relief.

EIGHTEEN

The night air, cool and bracing, stung Anna's cheeks. Weary beyond words, she had allowed herself to be led through the bowels of the courthouse in an attempt to avert the press. The diversion had worked, partially because the newspeople, en masse, appeared to be as tired as everyone else, partially because Jake Lugaric in particular had disappeared midway through the proceedings.

"Stay right here," Harper said to Anna, "and I'll get the car." To Sloan he said, "I'm going to let Marilyn drop you off."

Anna caught the look that Sloan threw in his friend's direction. The look said that he was surprised. Since the beginning of the trial Harper had driven Sloan, while Marilyn had chauffeured Anna. Tonight, however, the rules had changed, and like Sloan, Anna couldn't help but wonder why.

"It'll take me only a minute to get the car," Marilyn said to Sloan in a tone that suggested she had known about the revised arrangement.

Once Anna and Sloan were alone, Sloan shrugged, saying with a slight, forced smile, "I guess Harper's tired of my company."

Anna smiled in kind. "Marilyn probably asked to be rid of me."

Sloan gave her a look that said Marilyn would have to be out of her mind to ask such a thing, while Anna's look said that no one could grow tired of Sloan's company. One lingering look followed another until both of them glanced away, memories dancing in two heavy hearts.

"I wonder where Lugaric got off to," Anna said, wondering why she was bringing up the reporter's name, except he'd been on her mind ever since the confrontation with Sloan. And then there was the way Sloan and Harper had closeted themselves in Harper's office, their heads low, their voices lower.

"It doesn't matter as long as the creep leaves us alone."

The sharpness of the words underscored Sloan's dislike of the newsman. Unless Anna was wrong, however, there was more than dislike going on. Sloan was afraid of the man.

"Are you all right?" Anna asked.

Her question startled Sloan. "What do you man?"

"You've seemed strange since that scene with Lugaric."

Sloan laughed harshly. "He's a jerk."

"I won't argue that, but—"

"There's nothing wrong," Sloan interrupted.

Anna thought about letting the subject drop. She sensed it was what Sloan wanted, but that very fact was reason enough to pursue it. In the distance she saw a pair of headlights flash on, followed by another pair.

Anna knew that Harper and Marilyn would soon be there, so whatever she had to say had to be said quickly.

"Is there something you're not telling me about Beirut?"

Again Sloan paled. Again fear mingled with the night. "Why do you ask?"

"Because Jake Lugaric upset you by asking that question."

"Hell, yeah! Beirut was an upsetting time in my life." He laughed without a trace of mirth. "I guess I'm just weird that way. I don't like being reminded of having been taken hostage and beaten within an inch of my life." At the stricken look on Anna's face, Sloan added, "I'm sorry."

"I didn't mean to imply that the experience wasn't upsetting."

Sloan's faint smile reappeared. "Look, you're tired, I'm tired, and we're both under a lot of stress. Let's just drop the subject, huh?"

Anna was very much aware that Sloan had yet to answer her question. In fact, he'd cleverly avoided it. There was something about Beirut that he wasn't telling her. That she would have bet her life on.

Anna had no choice but to honor Sloan's wish, for at that moment Harper's car pulled alongside the couple. After one last glance at Anna, Sloan opened the car door. She slipped into the vehicle.

"Good night," Sloan said to both Anna and Harper, though he kept his eyes trained on Anna.

"Good night," Harper echoed. "I'll pick you up in the morning."

"Right," Sloan said, closing the door and stepping away from the car.

Perhaps fearing a renegade reporter, Harper wasted no time in pulling the automobile from the parking lot and onto the street. When Anna saw the flash of headlights behind them, she suspected that Marilyn was operating under a similar concern. Everything seemed so cloak-and-daggerish, so theatrical, that Anna once more had the feeling that none of what had happened the last few weeks had been real. Harper's words put the lie to that, however.

"Look, Anna," her companion said, cutting to the chase, "I want to talk to you."

"I know." She smiled at Harper's how-did-you-know look. "Why else change the driving plans for this evening?"

Nodding at her logic, he said, "The state has another day or so before it rests its case, which means that Meg will be testifying soon."

At the mention of her daughter, Anna's heart constricted. No matter what else, who else, was on her mind, Meg was never far away. Never in her life had she gone this long without speaking with her daughter. For that reason, even though the purpose of her visit was a grim one, Anna welcomed her coming to town. Since they would be in the same house, Meg would be forced to talk to her. She'd be forced to listen.

"When is she coming in?"

"She came in this afternoon."

Harper's reply caught Anna unaware. For seconds she said nothing, then raced to the obvious conclusion. "She's at the house?"

Hesitation, then, "No."

"But I thought you said she was in town."

"She's staying with Carrie."

"At your request or Meg's?"

"Meg's," Harper said, forcing Anna to conclude that, even when she thought she couldn't be hurt any more, she could. "Listen to me—mothers and daughters have been at odds since the first daughter was born, and while I'm not minimizing your pain, I'm telling you that what's going on between you and Meg is going to have to take second place to what's going on in that courtroom.

"You're fighting for your future. While it's fair to say that things are going pretty well so far, we're a long way from the finish line. Hennessey's going to milk Meg for all she's worth. He's going to concentrate on the confrontation you and Meg had concerning the affair. He's going to concentrate on the rift between the two of you."

Out of a habit bred by years and circumstance, Anna tilted her chin. "I can handle it."

"That's just it, Anna. I don't want you to handle it."

Anna wasn't certain she'd heard correctly. "I don't understand."

"It's simple. Not everyone is as emotionally strong as you. In fact, most people aren't. I admire your strength, your composure, but that jury needs to see what you're feeling. Because you're not going to testify, all that the jury is going to know about you is what others say and what the jury sees. I'm not saying fake anything—God only knows that a jury can detect false emotion a mile away—but let them be privy to what you're feeling. Let them see that you're in pain because of the struggle going on between you and Meg."

"You don't understand. I survive by not feeling."

"No, Anna," Harper said softly, sagely. "You survive by pretending you don't."

Richard Hennessey lay in bed, pretending not to hear the dripping of the bathroom faucet. Instead he concentrated on the events that had transpired that day in court. It had been a decent day, with some witnesses proving weaker than he'd hoped, others stronger, but, then, that was the way it always went. Yeah, all in all, it had been a good day.

Drip . . . drip . . . drip . . .

Hennessey frowned. The only thing that even

vaguely bothered him was Fleming's defense of his clients. There was no way that Jack Ramey had taken his own life, but like water wearing away at a stone—drip ...drip...drip, the faucet whispered—sometimes a jury's common sense could be worn away by repetition. Even though Fleming couldn't prove Ramey had taken his life, all he had to do was suggest the possibility. Some juries were so cautious that they would bend over backward, flying in the face of all reason, overlooking the prosecutor's airtight case, to give the accused the benefit of the doubt.

Drip ... drip ... drip ...

"I pegged you as the kind of guy who liked to keep an ace in the hole."

Hennessey snorted. He didn't need an ace in the hole, and he resented Lugaric's inference that he did. He could take on Fleming, a man past his prime, any day of the week. Besides, although he didn't possess any scruples, he did have a healthy fear of getting caught. To do so would be death to his grandiose plans. On the other hand, he thought, as he rolled from bed and dressed to go to the local motel, there was no point in passing up anything that might beef up his case. The truth of the matter was that he was too damned smart to get caught.

The pale-faced woman was named Monique. Presently she sat in the middle of the bed in room 105, her lean legs folded into the lotus position of meditation. She was naked, with small, too-jutty breasts, an anorexically tiny waist, and long dark hair that floundered, rather than flowed, over her back and shoulders. Neither she nor Jake had spoken since Richard Hennessey had come and gone.

"So can you get into those files?" she asked.

Jake Lugaric, as naked as Monique and, strangely, looking as rumpled as he did when clothed, glanced toward her from his side of the bed as the credits of the nightly news scrolled on the television screen. Monique had known not to interrupt until the program was over. Jake had one passion in life: the news. Or, rather, who was delivering it. More precisely still, he was obsessed with moving from one high-exposure job to another. Monique knew that Jake was with her for only two reasons: one, she gave great head, and two, her daddy was a major stockholder of a television news network. She thought of these reasons not necessarily in the order of their importance.

"Hell, yeah," Jake said in answer to her question.

"You made it sound like it was going to be next to impossible."

Jake turned off the TV and tossed the remote control onto the bedside table. "I never said that it was going to be easy, only that I could do it. I've already put out my feelers. I wanted to know what was in those files even if Mr. Prosecutor didn't. Besides, let the little prick worry. And let him cough up the money." He laughed. "This jerk's so busy thinking that he's smart—all this high IQ, Mensa crap—that he doesn't have enough street sense to know that you can buy info for a lot less."

Monique looked surprised, then giggled. "You stiffed him?"

"Never did like the son of a bitch," he said in way of an answer. Grinning, he added, "Where do you want to go on vacation?"

"Let me think."

Slipping from the bed, Jake said, "You do that, babe, while I make a call."

Jake spent the next few minutes in conversation with a fellow reporter who had a D.C. beat and knew a guy who knew a guy who worked in the State Department.

"Will he do it?" Monique asked when Jake hung up the phone.

He shrugged. "Looks promising."

"Ricky"—Hennessey would have hated her abbreviation of his name—"needs it no later than tomorrow evening."

"If this guy comes through, the info will be deep-throated to me by morning."

At his choice of words Monique licked her lips. "Speaking of deep throat, how do you think we ought to spend the time?"

The question produced an instant physical response in Jake. Laughing, he crawled back into bed. The last thing he heard before Monique's warm, wet mouth closed around him was, "Acapulco."

That night, as Anna tossed and Sloan turned, two people they'd never known, and never would, changed the course of their lives. One was George Oberle; the other Esther Wright. George, whose wife was expecting their fifth child, was a government employee disgruntled because he'd been repeatedly passed over for promotion. At a little before midnight, his hands shaking, he removed a classified file, scanned the information, and, relieved that it contained nothing to jeopardize national security—he'd told himself that he wouldn't go that far—copied a couple of sheets and returned the folder to its slot.

Later that night Esther Wright, who at ninety-eight was Cook's Bay's oldest resident, died peacefully in her sleep. Rosa Wright McDay, Esther's seventy-six-year-old daughter, was notified in Jacksonville, Florida. In hours, plans were set into motion. Rosa would arrive in Maine on an early-afternoon flight, and Morganstern's Mortuary, as a courtesy, would send the limousine for her. As Anna and Sloan were struggling with the new day, Arty Watteau was notified that he was to pick up Rosa at the airport at 1:15.

* * *

The trial resumed at nine o'clock. The state's first witness on this Thursday morning was Inez Gouge. Primly, under the skilled guidance of Richard Hennessey, she related a couple of incidents she'd observed at the general store. She told of overhearing a conversation between Anna and Sloan in July. During this softly spoken discourse, the two participants had been friendly—very friendly, indeed, according to Ms. Gouge. She was certain that she'd heard the man living in the lighthouse speak of leaving Cook's Bay for some new job. Why, he'd wanted Mrs. Ramey to run away with him! Mrs. Ramey had been upset. Very upset, indeed. Then, a short while later, both she and he—here Inez Gouge sent an accusing look in the defendants' direction—had been upset to realize that they were being watched. Why, they'd tried to pretend that they were just two acquaintances babbling on about nothing in particular. But she hadn't been fooled. No, siree, not one little bit.

On one other occasion, in fact on the afternoon of the night that poor Jack Ramey had died, she'd witnessed those two—another withering glance in Anna and Sloan's direction—in the store. This time the man in the lighthouse had told Mrs. Ramey that the job offer had come through, that he was leaving town, and that it was best for everyone because they couldn't go on as they were. And then—why, she hadn't believed her ears!—she'd overheard the man declare his love. Right there in the middle of the store, before God and country, and with her poor husband sick as a dog.

As might have been expected, Sloan's reported declaration of love sent shock waves rippling through the spectators. A couple of reporters actually vacated their seats in order to phone in the news to their news centers. One of the two was Jake Lugaric. In the heat of the outburst the judge hammered away with the gavel.

"Silence! Now!" Howard Waynon roared.

In the quiet aftermath Harper edged back his chair and stood. He stepped forward, moving unhurriedly toward the woman with the severe bun and the sanctimonious stare. Careful to touch only marginally on what she'd observed—he did get her to admit that she hadn't actually heard the man ask the woman to run away with him—Harper began to question her. It took only a short while to establish that Inez Gouge knew more about the lives of the inhabitants of Cook's Bay than they knew themselves, and that half the time she couldn't even remember their names. The fact that she was giving such damaging testimony about a man whose name she didn't even know, and a woman whose first name eluded her—she remembered Anna's last name only because it was a prominent name in the community—made the store owner look small and petty. By the end of cross-examination the jury saw a lonely woman to be pitied, and the fact that she herself could not see what Harper had skillfully led her to reveal only made her more pathetic.

As Harper took his seat, the state called Bendy Webber to the stand. The seaman, his skin dark and leathery from the sun and the wind, an index finger nubbed at the knuckle by a lobster, testified that he'd seen Anna and Sloan on the beach a little after eleven o'clock the night Jack Ramey died. While he'd seen only an embrace, a kiss, then the couple's disappearance inside a little cove, Hennessey made as much of the sighting as was legally possible. Even after Harper reminded Hennessey that the defense had admitted to an affair, that it was part of the court record, Hennessey still searched for lurid details. Only after the judge forced him to move on did the prosecutor venture into another area, and that turned out to be the sighting of Sloan at the Ramey house, somewhere around one-fifteen to one-twenty. This was followed by testimony indicating that the witness had seen an agitated Sloan throw something into the sea around one-thirty to one-thirty-five.

Richard Hennessey, wearing a self-satisfied expression, took his seat. As he did so, he noticed that Jake Lugaric was no longer in the courtroom.

"Mr. Webber," Harper said, "is it your habit to be out tending lobster traps that late at night?"

"No, that night was in no way typical."

"What was so atypical about the twenty-first of August?"

"One of my grandsons broke his arm playing baseball. It was a pretty bad break and took a while to set. After he was sent home, I stayed with him until his mom—she's divorced—could get the other children settled in for the night. Even then, though, I wouldn't have gone out that late to check the traps, except it had been a while since I'd emptied them."

"I see. And it took you a couple of hours to check the traps?"

"Yes, sir. I have about twenty-five traps along that area of the bay, and it takes time to get around to them all. Especially at night."

Avoiding any question about his first sighting, Harper keyed in on the second, beginning with a simple question. "Mr. Webber, did you ever come ashore that night?"

"No, sir, but when I saw someone making his way from the Ramey house down to the sea, I cut the lights and engine on the boat and waited. I admit that I was curious. I thought it was Mr. Marshall, but I wanted to be sure."

"And of course it was, wasn't it?"

"Yes, sir. With the moon full that way, I'd stake my life on it."

Harper smiled. "We won't ask you to do that. You *did* see Sloan Marshall. What I will ask you is if you have any idea what he was agitated about? You did say that he appeared agitated, didn't you?"

"Yes, sir, he did appear agitated, but I have no idea why he was."

"You don't have any idea whether he and Anna Ramey had just killed her husband?"

The very idea that he might possess such knowledge shocked Bendy Webber. "Good heavens, no."

"To your knowledge, or lack thereof, he could have been agitated about any number of things, then?"

"Yes, sir."

"He could have been upset because he'd just committed adultery?"

"Yes, sir."

"He could have been upset because Anna Ramey had asked him to leave?"

"Yes, sir."

"He could have been upset because he knew this might be the last time he saw Anna Ramey?"

"Objection, Your Honor," Hennessey said. "Mr. Webber has already stated that he has no idea as to the cause of Mr. Marshall's agitation."

"Sustained."

"Let me ask you another question, sir," Harper said, gracefully conceding since he'd already proved his point. "You said that Sloan Marshall threw something into the sea."

"Yes, sir, he did."

"What did he throw into the sea, Mr. Webber?"

The older man looked surprised that he'd even been asked the question. "I have no idea. I mean, I could see him slinging something"—here he executed the overhand motion of throwing it—"but I couldn't see what that something was."

"You couldn't tell if it was a syringe and an empty bottle of insulin?"

"No, sir."

"Could it have been a seashell?"

"Yes, sir, I suppose it could have been."

Harper smiled. "No further questions of this witness."

"Redirect, Mr. Hennessey?"

"No, Your Honor."

"Call your next witness."

"The state calls Carrie Ramey Douglas."

Carrie entered the courtroom to the accompaniment of the spectators' murmurs. Dressed in a tomato-red suit, she climbed onto the witness stand, was sworn in, and took her seat. Immediately she glanced over at Anna, as though in apology.

Anna smiled faintly, noting as she did so that one of the combs in Carrie's hair was higher than the other. Anna had a vision of its having fallen out recently and having been replaced, hastily, carelessly, at the last second.

"Mrs. Douglas," Hennessey began, "how were you related to Jack Ramey?"

"He was my brother."

"Mrs. Douglas, would you please speak up so the jury can hear you?" Judge Waynon said in something other than his blustery tone.

Carrie cleared her throat. "Yes, Your Honor." Then she added, "Jack was my brother."

When Carrie looked over to see if this met with the judge's approval, the magistrate nodded.

"How would you describe your relationship with your brother?" Hennessey asked.

"We were very close." The words were delivered with such emotion that they demanded no further comment, by either witness or prosecutor.

"Mrs. Douglas, Dr. Goodman testified that you borrowed a large syringe from his office. Please tell us what the circumstances were."

Carrie hesitated, as though trying to decide where to begin. Finally she said, "Every year I give a Fourth of July party. It's a tradition that goes way back in my family. For over two hundred years whoever has lived in the Ramey house has thrown a July Fourth party. Everyone in town is invited. Of course, not everyone comes, but . . ." Realizing she was babbling, she stopped, then changed tacks. "Anyway, I wanted to prepare a recipe that I'd read about in a magazine I bought—*Fancy Cuisine*. Actually, it wasn't really a recipe. I mean, it was so simple. It was more like one of ten tips to make a summer party unforgettable."

"And what was that tip?" Hennessey said, trying to keep Carrie's train on track.

"To inject liqueur into your fruit. Like watermelon, cantaloupe, whatever."

"I see. And that's why you borrowed the large syringe?"

"Yes. You were supposed to inject the fruit and refrigerate it overnight."

"I see. And did you do that?"

"Yes and no."

"What do you mean, Mrs. Douglas?"

"The fruit was injected, but I didn't do it. I took it to Anna." Once more she looked over at the defense table.

"Why did you do that?"

Carrie smiled, and Anna thought that she looked very much like a young girl, a fact her freckles only enhanced. "I, uh, I'm afraid of needles."

Several jurors smiled too.

"When you say you took it to Anna, what do you mean?"

"I took the fruit and syringe to Anna for her to inject the fruit with liqueur."

"And then what happened?"

"I forgot and left the syringe. And I kept forgetting it." She shrugged. "With Jack's illness I guess I had other things on my mind."

"You're certain that you left the syringe at the Ramey house?"

"Yes. Positive. But Anna didn't use it to kill Jack."

"Move to strike the last," Hennessey said.

"The last comment will be stricken," Judge Waynon ordered before directing his attention to Carrie. "Don't volunteer information."

"Yes, sir."

"Do you know what happened to that syringe?" Hennessey asked.

Hesitation, then, "No."

"One last question, Mrs. Douglas. Did you suspect that your sister-in-law was having an affair?"

Harper let the question stand. Anna thought that perhaps he was curious to know the answer. She knew she was.

Carrie straightened her shoulders, saying, "I learned a long time ago that things are not always what they appear."

Hennessey smiled. "While a very astute answer, it's nonetheless unresponsive to my question." Pause. Then he repeated, "Did you suspect that your sister-in-law was having an affair?"

"I accepted the possibility."

This time Hennessey laughed. "You've avoided my question again."

"No, Mr. Hennessey, you've avoided hearing my answer. I neither suspected nor didn't suspect that Anna was having an affair. I merely accepted the possibility."

"Forgive me, Mrs. Douglas, but to accept the possibility of an affair, don't you have to have suspected that affair?"

"No," she answered flatly. "I accept the possibility that it might rain this afternoon, but I neither suspect that it will or that it won't. I stop short of making any such judgment."

"You don't suspect that the gathering gray clouds portend anything?"

"As I said, things are not always what they appear."

"Your Honor," Harper interrupted, "the prosecutor is badgering his own witness."

"I'm merely seeking an answer to my question."

"And she's given him one. Obviously, however, it isn't the answer he wanted."

"Mr. Hennessey, move on or rephrase the question."

"Mrs. Douglas, were you surprised to learn that your sister-in-law was having an affair with Sloan Marshall? Yes or no?"

Hesitation, then, "No."

"Thank you, Mrs. Douglas. No further questions."

As Hennessey made his way back to the prosecution's table, he was full of his importance at having scored this final point. Out of the corner of his eye he noted that Jake Lugaric had returned to the courtroom. In fact, he leaned against the back wall in an attitude that defined cocky. Their gazes met for just a second, and in that time the newsman ever so slightly drew attention to a folder he held. Hennessey's self-importance grew.

Harper stood and, fastening the button of his jacket, stepped toward the witness stand. Given his formal demeanor, Anna never would have suspected that Harper even knew Carrie, much less that they were dating, and probably lovers in the bargain.

"Mrs. Douglas, you said that you and your brother were close."

"Yes, we were."

"How would you describe your relationship with your sister-in-law?"

"We were—are—very close too." Carrie smiled and glanced over at Anna. "She's more like my sister than my sister-in-law."

"You can still say that knowing she had an affair?"

"Yes."

"That's a very generous gesture, Mrs. Douglas. How is it that you're able to make it?"

"As I told Mr. Hennessey, I stop short of making judgments."

"Isn't it true that you watched Anna Ramey struggle to keep her marriage intact? Isn't it true that, although you loved your brother deeply, you saw him time and again strike out at her—not intentionally, not maliciously, but because he was caught up in his own struggle, his own suffering?"

"Your Honor," Hennessey said, "although Mr. Fleming is putting words in the mouth of the witness, I might not object so strenuously if they didn't sound like the script of a second-rate soap opera."

Harper retaliated. "While it may sound like a second-rate soap opera, Your Honor, it is nonetheless the life my client has been leading. Furthermore, Mrs. Douglas is in the unique position of having witnessed this marriage over a period of years, and in the even more unique position of having perhaps the most objective point of view of anyone testifying in this trial. She cared for both Jack and Anna Ramey. She has no ax to grind against either."

Judge Waynon sighed, as though the decision were a tough one. "I'm going to overrule your objection, Mr. Hennessey. I think Mr. Fleming has made a valid point, but I would caution you, Mr. Fleming, not to dwell upon this."

"Yes, sir," Harper said, repeating his question to Carrie.

Anna held her breath as she watched the war being waged inside her sister-in-law. Would she be able to slip off the rose-colored glass through which she safely viewed the world? Anna saw, too, that Harper watched and waited, this question prowling his own mind.

Finally Carrie said, "Yes, Anna did struggle, and yes, my brother did strike out at her."

Harper smiled. "Thank you, Mrs. Douglas, for your honesty, and now I have one last question. Do you think that Anna Ramey killed her husband?"

Carried responded with an emphatic, "No!"

"Objection. Calls for a conclusion."

"I don't believe it does, Your Honor, but I'll withdraw the question," Harper said, satisfied that the jury had heard what he'd wanted them to. "I'll also dismiss this witness."

"Redirect, Mr. Hennessey?"

"No, Your Honor."

"Then call your next witness."

"I'd like to call Megan Elizabeth Ramey as a hostile witness."

"Proceed."

Anna heard the excitement skip through the courtroom, just as she felt her own heart skip a beat. Remnants of the conversation she'd had with Harper came rushing back.

". . . let the jury be privy to what you're feeling . . ."

She honestly didn't know if she could do that, not even to save herself, and Sloan, from incarceration.

At her side Sloan whispered, "It'll be all right."

But would it? Would time ever right the wrong that had occurred that fateful night? Anna left the future to the future, knowing that the present was going to be all too difficult to get through. That in mind, she steeled herself against seeing her daughter again. But it was a futile exercise. Nothing could have prepared her for the Meg who took the stand.

Hostile. In Anna's opinion that about summed up her daughter. Even though she still wore her hair in a youthful braid, she looked older, but not necessarily wiser. In fact, Anna sensed her confusion, her forced realization that the people she loved were not always what she wanted them to be. Meg, just as the young often did, had turned to rebellion to cover her bewilderment, her hurt, her pain.

"Ms. Ramey," Hennessey began, "you are the daughter of Anna Ramey and the late Jack Ramey?"

Deliberately keeping her eyes from her mother, Meg answered, "I am."

"Would you please characterize for this court the relationship that presently exists between you and your mother." When second after second dragged by without a response, Hennessey rephrased the question. "Ms. Ramey, isn't it true that your relationship with your mother is strained? In point of fact, you're not even speaking, are you?"

Silence.

"Ms. Ramey," the judge said, "you must answer the question or be held in contempt of court."

Meg raised her chin. "No, we're not speaking."

"And isn't the basis of that strained relationship the fact that you discovered that your mother had had an affair?"

Meg's chin tilted even higher. "Yes."

"What led you to believe that she had had an affair?"

"I could just tell. I knew the minute she walked into the room that night that she'd been with him ... and what they'd been doing."

"How? Was her hair messed up? Her clothes askew? What?"

"All of that. But mostly I knew because she wasn't wearing her wedding ring."

Anna heard the jury and the spectators digesting this information—digesting and judging.

"Did she confirm that she'd had an affair?"

"She didn't deny it, and that's the same thing."

"How did you feel when you knew she'd been unfaithful to your father?"

"How do you think I felt?"

"Ms. Ramey," Judge Waynon interceded, "please answer the question."

"I was hurt and angry."

"And you still are?"

"Yes, I'll never forgive her for what she did."

Anna's heart withered, died. She closed her eyes, as though in doing so she might also close her ears to her daughter's hurtful words. In her self-imposed darkness she felt Sloan offering her the only consolation he could. As unobtrusively as possible, he rested his hand alongside hers, little finger to little finger. The contact was minimal, and yet never had so little meant so much. Gratefully, hungrily, Anna drew from his strength. Where, though, would she find the strength to admit that she'd lost her daughter, perhaps for the rest of her life? And how, in God's name, could she allow a jury to see a pain so great, so overwhelming, that she was afraid that its very expression would destroy her?

"Your Honor," Harper intervened, "I would remind this court that this is not an alienation-of-affections case. So far this witness has offered nothing more than the defense has already admitted to. There *was* an affair, and frankly, the defense can't see what the strained relationship between mother and daughter has to do with the guilt or innocence of my client. She's been charged with murder, not with alienating her daughter."

"Mr. Hennessey—"

Anticipating the judge's ruling, Hennessey said, "No further questions."

"Ms. Ramey," Harper said, "do you believe your mother is capable of murder?"

Hennessey jumped to his feet. "Objection!"

"No," Meg said clearly, defiantly.

"Ms. Ramey," the judge chastised, "you must wait for me to rule."

"Question withdrawn," Harper said.

"Objection withdrawn," Hennessey said.

"Gentlemen, don't play with this court," Judge Waynon cautioned. Looking at Harper, he asked, "Mr. Fleming, do you have any more questions for this witness?"

"No, Your Honor."

"Does the state wish to redirect?"

Hennessey rushed forward with, "Ms. Ramey, did you believe your mother capable of adultery?"

Hesitation. "No."

"No further questions," Hennessey said.

"This court will then recess for lunch and resume at precisely one-thirty," the judge declared.

"All rise," the bailiff intoned.

Anna came to her feet but was barely aware of having done so. All she could see, hear, feel, was her daughter's hostility, the hurtful fact that Meg had never once glanced her way, the positive, confident way she'd admitted that she didn't believe her mother guilty of murder. Oddly, this was the very last thing Anna wanted to hear.

NINETEEN

Clouds drifted across the gray sky. Richard Hennessey, parked on the same isolated back road that he'd parked on the day before, waited with the same impatience. He'd told his assistant that he had a personal errand to run. And the errand was, indeed, personal. The envelope of cash concealed in the breast pocket of his suit confirmed that. The information that Lugaric offered had better damn well be worth it!

In minutes the rented car wended its way into view and stopped. Lugaric swaggered toward the Porsche and climbed into the passenger seat. Wordlessly, as though the information would speak for itself, he handed the folder to Hennessey. The prosecutor just as quietly leafed through the half-dozen sheaves of paper that had been faxed to Lugaric.

Lugaric asked, "So, counselor, what do you think?"

What Hennessey thought was that he'd lucked out. But good. While the information wouldn't, in and of itself, win the trial, it would go a long way toward the character assassination of Sloan Marshall. It was just the kind of information that the jury wouldn't forget. Even when told to.

"Not bad," Hennessey said, trying to downplay his excitement.

"Not bad?" Lugaric asked. "C'mon, man, you know it's a whole lot better than that. It'll win your case."

"No, *I'll* win the case, and would have without this." He tapped the edge of the folder against the palm of his hand. "This'll just help to tighten the noose."

Lugaric gave a look that said that Hennessey's cockiness amused him. "Sure. Whatever you say."

A troubling thought suddenly occurred to Hennessey. "This isn't hitting the news even as we speak, is it?"

"I'm going to run it on the evening news. The defrocking of an American hero." Lugaric grinned. "People just love to have the pedestals knocked from under the gods."

The only people Hennessey cared about were those on the jury, but he didn't say so. Instead he asked, "Is this going to be the media event you came down to create?" The tone of the question implied that Hennessey wasn't all that impressed.

"Hey, the evening news won't be too shabby. Take my word for it. Besides, the trial isn't over with yet. If I were you, I'd spend my time figuring out how you're going to get classified information heard in court."

Not without risking contempt of court, Hennessey knew, but he had a plan, too gutsy and ballsy for some, but not for him. Once the shit hit the fan and settled, no one would remember anything except the information he introduced. And it was perfect that Nichols wouldn't be able to refute anything. He wouldn't be able to lift a finger in Marshall's defense. None of this, however, did Hennessey want to share with Jake Lugaric.

"Let me worry about that," he said in response to the reporter's question.

"Like I said, whatever you say," Lugaric said. "You got the money?"

Hennessey gave him a how-gauche-can-you-get look, but slipped a hand into his pocket and removed the packet. The sooner he was finished with this guy, the better.

When Lugaric took the envelope, he counted the money, bill by bill.

"You've got to be kidding," Hennessey sneered.

"Hey, a guy can't be too careful, and I've already shelled out money on this. I just want to get it back."

"Well, you got it," Hennessey said, starting up the engine and thereby calling the clandestine meeting to an official halt.

Lugaric took the less-than-subtle hint and flung open the car door. "It's been nice doing business with you."

"Hey, Lugaric," Hennessey called, and the reporter, who had just exited the car, peered back inside. "Don't get in touch with me again."

Lugaric grinned. "Sure thing, counselor." He shut the door. As he passed by the hood of the Porsche, he slammed down his hand.

"Son of a bitch!" Hennessey mumbled, gunning the car and pulling it from the side of the road. He left a cloud of white dust swirling around the newsman.

"It's going to storm," Anna said, staring up at the clouds perched low in the sky. Her tailored suit was as gray as the encroaching weather.

After a quick lunch spent dodging the press, the quartet had returned to the courtroom, which at the moment was empty. Anticipating that the state would soon rest its case, Harper was head-to-head with Marilyn, going over some last-minute details.

To the accompaniment of a soft growl of thunder, Anna said, "Jack used to hate storms, but I never minded them. Until now." A shudder accompanied her statement.

"You're safe," Sloan said.

Anna turned toward him and gave a small laugh. "Our lives are falling apart around us, Sloan, and you tell me that I'm safe? We're standing trial for murder, my daughter, whom I love dearly, stated before a roomful of strangers that she hates me, and will for the rest of her life, Harper is angry with me because I can't show the jury that I'm hurting, and you tell me that I'm safe?"

That Anna spoke calmly was far more disturbing to Sloan than had she shouted the words. Forcefully, he answered with, "The trial is going well, in time you'll patch things up with your daughter, and Harper isn't angry with you."

"Okay, *disappointed* might be a better word. Harper's *disappointed* with me. And perhaps rightly so. The jury probably sees me as cold and heartless." Before Sloan could comment, she said, "I wish I could cry. For you, for me, for Jack, but I can't." She glanced up at Sloan, as though deeply puzzled. "Why do you think that is?"

The question tore at Sloan's heart. He had his own theory as to why she couldn't cry—namely, that it was just too human an act—but, then, who was he to encourage her to be human when he hated himself for being just that?

"It doesn't matter, Anna," he said. "You did fine today."

Looking into his dark eyes, she found it so easy to believe everything he said. It was even easier to remember their past—the first time their hands had touched, their first kiss, his telling her he loved her.

Oddly, his admission had occurred in the general store, not when they'd made love; but, then, saying it when they'd made love would have been unnecessary, because his every touch had said as much. She often wished—like now—that she hadn't made him promise that he'd never declare his love again. But she had made him promise, because it was the worst punishment she could exact upon herself.

"I'm scared," she whispered. "Of this trial, of losing my daughter, of never again feeling the way I did in your arms."

Her words made Sloan feel as empty as all the years he'd spent without her.

"I'm scared too," he said. "Of spending the rest of my life in prison, of never again being allowed to tell you that I love you, of never hearing you say that you love me."

Time stood still as silence followed Sloan's confession.

"Don't worry, Anna," Sloan whispered at last. "Everything's going to be all right."

Anna realized that this was the second time Sloan had so remarked. It was the first time, however, that a troubling thought occurred to her. If worse came to worst, just how far would he go to protect her?

When Jake Lugaric entered the courtroom, the hair on the back of Sloan's neck stood at attention. Unable to stop himself, he glanced toward the press gallery. The reporter was looking his way, nothing short of smugness curling his full lips. Sloan found the look unsettling, as unsettling as the man himself.

"Looks like Dracula just found a juicy jugular," Harper said.

The comment only added to Sloan's unsettled feeling, because it eliminated the possibility that he had imagined the reporter's self-satisfaction. Panic, pure and simple, skipped down Sloan's spine, but he forced himself to rein it in, particularly since he knew that Anna was watching him closely. She was still leery of Lugaric, leery of his question about Beirut.

"Looks like he found that juicy jugular in Africa," Harper added.

This addendum caused Sloan's gaze to wander over the wrinkled safari jacket that the reporter wore, along with faded jeans and a T-shirt emblazoned with the call letters of the television station he worked for. Sloan then noted his shoes—Dock-siders. At the white powder that covered them, Sloan frowned, and instinctively he glanced toward the prosecutor, who had only minutes before entered the courtroom. Sloan's gaze lowered to his shoes. Unlike the day before, they were perfectly clean, with a shine so bright it glared. Sloan wasn't quite certain what he'd expected, but he didn't have time to dwell on anything beyond the judge's abrupt entrance into the courtroom.

"All rise," the bailiff commanded.

As always Judge Waynon acted as though time were precious. "Mr. Hennessey, is the state ready to move forward with its case?"

"It is, Your Honor. The state calls Captain Sherwin Nichols."

Sloan had known that eventually his former commanding officer would testify, but as his name rang out, Sloan realized that he wasn't at all prepared for that testimony. He wasn't prepared for the possible memories that it might invoke. Nor could he escape the feeling that this man posed his greatest threat. Sloan fought the urge to look in Harper's direction and, in doing so, seek reassurance that everything would be all right.

Instead Sloan took notice of the rain that had begun to pepper the windowpanes, the smug look on the prosecutor's face—no need to panic, the man always looked smug—the familiar figure, dressed in a navy uniform, who mounted the witness stand. After being sworn in, that familiar, and always friendly, figure sat down and glanced briefly in Sloan's direction. Sloan allowed himself to relax.

Hennessey stepped forward briskly. "Captain Nichols, please state your occupation."

Captain Nichols, tall and with the craggy features of a Clint Eastwood, set his visored hat upon the wide railing and replied with the commanding air of authority, "I'm an officer in the United States Navy."

"In what capacity do you presently serve the navy?"

The crisp reply of, "I'm a member of the Navy Seals," was followed by a crisper roll of thunder, which startled the crowd. Sloan's stomach tightened. He wasn't certain if his reaction was to the impending storm or the result of hearing the words *Navy Seals*, though he'd known all along that Hennessey would pursue this part of his past.

When the thunder, and the reaction to it, died away, Hennessey asked, "Please tell the court about this group known as Navy Seals."

"They're elite. Not only the elite of the United States Navy, but the elite among all of the United States military. In fact, they're the best fighting force in the world."

"They're special, then?"

"Very."

"And what special job do they perform?"

"Actually, we have a couple of missions," he said, his pride necessitating a change in pronouns. "In times of war we go in first to pave the way for other military forces. At other times we're simply called upon to rout trouble in one of the world's many hot spots."

"In regard to the latter, the Navy Seals might be called upon to rescue Americans held as hostages in a foreign country?"

Sloan's stomach tightened another notch. Yeah, the jerk was moving in exactly the direction he knew he would.

"Correct," Captain Nichols replied.

"Describe the type of man who belongs to this elite group."

"He's the best-trained fighting man in the world. He's an independent thinker, but a team player. He's a man who can get the job done."

"At any cost?"

It was an innocent enough question, but Sloan understood all too well its insidious implications. Apparently, so did Captain Nichols.

"He's a man who can get the job done at the appropriate cost."

"Ah, the appropriate cost," Hennessey repeated, making the words somehow sound sinister. Not dwelling on it, however, he moved on to another question, which was even more sinister. "Navy Seals are trained to kill, are they not?"

"Military men in general are trained to kill."

"Your Honor," Harper objected, "I'm not at all certain where this line of questioning is going." But, of course, he was. As was Sloan. As was every other even remotely intelligent person in the courtroom.

"Make your point, counselor, or move on," the judge ordered.

"Yes, Your Honor." Pause. "Captain Nichols, do you know Sloan Marshall?"

"I do. I had both the honor and the pleasure of serving with him before his retirement from the navy."

"He, too, was a Navy Seal?"

"Yes."

"In fact, he was an officer, was he not?"

"He was. One of the finest."

"I assume, then, that Commander Marshall"—Sloan noted how cleverly Hennessey referred to him in military terms—"was a well-trained fighting man, a man trained to kill, a man who, as an officer, was also trained to take charge and get the job done."

"Your Honor," Harper said, "the prosecutor is putting words in the mouth of the witness."

"I am not, Your Honor," Hennessey said in his defense. "I merely repeated the same words that Captain Nichols himself used to describe any member of this special group. No, no," Hennessey corrected, "I did make the assumption that, as an officer, Commander Marshall would have been trained to take charge. If that's an incorrect statement, Captain Nichols can refute it."

"Overruled," the judge said, then turned his attention to the witness. "However, Captain, should you like to refute any of the prosecutor's dramatic presentation, do so."

"What he said is correct."

Hennessey beamed. "He was also trained in the rudiments of emergency medicine, was he not?"

"Navy Seals are often shut off from everything, everyone. We have to know how to take care of our injured."

"Is that a yes, Captain? Did Commander Marshall know how to . . . oh, say, give an injection?"

"That's hardly a complicated skill."

Insistently, Hennessey asked, "Did he have medical training?"

"Yes."

Taking another tack, and calling emphasis to it by the abruptness of the shift, Hennessey asked, "Did there come a time, roughly two years ago, when a team of Navy Seals was dispatched to liberate an American held hostage in Beirut?"

"Yes."

"Who led that team, Captain?"

As though anticipating the witness's answer, Hennessey, now almost bursting with smugness, faced Sloan. In that split second of eye-to-eye contact, Sloan knew that Hennessey had discovered all about his past. The classified files had been accessed. Not by Lugaric, as Sloan had feared, but by the prosecutor. Sloan wanted to come to his feet, shouting, "Don't do this!" but he remembered Harper's saying that the information couldn't be introduced into the court record. Legal protocol would keep out his unsavory past. Sloan tried to relax, but he felt Anna watching him and tensed even more. *God, don't let her find out!* he prayed.

"Your Honor," Harper interrupted, "I fail to see what Sloan Marshall's military past has to do with the death of Jack Ramey."

"I confess, Mr. Hennessey, that I'm having the same trouble," Judge Waynon said.

"Goes toward establishing the character of Sloan Marshall," Hennessey said.

"Then perhaps," Harper said, "the defense can again save this court some time by stipulating certain facts, facts that eloquently establish the character of Sloan Marshall." He paused. "Sloan Marshall headed the force that liberated an American held in Beirut, was himself taken hostage, and held for a number of months, during which he was repeatedly and brutally tortured. After his release he was awarded the Congressional Medal of Honor for heroism."

A murmur rose at the same time that thunder rumbled through the heavens. A storm was imminent, both outside and inside the courtroom unless Sloan was mistaken. The information that Harper had provided should have displeased and defused Hennessey. Instead the man looked as though Harper had followed precisely where he'd led.

"Captain, isn't it true that Commander Marshall retired after his release?"

"It is."

"Probably because of the trauma he'd endured?"

"Your Honor—" Harper began, but was cut off by Captain Nichols.

"I couldn't say why he chose to retire."

"Then, again," Hennessey said, "maybe it was because he felt he no longer deserved to be in the military."

Sloan felt it coming, as inevitable as death.

"Your Honor, I object to this line of questioning," Harper said.

"Mr. Hennessey . . ." the judge cautioned.

Hennessey had no intention of being interrupted, however—not by Harper, not by the judge, not by God himself. "Cowards don't last in the military, do they?"

"Your Honor," Harper interjected, "this isn't even a line of questioning. The prosecutor is delivering nothing more than a soliloquy."

"Mr. Hennessey . . ." Judge Waynon repeated.

"Isn't it true, Captain, that our heroic commander broke under torture and revealed the name of an Israeli agent and that—"

"That's classified information," Captain Nichols said.

"Your Honor!" Harper cried as the storm closed in around them with thunder and lightning and driving rain.

"Mr. Hennessey, I'm warning you . . ."

Sloan listened to the four men speaking all at once and thought that this wasn't going to be like death. Death was an ending. This was going to be a beginning . . . of his disgrace.

". . . as a reward for that information, his Lebanese captors released him . . ."

"I couldn't comment on classified information," Captain Nichols said.

"Objection!"

". . . that to continue is to risk this court's wrath."

Hennessey, going for broke, risked it. "And isn't it true that the Israeli agent was suspiciously killed in an

automobile accident less than a week after our hero
was freed?"

"As I said, I can't comment on classified information."

"Objection!"

"Mr. Hennessey!"

"Our *hero* sacrificed another man when it suited his
purpose, just the way he sacrificed Jack Ramey when
he got in the way."

Captain Nichols didn't even bother to comment,
though he was one of the few in the courtroom who
didn't. Instead he just looked apologetically in Sloan's
direction.

"Objection, Your Honor!" Harper screamed.

"That's enough, Mr. Hennessey!" Judge Waynon said
to the tune of his pounding gavel.

Surging to his feet, along with most of the press,
Sloan roared, "No!"

A broad flash of lightning struck near the courthouse, causing a loud crackling. Seconds later thunder
jarred the courtroom, setting walls and windows to vi-
brating. Reporters scurried; spectators chattered; the
judge's gavel clattered. Slowly, chaos evolved into order.

"Your Honor," Harper said. "I would ask that you declare a mistrial."

Judge Waynon, red-faced and stern-eyed, spoke. "Mr.
Marshall, please be seated. Mr. Fleming, Mr. Hennessey, please approach the bench."

Surprised to find himself standing, Sloan edged back
into his chair. His survival mode automatically kicking
in, he forced himself to think of cool streams and
speckled trout as he watched Harper and the prosecutor step forward.

Once the two lawyers stood before the judge, Harper
repeated, "I move for a mistrial, Your Honor."

Judge Waynon sighed, considered, then sighed again.

"Mr. Hennessey, your behavior at the very best has been egregious."

Hennessey tried to appear contrite, but it was clear that he hadn't a clue as to how to go about it.

"However," the judge added, "I'm not inclined to declare a mistrial."

"But, Your Honor, you just said—"

"I know what I just said, Mr. Fleming, and I meant every word of it. The prosecutor's behavior was inexcusable and will not be tolerated in this courtroom. Do I make myself clear, Mr. Hennessey?"

"Yes, sir," the prosecutor said, but the man was no nearer contrition than before. In fact, he appeared to be smothering a shout of joy.

"I'm going to instruct the jury to disregard anything said regarding classified material." Pause. "Gentlemen, please take your seats."

As they did so, Judge Waynon so instructed the jury, after which he said, "Mr. Fleming, do you wish to cross-examine this witness?"

Harper, hiding his disappointment, stepped forward and made the best of a bad situation. "Captain Nichols, isn't it true that you can neither confirm nor deny classified information?"

"It is."

"One last question, sir. In your opinion, did Sloan Marshall deserve the Congressional Medal of Honor?"

"In my opinion he deserved a half dozen of them."

As Sloan watched Harper make his way back to his chair, he knew that the jury would probably remember nothing of this last bit of testimony, yet every word of Hennessey's tawdry allegation. Sadly, the allegation was all too true.

"Redirect, Mr. Hennessey?"

"No, Your Honor."

"Because of the storm, this court will recess until nine o'clock tomorrow morning."

"All rise."

Those remaining in the courtroom stood, the judge disappeared, and without a word, without a glance in either Harper's or Anna's direction, Sloan turned and walked down the center aisle. Even in his dazed state he wondered why Jake Lugaric wasn't out filing his story. He also wondered if he heard Anna calling his name. In either case it didn't matter. The truth was that not a whole lot of anything mattered anymore.

The storm raged.

At five o'clock, with the sky as black as pitch, the wind whining around the eaves of the house, the rain hammering the earth, Anna built a fire. She wasn't certain whether it was the warmth or the light she craved. Standing before the fireplace, the kindling flame leaping to life, she thought back to the courtroom, to the prosecutor's revelation, to Sloan's hasty retreat.

The news had been shocking, yet not shocking. She had known that there was something about the hostage incident that Sloan wasn't telling her. So much made sense now, particularly her instant bonding with Sloan. Both had been wounded by circumstances beyond their control. And both were virtually alone. The vision of Sloan leaving the courtroom, solitary, trying to bear the burden of guilt that no pair of shoulders could bear, haunted her, tormented her. So much so that she had defied Harper's order that she and Sloan have no personal contact for the duration of the trial. Shortly after arriving home, a couple of hours ago now, she'd called the lighthouse. There had been no answer—then or all the other times she'd called.

Where was he?

Of course, there was always the possibility that, fearing the calls were from reporters, he'd chosen to ignore the telephone. But in that case why not take the receiver off the hook and eliminate the bothersome ringing? No, somehow she just knew that he wasn't at the lighthouse. Which left the possibility that he was with Harper. Yes, that made sense, but still she didn't quite believe it. As he'd exited the courtroom, Sloan had looked as though the last thing he'd wanted was company. Even his best friend's.

Again Anna walked to the kitchen, reached for the telephone, and dialed the number of the lighthouse. She listened to the incessant ringing. After a frustrated sigh she replaced the receiver, and folding her arms about her, she walked to the window in the breakfast room. From the single vantage point the house offered, she saw the sea heaving with its own restless rhythm, surging in deep swells.

Restless. She, too, was restless, straining to break out of some emotional straitjacket. She wanted to be with Sloan. She had forbade herself to want this, but still she did.

Angry with herself for this weakness, she once more picked up the telephone, this time to call Carrie. When she wasn't being tortured by thoughts of Sloan, thoughts of Meg tormented her. Anna kept Carrie for only a minute, just long enough to make certain that Meg was all right. She didn't ask to speak to her daughter. She knew it was a waste of time. Neither did she believe Carrie when she told her to hang tough, that everything would be all right. Following this call, as though she had no will, she dialed the lighthouse again. Still no answer.

Where was he?

TWENTY

August

Y ou did what?"

Carrie, who sat at her brother's bedside, glanced up at Anna. "I talked to Sloan Marshall about helping you and Jack out. Only for a while, of course. During the weekends. Just to give you a break."

Anna forced herself to be calm. She forced her voice to sound normal. "I really don't need any help."

She was lying. The truth was that she was ready to drop, and if she did, she wasn't certain she'd ever get back up. For the second time that summer Jack had had to be hospitalized. Because the kidney infection refused to respond to antibiotics, because the sore on his leg wasn't healing, because the insulin dosage had had to be adjusted yet again, he'd spent the previous week at the Good Shepherd Hospital. Anna had remained by his side night and day, returning to the house only to shower and change into clean clothes.

He'd been discharged the tenth day of August, two days ago now, and Anna hadn't slept an uninterrupted hour since. She longed for the nurses she'd left behind, she longed for the help Carrie was suggesting, but dear God, that help could not come from Sloan!

"You need help," Carrie contradicted. "You're worn out. We all are. Kenny's been working longer hours, and Meg is nearing the end of the summer session and can't keep running the roads between here and school. She has to concentrate on her studies. As for me, I've stopped by two and three times a day, both at the hospital and here. Plus I'm working at the office. I'm exhausted, Kenny's exhausted, Meg's exhausted, and so are you. For heaven's sake, Anna, just look at you."

No, she'd rather not, Anna thought. Truth was that she'd stopped peering into mirrors. They were too honest, too blunt. They seemed to take too much delight in pointing out the dullness in her eyes, the baggy dark circles underneath, the paleness of her skin. Even her hair, which she'd had cut shorter than usual, seldom received more than a few strokes of the brush.

"Of course, you and Ken need to cut back. I'm sorry I didn't think of it myself."

Carrie held firm. "You need to cut back, as well." Suddenly realizing that Jack was hearing every word of the conversation, she turned to him and took his hand. The shocking pink of her dress made his color seem even more washed out. "We're not complaining, darling, and none of this is your fault. In fact, you're improving so rapidly that extra help would only be temporary."

Once more it amazed Anna how selective Carrie could be in her vision. She recognized that Anna was exhausted, yet couldn't see that not only wasn't Jack improving, he was steadily worsening. Even Dr. Goodman's prognosis for Jack's future had been guarded. His physical health notwithstanding, Jack's emotional health was at rock bottom. He was withdrawn, uncommunicative, and hadn't participated in his exercises since July. What Ken was presently putting him through was a series of passive movements often practiced on unconscious patients. As might have been expected, Jack made no response to Carrie's comment.

"Perhaps it's not my place to express an opinion," Ken said, "but I think that Mrs. Douglas is right. You *are* tired. You *do* need some help."

"See?" Carrie said. "And Kenny and I haven't even talked about this."

Anna could tell that she was losing the battle fast. She couldn't afford to lose the war, however. Sloan mustn't set foot in this house. She mustn't see him again. Simply because it was the one thing she most wanted. She had neither seen him, nor spoken with him, since that July afternoon when she'd found herself at the lighthouse, and in his arms.

"Fine," she said, "so we—I—need some temporary help, but I don't think that should be Sloan Marshall."

"Why not?" Carrie said. "I ran into him at the drugstore yesterday, spoke to him about it, and he was interested."

Anna couldn't believe any such thing. Sloan had made it perfectly clear that he didn't want to see her again. More likely than not, Carrie had backed him into a corner, in the process interpreting his response as she chose.

"For one thing he's leaving Cook's Bay. Probably by the end of the month." At the realization that her possessing this knowledge might appear odd, she added, "I heard Doris talking about it over at the Snappy Scissors." She didn't mention that she'd encouraged Doris—discreetly, she hoped—in this conversational direction.

"He doesn't know when he's leaving," Carrie said.

"The job's going through, but there's some sort of glitch holding things up."

"But why not hire someone who's going to be here for as long as I might need help?"

"Like who?" Carrie asked.

"There's a nursing service here in town," Anna insisted. "After all, we hired Ken."

"Ideally, you need someone who can lift, which translates to you need a male," Ken pointed out. "I'm the only male nurse registered with the in-home service. In fact, there are only two male nurses in Cook's Bay. The other works over at the Good Shepherd."

"Why does it have to be a nurse?" Anna asked. "I'm not a nurse. Sloan isn't a nurse."

"You're right," Ken said. "And there is a sitter service here in town. It's small, but there is one. Of course, it's all female staff."

"Yeah, five little old ladies supplementing their social security," Carrie said. "And not a one of them would know a hypoglycemic attack from a raging elephant."

"She's right," Ken said. "Most of them sit patients in hospitals, where all they have to do is buzz a nurse if they feel uncomfortable with a patient's condition."

"If they were worried, they could call me," Anna insisted.

"True," Ken agreed.

Anna's desperation escalated, a fact evinced by the shrillness in her voice. "There has to be someone I can hire!"

"There is someone," Carrie said. "Sloan Marshall."

Ken took this opportunity to state the obvious. "Mrs. Ramey, this is Cook's Bay, population thirty-five hundred max. We're not talking Bar Harbor, or Portland, or Augusta. And, again, I have to agree with Mrs. Douglas. A man might be better. Your husband would probably feel more comfortable with one."

"I don't understand," Carrie said, making no attempt to conceal her perplexity. "I thought you liked Sloan. I mean, he's a real nice guy."

"Of course he is, but—"

A grunt from Jack stopped Anna in midsentence. She, along with Carrie and Ken, seemed mildly surprised that Jack was in the room, on the planet, in the universe, and greatly surprised that he'd actually intruded into the conversation. When he nodded toward his pad, it was obvious that he wanted, in his own way, to speak.

Slowly, he wrote: *call him.*

When Carrie read the message aloud, Anna rose from her chair and started toward the bed. "Jack—"

Again he cut her off, this time with a sharp nod of his had. He wrote: *u need rest.*

"I'm fine. Really I am."

Jack tapped the earlier message, instructing her to call Sloan. Something in the way he tapped told her that the issue wasn't negotiable.

Anna studied her husband, and from out of nowhere came the oddest feeling that, just like Meg, Jack sensed something between her and Sloan and was forcing them together. The absurdity of the notion caused Anna to abandon it as quickly as it had dawned on her. Sighing, Anna knew that to continue protesting would be to court suspicion.

"All right. I'll call him."

"Now," Carrie said, delighted with her sister-in-law's acquiescence. "C'mon, I have his telephone number in my purse."

Anna gave her husband one last look—he, too, was looking at her—then followed Carrie into the kitchen.

Rummaging through her handbag, Carrie finally produced a piece of paper on which a number had been scrawled. Even the sight of the number sent Anna's heart scurrying. She prayed that Carrie would give her some privacy, but knew that she wouldn't. Her sister-in-law had already positioned herself against the counter, her eyes bright with expectation, her lips covered with a satisfied smile.

Anna dialed the number with fingers that had begun to tremble. Her heart pounded so heavily that she could hardly hear the ringing of the telephone. One ring, then another, followed by yet another. She had just decided that maybe the gods were on her side, and that Sloan wasn't at home, when he picked up. Salvation came crashing down around her.

"Hello?"

"I feel only when I'm with you . . . things I shouldn't feel at all . . . because I'm married."

"Hello?"

"Don't come back, Anna. If you do, I'm pretty sure I'll do anything I can to try and make you my lover."

"Hello?" The voice had grown impatient.

Anna started to speak, found the words clogged, and cleared her throat. Then, "Mr. Marshall."

Recognition. Silence. More silence.

Anna heard Sloan's breath. It rasped against the receiver with a cadence as uneven as hers. Had he been expecting her call with the same reluctance with which she'd made it?

"This is Anna Ramey. My sister-in-law, Carrie Douglas, gave me your number and said that I should call you. She said that you might be interested in helping me—Jack and me—out. Temporarily. By doing some weekend sitting with Jack."

Her stilted tone must have alerted Sloan to the fact that she was not alone, because he asked, "Is she there?"

"Yes," Anna said, relieved that he'd understood.

"Anna, there was no way I could talk her out of it. I tried. I swear it."

The way he said her name, in desperation, with possession, made her want to cry. Right then. Right there. With Carrie watching. Instead she said, "I certainly understand that."

"I didn't know what to do. She kept insisting, I kept trying to get out of it, but finally I thought that saying anything more would only cause her to start wondering why I was protesting so much."

"I know. It's just that I was surprised that you'd be interested. Carrie had told me that you were leaving town soon."

"Yeah, soon, but I don't know exactly when. Look, she said that you needed someone badly, that you were exhausted."

"I'm tired, Mr. Marshall, but I think Carrie exaggerated a bit."

"I did not," Carrie cried, reaching for the telephone and speaking directly to Sloan. "She's about to cave in. Do you think you can stay Saturday and Sunday nights? By then, with a little rest under her belt, I think she'll be ready to handle another week."

Silence. Sloan was speaking. What was he saying? Surely he'd find a delicate way of getting them out of this mess.

"Great," Carrie said, dashing Anna's hopes. "Well, look, I'll put her back on and you two can discuss the time." Carrie handed the receiver to Anna, saying, "See, all you had to do was ask."

She sashayed out of the room, as though she'd just brought about the greatest coup. Anna didn't know whether to laugh or to cry. She did neither. Numbly, she just listened to Sloan.

"We have no choice," he said, stating what she supposed she'd known all along.

When Anna opened the door Saturday night, Sloan realized that, had he known Anna looked so awful, he wouldn't have hesitated to come. Her eyes, normally so bright and beautiful, were listless, and fatigue etched her face. Worse, she was thin. So thin that she seemed lost in the baggy gray sweatsuit. There was still a prettiness about her, however, and a strength that said she would make it no matter how tough things got. He wanted to lessen her burden by just pulling her into his arms and holding her. That he couldn't sent an unpleasant emotion racing through him, an emotion remarkably akin to anger.

After speaking with her on the telephone, he'd wondered what their first encounter would be like. Anna quickly set the tone—polite, cool, very businesslike. All of which seemed for the best. He wanted to help her— God, she needed some rest!—but he also wanted to keep his distance. Holding himself apart from her was the only way he could get through the weekend, the only thing capable of saving his sanity. He'd told her when they'd parted that July day at the lighthouse that, should she not stay away, he wouldn't be noble a second time, that he'd try to make her his lover; but she hadn't come to him. She, like him, had been forced into this situation. Because of that, he owed her restraint.

After helping to settle Jack in for the night, she said at the foot of the stairway, her eyes not quite meeting Sloan's, "I think I'll go on to bed."

"I think that's a good idea."

"If you, uh, need me during the night . . ." She trailed off, perhaps, Sloan thought, because the words were ripe with suggestion. He wondered what she'd say if he told her that he needed her like hell right now. That he had night and day since the episode at the lighthouse, and maybe would for the rest of his life.

"I know where to find you," he said, the words sounding just as suggestive, though he honestly hadn't meant them to. Brusquely, he said, "Get some sleep."

He watched her ascend the stairs. She must have felt his gaze on her, but she never turned back. Not once.

He both admired and despised her control, particularly since it seemed to be entirely missing from his life of late.

At her disappearance Sloan walked back to Jack's bedroom. Though remaining aloof, Jack, nonetheless, had been friendly enough. He'd even thanked Sloan for helping out, stating the obvious, which was that Anna needed some rest. He'd added that she was the kind of person who took responsibility to heart, but he guessed that Sloan knew that about her. Sloan had thought the comment an odd one. He shouldn't have known this about Anna, and wouldn't have had their relationship not progressed beyond the casual. It made Sloan wonder if Jack Ramey suspected something. He dismissed the thought as ludicrous. The fact that he was in the house pretty much indicated that Jack suspected nothing.

Seeing that Jack was still awake, Sloan asked, "Is there anything else I can do for you?"

Jack indicated the nearby pitcher, and Sloan poured a glass of water. Taking it with his good hand, Jack managed several slow swallows, then returned the glass to Sloan. Slowly, Jack lay back on the pristine-white pillow of the hospital bed, looking both pitiful and proud. Sloan thought of the unfairness of life, of the uncaring way it had cut down this man long before his time, of the merciless way it had also called for the sacrifice of the woman upstairs, of the unfeeling way it was now demanding a smaller, though painful, oblation from him.

When Sloan realized that Jack was watching him, he grew uncomfortable. Were his thoughts in any way transparent? He asked again if there was anything he could do for Jack. Jack nodded toward the door.

"You want it closed?"

Jack shook his head.

"Oh, you mean Anna?" The instant Sloan used such

a familiar reference, he wished that he hadn't. At Jack's nod Sloan added, "Your wife went to bed."

Again Jack nodded, as though in approval, then indicated the lamp. Sloan cut it off, plunging the room into darkness, broken only by a faint night-light. He wished Jack a good night, then settled into an overstuffed chair that was actually quite comfortable. Did Anna ever sit in this chair? Did she ever think about him as she sat here? He couldn't believe that he'd even posed this question. How insensitive could he get? He wanted her to be sitting feet away from her husband and thinking about him? The answer was a simple, disgusting yes. Sloan shifted his position, his restlessness matching Jack's, and admitted one other disgusting thing. He hoped that this very minute she was upstairs, tucked in her cozy bed, thinking of him.

Anna tossed and turned and tried to think of anything besides the fact that Sloan was downstairs. From the moment she'd opened the door to him, his presence had filled every nook and cranny of the house. She'd assumed a distant position, an aloofness, even, but she didn't feel distant or aloof. In fact, as always when she was with him, she felt too much, too alive. When she'd climbed the staircase, his gaze had set her afire in ways that should have shamed her but, truthfully, had only made her feel hotter. What kind of demoralized creature was she that she could think of another man while her husband, her sick husband, lay nearby?

No answer came. Only a troubled sleep.

Suddenly Anna awoke, thinking that it was morning and that she'd overslept. She jerked her head in the direction of the clock to discover that its luminous dial read three-twelve. She heaved a sigh of relief as she coaxed her heart back into a normal rhythm. It had barely slowed when she remembered that Sloan was downstairs. The realization sent her heart tripping once more.

Go back to sleep. Do not—I repeat, do not—get up!

Anna knew the wisdom of going back to sleep. She knew the wisdom of not getting up. Wisdom, however, was obviously in short supply. Throwing back the cover, she reached for her robe, telling herself as she did so that perhaps she should check to see if everything was all right downstairs. After all, Sloan wasn't accustomed to tending to a diabetic. Maybe Jack needed something—water, to go to the bathroom, something—but was too proud to ask for it.

God, Anna, can't you even be honest with yourself?

The question halted her midway down the stairs and forced her to face the truth. It wasn't Jack she was concerned about. It was Sloan. The truth was that she just wanted to see him. On the other hand, there was some validity to her previous reasoning. Sloan wasn't familiar with a diabetic's needs, and Jack did possess his share of pride. In the end Anna had absolutely no idea whether what she was doing was justified. She knew only that her feet were taking her down the stairs. She knew only that a peek—and that's all she'd take, she swore—couldn't hurt anyone.

Anna stopped at the doorway of the bedroom—principle demanded that she not cross the threshold—and peered inside. The room glowed with a soft golden light; a stillness, muted and hushed, waited in the air.

Anna's gaze went first to her husband, whose motionless form suggested that he was sleeping; then slowly—perhaps if she did it slowly, it would excuse the act—she shifted her gaze to the nearby chair. Sloan slumped in a position guaranteed to produce aches and pains by morning. His long legs, clad in starched denim and no doubt numb from lack of proper circulation, stretched before him, one ankle crossed over the other, while his head lolled to the side. A swath of dark hair fell across his forehead. His arms folded into an X over his chest. His wide chest. His deep chest. The chest she remembered all too clearly being held against.

She urged the memory aside, trying to recall being held by her husband, but it had been too long ago. A lifetime ago. Even though she wasn't totally to blame, the fact that she couldn't remember filled her with remorse, and she would have turned from the door had not Sloan chosen that moment to sigh. A soft sigh. A sleep-riddled sigh. A sigh that spoke directly to her heart. A heaviness, an emotion that she thought wise not to identify, swept through her chest. It was both exhilarating and painful.

She told herself to leave.

She almost managed to obey herself.

Instead she became aware of Sloan watching her. She felt it, just as she'd once felt someone watching her on the beach. Her awareness now was disquieting, for it made that heaviness in her chest all the heavier.

Sloan, too, was experiencing discomfort. From the heartbeat that he'd come awake, he'd felt a quick, sharp stab that had not left him guessing as to its source. He had known that Anna was near. With a slow rolling of his head, he sought her out. The door. She stood at the door. *At,* not *inside,* as though crossing the portal was forbidden. Which seemed appropriate. Everything about their relationship was forbidden. But he could look, couldn't he?

Yes, he could.

And did.

Only to find that the quick, sharp stab was back, this time stealing away his breath. In the shrouded night, under the cover of darkness, he could barely see her. She was only a shadowy presence. A sweet glimmer of shape. A sensual specter. In his mind's eye, where his vision was perfectly, painfully, clear, he saw a swarm of blond curls and a delicately shaped face. He felt her breasts pressed against him, heard her heartbeat, tasted her honey-laden lips.

Do you remember? he wanted to shout.

Vibrations, both carnal and chaste, wafted across the room, wrapping themselves around Anna, giving birth to memories that would not die. Her heart quickened, her body thrummed.

Do you remember? she wanted to cry, unknowingly taking a step into the room.

A shaft of light draped itself across her, illuminating a simple cotton gown and a robe that revealed more than they covered. The sight of shadowed swells and shaded curves brought an agonizing pain to Sloan's heart, and his masculine body did what masculine bodies do best: it ached. It took all of the willpower he had to remain seated.

Go. Please, go!

Anna heard the words as clearly as if he'd spoken them, just as she felt his pain. With guilt chasing her every inch of the way, she raced back to her bedroom and her lonely bed. It had taken every ounce of strength she had to leave Sloan. It had taken every ounce of strength she had not to go to him. Even with her husband nearby. Surely that was a sin for which no god could offer forgiveness. Sitting on the edge of the bed, she closed her eyes and wondered how she could possibly endure the rest of the weekend.

Downstairs Sloan wondered the same thing, but he wasn't so concerned with sin, and the wages thereof. He was too angry, angry that the two of them were trapped, angry that she was legally, morally, bound to another man when she belonged to him.

The second time Anna awoke, it was six o'clock. The aroma of perking coffee and frying bacon had stolen its way upstairs. Anna's stomach, not caring one whit that she wasn't hungry—she couldn't remember the last time she had been—nonetheless growled in anticipation. Rolling from bed, she dressed in jeans and a black blouse and, after brushing her teeth and running a comb through her hair, headed for the kitchen. Once more she halted at the doorway and watched Sloan, who stood at the stove. He was scrambling eggs, the movement sending the muscles in his shoulders rippling beneath his shirt. His sleeves were rolled up, as they often were, revealing the black hair of his forearms. His jeans looked as if they'd been slept in, which, of course, they had been.

As she stepped into the kitchen, Anna put aside thoughts of rippling muscles, black hair, and wrinkled jeans. She could not ignore that exhilarating, painful heaviness that insisted on making its home in her chest. Neither could she allow herself to bestow a name on it.

"You didn't have to cook breakfast," she said, trying to hide her nervousness. She'd told herself a dozen times that she shouldn't have gone downstairs during the night. Nor should she remember so vividly the way his heated gaze had washed over her.

At the sound of her voice Sloan whirled. He'd been preoccupied with thoughts of his own, which also revolved around the evening before. With her standing before him, however, he realized how weak his memories had been. Suddenly the swells and curves barely glimpsed the night before could in no way rival those presently in view. Once more his body occupied itself in the act of appreciation, then in the act of self-chastisement.

Face-to-face, Anna first and foremost noticed Sloan's sunglasses, the gray-tinted, eyes-shielding sunglasses, the glasses that protected him from the world. And from her? She noted, too, the rakish stubble of beard and what looked remarkably like a scowl skulking about his lips. Surely she was mistaken about the latter, for why on earth should he be scowling?

Abandoning swells and curves for the stove and eggs, he said, "Someone has to take care of you. It's obvious you're not taking care of yourself."

The words had been pruned to a clipped shortness that startled Anna. "What does that mean?"

Sloan didn't look back, but rather reached for a couple of pieces of bread and plopped them into the toaster. "Just what I said. You look awful. You've lost too much weight."

Clippedness had turned to outright bluntness, which hurt and angered Anna. She found that she rather liked the anger. It fit her mood, set by the restless night, and the restless feeling that had begun to prowl through her from the moment she set eyes on Sloan this morning.

"I'm sorry about that," she said, walking to the refrigerator and pouring a glass of orange juice. "Life's been a little rough lately. I haven't had a lot of time to keep up a glamorous appearance."

At her reply Sloan glanced toward her. His eyes found hers, while hers tried to peer through his impenetrable gray lenses. He'd hurt her; but, then, he was hurting too. He'd also lied to her. Though thin, she didn't look awful, not with her features softened by sleep, her eyes hazy from dreams. Had she dreamed of him?

"Yeah," he said finally, raggedly, as though to acknowledge that she wasn't the only one life had been rough on.

The toast popped up, and relieved at the interruption, Sloan plucked up the two slices, buttered them, and placed them on a plate. He then dished up the eggs and bacon and handed the plate to Anna.

"Eat every bite."

"I don't eat much breakfast."

"You do this morning." He nodded toward the adjoining room with its table. "I'll bring you some milk and coffee."

"Just coffee," she said. "I need to check on Jack."

"He's fine. I bathed him, shaved him, and changed the linen on the bed. He said to tell you to eat breakfast, then come give him his shot."

Anna looked surprised. "You didn't have to do all that."

"That's what I'm being paid for."

His voice had grown brusque again. The truth was that he'd wanted to help Jack, simply because he liked the guy. He didn't like what Jack had done to Anna, certainly. But the fact that he'd been to hell and back, yet somehow managed to hang on to his dignity, commanded Sloan's respect. He himself had been to hell and back but had managed to come away with a lot less.

Stranger even than his liking Anna's husband was the feeling that Jack Ramey liked him. In a guarded kind of way. This morning Sloan had felt again that Jack suspected something was going on between him and Anna. Perhaps it was just a look Jack had given him. He worried that Jack might have witnessed the scene at the door.

"Go eat," Sloan ordered.

Upon entering the breakfast area Anna discovered that he'd laid a place setting for one. The sight was cozy, homey; he cared despite his lousy mood. What was he angry about, anyway? And he *was* angry; but, then, she wasn't in the best mood of her life, either.

In seconds Sloan brought in a glass of milk and two cups of coffee. "Coffee's all I want," she insisted.

"Drink the milk," he said, then motioned toward the plate. "Eat."

"You sound like a broken record," she said, picking up the fork. She could hear the tension in her voice. It matched the tension in her body, caused by the restless feeling sneaking around inside her, making a shambles of her usual composure.

"Then eat and shut me up," he said, dragging out the chair across from her, plopping down, and gulping a swallow of coffee.

Anna felt compelled to point out the obvious. "You're being paid to take care of my husband, not me."

My husband. Her choice of words didn't escape Sloan's attention. "Actually, at the moment I'm not being paid anything. We haven't even discussed wages."

Anna couldn't believe that they were having this conversation. She knew as well as she knew her name that he couldn't care less about the money. However, the prospect of fighting with him—with anyone, actually—felt good. When was the last time she'd snipped or snapped or shouted? Whenever it was, it just might have been too long ago. Maybe it was time to slip off her civilized bonds.

Tilting her head to a cocky pose, she said, "My, my, we've suddenly become mercenary, haven't we?"

"I'm working damned hard for this."

"I'll pay you what I pay Ken."

"Fine."

"You don't even know what that is."

"Whatever it is, it's fine."

"Fine!"

"Fine!"

They glared at each other, gazes hotter than the sun beginning to rise on the horizon. Anna glanced away first and crunched into a strip of bacon. Sloan downed a scalding shot of coffee. Both felt like taking a walk on the angry side.

"Are you always like this in the morning?" she asked.

"No, sometimes I'm grumpy."

The question conjured similar images in two minds, images of a man and a woman crawling from a rumpled bed following a night of passion. Hand in hand, they might walk the beach or wade into the sea, which at that instant could be heard tumbling its way shoreward.

Anna too easily recognized the man and woman and sought to change the subject to the first thing that had come into her head the moment she'd entered the kitchen. "I thought you were past the sunglasses."

"I like wearing sunglasses."

"In the house?"

Sloan shrugged. "In the house. Out of the house."

"What you mean is that you like hiding behind them."

"Hey, whatever gets you through the day, the night." He paused, fixing her with a steely eyed stare. "Speaking of night, what in hell did you think you were doing last night?"

His harshly delivered question startled her. This was not an area she wanted to pursue, and, flustered, she hedged. "What do you mean what was I doing last night?"

"Just what I said."

"I was checking on my husband."

"Like hell you were!"

That he'd so clearly seen though her actions angered Anna. She was already angry with herself for having gone downstairs. It had been incredibly stupid of her, incredibly brazen. Who was this brazen person she'd become?

"And just what do you think I was doing?" she asked, continuing to take the path of denial.

"I don't *think*, I *know*. We both know. You were courting disaster. Big time."

"Aren't you being just a little melodramatic?"

"No, I'm just being honest. Which was something you used to be. You were even being honest last night." Before Anna could respond, Sloan added clinically, as though saying it thus would make it easier to say, "I want you, and you want me, and if you don't give me a wide berth, nature's going to take its course."

Was he right? Was that what her anger was all about? A way to relieve the restlessness roaming her body? A way to douse the fire that his very presence built in her? She'd face the questions another time, when her heart wasn't racing so wildly.

Pushing back her chair, she stood, saying, "I need to give Jack his insulin."

As she walked past Sloan, he grabbed her wrist, his fingers manacling her with a sweetly painful pressure. Her gaze rushed to his and met a screen of gray. For forever-long seconds Sloan listened to the savage throbbing of her heart with his fingertips, while Anna listened to his unsteady breath.

"Stay away from me," Sloan rasped, and this time he couldn't conceal his desperation. "I'll help you out, but stay away from me. If you don't, I swear I'll take you right here, in this house, under the same roof with your husband. And afterward we're both going to hate ourselves. Maybe even each other."

Anna didn't have a lot of experience with threats, but she knew that the one Sloan had just issued should be taken seriously. For no other reason than the fact that she wished that he'd make good on it.

TWENTY-ONE

Anna was relieved when, at a few minutes before seven o'clock, Sloan called his night shift over and left. She spent the rest of the day trying to prepare herself for his return. Bit by bit she pulled into herself, leaving behind memories of heated gazes, sexy appearances, and tender threats. By day's end she had arrived in the world she so often inhabited, a world where feelings were not allowed. She would survive Sloan's being in the house by staying away from him, by feeling nothing.

When Sloan arrived that evening at six o'clock, his sunglasses still in place, he found an aloof Anna, an Anna whose eyes never quite met his, an Anna who, for the first time since he'd met her, appeared more stranger than friend. His first impulse was to rescind his warning, to shout, *Don't stay away from me! I can't stand to see you this way!* His second impulse was to ignore the first. He had to get through this night, and distance was his only hope of survival.

"Carrie's coming for dinner," Anna said as she walked beside Sloan toward Jack's bedroom.

"Good. I'll have a chance to tell her that I'm quitting." Even though Anna needed rest, she didn't need it at the risk of her emotional sanity.

Anna obviously agreed, for her relief was nearly tangible.

"I'll just tell her that sitting with Jack is more than I can handle, with my getting everything ready to leave town."

If the excuse sounded as shallow to Anna as it did to him, she didn't say so. Sloan suspected that she was as desperate as he, and consequently, willing to settle on anything even remotely plausible. The trick would be to make Carrie buy into it.

"She's also spending the night," Anna said.

Sloan shot Anna a quick look, which she didn't return.

"I didn't ask her to chaperon us, if that's what you think," Anna said. "She asked if she could stay. Actually, she announced that she was. She often does. Particularly when Harper's out of town."

What Sloan thought was that, although he'd had lunch with Harper, his good friend had failed to tell him that he was going out of town; but, then, Harper had had precious little time to mention anything beyond the fact that Sloan was playing with fire by sitting with Jack. Sloan wondered what his friend would say if Harper knew he'd already been burned by a kiss that he couldn't force from his mind.

"A chaperon isn't a bad idea," Sloan said.

Anna glanced over at him, her gaze colliding with the gray lenses of his glasses. "You're safe from me."

"But are you safe from me?"

Anna made no response. She just listened to the hot blood sizzling through her veins.

At six-thirty, just as Anna was administering Jack's shot of insulin, Carrie breezed in, wearing a mood as bright as her daffodil-yellow pantsuit.

Averting her gaze from the needle, she kissed her brother on the cheek, saying, "You look great. See, I told you you were getting better. And look at you, Anna," she added. "Didn't I tell you that all you needed was a good night's sleep?" Speaking at large, she said, "Doesn't she look rested?"

Suddenly Sloan felt a whole lot better about the lame excuse he'd be offering her later. Anyone who could buy into Jack's looking great, and most particularly, into Anna's looking rested, would buy into anything.

Dispensing with the disposable syringe, Anna diverted the subject from herself. "Something smells good."

"Shrimp scampi," Carrie announced proudly. "The recipe was in this month's *Gourmet* magazine." Without missing a beat she said to Sloan, "Tell me you haven't eaten."

"Actually, I have."

"Then you'll just have to eat again."

In the end Carrie, in her charming, no-one-could-say-no-to-her way, orchestrated the entire evening, which she'd planned with great deliberation. Not only had she brought dinner, but also a couple of candles, which she lit and set in the middle of the small table in the bedroom, along with a vase that held a single rose and some lacy greenery. She had insisted—"Oh, please, Jack, tell me that you feel like getting up!"—that they all sit around the table. Jack, with Anna's and Sloan's assistance, struggled into a bathrobe and the wheelchair.

"There," Carrie announced as Sloan slid Jack into place. "Isn't that perfect?"

Neither Jack nor Anna nor Sloan commented. Jack simply slouched in the chair, while Anna seated herself beside her husband. Sloan, after one more valiant effort to remove himself from the dinner scene, took the chair across from Anna. She didn't even glance his way, leaving Sloan to wonder at the thoughts roaming through her mind.

In truth Anna's mind was blank, which matched her feelings. No thoughts, no feelings. Every now and then a renegade thought would try to make itself known, but for the most part Anna held her ground and sent it scurrying. She *did* briefly hang on to the telephone conversation she'd had earlier that afternoon with her daughter. When Meg had asked how things were going, Anna hadn't mentioned Sloan's presence in the house. She'd feared her daughter's disapproval. But come tomorrow Sloan wouldn't be a presence in the house. This realization dented the armor she'd cloaked herself in. *Don't think,* she hastily reminded herself. *And above all, don't feel.*

And so the meal began, three traveling the road of silence, while the fourth chatted easily, endlessly. Carrie spoke of the past and of childhoods happily spent, of the present and shrimp scampi, of the future and of summer's end when Jack and Anna would leave Cook's Bay.

How odd, Jack thought as he watched the candlelight flicker across his wife's face. He suddenly realized he never thought in terms of leaving Cook's Bay. It was as though an unspoken covenant had been made between him and some unknown power, a covenant that would forever keep him here. And yet, he saw Anna leaving. What did that mean? And why did it make him feel both happy and sad?

Sloan tried to imagine that point in time, fast approaching, when Anna and Jack would return to their home in Connecticut, to their past life. Carefully, Sloan sneaked a peek at Anna, her face beautifully bathed in the candles' rich glow. He couldn't imagine her in Connecticut, only here by the seashore, by *their* seashore.

Anna, too, was trying to envision a return to her home, a return to her Sloan-less life. Her defenses down, a thought slipped in, and she stole a peek at his candlelit face. How would she survive without him? How would she survive knowing that he was half a world away?

"Where exactly is the North Sea?"

Carrie's query, which uncannily followed the direction of Anna's thoughts, startled Anna, and she glanced up to find Sloan's gaze on her. Without his sunglasses, which the evening had forced him to shed or else explain why he hadn't, he looked bare, naked. *Don't look, don't think, don't feel*, she told herself, and yet she waited eagerly for his reply.

Sloan allowed himself only a momentary glimpse of Anna. "It's part of the Atlantic. Between Great Britain and the North European mainland."

"Harper said that you'll be diving for an oil company."

Sloan shoved the shrimp around on the plate, in much the same way Anna was doing, in much the same way Jack was too. "That's right."

"He also said that you're retired military."

"Yeah," Sloan said, pruning his reply so as not to encourage further questions on the subject.

Carrie needed no encouragement, however. "Are you from this area?"

Despite herself Anna's interest was piqued. There was so very little that she really knew about this man. Only the warmth of his arms, only the sweet urgency of his kiss, only the fact that she would never know more. *Don't think, don't feel.*

"I've traveled so much of the world, it's hard to re-

member where I'm from," Sloan said, hanging on to his
privacy.

Carrie smiled. "And is there someone special waiting
in one of those ports of call?"

Anna's heart accelerated. So did Sloan's. Neither
looked in the other direction.

"No," he answered.

Carrie's grin grew. "I find that very hard to believe,
don't you, Anna?"

Given no choice, Anna glanced up. She found three
pairs of eyes glued to her—Carrie's, displaying her
usual spiritedness; Sloan's, clearly saying that he'd love
to be hiding behind his sunglasses; and Jack's . . . It was
difficult to read Jack's as he looked from Anna to Sloan
and back to Anna.

Calmly, as though the question ruffled her in no way,
Anna smiled, saying, "What I think is that you're embarrassing our guest."

At the end of the meal everyone told Carrie how de-
licious the shrimp scampi had been. Carrie ignored the
plates that were far from clean, clinging only to the
compliment. Jack, in particular, had eaten little and
seemed to wilt with sudden fatigue. He was put to bed,
whereupon Anna announced that she, too, was headed
in that direction. Which she was, with only a cursory
good night to all. Carrie herself seemed tired and, after stacking the dishes in the sink, after giving her
brother a kiss, recited the same nocturnal farewell. On
a relieved sigh Sloan cut the lights down and settled
into the chair.

Sleep, however, eluded him. The longer he sat, the
more unfriendly the chair became. He stretched his
legs, stacked his hands, tried to find any position even
remotely comfortable for his head. He fought and fret-
ted, listened to the house settle, and inhaled the lingering combined scent of the rose and melting wax.
Everything reminded him of Anna, and he grew to

hope, despite his warning her off, that she'd show up at the door the way she had the night before. With every whisper the house gave, he looked up hopefully, angry with himself for doing so. At twenty minutes till three o'clock, he decided that he could no longer sit still. He steered his tired body in the direction of the kitchen.

At the same time, Anna punched her pillow, knowing that no matter how many times she pummeled it, it wouldn't be enough to bring about sleep. The pillow wasn't the problem; but, then, with her no-think, no-feel policy, she hedged from admitting exactly what, who, that problem was. She obviously wasn't the only restless one in the house, however. An hour before, she'd heard Carrie open the door of the guest bedroom en route to the bathroom. Was Sloan as restless? *Don't think. Don't feel. Don't* . . . Throwing back the covers, Anna slipped from bed, grabbed her robe, and headed for the kitchen. She had no idea whether warm milk worked, but at this point she was willing to try anything.

At the sight of the kitchen light Anna frowned, though she concluded that Carrie was its cause. She was wrong, a fact she realized when she arrived at the doorway. Sloan, who'd obviously heard her approach, turned. Their gazes collided.

His heart racing, Sloan observed the way her golden curls tumbled wildly, the way she clutched her cotton robe to her, the way her bare feet peeked from beneath two hems.

Her heart racing, Anna noted the way Sloan's hair slanted across his forehead, the way his stockinged feet dug into the linoleum, the way his shirttail hung outside his jeans.

Anna backed away. "I'm sorry. I didn't know it was you."

Though he'd told her to stay away from him, he couldn't think of anything he wanted less.

"Don't go," he said, instantly justifying his order, if not his urgent tone, by adding, "This *is* your kitchen."

"I, uh, couldn't sleep. I thought some warm milk . . ." Anna trailed off.

"I couldn't sleep, either. Except I chose to give up the fight." A jar of instant coffee sat on the counter, alongside a cup and a spoon. "I just helped myself to what I wanted."

There was something innately sexy about his choice of words. Sloan knew that. Anna knew that. Both felt their breath falling too heavily in their chests.

Go back to the bedroom, Anna thought.

Get the hell out of here! Sloan thought.

"I don't need that coffee, after all," Sloan said. "What I really need is a shot of something far more potent."

"The top shelf of the right-hand cabinet," Anna said, knowing that she was courting trouble. "I'm not sure how potent it is, though. It's some sort of liqueur. Carrie brought it over."

"Are you telling me to stay?" he asked, thinking that the way she was looking at him was dangerous. Very dangerous.

"I don't know. Am I?"

She'd lobbed the ball back into his court. After all, he'd been the one who'd told her to keep her distance.

Hadn't he been the one who'd told her to stay away from him? He was pretty certain he had been, although right this minute he couldn't swear to anything except that his palms were burning with the fire that Harper had accused him of playing with.

"Actually, I think I could use a shot of something in my milk," Anna said, driving the ball even deeper, wondering if she was really participating in this reckless conversation.

"I'll make you a deal," Sloan said.

"What kind of deal?"

"I'll forget the coffee in favor of the hot milk. You heat the milk, I'll find the liqueur, and then we'll go our separate ways."

"That seems safe enough," she said, hiding behind her no-think, no-feel strategy, yet both thoughts and feelings were straining against their restrictive reins.

"Yeah, safe." He said the word as though he both loathed and loved it.

She stared. He stared. Finally she repeated, "Top shelf."

He turned, reluctantly, opened the right-hand cabinet, and stood on tiptoe. If she didn't stop looking at him with those sea-blue eyes, he was going to reconsider his stand on safety. That or have a couple of long, throat-burning, mind-numbing drafts of this liqueur. Could he get drunk on liqueur?

Sloan saw the bottle almost at once, although it had been shoved toward the back of the shelf. He stretched his arm forward, feeling the tail of his shirt rise upward.

Anna gasped at what she saw striping his back.

Sloan knew the mistake he'd made even before he whirled to confront her. Her eyes, wide and disbelieving, confirmed his error.

Anna knew the mistake she'd made. She thought of how naive she'd been. But then maybe she hadn't been naive at all. Maybe she'd deliberately chosen to believe that his being taken hostage was the no-big-deal he'd inferred it was. Now, however, every war movie she'd ever seen, every frame of news film she'd ever witnessed regarding hostages and maritime prisoners, came rushing back. She forgot that she wasn't supposed to think or to feel.

"Why didn't you tell me?" Anna asked, the question barely audible in the suddenly too-quiet kitchen. Even so, it was obviously tinged with anger, with hurt, with a million other emotions.

Sloan didn't pretend not to understand. "It's over. I didn't want to keep being reminded of it."

Her anger growing, she said, "But I specifically asked you if they'd hurt you. You told me that I'd been watching too many movies." Brushing the hair back from her eyes, she said, "You lied to me."

About that and more, Sloan thought, but said, "Isn't that what you really wanted me to do? Lie to you?" When Anna didn't answer, he said, "You didn't want to hear the truth. No one does." Silence. Then, "Look, Anna, fair is fair, and I'll admit that I didn't want to talk about it any more than you wanted to hear about it. I can't talk to anyone about what happened."

"Not even me?" she asked. The depth of the hurt in her voice surprised even her.

"Especially you." At her puzzled look he added, "I didn't, don't, want your pity."

Anna shook her head in disbelief as she started toward him. "Pity? What about compassion? What about my just wanting to share it with you? Didn't I deserve that much? Didn't you?"

"There was no reason for us to share it. We're nothing to each other. Just two strangers who met on a beach one summer."

Had he struck her, her pain could not have been more real. Why had he wanted to hurt her? Maybe because he himself was hurting so badly. Sloan leaned back against the counter and sighed. He refused to apologize for what he'd said, though.

"Tell me what happened to you in Beirut."

Sloan recoiled at the request. "Don't," he pleaded. "I've already told you that I don't want to talk about it." He swallowed hard. "I can't find the words."

"Was it terrible?" Anna knew that the question was stupid, but she hoped that Sloan, by a single word, would eradicate the horrible images spinning around in her head.

He didn't. His voice was harsh when he asked, "You want me to lie to you again, don't you? You want me to tell you that torture isn't bad, don't you? That I didn't prefer, and long for, death?"

The word *torture* stole Anna's breath away. "No! Yes! Yes, that's what I want you to tell me."

Sloan considered lying to her. It would be easy. So easy. "I know it's what you want to hear, but it's not what I'm going to tell you. Torture is hell."

Anna let the implications of what he'd said sink in. It hurt—deep in her heart. She tilted her chin. "I want to see what they did to you."

"No, you don't."

"Yes."

"Anna, don't do this to yourself. Don't do this to me. I'm begging you."

"I want to see, Sloan."

Sloan wasn't quite certain how she won her way. He knew only that she touched his arm, that she lifted his shirt, that silence, heavier than his heartbeat, thudded throughout the room. Maybe he'd allowed her this intimacy—and it was an intimacy of the most basic nature—because he'd really wanted to share his pain with her. Maybe he wanted her to see the physical ugliness of what he'd endured, so that maybe she could understand the emotional ugliness that he was still trying to cope with.

When she brushed her fingertips across one scar, then another, Sloan held his breath . . . and his heart. Closing his eyes, grasping the counter for support, he thought that he'd known all about torture, when the truth was that he'd known nothing about it. Nothing at all! This sweet torture, coming from a woman who would never be his, was the consummate form of punishment. And maybe the fact that she would never be his was the penance he must pay for his cowardly act.

With gentle strokes Anna traced the multitude of

scars scoring Sloan's back. What had happened to her no-think and no-feel resolution? Suddenly she seemed to be made up of nothing more than thoughts and feelings. Her thoughts ran the gamut of everything from how could any human being inflict such pain on another to how could anyone survive such torture. Sloan had been right. She didn't want to know any details. She didn't think that she was strong enough to withstand them. Even now her stomach crawled with nausea, and her heart felt as heavy as lead. Or maybe it was a return of that warm, heavy feeling that she'd felt before, that feeling that came to her when she thought of or saw Sloan, that feeling that she refused to give a name to, because she knew that doing so might well be the most dangerous thing she ever did.

Sloan, too, sensed the danger in the air, although he had no way of knowing the depth of that danger—until he felt Anna's lips, softer than fleece, replacing her fingertips. At the first kiss his breath escaped in a long hiss. At the second his knees threatened to buckle. At the third he whirled and grasped Anna's wrist. He manacled her with a pressure as tender as her caress, her kisses, had been. Sloan listened to the strong throbbing of her heart with his fingertips, while Anna listened to his unsteady breath. His eyes were hazed with passion.

"Don't!" he begged, with desperation and anger.

She matched his desperation, his anger. "Tell me that we're more than strangers who met on a beach one summer."

Her demand surprised him. "Does it really matter what we are?"

"Yes, it matters to me."

Sloan's eyes darkened. "Do you want the truth, Anna? Or another pretty lie?"

"I want the truth," she answered, knowing that she

couldn't return to Connecticut, to the rest of her life, without it.

Sloan studied her—the eyes staring so intently at him, ordering him to give her the answer she needed to hear.

"We're more than strangers who met on a beach one summer."

The soft sexiness of his voice lapped about Anna, and although he hadn't said exactly what they were, she knew. They were two people condemned to a lovers' purgatory, always hungering but never being fed.

Anna had just opened her mouth to thank Sloan for his honesty when she heard a noise at the door. Instinctively, she yanked her hand from Sloan's and whirled around. Her heart slammed into a fast gear.

Wrapping her robe about her, Carrie shuffled into the kitchen, her comment reflecting nothing out of the ordinary. "I'm glad to see I'm not the only one who couldn't sleep."

Anna smiled weakly, hoping beyond hope that Carrie hadn't seen enough to make her suspect anything, hoping beyond hope that she herself didn't look as guilty as she felt. When she spoke, however, she betrayed herself by stammering.

"I, we, couldn't sleep. Sloan—Mr. Marshall—wanted coffee. I thought warm milk would be nice. We were just about to make some. Warm milk, I mean."

Sloan, whose heart beat as erratically as Anna's, said with a deceptive calmness, "She's persuaded me that liqueur-laced warm milk would be better than coffee. Would you like to join us?"

"Sounds good," Carrie answered.

In uncomfortably long minutes, which Carried filled with nonstop talk, Anna held a mug of warm milk in her hands and excused herself. She thought she'd drink it in bed, she announced. Without meeting either Carrie's or Sloan's eyes, she left, headed for her bedroom.

Once there, she closed the door behind her. Quickly, as though it were medicine, she drank the milk, then lay down. She didn't fall asleep, however. Instead she thought of Sloan and of the sickening scars marring his back, of the soft, sexy way he'd proclaimed them more than strangers who'd met on a beach one summer, and of Carrie, who, despite the fact that Anna wanted to believe otherwise, had probably seen more than Anna had wanted her to.

Downstairs Sloan, who had no idea just how much Carrie had observed when she'd walked in on him and Anna, gave her his feeble excuse for having to quit.

"I certainly understand," she said. "Actually, I think Anna can manage on her own now. She looks rested, and Jack is doing so much better."

Sloan could think of no appropriate reply.

When morning came, Anna was relieved to discover that Sloan had already left the house. During the endless night she had wondered just how she could say good-bye, knowing that she'd probably never see him again. She told herself that in time she would forget him, and she honestly believed it that sunny Monday. All day, however, like the haunting refrain of a song, Sloan played over and over in her mind, in her senses. She heard his voice, saw the scars defiling his flesh, felt her fingertips reading them as though they were braille passages of his past. Mostly, though, she just felt that warm, heavy, nameless feeling in her heart.

By Tuesday she knew with certainty that she'd miscalculated the length of time it would take to forget Sloan. Oh, she'd forget him. It was just going to take longer than she'd first thought. Curiously, for the whole of two days she suspected that Jack was watching her. But, then, maybe she was mistaken. On the off chance that she wasn't, she tried to appear normal, which translated to chattering away as usual, talk that had no beginning, no end, no purpose. That night she dreamed that Jack died. She awoke upset—not so much because he had died, but because she had felt such relief at being free.

Come Wednesday morning, in punishment for the dream, Anna told herself that she wouldn't think of Sloan for the duration of the day. The resolution only seemed to strengthen him in her mind. Thursday followed the same troubling pattern, until she was left to conclude, Friday morning, as dawn brushed the unsettling night away, that, if she had two forevers, she wasn't going to forget Sloan. In retrospect she guessed she'd know that all along.

"More coffee?"

Sloan, seated across from Harper in a leather-padded booth, glanced up at the waitress whose name tag read Tammie. Every time he came into the Chat 'N' Chew, her hair was a different color. Today it was auburn, which actually went pretty well with her ivory complexion and green eyes. Despite her youthfulness, she had a used look, like a new car driven too hard and abandoned too soon to a secondhand lot. Still, she had a nice chassis, a firm body, and an engine, he'd bet, that could go from zero to a hundred within seconds of a man's touch.

"No, thanks," Sloan said, primarily because the cup was still three-quarters full. Upon his arrival, indeed upon his every arrival, Tammie rushed to wait on his table, hovering about with an embarrassing conspicuousness.

"We have some fresh blueberry pie," she said temptingly.

"None for me, thanks," Sloan answered.

Harper agreed, and Tammie reluctantly moved on to

another table filled with luncheon diners. Sloan knew that she'd find a reason to return—shortly.

"You know that she's interested in you," Harper said.

"She's a kid."

"She's single."

Sloan halted the cup midway to his lips, then brought it to his mouth. He took an unhurried swallow.

"I'm leaving town, remember?"

"And if you weren't, you still wouldn't be the slightest bit interested," Harper said, stating the obvious.

The statement required no response, although it did force Sloan to admit that no woman stood much of a chance holding his interest right now. Unless, of course, she had blond hair, blue eyes, and a face so ravaged by weariness, yet so sweet for all her fatigue, that it made him hurt to look at it. God, he'd hurt this week! In a way he didn't even know a human being could hurt. And what hurt most of all was the remembrance of her touch, her kiss, the way she'd stroked her fingertips, whispered her lips, across the scars on his back—gently, caringly, healingly. He wouldn't have been surprised to discover that the scars had disappeared entirely. Given enough time, could she also heal his emotional pain? The answer was totally irrelevant, because time was something they didn't have.

"When do you leave?" Harper asked, knowing that his friend had received a phone call that morning.

"Monday. At six forty-two A.M."

Harper paused before asking bluntly, "Are you going to be all right?"

"What's there not to be all right about? It's a great job offer."

"You know what I mean."

"I'm going to be fine," Sloan said, with just a tiny bit of testiness.

A few seconds lumbered by. "It's for the best, Sloan."

"Yeah," Sloan said, thinking that his buddy had spoken the truth. This way Anna could go on with her life and he could go on with his. This way she'd never know exactly what happened in Beirut. This way he could save face.

"Let's go out tomorrow night," Harper said. "A bon voyage fling. Just you and me and Jack Daniel's."

Sloan measured out a smile, saying, "Yeah. Maybe."

Even as he spoke, however, he was searching for a legitimate excuse not to go. He wasn't much for company these days. Anyone's. And that most certainly included Tammie, who was about to make another run on the table.

"C'mon, let's go," Sloan said, standing, pulling out enough money to pay for two coffees, and tossing it on the table.

As the two men headed for the door, Harper said, "You're breaking her heart."

Sloan said nothing. He knew that people didn't die of broken hearts. If they did, he'd be pushing up his share of daisies.

Anna's footsteps fell hollowly on the shiny wooden floor of Gouge's General Store. The sound was apropos. She, too, felt hollow. The week had used her up, stripping every feeling from her, every vital emotion—those few she had left—leaving her as empty as a carton needing to be tossed aside. She felt nothing. Absolutely nothing. Which, as always, was both wonderful and frightening. Within this emptiness, this nothingness, however, had come the knowledge that something was about to happen. Perhaps it was based on the fact that Anna knew things couldn't go on as they were—for Jack or for her. Even Carrie, who'd stopped by on her way to work, had broken from her characteristic optimism and had point-blank told Anna that she looked terrible. Jack, too, Carrie admitted—Anna knew what this had cost her sister-in-law—didn't look all that great.

At one o'clock—trying to escape the house, Jack, this feeling of nothingness—Anna had fled to Gouge's General Store. *Clippity-clip*, came the canine footfalls behind her. The dog, adorned in red, had followed Anna's every move, as had Inez Gouge out of the corner of her eye. The tinkling of the bell heralded the arrival of another customer, but still Anna felt nothing. She just kept gathering items—milk, bread, butter ... Were they out of eggs? She didn't know. And didn't care.

She had just turned the corner of the dairy aisle when she saw him. What astounded her, scared her, was the fact that she felt nothing even in his presence. The weekend before she had willed herself to feel nothing, but feelings had crept in anyway. Now, however, as she stood staring at Sloan, she felt no stirring of anything akin to emotion—no racing heartbeat, no catch in her breath, nothing. Only recognition.

Sloan stepped toward Anna. He'd seen her car parked in front of the store, and though he'd told himself not to stop, he'd found himself doing precisely that. He had not had the strength to do otherwise. The nearer he got to her, the faster his heart beat, the shallower his breath became. He halted directly in front of her. It was then he saw the emptiness in her eyes. The total and complete and frightening emptiness.

"Are you all right?" he whispered in a way of a greeting.

"No," she answered.

It was the first time she'd admitted as much. The fact that she was no longer willing to brave her way through a lie told Sloan something he didn't want to hear, namely, that she had reached the end of the emotional line.

"Oh, Anna, I'm so sorry I've done this to you," he said, his voice thick with regret.

"You've done nothing to me."

"That's not true. I took your complicated life and made it even more complicated."

"It wasn't deliberate."

"No, but it still happened." He paused, knowing that his next words might well be the hardest he'd ever say. "I'm leaving Cook's Bay."

"I know."

"No, I mean the job came through."

"I know."

She had known the moment she'd seen him what he'd come to tell her. For so long she had dreaded hearing it, but now that she had, she felt nothing. In fact, she heard herself asking calmly, "When?"

He told her. Come Monday morning he would walk from her life. For forever. Never to see her again. And she felt nothing.

"It's for the best," Sloan said. "You can go on with your life."

"I'm not sure that I have much of a life to go on with."

"Don't say that!" he said, then realized he'd spoken too loudly. Looking around, he saw nothing but the dog, but where there was the dog, could its owner be far behind?

"Sometimes it's just too late." She smiled, a gesture of pure mechanics. "I don't feel anything anymore. I didn't want to feel anything. At least, I thought I didn't, but now that I don't, it's scary."

Her admission gutted Sloan's stomach. He knew, not with masculine ego but with his heart, that he could make this woman feel—with kisses, with caresses, with tender words spoken in the heat of passion. But he could give her none of these things. The only thing he could give her was something she might not even want.

"I love you, Anna," he said, the words softer than moonlight falling on the silvery sea. Smiling just as softly, he added, "I think I must have fallen in love with you that first day on the beach. And just a little bit more every time I saw you." The smile faded. "I don't think, I *know*, that I'll love you for the rest of my life."

It had been so long since a man had said those words to her that Anna had forgotten how precious, how poetic, how promise-filled they were. She had forgotten how sweetly they could fall upon a woman's heart. Even though she still felt mired in an emotional numbness, she cherished his declaration. She raised her hand, her intent to cup his cheek, but stopped herself before doing so.

Sloan felt as though she had touched him. Anna knew that he wanted to hear the same words from her.

"I'm not free to say the words, Sloan. Please understand."

"I do," he said, admiring her loyalty even as disappointment raced through him. On a deep, ragged breath he added, "Promise me one thing. Promise me that you'll never forget me."

"I don't think there's even a remote chance of that."

Her reply was all he could hope for, and so, for a long, long while, he held it close. Into the silence he started to speak.

"Don't say good-bye," Anna said. "Just walk away."

Both stared, storing memories for a lifetime. Anna took in his dark hair, his dark eyes, the slant of his jaw, his chiseled chin, lips that had once moved over hers in an unforgettable fashion. Sloan took in a riot of blond curls, eyes bluer than a summer sky, her sweetness, her goodness, lips that had tasted as no other woman's ever had . . . or ever would again.

Suddenly, as though he could bear no more, Sloan turned and walked briskly down the aisle. At its end he hesitated.

No, don't look back! Anna pleaded silently.

One ragged heartbeat, then another, exploded against Sloan's chest, but he didn't look back, simply because he didn't trust himself to.

Anna watched him disappear, then heard the bell tinkling his departure. It sounded like what it was, a death knell ringing the demise of what might have been.

"Here, take these and go," Carrie said that evening as she tossed the car keys into Anna's lap.

Anna glanced not at her sister-in-law, but at her husband, who sat in the wheelchair in the kitchen. He gave a slow nod.

"But where would I go?" Anna asked.

"Anywhere. You just need to get out of this house. I should have seen this coming."

That Carrie saw her deterioration troubled Anna. She must be ready for a padded cell if her sister-in-law noticed that she was stressed out. The truth was that she wasn't stressed out. One had to feel something to be stressed out, and she still felt nothing. Sloan had told her that he loved her, then had walked out of her life, and she felt nothing. It was a bizarre feeling, one, she supposed, that meant she was in serious emotional trouble.

"Go to the movies," Carrie suggested. With a sweep of her hand, as though she were swishing away a flock of birds, Carrie cried, "Go, go, go! Anywhere! And don't be in any hurry to come back. We can manage fine, can't we, Jack?"

Jack said nothing. He simply watched his wife.

Anna obeyed because she didn't have the strength to resist. Once in the car, she started the engine and just sat listening to it hum. Was Sloan packing to leave? Probably. She envied him his new surroundings, his new beginning, his new life. Putting the car in gear, she headed for town, though once there, she drove past the theater with its flashing marquee. She just kept driving and driving until she had cleared town, until the countryside ebbed and flowed before her, until the next little town appeared. She drove through it, too, and the town beyond. Her thoughts were all of Sloan and of snippets of conversation they'd shared.

"Disappointment is part of life."
"Disappointment is part of death."
"Maybe the death of the spirit is as inevitable as the death of the body."

"Do you really have dark eyes beneath those sunglasses?"
"Yeah, I'll show you tomorrow."
"Do you have a given name?"
"Yes, I'll tell you tomorrow."

"Being human is intolerable."

"Why only whole shells?"
"I respect survival."

"Hunger eventually leads to recklessness."

"What was the name of the ship?"
"The Mary Jane ... at the full of the moon the beautiful figurehead rises from the sea, takes human form, and walks this very beach in search of the man she loved. For one night, every month, they become lovers."

"Hunger eventually leads to recklessness."

"Don't, Anna. Don't make me talk about the scars on my back, I can't find the words."

"I love you. I think I must have fallen in love with you that first day on the beach. I don't think, I know, I'll love you for the rest of my life."

"Hunger eventually leads to recklessness."

Anna pulled the car to the side of the road and, without hesitation, spun a U-turn and headed back to

Cook's Bay . . . not to her house, not to her husband, not to the marriage that lay in shambles, but to the sea. The sea where she'd first met Sloan. She heard the waves, quiet yet provocative, calling her name, promising to be her friend, promising to be her lover, promising to fill the emptiness that lived deep inside her.

TWENTY-TWO

The moon, hanging low and full in the satin sky, splashed its silver splendor on sea and sand. Like reveling surfers, moonbeams rode the spirited waves, laughing, dancing the surging, white-tipped crests, then sighing softly as the spent swells rolled shoreward. The stars seemed suspended in anticipation, as though they were holding their bright breaths for something that stood on the verge of happening.

Sloan, the beach wet and cool beneath his bare feet, felt this rare expectancy. He didn't know how to interpret it, but he felt it. Just as he felt the cruel joke that life had played on him that afternoon. Irony to beat all ironies, he had found a bivalve shell like the one Anna had so persistently sought all summer. And he hadn't even been looking for it. He'd just glanced down and there it had been, partially buried within the ivory-white sand. It had taken every ounce of strength he'd had not to destroy the shell. It now symbolized nothing—only a survival that hurt more deeply than anything he'd had to endure. And love didn't survive. He and Anna were going their separate ways, while she and her husband were barely hanging on to a meaningless marriage.

The unfairness of life angered him and was partly responsible for his restlessness. Anna was responsible for her fair share, as well. Every time he tried to settle down at the lighthouse, her face loomed before him. The emptiness in her eyes haunted him. God, what had he done to her? What had he done to himself? Why had he gone and fallen in love with a married woman? What kind of unmitigated insanity was that?

And why was he walking this beach, as if by doing so he could conjure her up? Moonlight and starshine teased and taunted him, making him think that he saw her in every shadow, behind every boulder, in every wave that washed ashore. When he saw the figure roaming the beach, Sloan thought that he'd simply imagined it. When he noted the figure's similarity to Anna, he thought he was sailing high on a wistful flight of fancy. Even when the figure stopped, as though it, too, questioned what it saw, Sloan doubted. Only when the figure walked resolutely toward him, golden curls fluttering in the breeze, did Sloan dare to believe.

From the moment Anna stepped onto the beach, she was aware of a strange magical feeling that seemed to sweep through the sultry night. She wouldn't have been the least surprised, especially with the full moon, to see the lovers in Sloan's story combing the beach in search of one another. In fact, when she first saw the figure, she was quite certain it was the heartbroken sea captain. Only when the figure stopped, obviously weighing the sight of her, did she realize that it was Sloan.

Sloan.

Again she felt nothing. Only an exacerbation of the feeling that something was about to happen. Yes. She felt as if the sea, the stars, the moon, were collectively holding their breath, waiting, waiting, waiting. . . .

Tonight will never come again, the sea murmured.

He'll soon be walking out of your life, the stars whispered.

Is it so wrong to want one night for yourself? the moon chimed in.

Right and wrong. They were concepts too civilized for the primitive need flowing through Anna. Need. Not feeling. Just need. As basic as the sensual rhythm of the sea. As elemental as the hunger gnawing at her belly, her heart.

"Hunger eventually leads to recklessness."

Stepping toward Sloan, Anna embraced a kind of reckless reasoning that, under the circumstances, made sense. Surely the kind, benevolent sea, which had called her to its shore, had meant her to find Sloan. She had waited for the sea to nourish her, to replenish her, and now it was. It was offering her this man, and everyone knew that one didn't, couldn't, reject a gift from the sea. Especially when one wanted that gift so desperately.

"Anna?"

The single word, spoken with their standing only inches from each other, asked for direction. What did she want from him? What would she allow him to give her? How far was he himself prepared to go?

"Make me feel," she said softly, yet demandingly, as though she couldn't live another minute with the barrenness that had become her life.

Her plea shattered what little restraint Sloan had managed to hang on to. It also answered his question about how far he was prepared to go. As far as she wanted him to. Tired of denial, weary from wanting, he sought only to ease his need, her need, their need. Right and wrong. There were no such moral provinces, not when his heart was bursting with love for this woman.

He hauled her to him, crushing her in his arms. She returned the embrace, her strength matching his. For endless heartbeats, his head bent over hers, they simply held each other. United, they stood as one against the sundering sea, against the waves breaking about their bare feet, against the wind lapping at her skirt and billowing his shirt. The magic of the night moved in.

As did instinct. Slowly, quickly, Sloan began a lowering, angling search for Anna's mouth. It was hers that found his, however—brazenly, ravenously, with consummate intent. The emptiness inside her ached so violently that she had to fill it—now!—with the taste of this man. Over and over their mouths collided, each shattered breath rasping against the other, their heads seeking new, more intimate angles. Finally, fearing that he was bruising her lips, Sloan snatched his mouth from hers. Cupping the back of her head in his hand, he buried her face in his chest.

Sloan could feel his heart beating out a wild rhythm, his masculine body responding instantaneously. The ache reached from head to toe, the result of a too-long abstinence, a too-severe denial. His heart, in particular, hurt. Did her body? Did her heart? He could feel it thudding against his chest, just as he could feel her warm, dewy breath seeping through the fabric of his shirt. He could feel her struggling to regain her composure. Did that mean she was feeling?

Anna could feel her her heart pounding, her feminine body responding instantaneously. Feeling. His kiss had left her with tiny trickles of feeling. They felt good. So good. Yet they reminded her of how empty she'd become, of how there was so much more of her left to fill. Still, she luxuriated in this small offering, just as she appreciated the way Sloan's heart hammered, the way his chest spread wide before her, the way he held her, both tightly and carefully. Most of all, she liked the honest response of his body. No, more than that, she liked the way his body demanded an honest response from hers. And what she was feeling now was as honest an emotion as she'd ever felt.

Pulling her head from his chest, she stared up at him. "Make love to me," she whispered.

Sloan had known what she was going to say—he had felt her need, a need that matched his own—yet the words, once spoken, were sobering. "Are you sure you know what you're asking?"

"Yes, I'm sure. More sure than I've ever been of anything."

"Anna—"

She lay a finger across his lips. "Don't say anything. Just make love to me. Here. Now." She rose on tiptoes and brushed her lips across his.

Sloan closed his eyes, dying a little from the pleasure of her simple kiss, dying a lot from her provocative proposition.

"Making love to you wouldn't be wrong," she whispered against his mouth. "I know that now."

Her mouth flowered beneath his, unfolding like a delicate sea plant, reaching, on this night, not for the sun, but for the lovers' moon. Unable to resist, Sloan returned her kiss—slowly, thoroughly, breathlessly. God, was he really holding her? Really kissing her? Or had desperation demanded that he concoct this elaborate fantasy?

Gazing up at him, her scattered breath purling across his face, she said, "I belong to you." Taking his hand in both of hers, she guided it to her heart. "I feel it here. I tried not to feel it, I tried to pretend that I didn't feel it, but I do."

Sloan felt her heart thrumming, felt the gentle slope of her breast. No, she was real. She *had* to be real.

"I know you tried," he said hoarsely. "I tried too." He reached for one of her hands and placed it over his heart. "I belong to you too."

As though in confirmation, he brought her hand to his lips and slow-kissed each fingertip, her palm, the whole of her hand. When his lips brushed the metal of her wedding ring, he halted. His gaze met hers.

"Take it off," Sloan whispered.

His voice, though soft, was more insistent that Anna had ever heard it. There was no way that her heart could refuse him. Removing the ring, she slipped it into the pocket of her skirt. Its absence made her feel strange, yet free.

Sloan brought her hand back to his lips and kissed where the ring had been. "I'll make you a ring—my ring—from the diamonds and rubies and emeralds washed up at your feet," he said, referring to the ship-wreck story he'd once so tenderly told her.

"We'll be those lovers tonight," Anna said.

"Yes," Sloan said as he pretended to slip a ring on Anna's finger. "With this ring, I thee wed. Be my love, my wife, for tonight, Anna."

His gesture, the way he spoke her name, as though it were the most precious of endearments, melted her heart. She whispered his name in return, a soft incan-tation that caught Sloan's breath.

"Come back to the lighthouse with me," he said, his patience as fragile as his restraint.

"Here," she said. "On the beach where we met."

"No."

"Yes. On our beach."

"Anna, we can't. Not here. Not—" Her lips touched his again, and for a moment he was lost, with no will to survive, but he had to survive, he had to think, he had to use a little common sense. Dragging his mouth from hers, taking her hand, he gasped, "Come with me."

Yes, Anna thought as Sloan, minutes later, drew her inside the quiet, silent, windless cove. This place would be perfect. Though she'd been here only once with Sloan, she had liked it. Now, as then, it had been like stepping into a cathedral, a place where only righteousness and goodness dwelled. Though she needed no justification for what she was about to do—the act had its own moral certitude—she, nonetheless, liked the idea of making love on this hallowed, sacred ground. By association, it sanctified, purified.

The instant Sloan cleared the sheltering entrance, he leaned against the rocky wall and yanked Anna into his arms. He roughly pressed his mouth over hers. Exacting a pressure, he forced her lips to part, then his tongue took a variety of hedonistic liberties. At the same time, he ran his hand across her back, drawing her flush against him. He felt her breasts, her stomach, her thighs. Then, easing his mouth from hers so he could watch her eyes, he pulled her into the heat of him. Beneath the jeans he was shamelessly hard and full. Just as shamelessly, his hands on her hips, he moved her against him, him against her.

Surprised not by his actions, but by her intense reaction, Anna gasped softly, sweetly. A heavy heat had jumped into the pit of her stomach, where it swelled with each stroke of their bodies. She liked the feeling. A lot. Greedily, she moved closer to the feeling-making source. Hungrily, she arched her hips more fully into him.

The act made Sloan feel as he'd never felt before. As always, he was awed by her honesty. And he was aroused by it—intensely, profoundly. He was also angered by it. How starved did a woman have to be to respond to something so minimal? No, there was no room for anger now. Just delight in her excitement, as he'd delighted a dozen times in her excitement at finding a shell. She was the mistress at appreciating simplicity. No, she wasn't a mistress. She was his lover, his wife. With this tender thought tucked in his heart, Sloan tightened his hold on Anna's hips. He drew her so close that he felt as if they'd melded into one. He heard her breathing accelerate, along with his own. He felt her body quickening.

Anna, too, felt the tension building, building, building, and she, too, heard her breath accelerating. Occasionally, a small sound at the back of her throat tried to escape. The heavy heat in the pit of her stomach burned now like a bed of hot coals. Her world had begun to spin dangerously out of control. To steady herself, she reached for Sloan's shoulders, just as she clung to his steady, sure gaze. It never crossed her mind to be embarrassed by what she knew was about to happen. It felt too natural. Too right. And she wanted it too much.

Sloan knew the instant tiny tremors racked Anna's body. They racked his, as well. Nothing had ever so moved him, especially the way she looked him right in the eye as the waves of pleasure washed over her, the way her breath cracked, the way her nails bit into his shoulders. And then, spent, she crumpled in his arms, breathing thickly, and quickly, her curl-tangled head tucked beneath his chin. Sloan held her fast, thinking that he liked this moment most of all. He liked the way she'd come apart in his arms, this woman who was always so consummately composed. Yes, he liked the way she'd trusted him to hold her together.

When her breathing had steadied, when she was aware of the simple surging of the sea beyond the cove walls, she raised her head. Again she exhibited not a shred of embarrassment when her gaze met his. "I hadn't planned that."

Sloan could feel his own gaze wading into the blue depths of hers. God, he could drown there! "I like spontaneity."

"It had been too long."

"I know," Sloan said, a sudden smile cocking a corner of his mouth. When he spoke, his voice was smoky soft. "Actually, I thought it was sexy."

Unexpectedly, a small smile tugged at Anna's lips. "Actually, so did I."

Sloan laughed gently, a hymn in the cove church, though no sooner had he laughed than he wanted to cry. Simply because there were far too few smiles in Anna's life.

Anna's smile faded. "Make me feel it again," she whispered. "This time with you inside me."

Sloan groaned, his heated lips finding the side of her neck, then her lips. From there each was lost in the feel of the other. From there time stood still.

Anna could hear the sea. It rose and fell as though breathing in the salted air. Anna realized, through the haze of her mounting passion, that Sloan was making love to her with the sea's rhythm. Each wave that crashed ashore did so just a little harder than the one before it. Yet each wave had its own pace—a mounting, a cresting, and then the slow building of yet another wave, this one stronger, wilder, willing to chart new and unexplored ground.

Nuzzling gave way to kissing, gentle kisses gave rise to not-so-gentle kisses, heated caresses gave way to those more bold. He unbuttoned her blouse and unfastened her bra. He kissed her breasts, then returned to her mouth to deliver almost chaste kisses. Anna moaned in frustration. He bared their bodies to the waist, nestling her breasts in the dark hair matting his chest, but still he stopped there. She kissed each scar on his back until he groaned her name. Finally he slid his hand beneath the gauzy fabric of her skirt, touching her in ways more intimate than any she'd ever known, and she bit her lip to keep from crying out, then cried out anyway. But still he didn't go any further.

"Give me tonight, Anna," he begged, sensing her impatience. "It's all I'll ever have of you."

In the end it was Sloan's patience that wore out, and it did so at exactly that point in time when Anna's knuckles grazed the zipper of his jeans. He swore. Releasing himself to her touch, he bore this sweetest of torture for only seconds before settling her down on a bed of sand, with moonlight bathing their bare bodies, with the sea whispering words of love. He entered her gently, shallowly, but with each liquid stroke he plunged deeper and deeper until the sea floor fell out from under Anna's feet, leaving her to sink into ecstasy, to drown in sublime feelings. Feelings? No. The world had been reduced to one feeling, but it was enough. For now. For always. It was the warm, heavy feeling she'd experienced before in her heart. Arching her neck, her back, she allowed it to fill her. As did the memories she'd made this night, memories that had to last a lifetime.

But, then, some memories were potent enough, magical enough, to do just that.

He had lost her.

Sloan knew this the moment their lovemaking ended. No one had ever made love to him with such abandon, with such sensual and emotional integrity, with such perfect wholeness. In fact, their bodies were still entwined, their sweat mingling, their breath coupling, their heartbeats so woven together that one couldn't be separated from the other. Ironically, he knew the end had come by the gentle, loving way she palmed his cheek, by the way she stared at him, by the way she whispered his name. Only once. With a purity that needed no repetition.

No! he wanted to scream as he saw her pulling deeply

into herself. Instead he let her roll from him. He watched as she brushed the sand from her as best she could, then slipped back into her clothes, coolly, calmly, aloofly. He watched as she, without a backward glance, walked from the cove. He called her name once, twice, thrice, but she didn't look back. He didn't call her again. Instead he sat listening to the sea, to the night, to his heart. All three told him that it wasn't Anna he'd just lost. It was himself.

Anna opened the back door of the house with a prayer at her lips. *Please, please let Carrie have gone to bed!* Immediately the prayer seemed answered. The house was dark, except for the usual faint light coming from Jack's bedroom. Tiptoeing in that direction, Anna peeked in. Jack was asleep, and alone. Anna breathed a sigh of relief. Standing in the doorway, she watched him, waiting to feel some guilt. Some came, but not as much as she'd expected. It was as though another woman had made love to Sloan, the woman who belonged to him. How odd that she'd feel that way, Anna thought as she started back toward the stairway. As though purposefully planned, the living room burst into light just as she placed her sandy foot on the first step.

Anna's heart jumped to her throat.

She waited for Carrie, but when she didn't appear, Anna felt obligated to walk to the living room. Straightening her clothes, running her fingers through her mussed hair—was it obvious what she'd been doing?—she walked into the room. She stopped dead in her tracks.

"Meg!"

The young woman, wearing jeans and a single braid, stood in front of the fireplace. Her stance, rigid and stern, suggested she'd been there a while. Waiting impatiently, no doubt, for her mother's return. Something in her daughter's presently cold eyes filled Anna with dread.

"I—I thought you were studying for finals," Anna replied, feeling more child than parent.

"I was worried about Daddy," Meg said, then cut to the chase. "Where have you been?"

The words didn't constitute a question, but rather an accusation. Anna's feeling of dread grew, though she cloaked herself in what dignity she could muster.

"Out," she said. "Your aunt, your father, suggested that I take in a movie."

"And did you?"

Anna stared at her daughter, whose eyes glinted with the intention of doing battle. Tilting her chin, Anna asked, "Why this interrogation?"

"Did you go to the movie?"

Anna paused, then answered candidly, "No, I didn't." Another hesitation. Then, "I went for a drive."

"And where did you leave your shoes?"

To her credit Anna didn't look down at her feet. Instead she answered truthfully, "In the car. I went for a walk on the beach after I returned."

At the mention of the word *beach*, Anna ran her fingers through her tangled hair, wondering if the curls looked as if a man's restless hand had whispered through them, wondering if there was telltale sand on her clothes, wondering if her lips were still swollen from her lover's kisses. And did she smell like the musty perfume of making love?

"And did you leave your wedding ring in the car too?"

Anna halted the tunneling of her hand through her hair. Again, to her credit, she didn't look down, this time at her ringless finger. She still felt the weight of the imaginary ring that Sloan had so sweetly bestowed upon her. She suspected she would for the rest of her life.

"No," Anna said. "It's in my skirt pocket."

"How convenient. Out of sight, out of mind."

"Meg—"

"You've been with *him*, haven't you?" Before Anna could even consider answering, Meg rushed ahead with, "My God, Mother, how could you?"

Instinctively, Anna stepped toward her daughter, as though proximity would somehow guarantee understanding. "Meg—"

"With Daddy lying in there?" Here Meg gestured toward his bedroom. "Sick. Maybe fighting for his life."

"Meg, listen—"

"I saw it coming. At the July Fourth party. The two of you couldn't keep your eyes off each other. It was embarrassing."

"Meg, will you listen to me?"

"No, I won't!" she cried. "I won't listen to you trying to explain why you took a lover. I won't listen to you trying to excuse yourself for acting like a bitch in heat!"

The harsh sound of Anna's palm striking her daughter's cheek crackled throughout the room. The act startled both women so much that conversation halted abruptly. Anna merely watched in stunned disbelief— had she really struck her daughter?—as tears jumped into Meg's doe-brown eyes. Disbelief quickly turned to heartsickness. Suddenly Meg, looking more like a little girl than a grown woman, stepped away from her mother. Anna reached for her, longing to comfort her.

"Meg, baby, I'm sorry."

Ignoring her mother's plea, Meg raced for the door.

"Wait! We have to talk!"

The younger woman didn't slow her pace, and Anna had to take off after her. Midway of the room she caught her and whirled her around.

Smugly, sanctimoniously, Meg shouted, "I have nothing to say to you! Now or ever!"

Jerking free, Meg continued her flight, but once at

the door, she turned and put the lie to her own pledge.
Her eyes, cold and tearless, found those of her mother.

"I'd rather see Daddy dead than ever have him learn
how you betrayed him."

Even if Anna had known what to say, she wouldn't
have had the heart to say it. It was difficult to speak
when her heart had just been ripped from her chest
and thrown at her feet.

Anna stood beneath the scalding shower spray, thinking that all the water in the world couldn't wash away
her sin. During the lonely trek up the stairway, her
daughter's frosty indictment ringing in her ears, Anna
had realized—*really* realized—the gravity of what had
occurred that evening. Until then she had been
shielded by the magic of what had happened between
her and Sloan, what she had encouraged to happen.
Until then she had been basking in the warmth of his
touch, the heat of his kiss, the fire of his passion. Cold
reality, dished up by Meg, had intruded and forced her
to face the fact that she was now an adulteress.

Adulteress.

Anna knew that, technically, the word applied to her,
and yet she didn't in the least feel like an adulteress.
An adulteress was a fast, loose woman who sneaked
around in the shadows, a woman in whom there was an
absence of moral content, a woman at whom women
sneered, a woman about whom men made crude remarks. An adulteress was not an ordinary woman from
Connecticut, a woman who worried about what was for
dinner and the cost of medical school, a woman who
loved her daughter to distraction, a woman who had
tried to stay in love with her husband, a woman who
had fought an attraction to another man until she'd
had nothing left to fight with.

Sighing, Anna turned off the shower and stepped
from the tub. Reaching for the towel, she enfolded her-

self in its softness and turned toward the mirror. She could see nothing for the coating of steam. She took her hand and cleared away an oval patch, in which her reflection appeared. No, with her face bare of makeup, with wet curls clinging to her head, she didn't look like a vampy adulteress.

So what was the value of a word?

The value of an act?

She'd read once that thought *was* action. If that was true, she'd been an adulteress long before tonight. That wasn't her sin, however, no more than the act itself had been. Her sin, quite simply, was her unrepentance, for she knew in her heart that, had she to do it over again, she would. Though ethics labeled it wrong, being with Sloan had seemed more right than anything in her life had ever seemed. He'd made her feel whole and replete. He'd awakened her to life again. He'd made her feel.

No, though it would never happen again, she couldn't regret what she'd done. And she'd find a way back into Meg's good graces. She'd find a way to make Meg understand that sometimes an adulteress was just an ordinary woman from Connecticut.

Though sleep was out of the question, Anna lay down on the bed. If she could just get a few hours of rest, perhaps she'd have the strength to cope with the new day that was already on its way. She'd decided to say nothing more to Meg until morning. Maybe with a little temporal distance, Meg would be more reasonable. At present Anna knew that her daughter must be in the adjacent guest bedroom, as restless as she, if the sounds she kept hearing were any indication.

At the pinging at the window Anna glanced up and listened. When she heard nothing more, she turned onto her side, tucked a hand beneath a cheek, and tried to erase Sloan from her mind. The attempt proved futile.

"With this ring, I thee wed. Be my love, my wife, for tonight, Anna . . . tonight . . . tonight . . . tonight . . ."

Anna's plaintive moan mingled with another sound, this one a sharp, piercing *plunk*. She sat up, knowing without a doubt that a pebble had struck the windowpane. She knew, too, who must have thrown it. Her heart began a rash rhythm. Anna couldn't have said whether it was because she knew Sloan was near or because she feared others discovering that he was near. Probably both, she admitted as she slipped from bed, crossed to the window, and parted the drapes. There he stood! Secreted in the lacy shadows of a leafy tree and causing her heart to stand completely still.

Exchanging her gown for a sweatsuit, she quietly opened the bedroom door and, even more quietly, crept down the stairs. Anna was halfway down the stairwell when she heard another bedroom door open—Carrie's, she thought. Pressing herself against the wall, she held her breath until the sounds indicated that her sister-in-law had walked to the nearby bathroom. Anna allowed herself to breathe again.

By the time Anna emerged from the house, Sloan stood at the foot of the back stairs. Though the outside light burned, he had managed to find a spot, flush against the house, where he was partially hidden. He waited for her to come to him.

"You shouldn't be here," she whispered.

"I know." And, God, did he ever know that he shouldn't! He'd paced the lighthouse, making promises to himself that he wouldn't go to her, and yet the promises came up empty. He simply had to go to her. He had turned her into the same thing he was, a betrayer of principles, and he, more than most, knew how devastating that could be. "I had to see if you were all right."

"I'm all right," she answered, though she wasn't at

all certain that she was. Despite her resolve to turn him away, despite her resolve never to repeat the intimacy they'd shared—that was her penance for breaking her wedding vow—she wanted to tumble into his arms, to lose herself in his strength, his sensuality, to know him again as her lover.

"Maybe I should apologize for letting tonight happen," he said, "but I can't, because I'm not sorry."

"Neither am I."

The words mesmerized Sloan with their beauty. He wanted to reach for her. God, he wanted to! Instead he raked his fingers through his hair—restlessly.

"Please leave, Sloan," Anna whispered. "You mustn't be found here. Meg knows what happened between us tonight. If she finds you here, I don't know what she'll do."

Sloan felt as if someone had poleaxed him. "Meg knows?"

"She showed up unexpectedly. She was waiting for me when I got in. I slapped her." Anna's voice trembled when she said, "I never laid a hand on her before tonight."

Though Anna didn't elaborate on what had led her to strike her daughter, Sloan could imagine the scene all too clearly. "I'm so sorry. I never meant my loving you to hurt you. In any way."

"Then, please leave," Anna repeated. Surely he must know that his very presence was hurting her.

With a sudden urgency he said, "We have to talk."

"There's nothing to talk about."

Unexpectedly, Anna's composure enraged Sloan. He was falling apart—hell, he'd already fallen apart!—and she was as cool as a spring night.

"You're telling me that we have nothing to talk about! You're telling me that what happened between us tonight meant nothing?"

"Keep your voice down," Anna begged.

Sloan ignored her and proceeded to answer his own question. "Don't tell me that tonight meant nothing to you. I was there. You felt exactly what I did."

"I'm not telling you that tonight meant nothing to me. On the contrary, it meant everything. Every-thing," she repeated, but the word fractured in two. Composing herself with a long sigh, she added, "But there's nothing to talk about. Tonight changes nothing."

"Like hell it doesn't!"

"Keep your voice down!" she admonished. Then, her own voice louder than she realized, she said, "What does it change? I'm still a married woman. With a husband who needs me."

"I need you too."

At this naked truth Anna's composure slipped. "What do you want from me, Sloan? For me to walk away from my husband? For me to turn my back on my responsibility the way I did on my vows? For me to run away with you and pretend that our doing so would hurt no one?"

"Yes, dammit, that's what I want!"

Anna's composure failed completely. "Well, maybe that's what I want too! But it doesn't matter what you and I want!"

Sloan took a step toward Anna, instinct demanding that he comfort her. He'd resented her composure, but now loathed her loss of it, especially since it had been his fault. When Anna stepped back from him, he thought that he would die right there and wished that he would. He hurt too much to go on living.

"Don't touch me!" she pleaded. "I need you too badly."

"How can this be happening?" he asked. "How can I have found you and lost you in the same summer?" Hanging his head, Sloan took a deep, cleansing breath. When he glanced up, his gaze met Anna's. "God forgive me for saying it, but your husband's death would be best for everyone."

His comment startled, frightened, Anna. "My God, Sloan, what are you suggesting?"

Her reaction equally startled, frightened, Sloan, for he realized for the first time how it must have sounded. "Nothing. God, nothing! I'm just saying that we're caught up in the bitterest of ironies."

That Anna couldn't deny. Neither could she deny that what had frightened her most about Sloan's comment was that it had mirrored her own thoughts. Sweet heaven, it had mirrored her own thoughts!

"Anna, I didn't mean it the way it sounded."

"I know."

And she did know. She'd never met a man as gentle as Sloan, a man to whom such a callous act would be so foreign. Which brought her full circle, reminding her of the gentle lover he'd been, the gentle lover she'd never know again.

"Please go," she begged. "While I have the strength to let you."

He did. Without another word. Because she'd begun to tremble. Because he could no longer be the source of her pain, her suffering.

Minutes later Anna leaned against her bedroom door, grateful that Sloan hadn't been observed, wondering if the pain in her heart would ease, wondering if she'd been right earlier in thinking that thought was action. If it was, she'd just been guilty of killing her husband.

Sloan stood by the water's edge, staring at the shell in his hand. In the midst of the emotional conversation with Anna, he'd forgotten that he'd slipped the conjoined shells inside his pocket and had intended to give them to her. It didn't matter that he hadn't. At this moment nothing mattered. Except the fact that he would never see Anna again. The unfairness of this truth angered him, and he closed his fingers around the shells. He wanted to snap the two halves apart, the way he and Anna had been torn apart, but he couldn't bring himself to do so. No, the shells must remain together in a way that he and Anna could not. With a throw of his hand, he committed the bound shells to the sea. In the darkness he heard the sea receive them, and his heart rejoiced. He allowed himself one last, parting look at the house. As frightening, as horrifying as the thought might be, the simple truth was that Jack Ramey's death would free everyone.

He was gone, Jack realized, refusing to think of him by name. Ever since he'd heard Anna sneaking down the stairs, he'd known that she was meeting him. In the beginning it had hurt to think of them together, but tonight it didn't. Tonight, nothing seemed to hurt. His heart seemed light, his head lucid. He could swear that the sea spoke to him, as it did so often of late. He could hear the gentle rush of its waves beckoning him to its peaceful depths.

Join me, the sea whispered. *And I shall share with you all my wisdom.*

Jack sighed, thinking that maybe the sea had already shared its wisdom with him. For the first time, he could see his life with some perspective. He'd had to bear a heavy burden. Illness had destroyed the foundation of his life, leaving all other areas to stand on unstable ground. He wouldn't whitewash his every action. Too often he'd taken his frustration out on Anna, but always he'd done the best he could. He'd always reacted as a human being, struggling, always struggling, and in that struggle sometimes succeeding, sometimes failing.

Yes, the sea murmured, *you've learned my wisdom. All things can be only what they are. Human beings can be only hu-*

*man beings. Just as I, the sea, can never be less, can never be
more.*

A calmness came to Jack, along with a warm, heavy
feeling. The feeling he knew had a name. It was called
forgiveness.

The house was restless. Anna tossed and turned and
listened to sounds coming from both Carrie's and
Meg's rooms. She heard Carrie going back to the bathroom, and later she heard Meg moving down the stairway. Thinking that maybe she should talk to Meg now,
rather than waiting for morning, Anna slipped from
the bed, opened her door, and lost her courage. Instead
she watched as her daughter descended the staircase
and disappeared into her father's room. With a sigh
Anna went back to bed and, overcome by fatigue, fell
into a light sleep. Through it all she continued to hear
the noise of a restless house. Through it all she
couldn't abandon the thought that Jack's death would
give everyone what they wanted. It would especially
give Jack what he wanted. And the truth was that giving him what he desired would be so very simple.

Come morning Jack Ramey was dead. Carrie and
Meg cried softly, although Anna didn't shed a single
tear. Across town, when told of the news by Harper,
Sloan canceled his travel plans. For the first time,
Harper used the word *obsessed*. Sloan couldn't deny the
allegation.

TWENTY-THREE

September

Where was he?

Anna had dialed the number at the lighthouse until her fingers were sore, but still Sloan didn't answer. To keep from going totally crazy, she made herself a cup of tea and carried it to the living room and the now roaring fire. The tea was soon forgotten, however, in favor of pacing back and forth. She temporarily gave up pacing for the evening news, but when Jake Lugaric came on, cheerfully, gleefully repeating what the prosecutor had said concerning Sloan's past, she snapped off the television set. Regrettably, however, she couldn't stop the words from playing in her head.

"Coward . . . broke under torture . . . coward . . . didn't deserve to be in the military . . . coward . . . coward . . . cow—"

The word faded, lost in a sound so subtle that Anna wasn't certain she had imagined it. Cocking her head, she listened. All she heard, however, was the wail of the wind, the weeping of the rain. She sighed . . . and heard the mysterious noise again. It was louder this time, and clearly coming from the rear of the house. Frowning, she headed in search of its source. Once she entered the kitchen, she could identify the sound—the frantic banging of a fist on wood, the distraught jarring of glass. Anna hastened toward the back door. Even with the darkening storm she could see the hulk of a man. She recognized him instantly. Fighting the lock with hands that were suddenly unsteady, she yanked open the door.

The wind sailed in, bringing with it a mist of rain, but Sloan made no move to enter. Eerily illuminated in a flash of white lightning, he simply stared at Anna. After several moments he said with a quiet desperation, "Don't send me away."

Anna's thoughts whirled so frantically, so rashly, that words were impossible to come by. She just stepped aside, her gesture a silent invitation, which he accepted.

Once he stood inside the house, inside the mudroom, Anna studied him. He wore jeans and a yellow slicker, not his military raincoat. The legs of the jeans were drenched, while rivulets of water ran off the vinyl slicker, pooling onto the tile floor. Similar streams plunged from his thoroughly wet hair onto his face, collecting in crevices and creases that seemed to have been forged within the last few hours. He looked older, lost, unaware that he was both soaked and shivering.

She held out her hand. "Give me the slicker."

When Sloan looked as if she'd spoken in a foreign language, Anna realized that he was far more lost than she'd thought. She wanted to be there for him, just the way he'd been there for her so many times that summer. His vulnerability made her strong, so strong that she would have fought anyone—Harper, the hounds of hell—to comfort him.

"Give me your raincoat, Sloan. You're drenched."

He began to unfasten the slicker, saying as though he'd just made the discovery, "It's raining."

"I know."

"I'm messing up your floor."

"It doesn't matter," she said, taking the dripping raincoat and laying it on the washing machine. "Here," she said, handing him a towel. "I've built a fire in the living room. Go warm yourself."

Anna paused long enough in the kitchen to make another mug of tea. She found Sloan standing before the fireplace, hands braced against the mantel, basking in the heat. He'd removed his shoes; even at first glance she could tell that his socks were soggy. The towel she'd given him, which he'd haphazardly run through his hair, lay draped about his neck. His short-sleeved T-shirt, which had managed to get wet despite the slicker's best efforts, clung to his shaking shoulders.

"Here," she said, and when he turned, she handed him the mug. He took it, and though its contents were scalding, he downed a generous swallow.

She could feel his eyes, unnervingly vacant, on her as she stepped to the sofa and picked up a garishly plaid afghan that had come with the furnished home. She walked toward him and, leaning into him, gathered the afghan about his shoulders. The task required that their bodies come into contact, hers lightly brushing against his. Beneath her hands, as she lapped the edges of the afghan together, he shuddered, and she suspected strongly that it had nothing to do with his being cold.

With a will of its own her gaze traveled from his strong chin to cheeks shadowed by stubble, stopping at lips still moist from trickles of rain. With a force that made her dizzy, she realized that, despite the price they were paying for their intimacy, despite the fact that she was punishing herself for it by never allowing that intimacy again, she wanted to kiss him.

Removing herself from harm's way, she approached the sofa and sat on its arm. "Where've you been? I called the lighthouse a dozen times."

Ever since Richard Hennessey had blurted out the sordid facts of his past, Sloan hadn't felt much of anything—not when the rain had stung his face, not when lightning had bolted about him, not when the autumn chill had crept into his bones. He hadn't even felt his feet carrying him to Anna's, or the fire blazing behind him, or the hot, sugary tea slipping down his throat. He *had* felt her body brush against his, but, here again, in no solid, substantial way. She might easily have been brushing against someone he'd once known. Her question, her statement, however, penetrated his numbness as nothing else had.

"You called me?"

"Yes. I was worried about you." Pause. Then, "Where have you been?"

He answered without hesitation. "In Colorado. Fishing for speckled trout." At Anna's frown he said, "Actually, I took a cab back to the lighthouse, but its walls closed in around me. Next thing I knew I was at the cove. I crawled under a ledge and just sat there, listening to the rain, living in one fantasy after another. I'm good—no, excellent—at creating fantasies. Anything you want—a moonwalk, sailing around the world in a balloon, breaking the bank at Monte Carlo, sunning on the Riviera . . ." He shrugged. "Anything to survive harsh reality."

Harsh reality? Anna knew that he must mean his imprisonment. She thought of the shipwreck story that he'd spun so effortlessly when their relationship had been new and pure. It all made such poignant sense now. He had survived the indignities perpetrated against his body by seeking sanctuary in his mind.

"I soon realized, though," he continued, "that all of the fantasies were trailing off into one. A fantasy in which I somehow made you understand what happened in Beirut." He laughed bitterly. "But even I'm not good enough to concoct that kind of fantasy. I can't make you understand what I don't understand myself."

"Try me," Anna said.

Something in the sweet acceptance of her voice angered Sloan. "I'm not here for forgiveness. I don't want it. I don't deserve it. So don't give it to me."

Anna doubted that what he'd just said was true. She suspected that he both deserved and wanted forgiveness, but she said simply, "All right. Just tell me what happened. But before you do," she added, "I want you to know that I could have asked Harper about Hennessey's allegations, but I didn't. I waited to hear the truth from you. I think that's earned me the right to share your past. All of it."

Sloan downed the remainder of the tea, set the mug on the mantel next to the one Anna had earlier abandoned, and hugged the ugly afghan to himself. Finally, his eyes directly on hers, he said, "The truth, my past, is really quite simple. I'm a fraud, a coward, and a liar. I lied even to you. You sensed something wasn't right about Beirut, and I deliberately kept the truth from you. A lie of silence. It's the worst kind."

Anna waited, then asked, "Is that your attempt at trying to make me understand?"

Sloan sighed heavily, saying, "Harper would kill me if he knew I was here."

"Probably. And you're avoiding my question."

"Yes, dammit! I'm avoiding it because I can't find the words."

"Just say it straight out."

"Straight out? Okay, straight out, I consorted with the enemy, which, as a military man, I'd pledged never to do. They wanted the name of an Israeli agent, I gave it to them, they freed me and killed him." Hesitation. "I'd say that pretty much makes me a coward, wouldn't you? No matter how many damned medals they hang on me."

"Yes, I would say that it did," she said, and she could see her agreement slicing through him like a sharp knife. "If that's all there is to it. Is that all there is to it?" She gave him no time to answer. "Did they hold this little civilized party, where they served tea and cakes, and did they say to you, 'Commander Marshall, we would just be ever so pleased if you'd give us the name of that Israeli agent so we could kill him and let you go free'? And did you tell them that you couldn't think of anything you'd rather do, except perhaps have another cup of tea?"

She let the absurdity of the scenario sink in.

"It wasn't quite like that, was it, Sloan? We're not talking civilized little tea-and-cake party, are we?" She bit her lip, as though in thought, then said, "It always struck me as odd how you downplay what happened to you. The first time you mentioned being taken hostage, you made it sound like a minor detainment, the kind of incident that happens to everyone. No big deal. Even when I saw your back and realized that it *was* a big deal, we still never really talked about it. We talked around it, but not about it."

Again she let her words find their mark.

"You won't talk about it. I won't talk about it. It's as though neither one of us can find the words. And it has just now dawned on me why we can't. The truth is, Sloan, that what they did to you was, is, unspeakable."

The word fell softly, quietly, underscoring the very essence of its meaning.

"They—and it's not some benign they—*they* were your captors. *They* were the ones who tortured you unmercifully. A part of me recoils even now from thinking about what they must have done to you, and the part willing to think about it can't really begin to imagine what it must have been like. They treated you savagely, brutally, as no human being has the right to treat another. Accept that fact, Sloan."

A hundred hideous memories came rushing back at Sloan, memories not only unspeakable, but unthinkable, so unthinkable that he'd built a wall around them, never quite letting himself see over the top. Anna's words toppled the wall, leaving him no choice but to look head-on at the fiery-eyed demons. The sight weakened his knees, forcing him to ease to the hearth. There he sat, his legs spread, his head held in his hands.

Anna wanted to go to him, but she wouldn't let herself. She couldn't trust herself not to comfort him in whatever way he needed. And so she, too, sat quietly, silently, until he finally raised his head. His eyes looked glazed, as though tears might be only words away.

"His name was Ezra Eshkol—Ezzie. He was thirty-five, married, the father of three daughters. He was also an Israeli secret agent, a member of the Mossad. Although I didn't know him well—we'd worked together on only a couple of classified missions—I knew that he was a decent man. I liked him."

This last admission momentarily stole Sloan's breath, compelling him to take a few seconds to compose himself.

"From the moment that they—my captors—took me hostage, they made it plain they wanted me to divulge Ezzie's identity. They knew him only by a code name, but they knew that I could identify him. They thought he'd been responsible—and maybe they were right, I don't know—for a couple of retaliatory raids against Lebanese terrorists who'd blown up a school bus full of Israeli children."

"They sound like great people."

"Yeah. Great." Silence. A sigh. "I wanted them to kill

me. I prayed they would. When it was obvious that they weren't going to, I began to devise my own plan, ways I could kill myself, if they'd give me a chance— hanging, eating glass, slashing my wrists, on and on my imagination ran. There was only one problem. They were hell-bent on protecting me from myself." Sloan laughed. "I even tried to will myself to die, but that didn't work, either."

Anna's stomach knotted at the callous, matter-of-fact way that he spoke of his death. If he'd gotten his way, she would never have known him. She never would have known the warmth of his arms, the tenderness of his kiss, the passion of his lovemaking.

When Sloan spoke again, his voice was unsteady, and his words shot Anna's heart with pain. "I, uh, I never knew that one could survive that kind of pain. But I did. Again ... and again ... and again."

Restless from these painful memories, Sloan stood and once more sought out the warmth of the fire. With his back to her, he said, "I'm not really sure what happened. I just broke one day. I heard myself giving them Ezzie's name. No, that's not true. I heard Ezzie's name and wondered who was screaming it. I finally decided that it was me."

The word *screaming* said far more than Anna wanted to know. She couldn't even begin to contemplate the severity of the torture that had led to that moment of disclosure. Again she wanted to go to Sloan, but she was no longer sure that she merely wanted to comfort him. Suddenly she, too, needed to be comforted.

"I thought they'd kill me after that. I mean, what good was I to them any longer? More than ever, I wanted them to kill me. At least I wouldn't have to live with what I'd done." He sneered. "But the bastards let me go, and the first thing I learned when I was freed was that Ezzie was dead. He'd missed a turn on a curvy road, and his car plunged off a cliff. It was ruled an accident, but I knew better."

Anna took in this last bit of information, processed it, and said, "You don't know for a fact that you were responsible for his death?"

Sloan whirled, anger once more shaping his features. "Don't you and Harper understand that it doesn't matter whether it was an accident? I betrayed Ezzie. I betrayed myself. I betrayed the most basic principle of being in the military. I was a coward, Anna. A stinking, yellow coward!"

The word rumbled through the room to the accompaniment of a groaning round of thunder. As though the noise had brought him to himself, Sloan raked one hand through his hair while he clasped the afghan to him with his other.

"Sorry. I have no right to take this out on you."

"Just on yourself," Anna said.

"That seems fitting, don't you think?"

Anna didn't waste an answer on something that had already been answered in Sloan's mind. Instead she said, "And so you came home, traveled around for a while, then settled here?"

"I went to see Ezzie's wife first." He didn't mention how the doctors had counseled against his going, stating that he was in no condition to travel. Neither did he mention how he'd told them all to go to hell. Nor did he mention how he and Ezzie's wife had simply held each other and wept. "I told her everything. I told her how I'd broken, how I'd probably caused her husband's death."

"And did she blame you?"

"No."

"Which only made you feel guiltier."

"Yes," Sloan said, somewhere between anger and anguish.

In the silence that followed, the fire crackled, and a

log shifted, sending forth a shower of orange sparks. Rain pounded the house.

"Tell me something," Anna said quietly. "If the circumstances were reversed, if Ezzie had given them your name, if he was standing here feeling guilty and you were the one dead, would you blame him?"

Sloan said nothing.

"I don't think you would," Anna answered for him. "I think you'd feel that no human being could have withstood that kind of punishment."

Silence.

"Yet you demand of yourself that you be superhuman."

As she spoke, she realized that the accusation could just as easily apply to her. Uncomfortable with this line of thinking, she let herself off the hook by telling herself that this conversation wasn't about her.

"Why is that, Sloan?" she asked, anxious to refocus her thoughts.

"Don't, Anna. Don't you dare forgive me."

"It doesn't matter whether I do or not. Redemption lies only in forgiving yourself." Again she didn't want to think of how this might relate to herself.

"Then I'll never be redeemed."

The words were stark, cold, self-condemning. They, along with the tears that threatened Sloan's eyes and the sway of his burdened shoulders, speared Anna's heart with pain. His pain. Her pain. Maybe one-and-the-same pain. Hers she might have been able to bear. His she could not. And so, without giving any thought to what she was doing, she rose from the arm of the sofa and walked toward Sloan.

Sloan watched her approach, silently pleading with her not to touch him. He wasn't at all certain what he might do if she did. When she spoke, it was her words that caressed him, more fully, more completely, than her hands ever could have.

"You're not a coward," she said, her statement boldly stroking him.

"Don't, Anna," he said hoarsely.

"A coward wouldn't have gone to see Ezzie's wife." Again her words brushed daringly against his battered soul.

"Don't. I don't deserve—"

"A coward wouldn't have come here tonight." Her voice, like teasing fingers, grazed over Sloan's empty heart. "Don't you see that?"

What Sloan saw was what he always saw when he looked at Anna: woman, friend, lover, himself. For a moment he thought he saw something else, as well. The possibility—distant, though near enough to contemplate—that in her forgiveness of him might lie his forgiveness of himself.

"What I see is a woman so like me that she could be my mirror image, a woman who knows all about being superhuman, a woman who hasn't the least idea of how to begin forgiving herself." He smiled sadly. "What a pair we make, Anna."

"Yes," she said, smiling sadly too. "What a pair."

A single tear slipped from the corner of Sloan's eye. Embarrassed by it, he tried to look away. Anna cradled his cheek with the palm of her hand, bringing his gaze back to hers. She had tried words, and they had failed. She now spoke with her heart. Raising her head, she placed her mouth against his—softly, tenderly, healingly. His lips, passive beneath her gentle aggression, tasted warm and sugary sweet. And they trembled. Or maybe it was her lips trembling. Perhaps even her body, for she felt that restlessness again, the need to surge beyond constraints, the need to be comforted even as she comforted. Perhaps even the need to forgive herself even as she forgave him?

At her trembling Sloan's mouth moved from passive to active. The kiss deepened, progressing from an ur-

gent passion to a passionate desperation. And then the
kiss ended abruptly, and he hauled her to him. The afghan, like their past restraints, fell away, and they simply held each other—tightly, fiercely, as lovers do when
they fear they have no future.

Future. Anna could not let him think that her actions that night granted them a future, and so she said,
"Tonight changes nothing."

But they both knew that it had. He had come to her
with the worst of his secrets, and instead of dividing
them, an even stronger bond had been forged between
them. Furthermore, each had glimpsed redemption.

The following day the world fell apart. The morning
news ran footage of Sloan entering and leaving Anna's
house the night before. Jake Lugaric, no doubt expecting Sloan to run to Anna for solace, had obviously
been lying in wait. That they had been such fools hurt.
It hurt even worse to know that they'd disappointed
Harper. He said nothing, not a word of condemnation,
not a single didn't-I-tell-you-to-stay-away-from-each-
other. Sloan and Anna thought that they'd reached the
nadir of the trial. They were mistaken.

Always cocky, Hennessey literally strutted into court
and announced his final witness: Arty Watteau. When
Harper objected, saying that Mr. Watteau's name
hadn't been on the list of prospective witnesses,
Hennessey apologized, saying that new evidence had
come to light. Mr. Watteau was allowed to testify. Actually, he was allowed to ramble, telling the court of Esther Wright's passing and of her daughter's arrival in
Cook's Bay. He spoke of being sent to pick up Mrs.
McDay at the airport, but forgetting exactly where he
was headed. The simple man unashamedly told the
court that he sometimes forgot where he was going. As
always he'd ended up at the sea, where he'd found the
strangest thing washed up on the shore. It had been his

mother, however, who'd recognized the significance of his find and had turned it over to Sheriff Tate.

A gloating Hennessey then introduced the find into evidence: an empty bottle of regular insulin, a large syringe, a thin black belt—all neatly tied up in a butter-yellow scarf. In regard to the scarf, Hennessey recalled two witnesses, Meg and Carrie, who testified that it belonged to Anna.

The courtroom edged into chaos.

Anna and Sloan slipped into shock.

"Mr. Fleming, is the defense ready to proceed with its case?"

"Yes, Your Honor, it is."

Despite her stupor, Anna heard the enthusiasm in Harper's voice and knew that it was faked. During the ten-minute recess that had followed Hennessey's introduction of Arty Watteau's discovery into evidence and the resting of the prosecution's case, no one—not Sloan, not Harper, not she herself—had spoken a word. Not a single, solitary word.

"The defense calls Dr. Philip Goodman," Harper said.

The physician came forward and was duly sworn and seated.

With a smile Harper moved toward the witness stand. "Doctor, I want to refresh the jury's mind in regard to your earlier testimony. You stated that, in your best medical judgment, Jack Ramey's prognosis was poor, that in all likelihood his health would have continued to deteriorate. Have you changed your mind in regard to that medical assessment?"

"No, I have not."

"You testified, too, that—again in your opinion—Jack Ramey knew how ill he was. Do you still believe that to be the case?"

"I do."

"You also testified that you thought he was afraid, and when I asked if you thought he was afraid that he would die, you said that you thought he was afraid he wouldn't." Here Harper consulted his notes. "Your exact words were 'that his health would keep deteriorating, and that his life would become less and less viable. He seemed particularly obsessed with the possibility of another stroke.'" Harper paused. "Have you changed your mind in regard to any of that testimony?"

"No, I have not."

"You also testified that you weren't surprised to learn of Jack Ramey's suicide request. Does this testimony still accurately describe your feelings?"

"It does."

"One last question, Doctor. Can you, beyond all doubt, tell this court that Jack did not administer the fatal does of insulin?"

Dr. Goodman hesitated, then said, "No, I cannot. Not beyond all doubt."

"No further questions," Harper said, stepping back to the defense table.

Richard Hennessey stood, still basking in the glow of the triumphant denouement of the prosecution's case.

"You testified earlier that you would be surprised to discover that Jack Ramey had killed himself, that, in your opinion, he was physically incapable of administering the fatal dose in the way it was administered, that is, directly into the vein in his arm. Do you still believe that?"

"Yes."

His glow brightening, Hennessey pranced back to his chair, tossing over his confidently squared shoulder, "No further questions."

Anna glanced over at Sloan, he at her. His look said that he, too, remained in a state of shock over the events that had unfolded that morning. He smiled slightly, however, a gesture of reassurance. Anna closed her eyes, trying to remember the kiss they'd shared the evening before, but remembering only the sight of a syringe and a bottle, a belt and a scarf. My God, what were the chances of that evidence being found?

"The defense calls Mrs. Alice Gay."

The name meant nothing to Anna, although when the young woman walked into the courtroom, Anna knew she'd seen her somewhere before. But where?

After Mrs. Gay had stated her name and occupation, Harper asked, "And where are you employed as a nurse?"

"At the Good Shepherd."

Anna immediately recognized the woman as one of the night nurses. She was the one with the ever-ready sense of humor.

"Did you have occasion to know Jack Ramey?"

"Yes, I nursed him during his last stay in the hospital."

"Tell us about a conversation that took place between the two of you."

"I can't remember the exact date. I just remember that it was during his last hospitalization. Anyway, it was one evening. His wife had gone down to the cafeteria, and I was giving him his usual insulin injection." She smiled. "I kid with my patients. If I can get a laugh, a smile, from them, it pleases me. I told him that I was going to give him a dose of dancing medicine, and that he and I were going to boogie out of the hospital."

"What, if anything, did he say to that?"

"He asked me if I'd ever given anyone an overdose of dancing medicine. I laughed and told him that you couldn't OD on dancing medicine. He smiled and said something about my being careful measuring out the insulin because he knew one could OD on it. He said fifty units of insulin, and he'd be a goner. Something like that, and I answered that it would probably take less than that."

"How did his comment strike you at the time?"

"I thought he was making conversation, kidding around."

"Did you later have occasion to wonder about his comment?"

"Yes, sir."

"When was that?"

"When I started following the trial in the newspaper. When I read that there was the possibility that Mr. Ramey had taken his own life."

"In the context of that possibility, how did Jack Ramey's comment then strike you?"

"I thought that maybe he was fishing around for what would constitute a lethal dose of insulin. That's when I contacted you."

Harper smile as this information resounded throughout the room. "Thank you for your testimony."

"Cross-examine, Mr. Hennessey?"

"Yes, Your Honor," the prosecutor said, standing. "Mrs. Gay, by word or deed, did Jack Ramey indicate, beyond all doubt, that he wanted this information so that he could execute his own death?"

"No."

"No further questions."

"Redirect, Mr. Fleming?"

"No, Your Honor. The defense would now like to call Father Edward Santelices."

Harper's announcement took Anna by surprise. She hadn't realized that he'd intended to call the priest. She watched with curiosity as Father Santelices stepped forward, was sworn in and seated. Harper approached the cleric.

"Father, did you have occasion to visit Jack Ramey?"

"Yes. Though he wasn't a member of St. Catherine's,

his sister is. Carrie—Mrs. Douglas—asked me to call on him and I did."

"More than once?"

"Yes. At the house and at the hospital. Altogether, three or four times."

"What did the two of you talk about, Father?"

"The usual smattering of subjects. The weather, baseball—Jack Ramey was interested in the Red Sox—Cook's Bay, his health, his wife and daughter. The usual."

"Did you ever discuss Catholicism?"

"Yes, we did on one occasion."

"And did you come away from that discussion with any opinion as to Jack Ramey's attitude toward the Catholic Church?"

The priest smiled. "His attitude was interesting, though not all that unique. As a child he'd been raised in a strongly Catholic home, but as an adult he'd drifted away from the Church, though he'd never drifted from the tenets of the Church."

"Were the tenets important to him?"

"They appeared to be."

"Objection, Your Honor, this line of testimony is going nowhere. Jack Ramey's religious beliefs are not at issue here."

"Your Honor," Harper said, "Jack Ramey was a man who'd asked his wife to help him die. It's not inconceivable—in fact, it's highly probable—that thoughts of religion were on his mind."

"While the prosecution is willing to concede that Jack Ramey might, indeed, have had religion on his mind, it is not willing to concede that his views on Catholicism have anything to do with this trial."

"Objection overruled, but make your point quickly, Mr. Fleming."

Turning his attention back to the priest, Harper

asked, "Did Jack Ramey ever discuss the subject of suicide with you?"

"No, he didn't."

Richard Hennessey leaned over to his assistant and, a smug smile at his lips, whispered something.

"At least not overtly," Father Santelices added.

Hennessey's smug smile disappeared.

"What do you mean, Father?" Harper prodded.

"When we were discussing Catholicism, he indicated that one of the things that had turned him off about attending mass was the Church's rigidity in certain areas. He specifically mentioned birth control, abortion, and suicide. At the time, I thought nothing of his bringing up the subject of suicide. I had no idea that he was contemplating taking his life."

"What is the Catholic Church's view concerning suicide?"

"Your Honor, while all of this is interesting, I hardly see—"

Harper interrupted. "Father Santelices has testified that Jack Ramey embraced the tenets of Catholicism. I think it only fair that the non-Catholic members of this jury have some idea of what he was embracing."

"I'm going to allow the question," Judge Waynon said.

The priest took a moment to collect his thoughts. "Jack Ramey had been correct. In the past, Church views were very rigid concerning suicide, defining it as the only unpardonable sin. Please understand that I'm not saying that the modern Church encourages or condones suicide, only that more recent Vatican rulings show a leniency in this area. In fact, it's called conditional absolution, which means that, at the time of death and judgment, no one can know the state of another's heart. Perhaps one is repentant, and based on that presumption, one cannot be denied a burial with full rites."

"Is it fair to say, however, this leniency notwithstanding, that there is still a stigma attached to suicide?"

"Yes, there is, and it transcends the bounds of Catholicism. It's a cultural stigma. Most people have, at best, a lack of understanding of, and at worst an aversion to, suicide. Maybe because it flies so in the face of our basic survival instinct. I've witnessed several deaths where loved ones have tried to cover up the fact that someone in the family committed suicide."

"You mention the family, Father. Have you had occasion to minister to many such grieving families?"

"As I said, several."

"And were there certain traits common to all?"

"Yes. All were hurt, angry, and in some way believed they were responsible. Most felt that they should have seen the suicide coming."

"One last question, Father. Were you surprised to learn that Jack Ramey had entertained thoughts of suicide?"

The cleric paused. "In the beginning I suspected nothing. As time went on, I increasingly recognized that Jack Ramey was troubled. I certainly knew that his health was worsening. All in all, I guess that I wasn't surprised."

"No further questions."

Judge Waynon looked in Richard Hennessey's direction.

"No questions," the prosecutor said, still looking smug.

"You may step down, Father," the judge pronounced.

While the testimony from both the cleric and the nurse seemed favorable enough, Anna thought with the sickest feeling, that the points scored must have been small, or else Richard Hennessey wouldn't be sitting there looking like the cat who'd lapped up the cream.

"Call your next witness, Mr. Fleming."

"The defense calls Carrie Ramey Douglas."

Again Anna was surprised, but watched silently as her sister-in-law took the stand. As before, no one would have suspected that Harper and Carrie were anything more than counselor and witness.

"Mrs. Douglas, the record indicates that, on the night of your brother's death, you slept at the Ramey home."

"That's correct."

"In fact, you were the last person to see your brother alive, weren't you?"

"Yes, that's apparently true. I saw him at midnight."

"But not thereafter?"

Hesitation. Then, "No."

"Was it customary for you not to check on him during the night when staying over?"

"Actually, no, but I assumed that Meg or Anna was checking on Jack."

"Why would you make that assumption?"

"I heard a lot of movement in the house and thought that Anna or Meg, or both, was up and would check on him."

"What kind of movement?"

"Stairs creaking, doors opening, footsteps—that sort of thing."

"I see. Now, Mrs. Douglas, let me ask you about that yellow scarf. You testified that it belonged to Anna Ramey."

"Yes, I did."

"Did you ever see her wear it?"

"Yes. She sometimes wore it down to the seashore. As protection against the wind."

"Your use of the word *sometimes* suggests that she didn't always wear it."

"No, she didn't."

"When she wasn't wearing it, where did she keep it?"

"Here and there."

"Would you define that, please?"

"I sometimes just saw it lying about the house. You know, here and there."

"At those time could anyone in the house have picked it up and used it for whatever purpose he or she chose? Say, for instance, the night Jack Ramey died?"

Hesitation, followed by a strongly delivered, "Of course."

"Mrs. Douglas, did you love your brother?"

The question took Carrie off guard, and she suddenly looked years older. "Yes. Very much."

"Enough to protect him from censure?"

Carrie's forehead wrinkled into a frown. "I-I'm not certain I understand what you mean."

"If you had found—bear in mind that I'm not saying you did—but *if* you had found that your brother had taken his own life, can you say unequivocally that, given the stigma associated with suicide, given the fact that suicide can be devastatingly traumatic on the family, can you say unequivocally that you wouldn't have removed the evidence to protect your brother and his family?"

Hennessey bounded to his feet. "Objection, Your Honor. Such a hypothetical question would be best asked at a hypothetical trial."

"I'm inclined to agree with Mr. Hennessey," Judge Waynon said.

"Your Honor," Harper said, "throughout this trial the prosecution has maintained that, had Jack Ramey killed himself, the instruments of death would have been found beside him. I'm merely trying to expose the jury to possibilities, not certainties, why they weren't."

"Still, Mr. Fleming—"

"Your Honor," Hennessey said, interrupting the judge, "the prosecution withdraws its objection."

Judge Waynon looked momentarily taken aback, then said, "Proceed, Mr. Fleming."

Harper repeated the question. "Can you say unequivocally that you wouldn't have removed the evidence to protect your brother?"

Carrie pondered the question before answering simply, "No, I can't say unequivocally that I wouldn't have."

Harper smiled. "Thank you, Mrs. Douglas."

Hennessey jumped to his feet. "Mrs. Douglas, *did* you remove such evidence from the scene?"

Without the slightest hesitation Carrie said, "No."

The prosecutor couldn't contain a smile. "No further questions."

Harper, on his way to the defense table, turned and said, "Mrs. Douglas, if you had gone to the trouble of protecting your brother and his family up to this point, is it likely that you'd stop protecting them now?" Before Carrie could answer, Harper rushed ahead with, "The defense withdraws the question."

The point had been scored with the jury. Anna knew, however, that it had been the first win of the morning. The second win came when Harper called Meg to the stand and, practically verbatim, repeated the discourse he'd had with Carrie, with virtually the same results: yes, the scarf was her mother's; yes, it was often just lying about; yes, anyone could have used it; yes, the night her father died, the house was filled with subtle sounds; yes, she assumed someone was checking on her father.

As always, at the sight of her daughter, Anna's heart had filled with sadness. That same heart had lurched when Meg had hesitated before her negative response to the prosecution's question about whether she had, indeed, moved the evidence. Looking about her, however, Anna concluded that no one but she had thought anything of the hesitation. As usual, Meg entered and exited the courtroom without once looking in her mother's direction.

"Call your next witness, Mr. Fleming," the judge ordered.

"Your Honor, the defense rests—"

"No!" Sloan bellowed.

Harper glanced over at Sloan, then up at the magistrate. Calmly, he said, "Your Honor, may I have a moment to confer with my client?"

"Since we're approaching the noon hour, we'll break for lunch and reconvene at one o'clock."

"All rise," the bailiff cried.

The court sounded like a herd of buffalo rising to their feet. Murmurs drifted throughout the crowd of spectators and reporters as all realized that the trial might well be nearing an end. Obviously, however, and this only added to the drama, one of the clients wasn't satisfied with resting the case.

Jake Lugaric turned to the woman beside him. "I wonder if Sloan Marshall's going to take the stand."

"Would that be bad?"

"Not for the prosecution," the reporter said. "Probably doesn't matter one way or the other. My guess is that they're both going to do time, anyway."

TWENTY-FOUR

No! I won't put either of you on the stand," Harper said. "And that's final."

"I'm not asking you to put Anna on the stand," Sloan said.

"I can't put you on the stand and not Anna. It would look as if she had something to hide."

Anna turned from the window of the small holding room they'd retreated to following the recession of court. Her gaze met Sloan's, then both of them glanced away. She looked back out the window, thinking how normal everything appeared outside—how wonderfully, how perfectly, normal.

"We've gone over this before," Sloan said. "If neither one of us takes the stand, it's going to look as if both of us have something to hide."

"You're right. We've gone over this. I told you that the judge will instruct the jury that your not testifying on your behalf is in no way to be construed as guilt."

"And I told you that the judge can instruct the jury all he wants, but that the jury will bring their own interpretation to our not testifying."

"Still, it's better than getting up there and giving them something to hang you with, and, believe me, Hennessey's just waiting for the chance. He'd love to show the jury how cool, calm, and collected Anna is. On the other hand, he'd love to show the jury how emotional you are."

At Harper's comment Anna again turned from the window. Cool, calm, collected? Didn't everyone see that, like rent fabric, she was torn and sundered? Unwanted images jumped to mind: a syringe, a bottle of insulin, a black belt—all so neatly bundled together in a scarf. Her scarf. She trembled, fearing that she was falling apart this very second. No, she must be strong. Now more than ever.

"I want to testify," Sloan insisted. "I want the jury to hear from me that I threw a shell into the sea, not what washed up on shore. I want the jury to hear that I *was* at the house that night, that I'd gone there to see if Anna was all right. I want them to hear from me that the affair was not some casual fling."

Harper keyed in to this last. "Don't you understand that it would be better for our case if the affair had been casual? Don't you see that Hennessey's just waiting for the opportunity to expose you as a man so besotted over a woman that you'd do anything to have her?"

Sloan stated the obvious. "C'mon, Harper, we all three know that we're in deep trouble. We have been ever since that news footage ran this morning—"

"The jury didn't see that footage. The jury doesn't know that you were together last night."

"When the judge polled them, they said they didn't

see the news, and maybe they didn't, but even so, they're bound to have sensed something negative."

Harper didn't bother with a denial, though he did repeat, "No, I won't do it. If you go on that stand, Hennessey will go right for the jugular and leave you to bleed to death right there."

"The news footage isn't the real problem, and you know it," Sloan continued. "The real problem is what Arty Watteau found. There isn't a man or woman on that jury who isn't seriously questioning if we committed murder."

"No, I won't let you do this."

Sloan had no option but to play hard ball. "Isn't it my legal right to testify on my own behalf?"

"Anna has rights, too, and as her counsel I have to protect hers."

Sloan glanced over at Anna, who said finally, "He's right. We haven't got anything to lose."

Harper swore, adding, "I want to go on record as saying that this is a hell of a bad idea."

"Mr. Fleming, do you intend to call another witness?" Judge Waynon asked at precisely one o'clock.

"Yes, Your Honor," Harper said, "but I'd like to approach the bench before I do."

"Do so," Judge Waynon replied.

Sloan watched as Richard Hennessey, following customary procedure, joined Harper. Not so customary was the fact that the prosecutor was beaming openly. His attitude seemed to be that he'd routed the defense, and to be truthful, Sloan couldn't argue the point. If he lived to be a hundred, he'd never forget the sight of the bundle that had washed up from the sea. What were the chances of something tossed into the sea ever being recovered? Maybe the storm was to blame, maybe it had been fate, maybe he would go crazy if he didn't focus on something else.

The lawyers stepped away from the bench, and Sloan took in Hennessey's impeccable appearance—everything from his expensive suit to his expensive tasseled loafers. For a reason he couldn't explain, he remembered the dust that had coated the loafers earlier in the week, the same dust he'd seen on Jake Lugaric's Dock-siders. Thoughts of the dust, of everything except the trial, disappeared when Sloan heard his name called. He hoped it hadn't been the heralding of Judgment Day.

His heart pounding, his hand on the Bible, Sloan swore to tell the truth and nothing but the truth. He then took the witness stand and sat listening to the judge address the jury.

"I have been informed by counsel for the defense that Anna Ramey will not be testifying during this trial. Her failure to do so cannot be construed, in any way, as an admission of guilt. Moreover, you are legally charged to reach a verdict based on the evidence presented, not on evidence not presented. Do each of you understand this?"

The jury assured the judge that they did.

"You may proceed, Mr. Fleming."

As Sloan watched Harper approach, his heart slowed, and a calmness settled over him. Regardless of the outcome of the trial, he'd have the consolation of knowing that he'd done everything he could. One look at Anna—her lovely face, the soft blue eyes staring back at him—convinced him fully that he was doing the right thing. He'd find a way to make the jury understand that his feelings for Anna, hers for him, were special and pure, not vulgar and tainted.

Confidently, looking as though Sloan's testifying was his idea all along, Harper said, "Mr. Marshall, please tell this court how you came to know Anna Ramey."

"We were, are, neighbors."

"In point of fact, you rent the keeper's cottage out by

the lighthouse and she, the nearest house, which she lived in with her husband until his death."

"That's correct."

"The two properties are a distance apart, are they not?"

"Yes."

"Then how did you meet?"

"I was accustomed to jogging every morning on the beach. In early June I saw a woman there—looking for shells."

Sloan thought it best not to mention how he'd watched her from afar, leaving shells for her before finally getting caught in the act.

"And so you first spoke to Anna Ramey because it was the neighborly thing to do?"

"Yes," Sloan said, knowing that he was bending the truth just a bit. By the time he'd spoken to her, he'd already developed a relationship with her.

"How would you characterize your relationship with Anna Ramey for most of the summer?"

"We were friends. I saw and talked with her any number of times. I even brought her some shells occasionally. When I could find whole ones."

"Did you discover that she was looking for one type of shell in particular?"

"Yes. A bivalve."

"Did she ever tell you why she was looking for this type of shell?"

Sloan glanced in Anna's direction before replying. He could remember, as though it were yesterday, sitting on the beach with her, she at first reluctantly, then eagerly, pouring out her heart. He was certain that she remembered, too.

Dragging his eyes from her, Sloan said, "It symbolized survival."

"And did you come to understand why survival was so important to her?"

"Yes. She was trying to survive some difficult times in her life. Her husband was ill and her marriage was floundering."

"Was her marriage floundering because her husband was ill?"

"Objection, Your Honor—"

"I'll rephrase the question. Was she ever specific about what she thought was the cause of her floundering marriage?"

"Yes. In dealing with his health problems, her husband had shut himself off from her. His isolation had hurt her."

"Isn't it true that at this juncture in your life, you, too, were preoccupied with survival?"

"I was still trying to come to grips with the horror of having been held hostage in Beirut, of having been tortured while in captivity," Sloan said, his voice barely audible.

"So the two of you began this innocent friendship based on a common understanding of survival?"

"Yes."

"But there came a time when you—when the two of you—realized that you had become more than friends. Isn't that true?"

"Yes, that's true."

"And what did the two of you do then?"

"We decided not to see each other again."

"Why?"

"Because both of us were concerned with ethics. She was a married woman. We both knew that only too well."

"Ultimately, how did you decide to handle this delicate situation?"

"I decided to leave Cook's Bay."

"But before you could what happened?"

"We became lovers." Again the words were whispered, but by this time the courtroom was so hushed that they were clearly audible to all.

"Why?"

Startled, Sloan just looked at Harper. "You mean why did we become lovers?"

"Exactly. You've already told this court that both of you had fought against doing that very thing, that you both were trying to act morally, but then suddenly, on August twenty-first, your restraint, your morals, flew right out the window."

Sloan raked his fingers through his hair. "Look, we didn't plan it. It just happened. We ran into each other on the beach, and . . ." He paused, sighing, trying to assemble the words he needed to make the jury understand. "We had fought against out feelings for so long. Anna was so . . . so emotionally and physically worn out—we both were. And we both knew that we'd probably never see each other again. The twenty-first was a Friday, and I was leaving early Monday morning. From the beginning there had never been any question about our future. Her marriage wasn't the best in the world, but she was committed to it." Sloan took another deep breath. "I guess we both knew that this was the only time we'd ever have."

"How did you feel afterward?"

"I didn't regret what had happened," Sloan said, "but I felt bad that I had been an accomplice to Anna's compromising her principles."

"Did you feel any guilt for what you'd done to Jack Ramey?"

"Of course. I liked Jack Ramey. I can't say that I approved of how he'd handled his illness—he'd hurt Anna badly—but I respected the fact that he'd had a difficult situation to deal with."

"Why did you go to the Ramey house later that night, on the very night, as it turned out, that Jack Ramey died?"

"I was concerned about Anna. As I said before, she's not an immoral woman, and I knew that she'd be struggling with what had just happened between us. I had to know if she was all right."

"And was she?"

"Naturally, she was upset. We both were."

"How long were you there?"

Sloan shrugged. "Five to ten minutes."

"Were you ever in the Ramey house that night?"

"No."

"One last question. What did you throw into the sea that night?"

"A shell. A bivalve. I'd found one that afternoon and I brought it to give to her, but as I said, we were pretty upset, and I forgot to. After I left the house, I threw it into the sea. It seemed a fitting and appropriate end to the shell and to our relationship."

"No further questions," Harper said, returning to his chair.

For several moments nothing, no one, stirred within the courtroom. Even the afternoon sunshine seemed poised at the windowpanes, peeking in to see what would happen next.

Slowly, in counterpoint to his usual haste, Richard Hennessey rose and, just as slowly, started toward Sloan. His shiny, dust-free tasseled loafers beat out a hollow—and disturbing, Sloan thought—rhythm on the wooden floor. The prosecutor reminded Sloan of a hunter stalking his prey. Maybe Harper had been right. Maybe his testifying hadn't been that great an idea, after all.

"Let me get this straight," Hennessey said, precisely adjusting one shirt cuff, then another.

At the tone of the prosecutor's voice, only shades away from sarcasm, Sloan steeled himself. No, unless he was mistaken, this had been an incredibly bad idea.

"The two of you met on the beach—by the way, how often did you meet?"

"Irregularly. Just whenever we ran into each other." Sloan thought it best not to mention that, in the beginning, irregularly had more often been regularly. Nor did he mention the notes they had inscribed in the sand to one another on those occasions when they hadn't met.

"So the two of you met on the beach, irregularly, became good friends, and then, one day out of the clear blue, you both realized that you had become more than friends. Is that right?"

"Yes, that's right."

"What happened to make you realize that you were more than friends?"

Sloan remembered only too well holding Anna's hand in his, of how startled they'd both been at the feelings the simple gesture had produced, but he had no intention of sharing this with Hennessey, and so he hedged on the truth. "Actually, it was more a gradual thing."

Hennessey nodded. "Ah, a gradual thing. And I suppose she just as gradually told you about her 'floundering' marriage, about how her husband had shut her out of his life, about how miserable she was? And you, just as gradually, poured out your heart to her about how you'd been held captive and how you'd broken under torture."

The latter, of course, wasn't true, but again Sloan had no intention of giving Hennessey anything more about his personal life than he had to. Instead he gave him an icy stare and said, "Something like that."

"Your Honor," Harper interrupted, "the prosecutor is interrogating, not cross-examining."

"Mr. Hennessey, I sense a lack of respect for this witness, and I will not tolerate such in this court."

Hennessey attempted to look as innocent as a choirboy. "I intended no such thing, Your Honor. My apologies to this court and to Mr. Marshall."

Sloan acknowledged the insincere apology in no way. He simply watched the hunter—warily.

Judge Waynon, sounding just as unconvinced of the apology's sincerity, said, "Proceed, Mr. Hennessey."

"Yes, Your Honor," the prosecutor said, turning his attention back to Sloan. "Mr. Marshall, you've already testified that Anna Ramey told you how ill her husband was."

"That's right."

"She also told you, didn't she, about his asking her to end his life?"

"Objection, Your Honor. Not addressed in direct examination."

Hennessey countered. "This court was made privy to the fact that these two talked openly to each other about their private lives. We have a right to know just how much they shared."

Judge Waynon considered, then ruled. "Since the prosecution maintains that the note might have acted as inspiration for the alleged murder, and since Mr. Marshall has elected to take the stand, I think this court has a right to know if Mr. Marshall knew of the suicide request."

"But, Your Honor—"

"I've ruled, Mr. Fleming."

With pleasure Hennessey repeated the question. "Did she tell you about the note her husband had written her?"

Sloan's throat tightened. "Yes, she told me."

Murmurs washed across the courtroom.

"Under what circumstances did she tell you?"

"I don't understand the question."

"Where did she tell you? When did she tell you? How did she tell you?"

Sloan stalled for time by shifting in his seat. "She

came to the lighthouse. It was the only time she ever did," Sloan hastened to add. "And she was upset."

"She was upset?"

"Of course she was upset. Her husband had just asked her to help him end his life!"

"Let me see if I've got this straight. Anna Ramey's husband asked her to help him end his life, and she, instead of going to family or friends, to his priest or to his doctor, who might have gotten help for his obvious depression, ran to her lover."

"We weren't lovers!"

"Your Honor, Mr. Hennessey is badgering the witness."

"Mr. Hennessey," the judge cautioned.

"I stand corrected," the prosecutor said. "She ran to the man she wanted to take as her lover, but couldn't because of ethics. Is that right, Mr. Marshall?"

"Mr. Hennessey," the judge repeated.

"Sorry, Your Honor."

"She was upset," Sloan said in response to the prosecutor's question.

"So you said," Hennessey responded. "And what was your reaction to the suicide request?"

"I was just as stunned and upset as Anna was."

"Are you in love with Anna Ramey?"

The question leaped at Sloan. "Yes," he answered.

"And did she ever tell you that she loved you?"

Sloan glanced over at Anna, his gaze sinking into hers. He wondered if she knew just how much he wished that he could answer affirmatively. But he couldn't.

"No," Sloan responded, feeling at least a modicum of pleasure in the fact that he had cheated the prosecutor out of the answer he'd expected.

Obviously surprised and disappointed, Hennessey, nonetheless, tried to salvage what he could. "And to what lengths did this love you felt for her lead you?"

"Objection!"

"Sustained!"

"Question withdrawn," Hennessey said, starting back toward the prosecution's table. His body language indicated that he'd finished with this witness.

Sloan breathed a sigh of relief—the damage could have been worse—and stood. Suddenly Hennessey stopped dramatically in midstride and turned. Sloan's sixth sense, the one that always warned him of danger, kicked in loud and clear.

"On the night that you and Anna Ramey became lovers, perhaps while you held her in your arms, perhaps later when you went to the house to see if she was all right, did either of you mention Jack Ramey's suicide request?"

Dead silence swept across the room. Everyone seemed to move closer to the edge of his or her seat. As for Sloan, his knees grew weak. At Hennessey's next question those knees threatened to buckle.

"Did either of you mention that all of you would be better off if Jack Ramey was dead?"

It had been a calculated shot in the dark, which had hit its mark with a bull's-eye accuracy. Yes, the man had gone for the jugular exactly as Harper had predicted he would. Sloan thought about lying and, in the end, might have done just that, except that his silence, or maybe the stunned look on his face, tipped Hennessey to the fact that he'd struck pay dirt. The lawyer made no attempt to conceal his pleasure. The courtroom was now as silent as a tomb.

"Yes or no, Mr. Marshall."

"I can't answer the question with a yes or no."

"A simple yes or no, Mr. Marshall."

"The irony didn't escape us, but—"

Hennessey's cold voice cut through Sloan's attempted comment. "Yes or no!"

"Yes!"

The courtroom erupted into a cacophony of sounds.

With immense self-satisfaction, Hennessey said, "I have no further questions of this witness."

The judge looked over at Harper, who said with bravado, "No questions."

It was only as Sloan stepped down from the witness stand, with legs barely able to support him, that he realized the extent of Hennessey's cleverness. He had not posed the one question that would have allowed Sloan to deny his, their, guilt. But, then, his own lawyer had not met the question head-on, either.

The following morning, a cool, nippy autumn Saturday, the case went to the jury, but not before each lawyer delivered a lengthy, impassioned closing argument. The prosecution maintained that, though Jack Ramey had obviously entertained thoughts of suicide, his paralysis had left him incapable of taking his life in the manner in which he died. Furthermore, only two people had motive, means, and opportunity, and these two people had spoken, on the very night of Jack Ramey's demise, about how everyone would be better off at his death. The reminder of what Sloan had admitted to fell heavily on those gathered in the courtroom, producing even a day later a round of unsettling whispers, which Harper's comments failed to hush. Basically, he contended that the evidence against Anna and Sloan was circumstantial, that murder wasn't a natural outgrowth of infidelity, that no one could say with absolute certainty that Jack hadn't taken his own life and that others had not lovingly conspired to cover up that fact. From there the judge charged the jury, and the wait began.

It was nearing eleven-thirty when a very quiet, extremely subdued, quartet entered Harper's law office. Harper walked straight to the bar and poured himself a drink, inquiring as to whether anyone wanted to join him. Everyone passed. Sloan shed his suit coat and tie, which he tossed onto the back of a chair, then slumped into the chair, his forehead buried in one hand. Anna merely took up a stance at the window, her arms folded across her chest. Marilyn went to the kitchen to prepare sandwiches that no one was likely to touch.

"Is it good or bad when a jury reaches a quick verdict?" Sloan asked after several minutes of silence.

Harper, uncharacteristically pacing about the room, sighed. "As I've said all along, there's no way to outguess a jury, but the longer they take, the more uneasy I get."

The remark set the tone for the long afternoon.

At twelve-thirty, his sandwich uneaten, Sloan sighed. "It's all my fault. I never should have taken the stand."

"You did what you had to," Harper said.

Anna turned from the window, her gaze meeting Sloan's. "I gave you my permission. That makes it as much my fault as yours."

"I pressured you and Harper, and we all know it," Sloan replied.

"Look, let's don't waste our energy assigning blame," Harper said.

Instead they wasted their energy on a vast assortment of other things. They paced. They stared out windows and at the telephone and at each other. Sloan, in an attempt to save what little sanity he had left, started counting the law books in Harper's office, but gave up when he couldn't concentrate on even that small a thing. The truth was that he kept hearing the clanking of steel bars, kept inhaling fetid smells, kept fighting the claustrophobic feeling that finally sent him catapulting out of the chair. He paced the room again, ending up at the bar, where he availed himself of the drink that Harper had earlier offered him.

At one-thirty, as though he were picking up the threads of a recent conversation and not one that had occurred more than an hour before, Sloan said, "It all went downhill after Beirut came out. How in hell did Hennessey access classified files?"

"It's unimportant how," Harper said. "He did and that's that."

At the mention of Beirut, Anna, who still felt on the verge of falling apart, glanced over at Sloan. Incredibly, even under the gravity of their circumstances, Anna wanted to throw herself into his arms, to burrow into his strength, to taste again the sweetness of his lips. Presently those lips no doubt tasted of liquor, which seemed fitting because even the sight of them made her more than a little drunk. But not drunk enough. She wanted to erase the image that simply would not leave her mind—an image of the syringe, the bottle, the black belt, and the yellow scarf. Why hadn't they stayed buried at sea?

It was incredible, Sloan thought. Here he was, flirting with a lifetime of imprisonment, and all he really cared about was taking Anna in his arms—holding her, kissing her, making love to her. Maybe his wanting to do so made sense considering the fact that his chances were poor that he'd ever again know her in any intimate way. Their cause had been desperate, he knew, from the moment that evidence had washed ashore. Dammit all to hell, why hadn't it stayed buried at sea?

The ringing of the telephone stopped four hearts. Marilyn, who'd been picking up plates of nibbled-at sandwiches, looked at the telephone, at Harper, at the telephone again. Setting down the plates, she walked to the desk.

"Good afternoon. Harper Fleming's office." She listened, then said, "Just a moment, please." Looking over at Harper, she said, "It's Mrs. Douglas."

Anna felt both relieved and frustrated. Mostly, though, she just felt herself falling apart. It was finally going to happen. She was finally going to do it, body part by body part. Or maybe she'd just disintegrate in one gigantic poof. But maybe not if she kept moving, instinct whispered, so she headed for the door even as Harper excused himself and headed for the telephone.

"Anna?" Sloan said.

She stopped, turned, smiled. "Tell Harper I'll be in the yard."

Unspoken was the fact that she needed to be alone, and so Sloan let her go. Maybe that's what he needed too. What he needed was to think. Clearly. Which he couldn't do in Anna's presence. The ringing of the phone had put the wait into perspective. When the telephone rang again, it would no doubt be to announce that the jury had reached a verdict. His time was running out, as were his options.

Stepping to the window, he watched as Anna came into view. She paused at the edge of the multiflowered garden. Sloan emptied his mind of everything, save the woman staring into space. There were times, such as now, when he could almost believe that he was still a captive and she just one of his many fantasies.

In the background he heard Harper speaking low to the woman he no doubt loved, a woman worried about her sister-in-law. Harper was comforting her, telling her that everything would be all right.

Would everything be all right?

Yes, it would, Sloan thought. Because he would make it all right. Perhaps that's what he'd intended all along, particularly since he'd seen the evidence that had washed ashore.

"And to what length did this love lead you?"

Sloan could hear the prosecutor's question and could answer that love had taken him all the way. While a part of him still feared being locked up, another part of him knew that he could endure what he had to. In a sense it was poetic justice. Because of his weakness he had in all probability taken the life of another human being. Instead of being punished for that, however, he'd been awarded the Congressional Medal of Honor. Now he would spend the rest of his life in prison for a murder he didn't commit, but in doing so he would protect the woman he loved.

A strange, and quite wonderful, calmness crept over him.

When he heard Harper hang up the phone, he turned and said, "There's something I need to tell you."

At the same time that Sloan was speaking to Harper, Anna raised her face to the cool autumn breeze blowing so teasingly, so freely, about her. Free. She was but one phone call away from losing every freedom precious to her. Sloan would lose his, as well, and he'd already had far too much captivity. In the distance she heard the sea whispering the question the prosecution had asked earlier.

"And did she ever tell you that she loved you?"

"No ..." No ... no ...

A strange and quite wonderful calmness crept over Anna. No, she had never said the words, but at this moment she knew that no words had ever been truer. She *did* love Sloan, and because she did, she wouldn't let him suffer, any more than he already had, for a crime he didn't commit. Jack was dead because of her. His death was her folly. His blood stained only her hands. For that she would be the one to pay the price.

Slowly, resolutely, Anna started back for the house. Freedom shrank with each step she took. Upon entering the office she glanced first at Sloan—a long, lingering look—then said to Harper, "I'd like to speak to you alone."

Her talk with Harper hadn't gone quite as she'd planned, Anna thought en route to the courthouse. He had listened quietly, unemotionally, to her admission of guilt, then had said, calmly, "I see. This is something we need to discuss with the judge as soon as possible."

The two of them had gotten into Harper's car and started for the courthouse. Marilyn and Sloan, at Harper's request, had left for the courthouse even before her conversation with Harper, which seemed odd. Why would Harper have wanted Marilyn and Sloan to return to the courthouse before his talk with her? She could understand the need to apprise the judge of this new turn of events, but Marilyn and Sloan had been ordered back before Harper had known there was a new turn of events. A sudden thought occurred to Anna, and she jerked her head toward Harper.

"Has the jury reached a verdict?"

A blank-faced Harper glanced over at her. "Not to my knowledge."

So that wasn't it, Anna thought, but there *was* something going on, something that didn't quite make sense. Another thought, as troubling as the first, crossed her mind, this one founded on the remembrance that Sloan had not once, but twice, told her that everything would be all right. Surely he wouldn't be crazy enough to confess to killing Jack.

"Has, uh, Sloan said anything to you?" she asked, trying to sound as casual as Harper was acting.

"Like what?"

Like what? Anna stammered around in her mind before saying, "Nothing."

Not another word was spoken until they reached the courthouse, but with each mile Anna became more and more convinced that something was amiss. Not even the press, which usually had to be swatted off like a swarm of bees, greeted her.

It was exactly ten minutes after six o'clock when they pushed through the doors of the courthouse. Marilyn was the first person Anna saw. It was obvious that she'd been waiting for them, because she rushed toward them at their appearance. Sloan was nowhere to be seen.

"The jury's reached a verdict," she announced.

Anna's heart fell to her feet. Now that she'd made the decision to admit her culpability, she didn't want the sacrifice to have been made in vain. Strangely, she was more than ever committed to her decision.

"It's not too late, is it?" she asked.

Without breaking stride, as though he hadn't even heard Anna, Harper expressed his own feelings, which turned out to be a curt, "Damn!"

"Great timing, huh?" Marilyn said.

"Did you contact Judge Waynon?"

"I tried to, but he'd already been informed of the jury's decision and was on his way back to the courthouse."

"Is he in his chambers yet?"

"Not when I asked last, which was about five minutes ago."

"Where's Sloan?"

"In the courtroom. Along with a standing-room-only crowd. Apparently, word about the verdict has leaked out. Everyone, particularly the press, was afraid of not getting a seat."

"It isn't too late, is it?" Anna asked again.

This time Harper's response was cut short by Jake Lugaric, who materialized from out of nowhere.

"How do you feel on the eve of the verdict?" he asked Anna.

"No comment," Harper said, ushering Anna forward, their brisk footsteps striking a bulletlike beat.

"Are you afraid, confident, what?" the reporter insisted.

"Get out of the way," Harper said, pushing him aside.

"Okay, okay," Lugaric said, falling back, but not so

far that he didn't hear the next exchange of conversation.

"Is it too late?" Anna insisted as Harper led her into the crowded courtroom.

"No," he said, then added to Marilyn, "Go check again on the judge. Make certain that we see him before court resumes."

Jake Lugaric frowned as the trio started down the aisle. Richard Hennessey, looking excessively confident, had already taken his place at the prosecution's table. Without warning, the bailiff announced that all present should rise. On the heels of that, the judge bounded toward his chair.

Harper swore and called from the aisle, "Your Honor, I need to speak with you."

Not only did Harper have the judge's attention, but also everyone else's in the courtroom, particularly Richard Hennessey's and Jake Lugaric's. The serious tone of Harper's imperative had sent up a red flag. Even as Harper had spoken, the clerk of court, whose flustered appearance suggested that she hadn't known that court was about to resume, approached Judge Waynon with Harper's earlier request.

Judge Waynon glanced at Harper. "I'm sorry, Mr. Fleming, I had no idea you'd requested a meeting."

"May I approach the bench?"

"Certainly."

As Anna slipped into her chair, Harper, with Hennessey close on his heels, stepped forward. Sloan glanced over at Anna and smiled reassuringly. Anna smiled back, knowing that she'd made the right decision. Even so, now that the moment of truth was here, she was afraid. She told herself that it was all right to be, that anyone would be frightened under the circumstance. Whatever happened from this point on, she'd survive. Surviving was what she did best.

Sloan, too, was well aware that he'd crossed his Ru-

bicon. There would be no turning back. Nor would he
if he could. There was a rightness in what he was
doing. Even so, his heart beat with fear. He told himself that his feelings were natural, and that he'd survive whatever the future held.

Although neither Anna nor Sloan could hear what
was being said at the bench with any clarity, they did
catch snippets. Enough to surmise that the judge was
surprised—"Highly irregular," he said twice—and that
the prosecutor was angry—"Ploy . . . protect . . . shambles of court . . ." It struck both Anna and Sloan as odd
that Hennessey had spent the trial's entirety trying to
convince the jury of their guilt, but now that the defense was admitting culpability, at least in half measure, he seemed upset.

"What's going on?" Monique whispered at Jake
Lugaric's side.

"I don't know, but I've got the strangest feeling that
the shit just hit the fan."

Hennessey, his voice low and clipped, had just
started to make an objection when Judge Waynon said,
"Counselors, take your seats."

"But, Your Honor—" the prosecutor began.

"Take your seat, Mr. Hennessey."

Both lawyers complied, against a backdrop of murmurs and mutters. Obviously, everyone in court had his
or her own idea of what was happening. The judge
rapped his gavel, then turned his attention to the defense table.

"Mr. Marshall"—Anna thought it peculiar that the
judge was addressing Sloan when she was admitting
her guilt—"is it your contention that you, acting alone,
murdered Jack Ramey?"

"Yes!"

"No!" Anna shouted. She could hardly believe what
she'd heard. Her look pleaded with Sloan not to do
what he was doing.

"Mrs. Ramey," Judge Waynon asked, "is it your contention that you, acting alone, aided your husband to take his life?"

"Yes," she said, defiantly adding, "Sloan had nothing to do with it."

Sloan could hardly believe what he was hearing. He couldn't let her spend the rest of her life in prison. He wouldn't!

"Your Honor, she's lying," Sloan said.

Hennessey jumped to his feet. "Your Honor, it's obvious that both are guilty and each is trying to save the other. Let the jury render its verdict. Let—"

The judge pounded his gavel. "Silence!" he shouted to both the prosecutor and the courtroom at large, but he might as well have been whistling in the wind. No one seemed to hear a word he said. Voices rose like an out-of-control choir, singing higher and higher, while half the press made a mad dash for the door. These individuals would later regret their haste, for even as the room erupted into chaos, a lone figure began to make her way down the aisle of the courtroom. Calm, resigned, she went unnoticed. Until she passed the bar separating spectator seating from the area holding the trial participants.

Slowly, one by one, the voices faded and Judge Waynon, his wrist weary from drumming gavel to wood, halted. He noticed the silence first, then the woman who stood adjacent to the defense table.

"They didn't kill him," she said. "I did."

TWENTY-FIVE

Anna and Sloan watched in disbelief as Carrie stepped forward, while Harper, who'd surged to his feet as though readying himself to come to Carrie's aid, merely stared in wordless shock. Even Judge Waynon looked as if he'd been struck upside the head. Only Richard Hennessey, who saw his hard-fought-for case, and probably his dreams for New York, exploding into smithereens, seemed capable of speech.

"Your Honor, how many more people are going to claim to have killed Jack Ramey? The evidence in no way indicates that Mrs. Douglas—"

"Sit down, Mr. Hennessey," the judge said.

"But, Your Honor—"

"Sit down!" Reluctantly, Hennessey did, at which time Judge Waynon turned his full attention to Carrie, who now stood directly before the bench. "Carrie"—it was a measure of the judge's astonishment that he used her given name—"do you understand the gravity of what you're saying?"

"Yes, I do."

"Are you telling this court that you killed your brother?"

"I helped him take his own life." She smiled faintly. "I suppose that's the same thing as killing him, isn't it?"

"Your Honor," Harper said after having found his voice, though only a wispy fraction of it, "Mrs. Douglas should speak with a lawyer."

"Mr. Fleming's right. You should—"

"No," she said softly, insistently, as she looked toward Harper. "It's all right," she told him. "I want to tell what happened that night. I always knew this moment would come. I'm glad that it finally has." Turning back to the judge, she said, "I really would like to sit down, though."

Judge Waynon indicated for the bailiff to step forward and assist Carrie onto the witness stand, which he did, as though Carrie were a delicate piece of porcelain.

Which was precisely what she looked like, Anna thought. A fragile piece of paper-thin bone china wrapped in a brilliant geranium-red suit. She also looked world-weary, as if the reality she'd spent her life running from had finally caught up with her. Why had she never even considered the possibility that Carrie had been guilty? The answer was simple. She'd been so certain that Meg had done it.

Judge Waynon spoke. "I'd like for the record to read that, although this testimony is highly irregular, I'm going to allow it in the interest of justice." He paused, then said, "Tell this court what happened the night your brother died."

Carrie nodded and squared her shoulders for the ordeal. "I had spent the night at the rented house. I was sitting with Jack, the way I often did. I had insisted that Anna go to the movie. I thought it important that she get out of the house. She was so tired, so worn-out, from taking care of Jack." Carrie smiled again. "I loved Jack, but he could be a handful—so demanding of himself and everybody else. I thought that Anna was near a breaking point. She didn't want to go, but I made her. Even Jack encouraged her to.

"After Anna left, Meg showed up unexpectedly. We all thought she was going to spend the weekend at school, but she'd been worried about her father—we all were—and so she'd come to check on him. I could tell, right from the second that she arrived, that she was upset that her mother wasn't there. She kept asking me where she'd gone, when she'd left, and when she was coming back. Though I didn't realize it at the time, I think now that she thought her mother was with Sloan."

Carrie looked over at Anna, as though in apology for this blatant admission. Anna smiled—reassuringly.

"Go on, Carrie," the judge prompted.

"Meg insisted on waiting up for her mother, and so I checked on Jack, then tried one last time to talk Meg into going on to bed, but she wouldn't, and so I did. A little later I heard Anna come in, and though I couldn't hear what they were saying, I could tell that Meg and Anna were having words. A few minutes later I heard Meg storming up the stairs and into her room. From there the night just got kind of crazy."

"What do you mean?"

"Nobody seemed able to settle down. I heard Meg prowling about in her bedroom, and Anna prowling about in hers. I even heard Anna go downstairs once. Then she came back upstairs, but I still continued to hear sounds from her room. I don't think she slept much, if any. Neither did Meg. I heard her go downstairs too. Then she came back up. Later—I think sometime after three o'clock—I decided to check on Jack myself. I mean, I couldn't sleep, and I wondered if he was as restless as everyone else seemed to be."

Here she stopped and didn't seem inclined to go on.

"Carrie," Judge Waynon prompted.

Carrie stared straight ahead, but it was obvious that she saw nothing but images of the past. Painful images. Her voice was cloud-soft when she finally spoke.

"When I approached the bedroom, I realized that there was more light than the night-light should have provided. I was surprised to see that the lamp was on and that Jack was sitting up. Well, sort of sitting up. He'd tried to prop himself up on some pillows, but mostly he just sort of slumped to the side. He looked startled to see me." Her voice cracked when she added, "When I stepped into the room, I could see why."

The judge gave her a few moments to compose herself before saying, "Carrie, what did you see?" Carrie glanced over at the judge, she herself looking a little startled that she was in a courtroom. "What did you see?" the judge repeated.

"At first I wasn't sure what I was seeing, or maybe I was certain and was only trying to block it out."

Again she hesitated, overwhelmed by past remembrances.

"Carrie, what did you see?"

"The black belt. Meg's belt. She got it for her birthday. Her mother bought it for her, and I got her some black jeans."

"What about the belt?"

"It was fastened around Jack's right arm." Here, perhaps unknowingly, she indicated her upper arm. "You know, like a tourniquet. And then I saw the syringe I'd borrowed from Dr. Goodman but kept forgetting to return, and a bottle of insulin. The bottle was almost empty, and the syringe was almost full. I told myself that there was a perfectly logical explanation, that Jack had just needed another shot and was trying to give it to himself." She closed her eyes, saying, "God, I wanted to believe that, but Jack wouldn't let me."

Even though Carrie's eyes were shut, a single tear escaped. It was so quiet in the room that Anna could have sworn that she heard the tear fall. She longed for the same self-expression, but knew that tears wouldn't come. They never did. They just welled within her heart, causing it to expand painfully. Not giving a damn what anyone thought, Sloan covered her hand with his. Not giving a similar damn, she let him. Beside her she felt Harper's heart breaking into a million pieces.

"Would you like a drink of water?" the judge asked.

Carrie shook her head, almost dislodging a comb. "No, thank you." She sniffed and said, "I'm fine. Really, I am. As I was saying, Jack made it very clear what he was doing. He told me in a halting but calm voice—in fact, I'd never seen him so calm—that he wanted to die, that it was time for him to, something about the sea had helped him to forgive himself, and that he knew he wasn't going to get better, and that he was tired of struggling. He said that he wanted to die now before he had another stroke and perhaps became so incapacitated that he couldn't end his life. He said that Anna deserved the opportunity to go on with hers. Surprisingly, his voice was strong, and even though it wasn't normal, I understood every word he said."

Anna's hand trembled; Sloan's hand tightened over hers.

"I told him that he was being silly," Carrie continued, "that he was getting better, that he wasn't going to have another stroke, but he said that I saw things the way I wanted them to be, not the way they were." She smiled. "I guess he was right. Maybe I do."

Again she paused, as though garnering courage. "He

asked me if I'd help him end his life. He said that he'd already stuck his arm once, but that he'd missed the vein. He was afraid that he'd miss it again."

"And what did you say?" the judge asked.

Carrie shook her head. "I really don't know what I said. Maybe nothing. My mind just went blank. I felt totally disassociated from what was happening, as though I were standing back watching. I may have said something about being afraid of needles. I'm not sure, though. I may have said something about giving the shot intramuscularly, or maybe he did. I just remember his saying that he could do that, but that it would take longer to die. He said that he wasn't afraid to die, but that he didn't want to suffer before he did. If he suffered, he didn't want it to last very long. He said that he'd already suffered too much."

Again she hesitated, looking as detached as she'd claimed to be that night. Again another tear fell.

"Did you help him, Carrie?"

"He begged me," she said, as though that, in and of itself, justified her actions. "I remember that he handed me the syringe. It felt odd in my hand, but I wasn't afraid, and I remember thinking how strange that I wasn't afraid because I'd always been afraid of needles. But I wasn't. The person watching from a distance was afraid, but the person holding the syringe wasn't. I remember thinking that, yes, this was the right thing to do because Jack was really sick. The person holding the syringe could see that."

Absently, she threaded the loose comb back through her hair, saying proudly, "I hit the vein the first time. The very first time. But then I hesitated. I couldn't bring myself to depress the plunger, so Jack put his thumb over mine and pushed. I could see the insulin disappearing into his arm. When the syringe was empty, I pulled the needle out and laid the syringe on the nightstand. He asked me to cut out the lamp and to sit beside him. I remember removing the pillows first, so that he could lie back, then I sat on the edge of the bed and took his hand in mine. He closed his eyes but didn't say anything, at least not for a few seconds. Then he said, 'Do you hear the sea?' And I said, 'Yes, I do.' And he said, 'Tell Mama that I'm going to go for a swim.' I told him that I would."

Her voice splintered, and she grew quiet. This time the judge said nothing. He merely honored her pain.

Finally she said, "I knew the second he died. His hand just went limp in mine. There weren't any convulsions, nothing agonizing. He just ... died. Peacefully. Calmly. I remember searching for his pulse, but I couldn't find one, and so I just held his hand for a long time. Five, ten, fifteen minutes. I don't know how long. I felt that, as long as I held on to him, he was still there."

"What happened next?"

"As I said, I don't know how much time passed, but slowly I became aware that, though I knew that what I'd done was right, in the eyes of the law I'd killed him, or I was an accomplice or something. That's when I got scared. I took everything—the belt, the syringe and needle, the insulin bottle—and put them in Anna's scarf. It was lying on the dresser. I tied everything up and slipped from the room, then out the back door of the house, and ran down to the beach. I threw it into the sea." She smiled, this time with irony. "The funny thing is that, if I'd just left everything where it was, it would have looked as if Jack had taken his own life. I mean that was the defense, wasn't it? And it was what Jack had intended to do—if he could have managed it."

A sudden thought crossed Carrie's mind, and she glanced over at Anna and Sloan.

"I never would have let you two go to prison. I swear it. I just thought that if the jury found you not guilty, what could be the harm? I mean, I know you suffered through the trial, and I'm sorry, but it was sort of like, if the jury found you not guilty, then maybe everything had happened as it should have. Do you know what I mean? Maybe it had been fate."

When she said nothing more, the judge asked, "Is there anything more you want to say?"

"Only that I'm not sorry. I'd do it again. Jack was my brother. I loved him." The words trailed off into a thin nothingness, and Carrie's eyes misted with tears. Through them she smiled sadly, then said, "He could always get me into more trouble."

In the days following the climactic conclusion to the trial, Sloan heard from Anna once and then only long enough to agree to speak later in the week. On Monday, Carrie had been arraigned before Judge Waynon, where she had pleaded guilty to aiding her brother to commit suicide. The sentencing was scheduled for Friday morning. Determined to stand by Carrie in her hour of need, Anna had moved in with her sister-in-law. Now that the truth behind Jack's death had come out, Carrie for the first time was truly mourning the loss of her brother. Though it was uncertain what would happen to Carrie, Sloan knew that Harper was optimistic. Harper felt—perhaps *hoped* and *prayed* were more fitting words—that the judge would be lenient. No one who'd heard Carrie's confession had been unmoved, including the usually rapacious press who, in general, had soft-pedaled their news stories. Even Jake Lugaric had shown an uncharacteristic degree of restraint.

If Anna was the rock on which Carrie leaned, Sloan was no less a bulwark for Harper. In all the years that Sloan had known him, Harper had never been so devastated—not by Carrie's guilt, but by the fact that he hadn't known to help her at this most trying time in her life. He had vowed to be there always for her in the future. Sloan knew what it felt like to make such a vow of love. He just didn't know if it was a vow he'd have the opportunity to fulfill. For all that he loved Anna, she still hadn't expressed her feelings for him, nor did he have any idea where she saw their relationship going. And so he waited impatiently for her to get in touch with him.

When the telephone rang on Wednesday afternoon, Sloan, his pride cast to the wind, rushed to answer it. It wasn't Anna, though Sloan did recognize the voice immediately. It belonged to Captain Nichols, his former superior office.

"I suppose that, under the circumstances, an unconditional congratulations wouldn't be in order," the naval office said. "Though I would be less than honest if I didn't say that I was pleased that you had been exonerated of all charges."

"Thank you, sir."

"How are you feeling these days?"

Sloan shared Anna's ambivalent feelings, a fact he expressed. "Relieved, though saddened that the relief comes at the expense it does."

"How is the sister-in-law?"

"Actually, she's doing pretty well. She has family and friends who've rallied about."

"That's good." There was a pause, which Sloan suspected heralded the purpose of this call. He was right. "Look, I've come across some information that I think you might be interested in."

"What's that?"

"After that debacle on the stand, in which classified information was revealed, I did a little checking around at the Pentagon. The authorities take a dim view of classified material being declassified without their permission."

The man certainly had Sloan's attention. "And what did you learn?"

"The authorities narrowed the leak down to a hand-

ful of individuals who could have had access to your
file. Under questioning one of them—a man by the
name of George Oberle—admitted to selling the information about your past. He was one of those disgruntled individuals who felt he'd been cheated out of a
promotion. Of course, he's been tossed out on his ear."

"Sold it? To whom?"

"To some reporter on the Washington beat, who, in-
cidentally, is looking for a new job these days too."

Sloan frowned. "That still doesn't explain how it got
into a courtroom in Maine."

"Well, actually, it does. Though the reporter refused
to divulge any information, his telephone records were
confiscated. Seems that he made a couple of calls to a
motel in Cook's Bay. To the same motel Jake Lugaric
stayed in."

"Jake Lugaric?"

"None other."

On this note Sloan eased into a nearby chair and
feathered his fingers through his hair. His mind was
racing a mile a minute. Ever since Lugaric had approached him, asking what had really happened in Beirut, Sloan had felt uncomfortable around the newsman.
He also sensed that he was as unscrupulous as a snake-
oil salesman. Jake Lugaric's involvement, however,
didn't explain how the prosecution had come into possession of the information, unless . . .

Interestingly, Captain Nichols echoed Sloan's thoughts.
"I'd say that there's some connection between Lugaric
and the prosecution."

"Yeah," Sloan said as visions of powdery dust danced
in his head. "The trick, however, is proving it."

The next afternoon, after a cryptic telephone call,
Richard Hennessey headed his red Porsche in the direction of a motel in Rockport. He had no idea what in
hell Lugaric wanted to see him about, although he was

grateful that the man had the common sense to meet outside Cook's Bay. He'd been surprised at the message his secretary had taken, principally because he'd thought Lugaric had already left town. He'd just assumed that, by now, the newsman was already sucking some other story dry.

Pressing the accelerator with his spotless loafer, he edged the speedometer to a reckless eighty miles per hour. As the wind molded itself around the car, Hennessey felt free . . . and luckier than any man had a right to be. The completion of the trial had been a disaster, the end, he'd thought, to any bettering of his career; but lo and behold, a well-known law firm in Boston had called him. Seems they liked the way he'd handled himself during the trial. They'd called him resourceful, energetic, possessed of courtroom courage. They wanted to talk about his possibly joining the firm.

Yes!

So Boston wasn't New York. It was a damned sight better than Cook's Bay. Boston was cosmopolitan, cultured, sophisticated, a place teeming with people who would appreciate Gucci loafers and Armani suits— already Botany 500 suits were gauche—a place where he could go to the theater and the Boston Philharmonic by night, a place where he could practice bigtime, big-money law by day. Yeah, he was going to like Boston just fine.

Twenty minutes and a thousand Bostonian dreams later, Hennessey pulled the Porsche into the parking lot of the motel. Thank God, the place was fairly deserted, with only a few scattered cars attesting to any occupancy. As he searched for the room number— 101—he realized that it must be in the back of the U-shaped court, which was another advantageous discovery. Now, he thought, stopping the car on a dime in the slot in front of the room, all he had to do was get rid of Lugaric. Once and for all.

Slipping on a pair of sunglasses, he stepped quickly to the door and knocked, hoping that he wasn't soiling his cuff on the dirty door. Instantly he heard movement within.

"C'mon, c'mon," he chanted, looking about. Suddenly the door opened. "Okay, Lugaric, what in hell—"

The words trailed off as Hennessey stared into the eyes of Judge Waynon. Inside the room he could see Sloan Marshall and Harper Fleming.

"Good afternoon, Mr. Hennessey," the judge said. "So glad that you could join us for this discussion on the repercussions of violating a gag order."

Hennessey stared in shock. He had the sickening feeling that the Boston Philharmonic would be performing without him in the audience.

Friday afternoon, her hands buried in her jacket pockets, Anna made her way to the lighthouse. A thick, melancholy fog had crept over Cook's Bay, closing it in gauzy, cloudlike patches. Billows of gray obscured the sea to her left and the forest to her right. It also obstructed her view, except for a few precious inches directly in front of her. More than anything, she was following the lonely-sounding *wa-wa* of the foghorn. Mingling with the forlorn wail came the desolate dashing of unseen waves as they crashed onto the shore, and the lonesome cry of a seabird.

In a way she could explain all too clearly, the fog fit her mood. With each sandy step she took, she moved forward by faith alone. In time she would find the lighthouse, but her emotional journey was not so guaranteed. That road was darkened by memories, shrouded by feelings that she couldn't yet cope with, shadowed by a guilt she had come to terms with. As she'd sat in court that morning, listening to the judge mete out his merciful verdict, Anna had realized that, unlike Carrie, she herself had not yet been sentenced for her moral crime. More important, she realized that she herself must be her judge and jury. Could she make Sloan understand this?

She didn't know, but she had to try.

At long last the keeper's cottage came into view. Fog swirled about the roof and chimney, erasing the simple lines and angles, hiding the uncomplicated composition of wood and workman's skill. Squinting at the structure, Anna hesitated, then forced herself to brave what lay ahead.

When Sloan heard the knock, he knew it was Anna at the door. He wasn't certain how he knew it—perhaps he'd grown so impatient that he had to believe it or go crazy—but knew it he did. He crossed quickly to the door.

Standing face-to-face with Anna, he felt as if forever had passed since he'd last seen her. Fog-moist tendrils of hair, a shade of blond by which Sloan compared all other shades, trailed onto her cheeks, while her eyes shone with the blueness of a thousand seas. As he stared into those eyes, he wondered if they didn't look just a bit sad. A feeling of dread, heavy and foreboding, settled about him. He released the feeling, telling himself that he was only being paranoid. What could go wrong on a day that, considering Carrie's compassionate sentence, had begun so promisingly?

He grinned. "Hi."

"Hi," Anna returned, thinking that he looked incredibly handsome in his worn jeans and old shirt, incredibly sexy with his hair mussed and disheveled. Did she really have the strength to walk away from him? Could she really steal away, with hurtful words, the most perfect smile she'd ever seen?

"Come in," he said.

Anna stepped into the cottage. A fire blazed in the fireplace, warming the chill that had wandered in with the vagrant fog. In welcome, the warmth surrounded her.

Reaching out his hand, Sloan said, "Let me have your jacket."

Anna obeyed. Her jeans were as worn as Sloan's, her untucked shirt as old.

Laying her jacket on the arm of the sofa, he motioned toward the kitchen. "Would you like anything? Coffee? Soda? Beer?"

"No," she said. "Thank you."

"I, uh, I talked to Harper a little bit ago. He said that everything went real well in court today."

"Yes, it did."

His perfect smile grew more perfect—painfully perfect. "Carrie can do a hundred hours of community service with one hand tied behind her."

Anna couldn't help but respond to Sloan's smile with one of her own. "She probably does that already."

"Yeah, probably." A pause. Then, "Look, you sure you don't want coffee or something?"

"No, nothing for me."

Sloan paused again, once more entertaining the vague feeling that something wasn't quite right. Once more, he sent the notion packing.

Plunging his hands into the back pockets of his jeans, he said, "I guess you heard about Hennessey being temporarily suspended."

Anna nodded. "Harper said that he and Lugaric were fraternity brothers at college."

"Yeah, he sent for Lugaric with orders for him to turn the trial into a media event. He was so sure that he was going to get a conviction that he wanted the whole world watching. He wanted to move into a big law firm somewhere and thought that this high-profile case could be his ticket."

"According to Harper, he almost got his wish."

"Can you believe that lucky stiff? Even after the trial turned out as it did, a prestigious firm in Boston contacted him. Of course, what with the suspension, the firm has backed down on their interest."

"I thought the suspension was only temporary."

"It is, but Harper said no reputable firm is going to hire him with that on his record. And then there's Lugaric's charge that Hennessey paid money for the classified information. Hennessey denies it, but with that bank withdrawal, it's suspicious."

"What does Harper think about Hennessey's possibly buying the information?"

"That he's guilty. Harper has had his doubts about Hennessey all along. He suspected at the arraignment that the prosecutor had leaked information to the press about the change in time, which resulted in our being mobbed. But that's what Hennessey wanted—us and him in front of the camera as much as possible."

"What about Jake Lugaric? What's going to happen to him?"

"Looks as if he's going to get nothing more than a slap on the wrist. Apparently the ends justify the means as far as some news executives go. Plus, it doesn't hurt that he's dating the daughter of the network's major stockholder."

"That's a shame. About the slap on the wrist. He deserves worse."

"Yeah."

Another pause ensued. When Sloan ended it by asking about her daughter, Anna was actually relieved, relieved to be postponing the purpose of her visit. She didn't want to hurt this man. She didn't want to hurt herself.

"She's back at college."

"Have you two patched things up?"

Suddenly chilled by the subject, Anna moved to stand in front of the fire. Orange flames shot upward to the accompaniment of loud, fiery crackles. "That may never happen, but we are at least talking—somewhat civilly."

"That's a start."

Anna smiled sadly. "I suppose."

"You thought she killed her father, didn't you?"

"Yes, for a number of reasons."

"Harper indicated that she'd said something during your fight that had worried you."

The remembrance of that night, her daughter's words, were painful. Perhaps they always would be, but Anna forced herself to repeat the dark statement that had lived in her heart like a poisonous viper.

"She told me she'd rather see her father dead than ever have him find out about my infidelity."

Sloan looked incredulous. "You thought she'd actually killed him that night because of your infidelity?"

"It wasn't quite that clear-cut. At the time, the statement hurt me badly, but I didn't take it as an indication that she meant it literally. People say a lot of things when they're mad or hurt. I certainly didn't think that night that it was anything she intended to act on. But of course Jack was still alive. It was only after he died, and in combination with other facts, that I worried that she might have taken her father's life.

"And, here again, I never thought she'd done it coldly and with calculation. I knew that she knew how ill her father was, and it even crossed my mind later that, although I'd tried to shield her from Jack's suicide request by burning the note, it was just possible that he had approached her with a similar request. Whatever her merciful reasoning, however, I felt that I was the cause of Jack's death. If I hadn't committed adultery, Meg never would have been motivated to act, to shield him from the pain of ever finding out what I'd done."

"But of course she hadn't killed her father."

"No, she was protecting Carrie. She wasn't certain

Carrie was guilty but strongly suspected it, which was another reason I suspected Meg. She'd had no qualms about confronting me with the affair, but she never once asked me if I killed her father, which I thought was a logical question under the circumstances. Plus, on the stand she was so adamant about believing that I hadn't killed him. I thought it only pointed the finger at Meg. I reasoned that she knew I wasn't guilty because she was. I knew she'd lied about checking on her father that night. The black belt cinched my suspicion."

"Why did she lie about checking on her father?"

"She didn't want Carrie to know that she'd seen her going into Jack's bedroom. If Meg had stayed in her room, she couldn't have seen or heard anything. Remember that Carrie said she hadn't gone downstairs that night. But Meg had seen and heard her. She'd even heard her leaving the house, which Meg thought strange. In retrospect she reasoned that Carrie was getting rid of the evidence, which, of course, she was.

"But what really convinced her of her aunt's guilt was the comb Meg found. When Carrie checked on Jack at midnight, right before she went up to bed, she stopped by the living room to try to persuade Meg to go on to bed too. Meg was certain that Carrie had both combs in her hair, yet the following morning she found one of Carrie's combs under one of the pillows in Jack's bed. Why lie about going to check on Jack, Meg concluded, if she didn't know something about Jack's death?"

"So you were willing to spend the rest of your life in prison for a crime you didn't commit?" Even the question sent shudders rippling down Sloan's spine.

"As I said, I felt responsible for what I believed to be Meg's actions. And I couldn't let you go to prison for something I knew you hadn't done." Before Sloan could respond, she added, her frustration still evident, "I couldn't believe it when you admitted to killing Jack. I mean, I knew all along that you probably thought I did it. After the appearance of the yellow scarf, what could you think? But still, I couldn't believe what you'd done."

"Is it so hard to understand? You were protecting a daughter you love. I was protecting the woman I love."

As always Sloan had a way of disarming her with the simplest of truths. Stepping toward Sloan, Anna placed her palm against his cheek.

"Sloan Marshall," she said, speaking his name in such a way that Sloan thought he'd die of pleasure, "you are the most incredible man, the most incredible person, I've ever met." Anna's voice lowered until it sounded like silk and lace and all things soft and sweet. "And I love you more than I ever thought it possible to love anyone."

If Sloan had disarmed Anna with the unadorned truth, she had stunned him with the same simplicity. Her words bound themselves to his lonely heart. Sighing roughly, he said, "I've waited a long time to hear that. There were times when I wondered if I ever would."

"Surely, you knew—know—that I love you."

Sloan said nothing. The words were trapped between his thundering heartbeats. Instead he covered her hand with his and drew her palm to his lips. The kiss was tender and warm and Anna's undoing. Slowly, while she still had the strength to, she pulled her hand away and walked from the warm fire to the fog-latticed window. Her back to Sloan, she stared out into the gray afternoon. It was then that Sloan knew with certainty that his feeling of dread had been justified.

"What is it, Anna?" he asked, wanting to know, not wanting to know.

She pulled no punches. The quicker it was said, the better. "I'm going back to Connecticut."

It took Sloan a few seconds to grasp what she'd said. When he did, he said, "Wait a minute. You're telling me that you love me, and in the same breath that you're leaving me?"

Anna turned, her eyes pleading for him to understand. "Please just hear me out." Pause. Then in a desperation-laced voice she added, "I beg you."

"Why do I have the feeling that I'm not going to like what I hear?"

"You're probably not, but I have to say it." Hesitating, she chose her words carefully. "What's between us has happened so quickly."

"It sometimes happens that way, but it doesn't minimize our feelings for each other."

"I know that, but there's been no time for us—for me—to think, to reflect. And even if there had been time, circumstances wouldn't have allowed it. For so long I've been mired in emotional quicksand. There's been Jack's illness, his growing progressively worse, his death, the trial, thinking that I might spend the rest of my life in prison for what I believed Meg was guilty of, her animosity toward me, Carrie's admission of guilt, the affair, falling in love with you . . ." Even the itemization took its toll, and Anna trailed off on a shattered sigh.

"Okay, so you need some time, but why can't you take that time here in Cook's Bay? We can take the time together."

"Because I can't think clearly around you." Anna regrouped her thoughts, trying to find the words that would come to the heart of the matter. "I don't regret anything that happened between us, and that's part of my problem."

Sloan frowned. "I don't understand."

"If I had it to do over, I'd do the same thing again.

What we shared was the most beautiful experience of my life, but it constituted the breaking of a vow that I held dear. I don't know what that says about me. I'm not sure I like what it says about me." Frustration ruled, and Anna raked her fingers through her hair. "I'm not sure who I am anymore."

Sloan's frustration matched Anna's. "You're Anna Ramey—human being."

"A philosopher once told me that being human was intolerable."

"Yeah, well maybe you ought to fire the bum and hire another philosopher."

"Maybe, but that same philosopher is still struggling with his own humanity. Can you honestly say that you've forgiven yourself for what happened in Beirut?" When Sloan said nothing, she answered for him, "See, you haven't. If we have a future, Sloan, we must enter into it as whole beings, not emotional fractions of what we should be. I told you once that your redemption lay in forgiving yourself. Mine does too. Don't you see that?"

What he saw was that he was losing her, at least temporarily, and that nothing he could say would change that. What he didn't want to admit, but couldn't ignore, was the fact that perhaps she was right. Maybe they did need time to think, time to heal. This realization didn't lessen his pain, however, which felt like a dagger being driven into his heart.

"How long will you be gone?"

"I don't know."

A sudden thought crossed Sloan's mind, which slowly twisted the dagger until he couldn't catch his breath. "You *are* coming back, aren't you?" When she didn't answer, his temper flared. "Dammit, Anna, you can't do this to us!"

"Please, Sloan," she whispered, "give me some time."

Finally, his voice rich with resolve, he said, "I'll

wait for you for the rest of my life, if that's what it takes."

They parted on that promise, though Sloan was all too aware that Anna had carefully refrained from making a commitment. She hadn't said that she was coming back.

TWENTY-SIX

The following week Sloan sat glued to the telephone. He was certain that any minute, any second, Anna would call, confessing that she missed him, loved him, couldn't stand to be without him. Surely distance—Connecticut seemed as far away as the farthest star—had helped her quickly to put everything that had happened between them in perspective. Surely she could see as clearly as he that, although their relationship had begun under less than ideal circumstances, the ethical fires under which it had been forged had strengthened it. Surely she could see that they had been guilty of nothing but answering destiny's call. More important, they had answered to their hearts.

Surely she could see this. Why, then, Sloan wondered at week's end, hadn't she called?

By Wednesday of the next week, during those moments when he allowed himself to be honest, he admitted he was getting a trifle worried . . . and running out of excuses why he couldn't leave the keeper's cottage. Harper had asked him to lunch a couple of times and out for coffee twice that number of times, but always to Sloan's refusal. Sloan knew that his excuses were pitiful. He knew, too, that Harper suspected the reason behind those refusals, a fact his friend revealed with one telling comment.

"Give her time," Harper said Friday afternoon when he called with yet another invitation to lunch.

Sloan didn't pretend not to understand what his friend meant. Neither did he try to conceal his ever-growing impatience. "It's been two weeks."

"Two weeks isn't all that long." Sloan could tell that Harper chose his next words carefully. "Maybe she's right. Maybe the two of you have to come together as whole individuals or not at all."

Though a private person, Sloan, in a share-or-go-crazy moment, had told Harper about his parting conversation with Anna. Sighing, he admitted what he'd acknowledged to himself even at the time of his talk with Anna. "Maybe."

"Whatever happens between you and Anna, you owe it to yourself to come to terms with what happened in Beirut."

Sloan thought about his friend's remark that night as he stood at the window watching the season's first snowfall. Nickel-sized flakes, as fleecy as the softest cotton, fluttered downward, dying a quick death as they struck the living sea. In the nearby woods, however, the flakes collected. In particular, Sloan was drawn to the snowflakes flittering through the skeletal branches of a grove of paper birches. White flakes. White bark. White on white. Camouflage at its most effective. Was he hiding his feelings about Beirut just as effectively?

His hands lost in the back pockets of his jeans, his

thoughts lost in the past, he had to admit that he just didn't know what his thoughts, his feeling, were concerning the incident. Except for only an occasional lapse, the horrifying nightmares had stopped. Each time he thought of his betrayal, however, his heart grew heavy, leaving him to conclude that he hadn't forgiven himself. And perhaps never would. Still, he longed to look himself fully in the mirror and see the man he'd once been ... or at least like the man he'd become.

Cursing, Sloan had gone to bed, angry with the fact that he at least had to admit he understood Anna's longing for redemption. That redemption, or lack thereof, might well keep them apart.

The next week saw a significant tapering off of what little patience Sloan had managed to hang on to. Monday, fearing a break in his sanity and no longer able to tell Harper no, he joined him for coffee at the Chat 'N' Chew. Hearing that Anna called Carrie on a regular basis, which he pried out of Harper, did nothing to sweeten his souring mood. Wednesday he even entertained the notion that Anna hadn't loved him, after all, that she'd simply come to him out of need, that he'd simply been a substitute for her husband, whose affection she'd wanted, needed, but had been denied. Knowing that true insanity lay in that line of thinking, he abandoned it ... or tried to. By Friday, perched beyond a doubt on the edge of going bonkers, Sloan slipped on his sunglasses—was he still hiding out from himself?—left the cottage, and jogged along the beach. He refused, however, to enter the territory where he and Anna had met, where they'd laughed and loved.

He returned home to a ringing telephone.

Taking the steps two at a time, he bounded onto the small porch and thrust the key into the lock. He turned the key the wrong way, then, a curse at his lips, he reversed the direction. The door gave way. He raced inside and yanked the receiver from its cradle.

"Hello?"

"Mr. Marshall?"

Sloan expressed his disappointment with a silent swear. He recognized the masculine voice as that belonging to the personnel director in charge of hiring divers for the North Sea oil operation. Sloan removed his sunglasses and, with a careless flick of his wrist, sent them sailing onto the sofa.

"Yeah, how are you doing?" Sloan asked.

"Fine. And yourself?"

"Fine," Sloan said, lying.

"Look, I just wanted to touch base with you and let you know that the position we spoke about is still open. Actually, we filled the position just as you encouraged us to do, but the truth is, it didn't work out. The man didn't have the diving experience we thought he had. We, uh, we were wondering if we could interest you again."

Sloan had been candid with the man about the trial—he really couldn't have been anything else—and though he hadn't spoken to him since the trial, the personnel director calling now clearly indicated how high-profile the case had been. Headquartered in Houston, the man had obviously heard the case's outcome.

"Are you interested, Mr. Marshall?"

Sloan rubbed the bridge of his nose with his thumb and forefinger. Was he interested? He had no idea, though he heard himself saying, "When do you have to know?"

The man laughed. "Yesterday."

"I've got some things that I can't walk away from now."

"I could give you until the first of the month," the man said, clearly eager to have Sloan accept the position. When Sloan said nothing, he said, "That's a little over a week off. How about if we talk then?"

Again Sloan heard himself saying, "Fine. I'll talk to you then."

Sloan spent the rest of the afternoon and evening avoiding the issue. After a cold meal and a hot shower he went to bed, where his tossing left the bedclothes looking passion-rumpled. Ironically, for the first time since she'd left Cook's Bay, he dreamed of Anna—her soft mouth devouring his, her sweet voice whispering his name, her body, as no other woman's before her, demanding a sensual response from his. Sloan awoke aroused, achy, and above all, angry. He'd had all he could take.

At midmorning, a cold, clear Saturday, he called Anna in Connecticut. He got the housekeeper, who politely told him that Anna was visiting her daughter at school. Sloan left a message for Anna to call him, then hung up. He was confident that she would call soon.

The café, cramped and crowded and looking like a near-campus eatery should, had not been Anna's choice. She would have preferred the quieter restaurant at the local motel, but Meg had insisted on this location. Anna thought that it had something to do with meeting on Meg's turf rather than on hers. It was a subtle, perhaps even unconscious, form of defiance and, no doubt, a harbinger of the meeting's outcome. Whatever the outcome, Anna, who hadn't spoken with her daughter except for one brief encounter following the trial, was adamant about seeing her and trying to bridge their differences. Not necessarily to make Meg understand about the affair—again, she felt ill equipped to explain what she herself didn't understand—but to offer the olive branch of peace.

Seated near the back of the room, her hands folded serenely on the wobbly-legged table, Anna waited for her daughter's arrival. All around her kids laughed and hollered, while the jukebox played a tempo-thumping song that was already giving her the beginning of a headache. Even considering the niggling ache, the noise was better than the sepulchral silence of the house in Connecticut. She had never known its kind of silence, a silence of the soul, a silence that swallowed all other sound. It greeted her in the morning; it tucked her in at night. It reminded her of how much she missed the sea.

And Sloan.

Most particularly, Sloan.

It was funny. Her thoughts were muddled, as though she'd brought with her the fog surrounding Cook's Bay on her last day there. On the other hand, her feelings were crystal clear. The ending of the trial had heralded a reawakening of her feelings. No, she had to admit she didn't think that was altogether true. From the instant she'd made love with Sloan, she'd felt. She'd tried to hide her feelings, but they had been there, oftentimes too abundantly. He'd filled her senses, making her feel refreshingly, painfully alive. Even the memory of him was so potent that, without warning, it left her breathless, giddy, wanting more of everything that defined him—hard kisses, alternately tender and passionate lovemaking, an integrity that he couldn't see had never been compromised despite the incident in Beirut. She loved him. She didn't try to delude herself into thinking otherwise. On the other hand, neither did she try to defend her actions. Morally, the affair had been wrong. And the jury was still out as to whether she'd ever come to terms with that.

Anna saw Meg the instant she stepped through the door of the diner. In those unguarded seconds as Meg searched for her mother, Anna observed her. She wore jeans, tennis shoes, and a braid. Her face, always showing the strain of study, bore the look of exceptional fatigue. She'd also dropped a few pounds. Was it possible that the last weeks had been as hard on her? Was she ready to reconcile their differences? Anna's hopes suffered a defeat when her daughter made eye contact, for she saw an unmistakable aloofness. To further dash Anna's hopes, Meg squared her shoulders, as though readying herself for combat, as she wended her way toward her mother.

So be it, Anna thought. She'd simply say what she came to say and let the chips fall where they would.

Meg pulled out the chair across from her mother, stating as she did so, "I have a class in an hour."

If Anna had had any doubts as to the frame of her daughter's mind, the terse announcement erased it. Though saddened, Anna said calmly, "Sounds as if they're working you hard."

"You wouldn't believe it," she said. "I have a test Monday that's going to be a killer." Before Anna could respond, Meg said, "The hamburgers are good here. A little greasy, but good. And the service is fast."

Anna motioned for the waiter and placed an order for two hamburgers. She then said into the lengthening, awkward silence, "How have you been?"

Meg shrugged her battle-squared shoulders and said formally, "Fine. How about you?"

"Fair. Some days I'm better than others."

Anna's honesty obviously rattled Meg, for she quickly changed the subject. "How's Aunt Carrie?"

"Actually, she's doing very well."

Defiantly, Meg said, "I'm not angry that she helped Daddy take his life."

"Neither am I. Under different circumstances I might have done the same thing." Anna paused, then plunged ahead. "You're still angry with me for what I did, though, aren't you?"

Meg's defiance deepened. "Yes. What Aunt Carrie did was for Daddy. What you did was for yourself."

"I can't very well argue with that, can I?"

Again Anna's honesty nonplussed her daughter. They lapsed into a silence that was growing uncomfortable, when, fortunately, the hamburgers came. After the waiter stepped away, Meg asked bluntly, "Why did you want to see me?"

"You're my daughter. I love you. I want you in my life. Even if you can't forgive me, I'd like for you at least to try to understand."

Meg stalled for a reply by picking up her hamburger and taking a bite. Anna did the same, glad that Meg wasn't rushing into a negative response. At last Meg spoke.

"I don't know if I can ever forgive you. I don't know if I want to forgive you."

Anna knew that the former depended on the latter. She had come to this incredibly simple conclusion in the dark of one silent night. It just wasn't a courtesy she was yet willing to extend to herself.

"That's fair enough," she said. "At this point I'm interested only in your trying to forgive, only on your working to want to."

Another bite of hamburger, followed by a halfhearted sip of soda, and Meg asked, "What about him?"

"He has a name. It's Sloan. And I'm in love with him."

Meg tilted her chin in a gesture identical to the one her mother often posed. "Are you going to marry him?"

"I have no idea. The truth is, he hasn't asked me. We haven't discussed the future. In fact, I haven't spoken with him since I left Cook's Bay."

Meg's surprise was more than evident. Anna took advantage of it. "Contrary to what you seem to think, I didn't set out to fall in love with Sloan. I didn't enter into the affair lightly. You say you haven't forgiven me and maybe never will. The truth is that I haven't forgiven myself . . . and maybe I never will."

"Then why did you do it?" Meg asked, anger and hurt mingling as they always did when the young woman confronted this subject.

Anna replied honestly, though she doubted that Meg would appreciate her candor. "Because I loved Sloan."

Meg made a scoffing sound. "And that's supposed to excuse what you did?"

"No," she said, wondering why she couldn't forgive herself for the most human of emotions. Why couldn't simply being human be enough?

The hurt had returned when Meg said, "You were supposed to have loved Daddy."

"I did."

"Bullshit!"

The couple at the nearby table glanced up. Neither Anna nor Meg noticed. Meg was too occupied with being angry, Anna with remaining calm.

"Whether or not you choose to believe it," Anna said, "I *did* love your father. In the beginning I loved him as a friend and a lover. In the end I loved him as a friend, as someone I'd known for a long time, as someone I wished well, as the father of my daughter, a daughter I love very much."

This last seemed more than Meg could bear. "What do you want?"

"To know that whatever my future holds, you'll be a part of it."

"I can't promise that."

Meg's bluntness hurt, but Anna tried not to let it show. "I only ask that you promise to think about what I've said."

Meg shrugged and suddenly, as she sometimes could, she looked vulnerable, youthful. Her next words added to that image. "A part of me hates you for what you did."

Anna saw her daughter's pain and would have done

anything to ease it, but the truth was that she couldn't. What was done was done.

"And what about the other part of you?"

Meg's voice shook when she answered, "You're my mother."

On the drive home Anna dissected Meg's reply. It implied an intrinsic, unconditional caring. If Anna had hoped for more in the way of her daughter's forgiveness, she nonetheless had to admit that Meg's response was perhaps all she had a right to expect at this point. At least it was a beginning.

Anna found the note plastered to the refrigerator with a smiley-face magnet. At the sight of Sloan's name and telephone number, her heart skipped a beat. Removing the piece of paper left by her housekeeper, Anna traced the cursive pattern of letters, as if by doing so she could magically make Sloan appear before her. Her first impulse was to rush to the telephone and call him. Her second impulse was to reconsider. The degree of her desire dictated that she not do so. She could not call him simply because she needed, more than breath itself, to hear his voice. It wasn't fair to him. Or to her. The road to forgiveness had to be traveled alone.

That night Anna lay in bed, the note held tightly in the fist settled over her heart. She listened to the earsplitting silence falling around her. She pretended that she could hear Sloan's voice calling her name. She pretended that the gentle rain tapping on her window was the sound of healing teardrops. She pretended that she could hear the sea. It sang of many things, but not of the one thing she most desired. It did not sing of forgiveness.

When Anna didn't call by Wednesday night, Sloan had to entertain the notion that she was not going to call. By Friday night Sloan had to accept the notion as fact. He crawled into bed feeling more desperate than he'd ever remembered feeling before.

At the dream's commencement Sloan was surprised. It had been a while since he'd had the nightmare. As always the adrenaline began to pump, the fear to pulse. He told himself to wake up, but he couldn't. The dream kept tugging at his ankles and towing him under.

"Ah, Commander," came the thickly accented voice, *"why don't you spare yourself the pain? Just tell me the name . . . the name . . . the name . . ."*

Sloan fought with the hazy demons, but he knew that he was destined to lose. He always lost. There was no combating the devils of his past. Yes, he was losing, slipping further and further away. He could hear the jangle of the key in the lock of his cell. He could see his pain-loving captor stepping out of the shadows. He could taste the terror trembling on his tongue. Someone yanked him to his feet, shackled his wrists, and dragged him down a dark hallway. He knew that each step took him closer and closer to pain and degradation. Harsh hands pushed him into a room. His shirt was stripped from him. A rope hoisted him from the ceiling like a side of beef.

"No," Sloan moaned, trying to avert what he knew was coming next.

Here the dream departed from the norm. There was no beating, no slashing of his skin, no bolts of hot electricity. Instead there was a torture the likes of which Sloan had never had to endure. At first Sloan couldn't believe what he was seeing. There shouldn't have been a golden-haired, blue-eyed woman there. And she shouldn't be stepping toward him with a sweet, but sad, smile.

"Anna?" Sloan whispered.

"I'm not coming back," she whispered. *"Please understand. I love you, but I betrayed my vows."*

"You were only being human," Sloan's captor chimed in.

"Being human is intolerable," Anna said, repeating Sloan's own words.

"No!" the Sloan in the dream cried, while the Sloan in bed sprang to a sitting position. Despite the chill, perspiration ran in the black spirals of hair matting his bare chest. He gulped air into his lungs even as he struggled to deny what he knew was true. Anna wasn't coming back to him. This realization slammed into him. Hard. Sickeningly. With finality.

Sloan threw back the bedcovers, grabbed his sweatsuit and jogging shoes from the floor, and threw them on. He then raced for the front door—all in an attempt to keep the walls from crashing in on him. The cold night air struck him in the face as he crunched his feet in the pea-sized gravel. From there he streaked down the stone steps and onto the beach. He ran full out, stopping only when he could run no more. When his knees gave way, he sank into the moist sand. A sound clawed at the back of his throat. Finally it escaped, a keening, animallike wail that surprised even him. Had he made that sound? Were those tears coursing down his cheeks?

Yes, the sad sea answered.

"She isn't coming back," Sloan whispered.

Don't think about it now. Don't think about anything now.

Sloan obeyed, whether by choice or design he didn't know. All he knew was that the gentle beast beside him, in an undulating pattern that was always the same, yet always different, erased all thought, all feeling, from his being. He was aware of nothing beyond the primordial essence of life—the splash of waves, the sparkling of stardust, the stinging of winterlike wind.

Time passed. How much of it, Sloan didn't know. Gradually, though, the night imprinted itself on him. He felt the cold, the dampness, his love, pure and abiding, for Anna. He'd never loved, and never would again, the way he loved her. He almost could believe that she'd magically, mystically, been sent to him for this one summer of his life.

Yes, the sea soughed.

But why?

Don't you know?

No, he didn't know. He knew only that both of them had been wounded by events in the past, and that neither could forgive or forget. Each had failed. Each had become less than he or she had wanted to be. Under pressure, each had been all too human.

Is that so wrong?

Yes. No. He didn't know! At this he passed his hand across his whiskered cheek and, with a deep sigh, turned his face toward the heavens. A three-quarter slice of silver moon rode high in the sky. He'd seen it hundreds of times, yet never had it shone so brightly. As though it were trying to tell him something? Maybe. But what? As though on cue Sloan realized that the tide had shifted, prompting wavelets to purl just at his feet. Tide?

Yes, tide, the sea whispered. *As great as I am, I must bow to the moon. As great as I am, I am only what I am. Just as you are only what you are.*

And what was that? Even as Sloan pondered the question, he knew the answer. He was human. Nothing less, nothing more. He'd tried to be more. He'd castigated himself for not being more, but when push had come to shove, he'd had no choice in the matter. Just as the sea was influenced by the moon, so had he been influenced by the torture he'd endured. He had done what any human being would have done under similar circumstances. He had done what was necessary to end the unbearable pain. Simply because human beings were physically, emotionally, spiritually coded to do so. He hadn't dishonored himself. Being human, with its strengths and its weaknesses, was all a human being could ever be.

Slowly, a warm, heavy feeling filled Sloan. The feeling had a name. It was love. His love for Anna had grown and changed until it now encompassed a self-love, a forgiveness. From the moment he'd met her, he'd felt his redemption lay with her, and it had. She had been sent to him, a gift from the sea, to heal him, to restore him.

The gift had been his to keep, but not the giver of the gift. He'd known that when she hadn't returned his call. He'd known that when the dream had occurred. That realization saddened him, but he could not change what was meant to be. Forever he would hold her memory close. Forever he would remember this special summer. Forever he would hold a place for her in his heart.

As moonlight gave way to dawn, Sloan stood and walked the distance to the lighthouse cottage. Once there, he called the personnel director and accepted the job offer. He then called the airport and arranged for a flight early the next morning. Next he called Harper, asking if he could take him to the airport.

"Are you all right?" Harper asked at conversation's end.

"Yeah," Sloan replied.

And, curiously, he was. He hurt badly, but the pain was not altogether unwelcome. It was validation of his newfound humanity.

When Anna crawled from bed that Saturday morning, something felt different. Ordinarily, mornings were cold and stale, nothing more than the residue of another sleepless night. This morning, however, seemed full and fresh and filled with secrets just waiting to be revealed to those clever enough to hear them. Anna told herself that part of the matin magic was caused by the shower that had fallen during the night. Raindrops, like diamonds, twinkled from the leaves of the evergreen trees. But there was something more that she couldn't quite define.

After breakfast, Anna tried to settle down with a book but couldn't. The secrets had begun to whisper—from behind the closed doors, from among the lacy fronds of the hanging fern, from within the fragile shadows that shimmered in the corners. What were they trying to tell her? She didn't know, but a sense of expectancy welled within her.

Restless, she wandered the house. Here and there. There and here. She longed, as she never had before, for the comforting sea. Surely it would calm her. Surely it would decipher the secrets moving ever and ever closer. Her need for the sea ultimately led her to the seashells she'd collected that summer. As she often did, she took them out of the brass chest in which she'd placed them—they seemed treasures worthy of a chest—and merely spent time with them. She held them—the small, the large, the plain, the beautiful. She put them to her ear, imagining that she could hear the sea serenading her, making her feel once more that she strolled its shores.

She picked one up, noting its pink iridescent underbelly. As she turned it, she could have sworn the whispers grew louder. She lay it back in the chest and selected another shell, this one more oblong than round, this one with a rippling pattern that reminded Anna of the waves that rushed forward in greeting. The whispers grew louder still. This time Anna thought she heard the word *perfect*.

Perfect?

Yes, the silent voices spoke. *Each shell is perfect unto itself. Even those imperfect shells you left on the beach are perfect, for each shell met the needs of the animal that had once called it home. All creatures have needs.*

Even human beings?

Most particularly human beings.

Yes, Anna thought, the truth coming so quickly that it stunned her with its innate simplicity. Just as her husband had had needs, so had she, needs that he, not purposefully, but because he'd been caught up in his own fight for survival, had denied her. She'd needed love, companionship, someone with whom she could share her life. Sloan had offered her this. She had taken it, doing as her human heart had guided. Loving was never wrong. Being human was never wrong, for it was what she was—all that she could ever be.

Placing the shell to her ear, Anna heard the sea applauding her newly gained wisdom. It was a wisdom the sea promised that her daughter would know in time. Slowly, as though she'd been touched by the golden sun beaming through the window, a warmth eddied through her. The warmth of forgiveness. Anna smiled and touched her cheek. It was moist, from long-awaited tears.

She felt free.
She felt happy.
She felt human.

It was sad, Sloan thought Sunday morning, that all of a man's possessions could be stuffed within a single duffel bag and still have room to spare. Not that the scarcity of his worldly goods really mattered, for he was taking with him a heartful of memories. That in mind, he had arisen early, his intent to walk the beach one last time before he left Cook's Bay. Since Anna's departure, he hadn't visited the stretch of shoreline where they'd met, talked, and laughed, where they'd fallen in love. And she *had* fallen in love with him. He'd doubted it once, but never again. A woman like Anna didn't profess a lie. He only hoped that the day would come when she would allow herself to be human, when she would forgive herself for her—for their—very human transgression.

Setting the bag by the front door, Sloan checked his

watch, assuring himself that, as planned, he had an hour before Harper's arrival. Reaching for his coat, he threw his arms into it, then automatically grabbed the sunglasses that lay on the coffee table. He hesitated. No, he concluded, he didn't need the sunglasses. He was no longer hiding out from others or from himself. The realization was liberating.

As Sloan stepped from the cottage and traveled the familiar path to the beach, a cold predawn morning greeted him. Overnight the temperature had plunged to the season's lowest, leaving a brisk brittleness hovering about the bay. The sea shivered in the wake of the blustery wind, as did Sloan, who turned up the collar of his coat and buried his hands in its warm pockets. Overhead the gray and navy of night were getting ready to give way to a glorious new day. Sloan wondered if the same perfect day was breaking across Connecticut skies.

What would Anna think, feel, when she knew that he was gone? Though he wanted her to miss him, he didn't want her to be sad. There had been too much sadness in her life. He only wanted her to remember the summer with the same kindness he would. He only hoped that for the rest of her life, her heart would skip a small beat at any remembrance of him.

Entering their domain was like entering sacred ground. From the moment Sloan did, bittersweet memories rushed at him, causing him to pause for breath. His heart felt achingly full. Still, he forced himself forward, past the pile of rocks that looked like beached dolphins, past the place where they'd fed the hungry sea gull, to the spot, most sacred of all, where he'd first seen Anna wading in the water. He paused, summoning up the bewitching image of the woman zealously looking for shells. A smile softened Sloan's lips. No search had ever been more ardent, not even that for the Holy Grail.

Slowly, the smile at Sloan's lips died. Anna had been misguided in her search. She had been wrong to seek only whole, perfect shells. Imperfect shells, like imperfect human beings, survived too. As though to underscore this sentiment, a shell, chipped and worn, came into view. Sloan stooped and picked it up from the sand. Yes, he mused, displaying it in the palm of his hand, it was magnificently imperfect. The thought came to him quickly. He would leave this shell in the very spot where he'd left so many perfect shells. It seemed a fitting tribute to a summer that was gone.

Sloan headed for that special spot on the beach, but midway there, he stopped.

Surely the slowly rising sun was playing tricks with his vision. There was no way he could be seeing what he thought he was seeing. Was there? No, gold chests washed ashore on beaches only in legends. Still, the chest appeared so real that Sloan had no option but to prove or disprove its existence. Perhaps he would discover that he was only hallucinating. Perhaps the chest would vanish as he drew near.

It didn't. In fact, as he stooped before it, he concluded that nothing had ever appeared more real. Neither had anything ever felt more real. As he raised the chilled lid, a sense of expectancy gripped him, as though he stood on the verge of some great discovery. In disbelief he stared at the shells nestled inside the chest. Who would have placed this odd offering here? And why? An answer came to Sloan, an answer that caused his heart to thump against the walls of his chest. He dared not hope, and yet that very thing sent him rummaging through the shells. The perfect shells. The shells he recognized as those he and Anna had collected that summer. His heart crashing in a wild crescendo, he whirled around.

It was then he saw her.

Though she was bundled against the wind, it had

nonetheless tossed her golden curls into a disarray that reminded Sloan of the first time he'd seen her. Then, too, her hair had been wild with the morning wind. Today, though, he knew that something was different about her. She was no longer the woman he'd seen that fair June day. A gentleness had settled about her. Her shoulders were no longer squared in defiance of life's unfairness. Her chin was no longer tilted for battle. She looked at peace with life and with herself.

The hope he'd dared himself not to feel blossomed.

The hope she'd dared herself not to feel blossomed.

Anna had hoped beyond hope to find Sloan on the beach. She'd driven through the dark hours of the night just to be in this spot come dawn. Once she'd confronted her humanness, once she'd experienced the warm balm of forgiveness, she'd had to seek out Sloan. An urgency had seized her. It was as though she instinctively knew that, although he'd promised to wait for her for the rest of his life, time was running out, that she must go to him now, with not even minutes or seconds to spare. Seeing him, tall and windblown, Anna sensed that he was no longer the man she'd once known. There was a softness to his unconcealed eyes, an acceptance in his stance. Had he, too, been blessed with forgiveness?

Go to him, the sea commanded.

Again an urgency filled Anna's heart. Once more she had to feel the strength of his arms, the softness of his lips. Later there would be time for words, for declarations of love, for the chanting of a lover's name, but now, this moment, she had to *feel* him.

Sloan watched her purposeful approach. Yes, she was different, his heart sang. The tears, which glazed her mascara-lush eyes with a beauty beyond compare, confirmed this. Through his own tears he fought to keep her image clear, to lock this moment away in the treasury of his heart.

Slowly, she walked toward him.

Slowly, he walked toward her.

Two people making one last lone voyage. The walk seemed endless, but just when each would have despaired, she stepped into his eager arms. The imperfect shell fell at their feet, a tribute to all that was human within them. At that precise instant when his arms closed around her, and hers around him, dawn broke across the sky, an oyster-pink glow that illuminated the heavens and sailed high above the ice-chilled sea.

For both, the dark journey had ended.

ABOUT THE AUTHOR

Sandra Canfield, a.k.a. Karen Keast, lives in Shreveport with her husband, Charles, her staunchest supporter. Sandra, a very diverse writer has published mainstream, contemporary, and historical romances. Sandra's fans say they read her books because of their humor, sexual tension and unusual plots. Sandra's favorite reads are bloody murder mysteries. Her favorite author is Agatha Christie, to whom Sandra wrote her first fan letter.

The Very Best in Contemporary Women's Fiction

Sandra Brown

_____	28951-9 TEXAS! LUCKY	$5.99/6.99 in Canada
_____	28990-X TEXAS! CHASE	$5.99/6.99
_____	29500-4 TEXAS! SAGE	$5.99/6.99
_____	29085-1 22 INDIGO PLACE	$5.99/6.99
_____	29783-X A WHOLE NEW LIGHT	$5.99/6.99
_____	56045-X TEMPERATURES RISING	$5.99/6.99
_____	56274-6 FANTA C	$4.99/5.99
_____	56278-9 LONG TIME COMING	$4.99/5.99

Tami Hoag

_____	29534-9 LUCKY'S LADY	$4.99/5.99
_____	29053-3 MAGIC	$4.99/5.99
_____	56050-6 SARAH'S SIN	$4.50/5.50
_____	29272-2 STILL WATERS	$4.99/5.99
_____	56160-X CRY WOLF	$5.50/6.50
_____	56161-8 DARK PARADISE	$5.99/7.50

Nora Roberts

_____	29078-9 GENUINE LIES	$5.99/6.99
_____	28578-5 PUBLIC SECRETS	$5.99/6.99
_____	26461-3 HOT ICE	$5.99/6.99
_____	26574-1 SACRED SINS	$5.99/6.99
_____	27859-2 SWEET REVENGE	$5.99/6.99
_____	27283-7 BRAZEN VIRTUE	$5.99/6.99
_____	29597-7 CARNAL INNOCENCE	$5.50/6.50
_____	29490-3 DIVINE EVIL	$5.99/6.99

Deborah Smith

_____	29107-6 MIRACLE	$4.50/5.50
_____	29092-4 FOLLOW THE SUN	$4.99/5.99
_____	28759-1 THE BELOVED WOMAN	$4.50/5.50
_____	29690-6 BLUE WILLOW	$5.50/6.50
_____	29689-2 SILK AND STONE	$5.99/6.99

Theresa Weir

_____	56092-1 LAST SUMMER	$4.99/5.99
_____	56378-5 ONE FINE DAY	$4.99/5.99

Ask for these titles at your bookstore or use this page to order.

Please send me the books I have checked above. I am enclosing $ _____ (add $2.50 to cover postage and handling). Send check or money order, no cash or C. O. D.'s please.

Mr./ Ms. _____

Address _____

City/ State/ Zip _____

Send order to: Bantam Books, Dept. FN 24, 2451 S. Wolf Road, Des Plaines, IL 60018
Please allow four to six weeks for delivery.
Prices and availability subject to change without notice.

FN 24 4/94